THE SPOIL OF BEASTS

IRON ON IRON

BOOK THREE

GREGORY ASHE

H&B

The Spoil of Beasts
Copyright © 2023 Gregory Ashe

Published by Hodgkin & Blount
https://www.hodgkinandblount.com/
contact@hodgkinandblount.com

Published 2023
Printed in the United States of America

Version 1.05

Trade Paperback ISBN: 978-1-63621-069-8
eBook ISBN: 978-1-63621-068-1

1

Shaw tried to make sense of the words.

There's been an incident.

Ambyr Hobbs hanged herself.

North's hand squeezed Shaw's shoulder, and Shaw felt himself sink down into the moment. It was surreal, sitting in the Cock of the Walk, with country music playing in the background and the smell of fried chicken hanging in the air. John-Henry still stood with the phone pressed to his ear; Emery sat next to Evie, the frozen amber of his eyes catching the light in a way that made them glow. Auggie leaned into Theo, happiness crumbling to ash behind the bandage on his face. Theo wrapped an arm around him, expression grim.

"Jesus," Jem said.

And then John-Henry spoke again. Even before the words came out, Shaw felt their force—destabilizing, undermining, like backwash dragging grains of sand out from under their feet.

"It gets worse. Someone killed Dalton Weber in his cell tonight. And they murdered Sheriff Engels in the process."

Tean shook his head. "That's not—" He stopped, but they all heard the word he hadn't said: *possible*. Because, of course, it was possible. Shaw only had to look at John-Henry's face to see the reality of it.

"I've got to go in," John-Henry said to Emery.

"Go," Emery said. "We'll be fine."

John-Henry ran for the door. In the background, the music changed to Dolly. "Wildflowers."

"We should—" Emery stood, scanning their table and then looking around the restaurant. Night made mirrors out of the windows, and in the glass, Shaw saw a group of frightened men. "Are the children done?"

"Lana's finished," Auggie said in a numb voice.

Pain flashed in Theo's face, but he nodded.

"Come on, baby," Emery said, lifting Evie.

"Where's Daddy?" she asked.

"He had to work," Emery said, and he sent a meaningful look toward the other men. "And we need to go home now."

"I'll check the parking lot," Jem said. Tean held on to his arm for a moment, but Jem slipped free and pushed off from the table, jogging not toward the exit, as Shaw had expected in that first moment, but toward the kitchen. The girl who had taken their order said something like she was trying to stop him, and Jem said something back. It must have worked, whatever it was, because the girl laughed and waved him on, and a moment later, Jem disappeared from view.

"Guess being slipperier than goose shit has its advantages," North grumbled.

Tean's face creased with displeasure, and Shaw elbowed North.

"Uh, that was quick thinking," North muttered.

"Oh my God," Shaw said under his breath.

A moment later, Tean's phone buzzed, and he answered it on speaker.

"Clear," Jem said.

"Are you sure—" Emery began.

"If Jem says it's clear," Tean said, "it's clear."

Shaw waited for the argument, but Emery only nodded. Carrying Evie, he headed toward the door. Auggie copied the move, picking up Lana even though she was definitely too big to be carried. It didn't stop Auggie, though, and he followed Emery. Theo was a step behind, his hand on Auggie's shoulder. North motioned for Shaw to go ahead with Tean, and he brought up the rear as they filtered out of the restaurant.

The summer evening was hot and waiting for them, like a wet cloth pressed against their faces. It was hard to believe that it was past eight, but the sun had almost set, and in spite of the peach-colored arc in the west, the parking lot had fallen into shadow. It was mostly empty.

"Our house," Emery said. "Everyone."

"We don't have—" Theo began.

"It's not a discussion. Theo, Auggie, you're with me. North, Shaw, are you good?"

"Good," North said.

Theo and Auggie hurried toward the minivan, where Emery was already loading Evie into her booster seat. North herded Tean and Shaw toward the GTO, where Jem waited, hands in his pockets.

Inside, the car smelled like American Crew hair gel and the faint hint of cleaner, whatever North had used last time, and maybe, possibly, just barely, the faintest whiff of cigarette smoke. The engine rumbled to life, and North eased the car forward.

"He thinks someone's going to try to kill us," Tean said. Under the GTO's growl, he was barely audible. "Doesn't he?"

Jem said, "Let 'em. We fucked them up last time."

"Last time," North said, "you and Theo barely got out with your lives, and Theo and Auggie's house burned down."

"It didn't burn down," Shaw said, "not entirely."

"And that time, the killer didn't even bring a gun. How well do you think you're going to do if four guys step out of an alley with shotguns?"

"We've managed to stay alive so far," Jem said.

"Because you're lucky. How long do you think you're going to be lucky?"

"We've stayed alive because—"

But when Shaw looked in the rearview mirror, Tean was shaking his head, and Jem cut off.

"Exactly," North said.

"North," Shaw said.

North grimaced, and his attention seemed to settle on driving. They rode the rest of the way in silence.

Instead of hotdogging it, as usual, North hung back a few car lengths and let the minivan lead them to the Hazard and Somerset home. He pulled up in front of the house as Emery was still guiding the Odyssey into the garage.

"I'll clear it," Jem said.

"We'll clear it," North said.

"But I'm lucky," Jem said, "and you're just an asshole."

North barked a laugh. He waited by the side of the GTO after he got out, and when Jem climbed out, North tried to swat him on the back of the head, which made Jem laugh in turn. Their laughter faded, though, as they headed toward the dark house.

Shaw traded a look with Tean. "Do you understand boys?"

Tean touched his glasses like he wanted to resettle them. "They're nervous, and they're finding outlets for that nervousness." Then a tiny smile curled the corner of his mouth. "But no. Not in the slightest."

They waited in silence. Shaw's mind began to branch and fork, a labyrinth of possibilities. First and clearest was the one North had suggested: men in the dark, men in masks, waiting with shotguns to deliver a rain of death. But it could be so many things. Gas filling the house, waiting for a single spark to explode. Or the man again, the one with the sickle, who

7

had come before. He pictured North caught off guard, North with nothing to defend himself against that black blade sweeping out of the darkness —

Tean touched his arm, and Shaw flinched.

"You need to take deep breaths," Tean said. "You're hyperventilating."

Shaw nodded and tried to breathe through the chaos of his own mind. For a moment, the frustration was worse than the fear itself: the old, familiar dismay that no matter what he tried — psychotherapy, psychedelics, weed, meditation, even exercise — he was a victim of neural wiring.

But the breathing helped, some, and after a moment, Tean dropped his hand.

Lights went on in the house, and then the front door opened, and North signaled. By the time Tean and Shaw stepped inside, Shaw could hear Emery and the others in the kitchen, where they'd entered through the garage. The house itself looked untouched: no vandalism, no destruction, no ominous threats or messages. It felt right, too, although Shaw knew North would dismiss that as woo-woo; the house still felt safe, comfortable, like a home.

"All good," Jem said.

"For now," North said. "Let's make it through tonight before the victory jackoff."

"So, cool fact, I actually didn't know victory jackoffs were a thing until literally right now, which means I've wasted, like, at least eight of them —"

"Go on, sweetheart," Emery said from the living room. "You and Lana go upstairs and play. I'll come check on you in a minute."

The little girls' voices faded in time with their steps. North led their group into the living room.

Theo and Auggie stood near the stairs, Auggie clutching Theo's hand like his body weight was an anchor to keep Theo from going after their daughter. Emery stood in the center of the room, head down, face empty. North dropped onto the couch, and Shaw joined him. Tean stayed near Jem, close to the entry hall.

"Is North right?" Tean asked, breaking the silence. "Is someone going to try to kill us tonight?"

"We don't know that," Shaw said.

"They'd be stupid not to," North said.

"We don't know what they're doing. We don't know anything."

"We know somebody tried to kill those bozos." North nodded at Jem and Tean. "And someone tried to kill those bozos." He nodded at Theo and Auggie. "And tonight, somebody killed the motherfucking sheriff. So, I'm going to go out on a limb and say somebody's cleaning up, and we're part of the mess."

"We have no idea what really happened tonight—"

Emery's head came up, and he broke in, saying, "North's right."

"Put that on a fucking plaque," North said.

"We had two leads that could connect us back to illegal activity at the Cottonmouth Club. Both of those leads are now dead. The sheriff is dead. And those three deaths took place inside a secure facility. We don't know everything, but we know enough: someone is tying off loose ends, and we—in particular, Theo, Auggie, Jem, and Tean—are a bundle of loose ends."

Shaw opened his mouth. Then he shut it again.

"Who's doing this?" Jem asked. "That's what's driving me crazy about the whole thing. It was one thing when we thought we'd stumbled onto a wildlife trafficking ring. And then—and then Theo and Auggie got caught up in it, and it turns out it's more than animals; they're trafficking people. But who's doing this? We don't have names. We don't even have faces. We've got a psycho in a mask, but that's one guy."

"That's not the real problem," North said.

"It felt like a pretty real problem when he tried to gut me." Jem touched his chest, where a cut was still healing.

"He came into our home," Theo said, his voice flat. "He tried to kill my family."

"North is—" Emery seemed to hear himself and managed to say, "—not wrong."

North snorted.

"The real issue," Emery said, "is whoever conducted these killings tonight, they have a reach and influence beyond our original estimation. This isn't a group of amateurs who have found a way to profit from illegal activities. We're dealing with people who are organized, who are ruthless, and who can strike into the heart of a law enforcement facility."

"Where's Colt?" Tean asked.

"Ashley's." Something in Emery's voice eased. "He's fine; I called on the drive over."

North rubbed his eyes. "Anybody want to go to Tahiti?"

Auggie raised his hand.

"What are we going to do?" Shaw asked.

Emery looked at him, but instead of answering, he reached into his pocket and took out his phone. He spoke quietly as he moved into the kitchen.

"You two should go home," North said with a glance at Tean and Jem. "Hell, I wasn't joking about Tahiti. Go to Tahiti."

Jem scratched his beard, but Tean shook his head. "They killed my friend."

"Our friend," Jem said.

"They were trying to kill us, and they killed her instead. We're not running away from that."

"Even though we don't exactly have unlimited vacation days. Well, I do. But that's because I'm a reprobate."

"We talked about this," Tean said, his voice dropping as he turned toward Jem. "It's my choice—"

"I know, I know, I know." Jem held up his hands. "Look, this is my fault. I'm the one who screwed up. I'm the one who got these fuckers after us."

"It's not anyone's fault," Shaw said.

"It's kind of his fault," North said. He twisted away from Shaw's elbow. "What? It is."

"It's not," Auggie said. "We stirred the pot too."

"He's being kind," Theo said. "I dragged him into this."

Auggie shook his head, but he didn't press the argument. After that, no one seemed to have anything to say. Silence gathered; it was thick in Shaw's throat, and he wiped his eyes and laid his head on North's shoulder. Emery's voice was a low rumble in the background. And then that ended too.

His steps moved back toward the living room, and everyone turned toward the sound. Emery looked at them, face grim. "John asked me to come in."

Theo glanced at Jem, who nodded, and said, "We'll keep an eye on things here."

"Good," Emery said, his voice suddenly dry. "Because he wants North and Shaw to come as well."

2

The Wahredua police station looked like it had, at one point, been a school. North had plenty of friends who'd gone to Catholic school, and he recognized the look: the grim severity of the redbrick walls, the cramped windows, the uninspired attempts at religious ornamentation. At some point—probably whenever the city had taken it over—someone had tried to get rid of the iconography. No more angels and devils, no more saints and sinners. Not on the taxpayers' dime. But, like most public works jobs, this one had been half-assed and, apparently, eventually given up. The decorative stonework above the main entrance, for example, still showed an angel with a bad hair day who was, apparently, pointing a pencil dick at the devil lying underneath him. No homo, North thought as he followed Emery into the building.

Emery led them past the front desk without slowing; the uniformed officer seated there opened her mouth in protest, but either she was familiar with Emery or didn't care enough to raise a ruckus, because she let them continue into the building. Her nametag said Ehlers.

John-Henry was waiting for them in his office. It was the kind of space North would have guessed John-Henry would create for himself: a comfortable chair, a fairly organized desk, photos of Emery and Evie and Colt. An annoying number of awards. Somehow, John-Henry had found time to change into uniform—a spare, North guessed, kept at the station for emergencies like this. Blue trousers. Crisp white shirt. It would be nice one day when John-Henry got a beer belly and his arms went all soft and wobbly the way a lot of old guys did. North was really looking forward to that.

For now, he said, "You look like a wiener in that uniform."

John-Henry's answering smile was startled and, for a moment, white-hot and genuine, and he glanced at Shaw's fuzzy shirt. "Better than a Muppet. Thanks for coming. Sit down."

"Just so everyone knows," Shaw said, "this is a cruelty-free pelt. This Muppet died in the wild of natural causes."

North made him sit down.

John-Henry paused to check a message on his phone. Then he looked up at them; he already looked tired, and North knew this was only the beginning of a lot of long days and nights for the chief of police. When he spoke, though, his voice was strong.

"I'd like to hire you to help with this investigation. In particular, with running down our primary suspect."

North shifted in his seat. "Ok."

"Ok?" John-Henry asked.

Shaw nodded. "Ok."

A tiny smile flickered. "I thought it might be a little more difficult than that."

"The difficult part," Emery said, "is going to happen the first time you try to tell them what to do."

"Oh, yeah," North said, "we're fucking terrible at taking orders."

"Very bad," Shaw said, nodding enthusiastically. "The worst."

"Uh huh," John-Henry said. "That's not exactly reassuring."

"Look, we're already tied up in this," North said.

"Because you're our friends," Shaw said.

"Because it's an interesting investigation."

"And we care about you," Shaw said. "We love you so much. Both of you, although mostly Emery. No offense, John-Henry."

"Are you kidding me? If anything, we're doing this because I feel sorry for John-Henry because he lives in this shithole, and in a place like this, beggars can't be choosers."

"What's that supposed to mean?" Shaw asked, bristling in his seat.

"Exactly what you think it means: if he could get any non-crazy, non-asshole dick in this bunghole of a town, he would have. Instead, he's got chuckle-fucks."

"That's you," Shaw said to Emery. "You're chuckle-fucks."

"I hadn't realized," Emery said.

"I'll have you know Emery is a top prospect," Shaw said. "In this town. In any town. He's a Wahredua ten. And he's a New York City ten and a half."

"It's a fucking ten scale, jackass. He can't be a New York City ten and a half."

"Really? Let's do the math. Thighs: ten. Ass: ten and a half. Dick—"

"Ok," John-Henry said. "As much as I would normally enjoy this, I've got to keep moving, guys. There's a lot to do."

"Of course," Shaw said. "I'm sorry for my colleague's unprofessional behavior."

"His dick would be a three because it's probably falling off from scurvy," North said.

"If anything, his dick would be—"

Emery clapped his hands. "Jackasses, enough."

North settled back into his seat.

"What have you got?" Emery asked.

"It's a mess," John-Henry said. "Where do I start? The cameras were deactivated, for one. For another, we've got a deputy missing, and an offender escaped."

"Jesus Christ. Why were the fucking cameras turned off?"

"Great question," John-Henry said.

Emery looked like he wanted to get his teeth into that, so North leaned forward. "Do you have a timeline?"

"Kind of. The cameras went off around seven. A deputy found the sheriff and Dalton a little after eight; they got a hold of me pretty quickly after that. We've got BOLOs out for the missing deputy and the offender, and Highway Patrol is putting up roadblocks and checkpoints."

"An hour," Emery said. "That's a lot of time."

John-Henry nodded. "They could be anywhere at this point, but if Highway Patrol moves fast, maybe they'll catch something."

"Do we know what happened?" Shaw asked. "Did Dalton attack the sheriff? Why was the sheriff even there?"

"We don't know. They run a skeleton crew at night. The deputy who found the sheriff was one of two who were supposed to be on duty in the men's unit."

"And the other one?" Emery asked.

"I'll get to him in a minute. The deputy who found them, his name is Glover."

"Jesus."

North cocked an eyebrow.

"He's not that bad," John-Henry said to the unasked question. "Well, he's pretty bad—lazy, aggressive, all-around incompetent."

"Oh," North said, "a cop. Got it."

"Incompetent doesn't begin to describe it," Emery said. "That's like saying the Hindenburg was a whoopsie."

John-Henry's smile was a shadow and then gone. "The point is, Glover might not be a good deputy, but nobody seems to think he's a corrupt one." Emery opened his mouth, but John-Henry kept talking. "We don't know that for sure, obviously; we're going to have a major case squad here tomorrow, possibly a special prosecutor, the Highway Patrol. Glover's going to have so many people crawling through his life, if he's dirty, we'll know pretty soon." For a moment, John-Henry was silent as though gathering his thoughts. "According to Glover, last night, another deputy should have been on duty. His name is Adam Ezell. He showed up for his shift and then left; Glover doesn't know why."

"That's not suspicious," Emery said. "If he was involved, he couldn't have picked a worse way to draw attention to himself."

"A little before eight, the sheriff left to do rounds; Glover insists that the sheriff offered to do it, which I have to admit is in keeping with Engels's personality. When Engels didn't come back, Glover tried to get him on the radio."

"Weren't they concerned because the cameras weren't working?" Shaw asked. "I think they'd try to call someone. Maybe go into lockdown."

"They probably should have, yes," John-Henry said. "But you've got to understand, this is a small jail in a small county."

"With a small budget," Emery said.

"That's true too. It's not a high-security prison, and it's—well, it's Wahredua. Glover said the sheriff was going to have someone come out first thing in the morning."

"But it's convenient," North said, "the cameras going out like that."

"It's more than convenient," Shaw said.

John-Henry nodded. "We don't know what happened in that cell, but by the time Glover went to check, both the sheriff and Dalton Weber were dead."

"When did they find Ambyr?" North asked.

"Not long after that. They did a head count, of course, and that's when they learned she'd hanged herself."

"Conveniently," Emery said sourly.

John-Henry gave a weary shrug. "That's also when they discovered that Philip Welch was missing. That's who I want you to find. Hold on, I've got his photo here."

He sorted through the papers in front of him and found a folder, which turned out to be Welch's file. North studied the photo clipped to the inside. The photo was only a headshot, but Welch's height and weight were given on the intake form—five-five, a hundred and eleven pounds. That might not qualify for a world record, but Welch was officially tiny, and in the photo, he looked even smaller because he was so young. The form listed his race as Black, but he was light-skinned and wore his hair buzzed. His lantern jaw gave his otherwise fine bone structure an oddly distended look.

Flipping through the rest of the file, North tried to paint a picture of the man in front of him. "He's a frequent flyer, huh? Gangbang stuff in Jeff City. Dealing in Columbia. What'd they pick him up for here?"

"Possession with intent to distribute," John-Henry said.

Emery grunted and held out a hand, and North, because he could, leaned back in the chair and fanned himself with the file. With a snort that could have been anything from amusement to murderous intent, Emery snatched the file from him and leaned against John-Henry's desk as he began to read.

"How did the sheriff die?" Shaw asked.

The emptiness of his voice made North take a considering look. Shaw wouldn't meet his gaze, but he hugged himself, angling his body toward John-Henry.

John-Henry said, "He was stabbed. I'm not even going to try to guess how many times, but a lot; the medical examiner has him now."

"Shiv," Emery said without looking up.

"That seems likely. Dalton died the same way."

"The sheriff didn't fight back?"

For a moment, frustration flared in John-Henry's face. He spread his hands. "We don't know. He didn't have his service weapon with him."

"What kind of rinky-dink operation is this?" North asked. "Aren't there doors that only open on buzzers, that kind of thing?"

"It's a county jail in rural Missouri," Emery said, his attention still fixed on the file. "It might as well be a popsicle stand."

"He had the sheriff's keys," John-Henry said. "It's not clear—not yet, anyway—what other security measures had been compromised like the cameras. We're going to have people going over this place with a fine-toothed comb. God, it's going to be a nightmare."

Emery looked up from the file to study his husband. Then he moved behind the desk to lay a hand on John-Henry's shoulder. He squeezed once, and John-Henry nodded and rubbed his forehead.

"Do we know anything about what happened with Ambyr?" Shaw asked. "Had she said anything about harming herself? Does anyone know what kind of condition she was in today?"

This time, North didn't have to look; he could hear it in Shaw's voice, the mind-fuck, like oil slicking clean water. "Shaw, maybe you and Emery want to go over that file together? You can see if he missed anything."

"I certainly didn't miss—" Emery began, but maybe, against all odds, even Emery Hazard could occasionally catch a hint because he glanced at Shaw and shut his mouth. "Yes. There is, I suppose, always a possibility. If you'd like to help me—"

Shaw shook his head, still not looking at North.

"If she'd talked about self-harm," John-Henry said, "she'd have been on suicide watch. They have female deputies on staff for the female offenders, but none of them heard or saw anything unusual."

"Sure," North said. "Why would they?"

"She must have been scared," Shaw said, his voice barely more than a whisper. "And humiliated, and alone."

"Shaw, I need you to hold it together for me."

Shaw nodded, eyes hooded and looking off into his own private nightmares.

John-Henry glanced at North, but North shook his head. "Did Welch take the sheriff's car?"

"Yeah," John-Henry said. "Private vehicle because the sheriff's department cruiser is in the shop."

"Which means no lo-jacking," Emery said. "Which is consistent with everything else in this case being fucking perfect."

"We're working on it; our guess is that Welch only took it to get clear of Wahredua. He'll ditch it as soon as he can if he's smart." John-Henry shook himself as though remembering something and plucked a sheet of paper from his desk. "Ezell, so you know what he looks like."

The picture showed a moon-faced white man with a perpetual flush. His blond hair was slicked back and thinning so that you could see the shape of his skull. He wore the khaki uniform of a sheriff's deputy.

"Another of Wahredua's finest," North said. He held the photo out for Shaw, but Shaw didn't seem to see it; after a few seconds, North passed it to Emery.

"He doesn't have any official complaints filed against him," John-Henry said, "and nobody seems to have any unofficial ones either. From what I could gather, nobody seemed to suspect he was dirty. Always showed up, did his job, went home."

North nodded.

"Are you comfortable if we do the contract tomorrow?" John-Henry asked. "I can ask one of our administrative assistants to draw up a version of the one we use when we contract Emery; I'm already an hour behind where I should be tonight, and there's a million more things to do."

Waving away the question, North settled himself in the chair. "Why do you want to hire us?"

"Fantastic question," Emery murmured.

"Because I need manpower," John-Henry said. "And I need results. And most importantly, I need someone I can trust. You're our friends, and I know I'm asking a lot, but I think you know we're neck deep in this already. Someone arranged these murders. The same someone who went after Jem and Tean. The same person who attacked Theo and Auggie in their home. This isn't over."

"They're barely getting started," Emery said, voice so low he might have been speaking to himself.

North gave him a long look.

"John's not wrong," Emery said. "I'd also add that your methods are…unconventional, which in this situation may prove to be an asset."

North nodded.

"Is there a problem?" John-Henry asked. "I understand if you don't want to—" He didn't quite look at Shaw, but he didn't need to; North could feel the pull, the way Shaw was acting on all of them like a dark gravity. "If you need to think about it first."

"No," North said. "We'll do it. I just wanted to hear both of you admit we're hot shit first."

"I never said—" Emery began.

Before he could finish, though, raised voices came from the bullpen: the words were indistinct, but the volume and tone suggested anger.

Emery, looking out the window, grimaced. "Brother Gary and Red Alvin."

"Problem?" North asked.

"The sheriff's department's on-call clowns."

"They're detectives for the sheriff's department," John-Henry said. "And they're not going to be happy when they find out I'm directing the investigation. You might want to clear out while you can."

"Can you call over to the jail?" North asked as he stood. Shaw didn't move, so he caught Shaw's elbow and helped him to his feet. "We'll start there."

John-Henry nodded. His eyes moved to Shaw. "North—"

"We'll be fine," North said.

He led Shaw out of the office, and instead of heading for the entrance, they broke right toward a fire door across the bullpen. He had a glimpse of two men arguing with a pair of uniformed officers—one man wore a white suit like Matlock, and the other, in a track suit, looked like death warmed over. John-Henry had been right: they didn't look happy, and North figured they were going to be even more upset by the time the night was over.

"Come on," he said, joggling Shaw's elbow. "We've got a murder to solve."

3

North got Shaw settled in the GTO, and then he started driving back to Emery and John-Henry's house. The streets of the small town seemed impossibly empty; in St. Louis, there was always the low-grade thrum of traffic. Here, though, they passed intersection after intersection, the lights all switched over to red blinkers, the streets like hollow places in the darkness.

Shaw stirred, blinked, looked around. "Where are we—North, no!"

"North, yes."

"I'm fine."

"You're most definitely not fine. You're going to call Dr. Farr—"

"It's the middle of the night!"

"—and I'm going to stay with you until I'm sure you're ok—"

"I'm fine! North, stop!"

"—and then I'm going to make Tean babysit you and Jem bully you until I can drive you home."

"No!"

North kept driving.

"Hey, are you listening to me? I said no. North, stop the car right now or—or I'll drive us into that Chick-fil-A!"

"You wouldn't dare."

"I would! I'll wreck your car."

"Nope. You won't even eat Chick-fil-A because you don't believe in giving your money to anti-LGBTQ organizations, so there's no way you'd sacrifice all your morals now and use their building to wreck my car."

Shaw gaped at him. "I'll use the Lee's!"

North rolled his eyes.

"This is central Missouri, you—you giant jackass! There are fried chicken places on every street!"

North couldn't help it: a laugh slipped out of him. Shaw grabbed the wheel, and North let him. Instead of death by Popeye's, though, Shaw steered them into a parking lot that had once been anchored by a Kmart. North slowed the car, and they ended up parked in a stall.

"Look at that," North said quietly. "Teamwork. And we're not dead."

"I decided it would dishonor the ghosts of all those chickens."

North nodded.

"If you knew how inhumane poultry farms were—"

"I am scared this is going to hurt you." North managed to hold back, at the very end, the rest of what he wanted to say: *more than you can bear.* "And I'm scared of seeing you like that. You don't know what it's like, what I feel like. It's like losing you. And I'm not going to lose you."

"I'll be fine," Shaw said. "I can do this."

"You don't have to be fine, Shaw. You don't have to do this."

"They're our friends—"

"Who cares? You are the one person who matters to me, get it? They can all go to hell if it means keeping you safe. This is their fucking mess." Shaw opened his mouth, and North said, "And I'm not talking about abandoning them, you horse's ass. I'm saying you should go back to St. Louis. We've put everything on hold at Borealis while we've been down here; Zion and Truck can't carry the load forever."

"I wish Truck had heard you say, 'Carry the load.' Ze would have cried out of pure happiness."

"We need to get back to work. So, this is perfect. You keep Borealis afloat, and I'll help these morons."

"This is too dangerous."

North couldn't help the sound he made.

"I'm serious," Shaw said. "Whoever's behind this, they killed a sheriff, North. That's not messing around. That's—that's crazy. And it's more than that. What if you got hurt? What if someone attacked you? Theo and Jem couldn't stop that guy when he came to Theo's house."

"Ok, well, first of all, I cannot fucking believe you'd compare me to those two. We're not even in the same league. Theo is literally a teacher. He teaches. Kids. About books. And he's ancient." North tried to repress a shudder. "Jesus, Shaw, for all we know, he could be forty. And Jem? That pansy ass in the windbreakers and the grandma sweaters and the dick-dangling shorts? I could kick their asses up and down the block and not break a sweat."

"That's very macho. I hate machismo."

"Yeah, but your Mr. Slinky kind of loves it."

"No, he doesn't. I mean, I don't. I hate it. And I own a lot of windbreakers."

"And you look like a horse's ass in them. As I've told you. Many times."

"And I own grandma sweaters."

"Yeah, but yours are cuter."

"And I always wear dick-dangling shorts."

North brushed a loose strand of hair away from Shaw's forehead and kissed him. Then he said, "That's fine because you've got such a pretty dick."

"I'm not leaving you," Shaw said. "We're a team. We're partners. In every way that matters." North opened his mouth, but Shaw said, "I know — I know I don't handle things well. Hard things, I mean. But I don't think that's different, not in the long run, from you risking your life. We're both taking risks, but we're safer when we're together."

It's different, North wanted to say, because it's you. It's different because the world is hard and meant to cut, and no matter how deeply it slices, you never heal, never scar. It's different because I can keep you safe from a lot of things, but I can't keep you safe from that.

"And Jem would be a terrible bully," Shaw said, sniffling and wiping his nose. "He let me let him braid my hair, and all I had to do was give him my Amex."

"Jesus Christ," North muttered.

He tried to think of a way to say no. He tried to find an escape hatch, a release valve. Hell, he'd settle for a Wonkavator. Anything to get Shaw out of this. But the sharp, fierce beauty of Shaw's face was set, and North recognized the expression, knew that he'd lost this fight the way he'd lost most of them. He brushed that errant strand of hair away again, kissed Shaw once more—just a brush of lips, but he went slowly, the way you move when you're holding glass. Then he pulled back, looked for the darkness in Shaw's eyes, and found only Shaw—hazel, the rims red.

"Well, then," North murmured, "fuck me."

4

The county jail was attached to the rear of the sheriff's station, which sat in the center of Wahredua alongside several other government buildings. A few of them, like city hall, were remarkable pieces for a town this size — built when civic pride meant spending the time and money to do things right, in limestone and bronze. Other buildings, though, showed the inspiration of budget restrictions and committee groupthink: long, low buildings that had been thrown up when land was cheap and available, and when the driving aesthetic imperative had been brown.

"Brown's making a comeback," Shaw decided to tell North.

"No, it's not."

Sheriff's department cruisers crowded the parking lot, many with their lights still flashing, and North parked a hundred yards off. Men and women milled around with the purposeless activity of people who didn't know what to do but didn't know how to leave, either. Many of them wore deputy uniforms — or, like one guy with sleep-tousled hair and boxer shorts to complement his uniform shirt, parts of their uniform — but others were clearly paramedics, and others had the look of administrative personnel. It was a small town, and tragedy meant people you knew.

North and Shaw made it through most of the restless crowd without more than a few side-eye glances, but as they drew closer to the sheriff's station, a square-jawed guy darted into their path and held up a hand. He wore a rumpled deputy's uniform, and he smelled — to borrow a phrase Shaw had heard from North and would never have used himself, on account of being sex positive — like a two-bit whorehouse.

"Hold on," the guy said, in case putting his hand up wasn't clear. "You can't go in there."

"We can," North said, detouring around him, "and we are."

"Hey!" the man barked, prancing backward, hand going to the gun at his side. "I'm ordering you to stop right now!"

North stopped. He gave the man a slow up-and-down look. It was similar, Shaw thought, to the time North had caught Shaw and the puppy arguing over who was going to get to sleep with North that night. That sounded silly, Shaw decided. Nobody argued with a puppy. They had been negotiating.

"Buzz off," North said.

The deputy's eyes flicked to him and back to North. "I don't know who you are, but—"

"Jackass, the chief of police sent us over here, so you can call Chief Somerset and clear it with him. While you do, my partner and I are going to get to work."

For a moment, the deputy looked like he might back down. Then his face hardened, and he opened his mouth.

"Let them through, Moore." The voice belonged to a woman who stood in the station's doorway, backlit by the yellow wash of interior light. "McKinney? Aldrich?"

"That's us," North said as they started forward.

She wore the brown uniform of a deputy, and her nametag said Weiss. She was past forty, on the stocky side, her brown hair cut short. She gave Shaw a familiar negotiating-with-the-puppy look, and when she turned to face North, Shaw caught a hint of a limp in the way she carried herself. Now, up close, Shaw could make out the film of shock covering her features, and beneath it, the deeper layer of grief. After checking their IDs, she jerked her head for them to follow, and they went inside.

They didn't go far. She stopped in the lobby and said, "Chief Somerset said to give you whatever you need. What do you need?"

"We'd like to see Dalton Weber's cell," North said, "as well as the route the sheriff would have taken. Then anything you can give us that might help with finding Welch: security footage from before the cameras went down, visitor logs, phone records."

Weiss nodded. "The cell's locked down until Highway Patrol can get here and process it—Chief Somerset's orders. But I can walk you past it, and you can take a look."

"That works."

She took them down a hallway that led toward the back of the building. The station looked like a lot of government facilities Shaw had been in: the high-traffic carpet squares with a microdot pattern meant to disguise dirt and wear; painted cinderblock walls that never quite looked like they were meant for human occupation; sterile pieces of non-art mixed with informational posters about how to run a neighborhood watch or what to do if someone left their briefcase at a bus station (SAY SOMETHING!). One of the posters had to be from the Depression—it showed a woman in a nightgown and curlers peering out her door at the suspicious outlines of two tramps, bindles over their shoulders. The words were simple: NOT IN OUR TOWN.

"Jesus," North muttered.

"I have those curlers," Shaw said.

North tried twice to slap him upside the head, but both times Shaw was faster.

It was silly, yes. It was stupid. It was, Shaw knew—because he could hear his mother and father saying it in their own distinct ways—wildly inappropriate. But it was the lifeline he and North threw each other when the darkness was too deep to swim in. Plus, it was fun, and it made North smile, and that went a long way toward pushing the nightmares back.

Instead of taking them through the visitors' entrance to the jail, Weiss unlocked a steel security door and led them through a suite of offices. She stopped where another security door was propped open. Inside, a bank of monitors showed empty screens. Large windows looked out into the jail's chow hall. "As you can see, the cameras are still out of order. The tech is supposed to come out tomorrow and tell us what happened."

"Is this where the sheriff would have been?"

Weiss shook her head. "Normally, the sheriff would have been in his office, but Ezell was gone—you know about that?"

"We heard something."

"The sheriff came back here to hold down the fort with Glover. This part is called the control center."

"Add that to the list," North said. "We want to talk to Glover."

"Get in line. He's already got his union rep, and he's not talking to anyone until Highway Patrol gets here."

North grunted. "So, how would the sheriff have gone to check on Weber?"

Weiss led them across the control center to a door. The door had a security window that looked into a small enclosure, with another door at the other end. The design was familiar—it was called a sally port, or a mantrap, and each door had to be unlocked in turn. In theory, this meant an offender couldn't jump a guard while he was entering or exiting the secure portion of the facility. Or rather, an offender could jump a guard, but they still wouldn't be able to escape.

Steps made Shaw turn. A thin-faced deputy with penciled-on eyebrows stood in the doorway. Her nametag said Lang.

"Deputy Lang was on tonight as well," Weiss said.

"Here?" North asked.

"The women's unit." Lang's voice was deeper than he'd expected. "We didn't know anything had happened until the alarm."

"We're going to want to talk to you," North said. "About Ambyr Hobbs."

"Chief Somerset sent them," Weiss said.

Lang's face remained skeptical. Or maybe that was just the eyebrows. All she said, though, was, "I can't help you. They found her in the laundry, not the women's unit."

Weiss produced a keycard and let them through first one door, then the other. North was frowning.

"It's called a sally port," Shaw said.

"I know what it's called," North snapped.

"Oh. Because it looked like you didn't."

North scowled at him as he strode off after Weiss.

The secure portion of the jail smelled like what Shaw thought of as hospital cleaner, with an underlying flush of warm bodies and warmed-over cafeteria food—tinned meats and overcooked grains. It looked well maintained, with panels of fluorescents providing unflinching light. There were no Alcatraz-style corridors of cells. Instead, Weiss led them past a door with a sign above it that said DORM 1, and men looked out at them from the inset security window. No one said anything. No catcalls or hoots or shouts. But the sound of restless movement came even through the closed door, and the animal part of Shaw's brain was aware of too many eyes focused on him. Ahead, North's shoulders were tight, and his head moved slowly from side to side.

Weiss had to stop at another sally port, where she used her keycard again to get them through.

"How big is this place?" North asked. "I thought we were talking about a county jail."

"You've seen most of it," Weiss said. "There's a second men's dorm, the rec room, the yard, the canteen. The women's facility is even smaller, and the isolation unit—that's what this is—doesn't get used unless we need it."

"Why was Dalton Weber in isolation?" Shaw asked.

"We usually have people in isolation for a few reasons. One, they're a danger to themselves. Two, they're a danger to the other offenders. Three, they're in danger, and we're trying to keep them safe. Sometimes a lawyer asks the judge for special housing. That happens if we've got someone with a gang affiliation, for example. LGBTQ offenders are another one."

"Is that why Dalton was in here? Because he was gay?"

"I don't know why the sheriff put Mr. Weber in isolation, but that seems like a good guess."

North waited for her to start walking again before he whispered, "Or the sheriff knew Dalton was an important witness because John-Henry told him."

"Or that," Shaw whispered back.

The isolation unit was much smaller, and instead of dorms, Shaw found the cells he had expected to see earlier. They were all empty. Two doors stood open, and a deputy stood watch—clearly responsible for making sure nobody tampered with the scene before the Highway Patrol forensic unit was able to process it. He looked like a farm boy about to pop out of his uniform—in a good way. His nametag said Andersen.

"Why don't you ask him to take his shirt off?" North said. "It'll make it easier to climb up on his tits."

"I didn't—"

"And try not to swallow your tongue if it's not too much trouble."

"I wasn't—North, I would never—I mean, yes, I looked—" Shaw managed to stop himself. "Don't say tits!"

"I'm sorry—" Andersen began automatically, holding up a hand.

"They're not going in there," Weiss said. "They're with Wahredua PD, and Chief Somerset sent them over to take a look."

Andersen seemed ok with that; he settled back into position. The uniform was exceptionally close fitting, and Shaw wasn't sure if it was a trick of the light or if—

"That's his dong," North whispered furiously.

"I know that! I mean, I thought I knew that. I mean, sometimes the way the fabric lies, the optics of the bulge, you know—"

"You know what? I changed my mind. I don't want to marry you."

"North!"

"I'm good with this weird thing we have. I'm a faithful and loyal partner, and you're this pervy little skeeve I drag around so you can stare at farm boys' dingalings."

"Oh my God, he does look like a farm boy, doesn't he?"

For whatever reason, that made North's face flash red, and he stomped a few paces closer to the cell, ignoring Andersen's warning look.

Shaw caught Deputy Weiss's side-eye and was suddenly aware of how he and North must seem—the poor taste of it all, the crassness, what must have looked like levity instead of what it really was: fear. The humor was a cheap veneer neither he nor North could risk letting fall. But Shaw didn't know where to start explaining it, or if this was one of those things people didn't say out loud.

So, instead, Shaw walked past Weiss and North and Andersen to inspect the other cell that was open. The room inside held only a metal bunk bolted to the wall, a thin mattress, and a stainless-steel toilet and sink.

"Who was in this room? Uh, cell. Who was in this cell?"

"Philip Welch," Weiss said.

"The inmate who escaped?"

Weiss nodded.

"Why was he in here?"

"Gang affiliations. It would have been too risky to house him with the general population."

"Because it's full of neo-Nazi white trash," North said.

Andersen stiffened.

"Because it would have been too risky," Weiss said again.

Shaw glanced around, but the other cells looked unoccupied. "Was anyone else in the isolation unit?"

"No," Weiss said.

"So, Welch was the only one who could have gotten to Dalton?"

Weiss grimaced. "Nobody should have been able to attack Mr. Weber in his cell. Everyone should have been locked down for the night. In the isolation unit, they're locked down twenty-three hours a day."

"But that's clearly not what happened," North said, and he directed a meaningful look at Shaw before turning his attention back to the cell. Shaw moved over to join him as North continued, "So, what did happen?"

"Ideally," Weiss said in a tone that Shaw couldn't pin down, "the explanation is that some sort of failure in the locking mechanism of the cell doors left both Welch and Weber unsecured."

"Yeah," North said, "that'd be great. What really happened?"

"We can't be sure until the doors are inspected—"

"You didn't have some sort of tragic coincidence when both doors magically unlocked themselves. Somebody made sure these two cell doors were open. The question is, who?"

Weiss's mouth twisted, but she didn't answer. Andersen's face was ruddled with what must have been anger.

"Do you need to see anything else?" Weiss asked. "Or are we finished here?"

For the first time, Shaw let himself look into Dalton Weber's cell. Both Weber's body and the sheriff's had been removed, but blood puddled on the floor, slowly drying on the concrete. More blood spattered the bunk, the walls, the sink. John-Henry had told them that the sheriff had been stabbed multiple times, but that didn't come close to describing what must have happened. Shaw could picture it: the rapid thrusts, the resistance of muscle as the shiv penetrated, the frantic, manic energy driving Welch to stab over and over again, the blood spraying out, black under the fluorescents, the sound of the dying men's breaths under the flurry of blows—

North squeezed Shaw's nape. Shaw drew in a ragged breath. He blinked his eyes clear and nodded.

"We're done here," North said.

Weiss led them back the way they'd come, and North kept his hand on Shaw's neck. Eyes followed them from the darkness. Shaw thought he could feel air moving against his skin, the collective breath of men caged like animals. Sweat slicked his neck where North's hand lay heavy on it. When they stepped back into the control center, safely behind the sally port and under the watchful gaze of Deputy Lang and her eyebrows, North let his hand slide down Shaw's back, Shaw felt cold, and he shivered in spite of himself.

"Question number one," North said. "How the fuck did Philip Welch walk out of here?"

Lang's mouth tightened at the swear, but Weiss just shrugged. "If you're talking about the sally ports, well, they all have a mechanical bypass."

"Let me guess: the sheriff is the only one with the keys."

"It's a security protocol." Weiss shrugged again. "He's not the only one, but he does have a set. In theory. If you want my guess, Welch did what he did and then waited. He stayed out of sight until Glover went to investigate why the sheriff had been gone so long. Then, while Glover was headed down to the isolation unit, he walked right out of here."

"Really good fucking system," North said. "They could do a whole 'Your Dollars at Work' show about this fuck-up."

"Why didn't the sheriff use his gun?" Shaw asked.

"Because he wasn't carrying it," Lang said, the words a little shrill, a little sharp. "Obviously."

North spared her a glare for *obviously*, but he turned his attention back to Weiss when she spoke.

"All firearms are stored in a locker outside the secure facility," Weiss said. "If there was an emergency, I guess maybe he'd take his with him. But walking back there with a gun is against protocol. I think Deputy Lang's right about the surprise. When the sheriff stepped out of the sally port—that would be a good place to get the jump on him."

"But there weren't any signs of a struggle," Shaw said.

"Inside the cell, then. He might have seen that Dalton was hurt, gone to check on him. It would have been a mistake, not following protocol, but everybody makes mistakes."

"Is his gun here?"

Weiss grimaced. "We don't have the key, but one of the lockers is still in use."

Hands on hips, North was silent for what felt like a long time. When he looked at Shaw, Shaw read the question in his face and shook his head.

"What kind of timeline are we talking here?"

"What do you mean?"

"Somebody unlocked those cells. When could that have happened?"

"If it was a mechanical failure—" Lang began.

But Weiss spoke over her. "We do rounds and checks once an hour, and five full head counts every day. You didn't see, because we didn't go in there, but the dorms have an observation room so a CO can keep an eye on things. Everyone's in their dorm by eight. When we've got someone in isolation, we do checks every fifteen minutes."

"That's why the sheriff went back there?" Shaw asked. "Routine?"

"And we have floor deputies in the rec room, the yard, the canteen," Lang said. "But that's only during the day, before lockdown."

"That's our best guess," Weiss said. "A routine check, and Welch got the jump on him. But, like I said, Glover isn't talking."

"So, whoever did the rounds before the sheriff must have unlocked the cell doors," North said.

"Not necessarily," Lang said. She gave him the eyebrows again. "They could have been unlocked for hours. It's not like we rattle the doors every time we do rounds."

Shaw caught North's eye and shook his head.

"Anything else we should be asking?" North said.

"About the jail?" Weiss frowned. "The only thing I'd say is that Welch had to know somebody was coming. Fifteen-minute intervals, right? As soon as someone did rounds, he would have killed Mr. Weber. Then he waited for the next deputy to do the rounds."

"So, it wasn't heat of the moment," North said. "It was an ambush."

"The real question," Shaw said, "is did he know it would be the sheriff."

Nobody seemed to have an answer for that.

"Let's see what else you've got," North said.

Weiss settled them in an office that was so spartan that it had to be communal: a particleboard desk, two back-punishing office chairs, another piece of non-art (a print of a waterfall), and a poster, black with yellow letters, that said, PRISON OFFICER—BECAUSE GOD WAS ALREADY TAKEN. North's eyebrows went up at that.

"I've already got the visitor logs," she said, pointing to a binder on the desk.

"That was fast," North said with something like approval in his voice.

"It wasn't hard. We've had Welch for a couple of weeks, but Weber's only been here a few days. That's the last six weeks. It's not like we're the Ritz."

"We can take this?" North asked.

Weiss laughed.

"It was worth a shot," North said with a grin. "Copies?"

"I'll make them before you leave. Chief Somerset has their files already; he took them with him."

"He let us look at them," North said.

Weiss moved the binder aside and revealed a folder underneath. She opened it to reveal what appeared to be printed stills from security cameras. The images were in black and white and suffered from the usual graininess that could be attributed to government spending and outdated technology, but they weren't terrible. Weiss flicked through them, and Shaw glimpsed several high-angle shots of a man in a suit.

"I did my best to match the face to the name," she said. "I went by the sign-in time. I guess it's possible the logs aren't accurate, but we're pretty good about that. You might find that hard to believe after tonight, but it's the truth."

North's eyebrows went up again. "That's helpful."

"Welch only had the one visitor, you see." She slid the folder of security stills aside and opened yet another folder. This one held phone records, with several lines highlighted. "He spoke on the phone to a few different people, but he only had the one visitor."

"Thank you for doing this," Shaw said.

"How'd you have time?" North asked.

Weiss snorted. "What was I supposed to do? Walk around in circles out there so everyone can see how useless I am?"

"You'd be in good company."

"You've got no idea."

North took the visitors' log and the security stills and pushed the phone records toward Shaw. It didn't take Shaw long to read through them. Philip Welch had spoken on the phone with four people: Liliana Cain, Melvin Welch, Carly Welch, and Maleah Donaldson. It wasn't hard to guess that at least one of the four was a lawyer, the other three were likely family.

When he glanced over, North was considering one of the security stills. It gave a surprisingly good look at the man's face: square jaw, dark hair in a businessman's special, old enough that nobody would ever think he was in his twenties again, but not so old he'd started to spread.

"Who's Eric Brey?" he asked. "And why is this guy visiting a small-time gangbanger and drug dealer?"

Weiss shrugged.

"What about Ambyr?" Shaw asked. "Did you have time to pull her visitors and calls?"

"She hasn't had any," Weiss said.

"None?"

"Zero. No visitors. No calls. I double checked."

"She didn't have a lawyer?" North asked.

"She had one. A public defender, I think. She was here barely twenty-four hours, so like I said: no visitors, no calls."

"And Dalton?"

"Mr. Weber didn't make any calls either, and he didn't have any visitors."

"He was in here longer than twenty-four hours."

"And I'm telling you I checked: he didn't make any calls."

North and Shaw exchanged a look, and finally North said, "All right."

Shaw took pictures of each page of the documents—there weren't that many—and then forwarded the images to a group chat with the other men. His phone buzzed a moment later with a message from Auggie: *On it.*

North rolled his eyes.

"Be nice," Shaw said.

"Fucking eager beaver."

"It's cute."

"You know he was a suck-up in school, right? That's how he ended up swinging on Theo's—" North seemed to remember Weiss at the last moment. His cheeks reddened, and he cleared his throat.

In a dry voice, Weiss said, "If there's nothing else..."

"A couple of things," North said. "What's your read on Glover?"

"He's a jackass and a shit deputy." Weiss delivered the words without a pause. "But he wasn't part of this, if that's what you're thinking."

"Why not?"

"He's too stupid, for one. For another, I saw him after the alarm went off. That man was about to piss himself. He walks around three hundred and sixty-five days a year trying to step on people's necks, and when shit goes down, he needs an extra pair of Depends."

"What about Ezell?"

This time, Weiss did hesitate, and when she spoke, she seemed to be choosing her words carefully. "Yesterday, I would have told you he's solid. He's a redneck, but he does his job, and he doesn't go looking for trouble the way some guys do."

"But?" Shaw asked.

"But where the hell is he?"

"And what about Ambyr?" North asked. "That business about her hanging herself."

"What's that supposed to mean?"

"It's a question."

"Are you asking me if I let somebody do that to her?"

"I'm asking you if there's anything else to say. From what I understood, hanging yourself isn't exactly uncommon in jail, but it doesn't have a high success rate."

Weiss snorted. "You saw the dorms. We've got a CO staring down their shorts every minute of the day. Sometimes, somebody tries in the bathroom, but there's nothing high enough—their feet can touch the floor no matter what they use." Rubbing her cheek, Weiss frowned. "You heard Lang: they found her in the laundry. The question is how she got in there after lockdown. Nobody went into the women's unit. Nobody. If you think I'm lying, you'd better say it to my face."

"I didn't say you were lying." But North was slouched in his chair, and he was wearing the look of his that made a lot of people want to punch him. "You're getting awfully worked up about a question."

"I'm getting worked up because it's my job and I'm damn good at it. And I don't need some yahoo off the street walking in here asking me if I let a girl get killed on my watch."

"I apologize."

Weiss let out a huff.

"You know people are going to ask," North said.

"I know. But screw them and screw you."

"Welch took the sheriff's personal vehicle?"

It took Weiss a moment to recalibrate for the new line of questioning. "That's what it looks like."

"What kind of car was it? Do you have the license plate?"

"They already sent all that to the Highway Patrol."

"Yeah, well, we're not on their Christmas card list. Mind giving it to us too?"

Weiss gave him a look that mixed annoyance and a kind of wry surrender. Then she took one of the folders and jotted down *2015 Subaru Outback, red* and a license plate number.

"You're wasted in here," North said. "They should make you sheriff next."

Weiss's smile lolled as she rocked back in her chair. "That'd be the day."

5

"Does everything in this town close at nine o'clock?" North asked as they drove past another darkened strip mall. "Where the fuck am I? Mayberry?"

"Pull over," Shaw said. "We'll use my hotspot."

"We get charged for the hotspot. There's got to be somewhere with Wi-Fi."

"North, it's five dollars. Or ten dollars. Or a hundred dollars."

"We should have free Wi-Fi everywhere. It's twenty-fucking-twenty."

"I'll pay for it. I'll use my own money. It won't even be a Borealis expense."

"A coffeeshop. A grocery store. For fuck's sake, have they ever heard of McDonald's?"

"You can charge it," Shaw said as genius struck. "You can expense it to the Wahredua PD."

North gave him a sidelong look and then made a hard right into the next parking lot.

They sat, the soft glow of the dash illuminating the car's interior, as Shaw set up his hot spot and North logged in to his laptop. North made a satisfied noise as his laptop picked up the internet connection, and then he began opening tabs.

"What are you going to do?" he asked as he started typing.

"Daydream," Shaw said. "I've been working on this particular fantasy about a world without boots."

North bent lower over the laptop, and it sounded like he might have said, "Jesus Christ."

"It's a fair and just and equitable world."

"Why don't you do something useful? Why don't you wander into traffic or chew on a high-voltage line or something? Oh, but leave the phone."

"Nobody gets their toes stepped on."

"It was one time, mother of God, and I'm never going to hear the end of it."

"Innocent puppies aren't viciously de-tailed by hulking, stomping men who are angry because their cartoons got canceled."

"The puppy still has his tail, thanks very much, and why the fuck would you slap an infomercial into that Saturday morning time slot?"

"Nobody is a secondhand victim of boot foot."

North's head came up. "I do not have boot foot. I don't even know what that is. I mean, it's not a thing."

"Oh, it's definitely a thing. It's when your socks get all crusty—"

"You know what would be fun? Let's see if your head fits inside the glove compartment. How's that sound for a game?"

For about a minute, North tried to grab Shaw—he even went so far as to open the glove box—and Shaw fought him off. North was hampered by the fact that they were still in their seats, as well as by the laptop. Shaw was a victim of a giggling curse an invisible witch put on him—which he tried to tell North about, and which only made North shout louder—so, all in all, they were about even.

Finally, North gave up and said, "Make some fucking phone calls!" And then he went back to work on the laptop.

So, Shaw took out the list of phone records that Deputy Weiss had assembled for them, and he began to work his way through the highlighted numbers. The most recent one, for Liliana Cain, connected him to a recorded message for a law firm. He made a note of the firm's name in the margin and moved on.

Next, he tried the number for Melvin Welch. The phone rang several times before connecting to a voicemail service. There was no prerecorded message; instead, a robotic voice read off the number Shaw had called. When the tone beeped, Shaw made his voice as stilted as he could and said, "Hello, this is a recorded message from the Missouri Department of the Treasury. We have unclaimed funds for Philip Welch. To learn more, please call us back at your convenience." Then he recited his phone number and disconnected.

Shaw looked over at North.

"Not your best," North said.

Shaw couldn't help the dismay. "Not my best?"

"Your Avon lady is better."

"But an Avon lady wouldn't be calling—you're an asshole! That was really good!"

North shrugged as he clicked the trackpad.

Shaw placed the next call to Carly Welch. This time, a woman answered. Shaw opened his mouth, and then all he could hear was North inside his head saying, *Not your best.* Out of reflex, he started up with his same spiel. "Hello, this is a recorded message from the Missouri Department of the Treasury. We have unclaimed funds for Philip Welch."

"Fuck!" North swore.

"Hello?" The woman—presumably Carly Welch—said. There was a tapping noise like she might be checking the phone. "Hello? I thought this message was recorded."

In a rush, Shaw finished, "To learn more, please call us back at your convenience." He gave his phone number again and disconnected.

"God damn it," North said to himself. "Connect, you piece of shit."

"She heard you!"

North flicked him an annoyed look, grunted, and went back to work.

"That's why it wasn't my best work," Shaw said as he began to place his final call. "Because you ruined it."

North did some subvocal muttering that sounded distinctly unflattering.

Maleah Donaldson's voicemail picked up the call, and Shaw repeated his message for the third time. The idea was simple: people were often reluctant to talk if you asked them questions. But if you let them think they had something to gain, and you made them work a tiny bit for it—well, that was a different story.

"Which one is the mom?" North asked.

"I think Carly might be the grandmother. Any luck?"

North sat back and angled the laptop for Shaw to see the map and the highlighted route.

One of the Borealis investments they'd agreed on—after much handwringing by North, and much, much, much "please, I can't talk about this anymore" from Shaw—was to begin paying for an online database geared toward private investigators. It was actually a set of databases, and it drew on public records as well as proprietary information. It gave them access to a number of tools that they hadn't had before, and one of those — which North was currently playing with—was a system that tracked license plates through traffic cameras.

It wasn't perfect, of course. Traffic cameras didn't always catch a license plate, and not all camera systems uploaded their information, and — well, on and on like that. But it was a tool, and it was often helpful. And it looked like tonight was one of the helpful nights because North had plotted out several appearances of the sheriff's license plate.

"These are from tonight?" Shaw asked.

"No, I figured I'd map every time his license plate has appeared on camera anytime in the last year."

"I know you use sarcasm as a shield, but I hope one day you'll shed your armor and let the healing warmth of human love—oh holy Buddha, my hair!"

When North released him, Shaw rubbed the de-scalped section—he had a fresh understanding of the puppy's suffering now, and he vowed, once again, to be more forgiving the next time the puppy bit him in the, er, private area. By accident, as North insisted. Then he leaned in for a closer look at the laptop.

The sheriff's license plate had appeared several times within Wahredua that evening—which made sense, since the city would have the highest concentration of traffic cameras. Then the trail went dark for a while until two hits in Eldon and then another hit in Versailles.

"He's going west," Shaw said, still rubbing his scalp. "He's past the roadblock; there's no way they're looking for him that far."

"Someone's going west," North said. "If Welch is smart, he's already ditched the sheriff's car. Or at least traded plates." He was quiet for a moment and then he panned the map to the west and pointed to a city called Auburn, where all this mess had started. "But then there's that, and what are the odds it's a coincidence?"

"The Cottonmouth Club," Shaw said.

"Or some jabroni with a fresh set of plates happens to be driving that way."

"North, it can't be a coincidence. Dalton was going to identify the man he met at the Cottonmouth Club. Ambyr was the one who introduced them. And now they're both dead before the investigation can even get off the ground, and the killer is driving straight toward the club."

Neither of them spoke for a moment. On the street, a Highlander rolled past, tires thrumming against the asphalt. Then stillness descended again. No wind. No night birds. Nothing but the GTO's rumble, and the air conditioning's valiant attempt to push back the sticky heat, and the flicker of an Amoco sign.

"The police have access to all this data," North said in a painfully neutral tone. "They'll figure out—"

"No," Shaw said. He made his voice gentler, as best he could, and said, "No. I know you're trying to—I appreciate it, North. But you know that they're going to take time to get mobilized, for the investigation to start moving. That's the nature of a bureaucracy."

"They also have big guns and bulletproof vests and a hell of a lot more bodies."

"North, he's not going to stay with the sheriff's car forever. He's going to ditch it, and then this lead goes cold."

North was silent, but the struggle showed in his face. "John-Henry could use you—"

"No."

"If I call Emery—"

"No."

Something snapped, and North burst out, "Well, God fucking damn it, will you let me finish a sentence?"

"Come on," Shaw said, and he found North's hand and squeezed it. "Let's go see which jabroni is driving around with the sheriff's license plates."

North's features twisted, and for a moment, the armor fell away. Behind it was fear, and fresh pain, and a kind of wildly grappling resolve to take control again. And then everything got buckled down again, and his face closed, and he started to drive.

6

North drove through the night, and as they left Wahredua's lights behind them, the darkness became a canvas for his nightmares. Shaw in the hospital after the West End Slasher had almost gutted him. Shaw lying at the bottom of the parking garage stairs, the night Marvin Hanson had almost killed him. Those horrible moments when North had been incapacitated after a bad car accident, and all he could do was stare as Tucker pushed Shaw down the stairs. He remembered, the moment frozen for an eternity inside his mind, the way Shaw's stupid slippers had seemed to float in the air.

He dragged himself back to the GTO, to the drive, to the darkness of old trees and the route between them—like driving through a tunnel, he thought. Like everything is leaning in, bending over you, bearing down. When they cleared the trees, they followed the swells and dips of rolling hills, passed faces of stone where they'd been blasted and cut to make way for modern roads. Those bare stretches were yellowish white in the moonlight. Like dirty teeth, he thought.

They had to stop twice to check the license plate tracking system. They got another hit in Lincoln, which wasn't too far north of Auburn, and so they kept driving. When they stopped the second time, they got a hit to the southeast—technically inside the city limits of Auburn, North thought, which wasn't what he'd expected at all. He'd expected the trail to go dark; there weren't any traffic cameras near the Cottonmouth Club itself. Instead, they'd gotten a hit on the outskirts of town.

When they reached the city limits, North kept a close eye on the speedometer, made sure to signal every turn, and sent up a silent prayer. He had no desire to get pulled over, not in this town. Running into Chief Cassidy again was at the bottom of his list—and only partially because it would give Shaw a reason to launch into that Cassidy bullshit all over again.

They found the traffic camera where the sheriff's license plate had been spotted most recently, and North eased the GTO onto the shoulder. Then he said, "Jesus fucking Christ."

"Yes," Shaw said with an enthusiastic nod. "Very good, North."

North chose to ignore that and stared at the massive building with the words EPIPHANY OF LIGHT CHURCH on its side. A fence marked the limit of the property, and another sign at the entrance—which was gated and shut—said EPIPHANY OF LIGHT CENTRAL CAMPUS.

"Which means what?" North asked.

"Campus is another word for—ow, ow, ow!"

The megachurch itself looked dark—a few windows suggested emergency lights, but the parking lot was empty. North considered the road they'd followed; technically, it was a divided highway, with two lanes in each direction. It was empty too, and he figured it was some sort of state road meant to serve an even smaller satellite community.

"Ok," North finally said. "All it means is that whoever has the sheriff's plates, he drove past this intersection." He indicated the stoplight and traffic camera whose sole purpose was clearly to let the faithful masses turn out of the church parking lot on a busy Sunday morning. "Maybe he drove straight through."

"Maybe."

Still no cars coming. North eased the GTO back onto the road. They rolled through the light. He checked the position of the traffic camera, but it didn't tell him anything useful. "Let's follow this road," North said, "and you check the database to see if the plate's been tagged anywhere else—"

"Or there's that," Shaw said.

That in this instance referred to a section of the Epiphany of Light fencing that had been torn from the support posts and now lay at an angle, half-fallen across the opening where it had originally hung. The spindles at the lower right corner were bent, some of them even popped out of the railing.

North swore.

"It's ok," Shaw said. "I'm a trained detective. That's probably why I noticed it."

"I would have seen it."

Shaw's silence lasted a beat too long. "Oh. Of course! Of course you would have seen it!"

"I would have! Someone crashed into the fucking fence, Shaw, it's not like it was some microscopic detail—you know what? I'm not going to do this."

Shaw nodded with the kind of patience that explained why so many murders were domestic. "Of course, of course. Nothing microscopic. Your vision is completely fine."

"My vision is—" North cut off with a strangled noise and cut the wheel to the right harder than he needed to. They bumped off the pavement and onto the gravel shoulder again, and North killed the engine.

He didn't slam the door. He didn't need to. But he did kick Shaw's door shut a few times to keep him from getting out of the car. Shaw still managed to ruin the whole thing, of course, by giggling as he yanked on the handle and tried to force the door open over and over again.

North finally gave up and got a high-powered flashlight from the trunk. He made his way across the drainage ditch and over to the damaged fence panel. Up close, with better light, he could see where tires had torn up the perfect lawn. When he played the flashlight over the wrought-iron fence, especially those damaged spindles in the corner, he caught traces of red. Like you might expect, North thought, if a red Subaru Outback hit the fence hard enough to knock the railings out of the support posts.

"So, where's the Subaru Outback?"

"Maybe if you squint," Shaw suggested. "Squinting isn't a replacement for glasses, but the properly trained squinter—"

North got him a good one in the ankle, and Shaw yelped and hopped on one foot as North slipped under the half-fallen section of fencing. He shone the light on the grass, taking his time, ignoring Shaw's whimpers and groans and mewling. The grass was thick—fertilized and watered and probably softer than the carpeting in the Borealis office. And that meant it took footprints surprisingly well, especially when they were less than a couple of hours old. Several sets milled around, which was interesting all by itself, but one set led across the lawn and toward the Epiphany of Light church.

"Ready to do some exploring?" North asked.

"No," Shaw moaned. "You shattered my ankle. I can't walk. I'll probably never walk again, not even after multiple reconstructive surgeries, and you'll have to carry me everywhere out of guilt—"

"You know what? I'm feeling surprisingly guilt free."

"—and when I have to go to the bathroom I'll scream, 'Nine-one-one, nine-one-one,' and that'll be code for a bathroom emergency—"

"Race you to the church."

"What do I get—"

But North took off before Shaw had time to finish the question. There was no squawk of outrage or protest, and that was a bad sign; for the first hundred yards, charging across the lawn, North focused on breathing, on finding his stride. But the Red Wings—although amazingly well made and incredibly tough and excellent protection for his feet under basically every possible circumstance—were heavy. Worse, as the first hundred yards began to close, North discovered he was having a difficult time catching his breath, and he resolved for the thousandth time…to do more cardio. Fewer resistance days. More days hitting the streets. Sprints. High-intensity interval training. And then his brain wasn't getting enough oxygen, so he had to stop planning and start focusing on not running like the Bride of Frankenstein. He pumped his arms. He pistoned his legs. He had the vague idea that he was supposed to engage his core, but that seemed like a fuckery of an expectation for someone whose entire body was shutting down under duress.

Shaw, of course, breezed past him and reached the small plaza in front of the church with seconds to spare.

Heaving for breath—and straddling that line between a stitch in his ribs and the need to puke—North finally reached him.

"What do I—"

North swatted him, or tried to, and then had to gasp for air, hands on knees.

"That bad?" Shaw asked with what might have been real sympathy. North needed more oxygen before he could decide. "You know, you might consider the fact that along with all the other terrible things it does to your body—"

North looked up. He was drooling, he realized. Only a tiny bit. He knuckled it away and sucked in some more air and, because God occasionally still performed miracles, managed to stand up straight.

"Er—" Shaw said. "That thing, you know. The one we don't talk about."

"Cardio," North said flatly.

Shaw looked like he might argue, but he must have read something on North's face because he nodded and said, "Yup. Cardio."

"It's the altitude," North finally said, shuffling in a circle as he continued to catch his breath. "The altitude must be different here."

"Yeah," Shaw muttered, "we're at sea level." But when North stopped and turned, he began nodding enthusiastically. "Yes, the altitude. That's got to be it."

He was wearing one of those looks of overenthusiastic agreement, the way he did right after North finished explaining that there was nothing wrong with a well-rounded diet that included the occasional snack, treat, and/or indulgence, and right before he was about to purge their fridge of everything delicious. North scowled.

"What do I win?" Shaw asked.

"A fiver."

"A fiver? I already get fivers—I mean that's wonderful! And so romantic! I can't wait!"

"God damn it," North muttered and started toward the church's main entrance.

From the street, the church had appeared dark and unoccupied, and nothing North saw now changed his opinion. When he tried the doors, they were locked. On the other side of the glass, an emergency light illuminated enough of the space for North to make out the shape of the lobby. But no one moved—no one responding to the sound of North trying the doors, and equally annoyingly, no one running away because two intrepid detectives had finally tracked him down.

North followed the perimeter of the building, but the rattle of machinery made him stop and look. The gate at the road was slowly opening, and a car was waiting to turn in. North motioned for Shaw to hunker down behind some of the bushes along the side of the church, and they crouched there and waited.

A minute later, tires hummed toward them, and in the distance, the gate rattled back into place. The car—a Ford Focus, dark—drove past them, and North snapped a picture of the license plate. North assumed that the vehicle was headed toward a private parking lot behind the church, but instead, it turned down what North had assumed, until now, was a service road. The car disappeared from view a moment later, and North realized that some sort of privacy fence or windscreen was there, blocking whatever was on the other side from view.

North took off at a jog—a light jog, what Shaw, when he wanted to be an asshole, might have called a lope, or even a brisk walk. Shaw kept pace with him, which was easy when you were skin and bird bones and had your underwear ventilated by an air elemental, or whatever the fuck Shaw had paid fifty dollars for. Not that Shaw even wore underwear. Not often. Not unless North ordered it on the grounds of not getting arrested.

The smell of pine sap and exhaust grew stronger as they approached the privacy barrier, and now North could make out the deeper darkness of a windscreen against the night. The road that the Focus had taken cut behind the windscreen, and as North came around the turn, he let out another string of swears. A hundred yards down the road was a house—a mansion, technically—with lights blazing.

It was hard to get all the details in the interplay of light and shadow, but North could tell enough: the house was stucco, with a mansard roof and lots of windows, all of them glowing. It crouched behind a second fence, which told North something about the people who lived here. Carriage house lanterns, manicured flower beds, copper accents—details, but details that became more and more suggestive as North considered the house. He summed it up as ten thousand square feet of a lot of naïve people's money.

Ahead of them, the gate was sliding shut behind the Focus.

"That's a big house," Shaw said.

"You know all that money that sits in your stupid trust fund, and we don't get to use it for anything, not even buying groceries?"

"Well, it's not my money; it's family money—"

"Why don't you use it to buy me a house like that?"

"Why would you want a house like that?"

"Because." North gestured. "It's fucking enormous."

"It's too big."

"There's no such thing."

"Who would do all the cleaning?"

"Not you, that's for fucking certain."

"You see? You're mean to me. This is why I never bought you a mansion. Plus it really is too big. You'd get lost. Or I'd get lost. Or we'd both get lost, and I'd never be able to find you."

"Jeez," North said as he started forward again. "Imagine that."

The fence wasn't topped by anything substantial—no C-wire, not even any decorative broken glass—so North made a saddle of his hands and gave Shaw a lift. Shaw dropped to the other side, reached between the wrought-iron spindles, and repeated North's movements. He added in a lot of grunting, a lot of noises like he was straining.

"I am going to kick your ass," North said when he fell-landed on the other side. "You know how long it's been since I kicked your ass? You are on a fucking tear tonight, you know that? You are seriously asking for it."

"When you keep repeating yourself like that, you start to sound a little excited."

North gave him a glare.

"Plus, it might be the carriage house lights, but I'm pretty sure you have a semi."

North took one threatening step, and Shaw danced backward, laughing.

"We're working, you jackass," North said. "Could you try to be a professional? Could you try for one night to be a professional fucking detective?"

"Do you hear it? You say the same thing over and over again, and your voice gets a little higher, you talk a little faster —"

North stalked off because it was either that or beat Shaw up, right then, right there, and North had professional standards to uphold. Plus, he'd kind of jinked up his foot when he'd come down hard on the landing, and he wondered if maybe some of Shaw's grunting and straining noises hadn't been entirely made up.

There were a lot of ways to go about approaching people you wanted to interview. Sometimes, it was helpful to have a story prepared. Sometimes, it was essential to get them talking before they realized who you were. Sometimes, in a way that left North mildly but perpetually astonished, telling the truth was the best way to get people to help you. But always, forever, exclusively, the absolute best thing to do was catch people by surprise.

He started toward the front of the house. He thought tonight, he'd start by knocking and announcing himself. He needed one of those wallets for his PI license so he could flip it open, right in their faces, so close maybe they had to take a step back. Then he thought of what Shaw would say about that—something about seeing it in a movie—and, of course, as with everything Shaw touched, it blackened and curdled and was absolutely ruined even before North could consider going on Amazon to buy one of those flip-openable wallets.

He was working on a way to order the wallet but have it delivered to their neighbors, then tell the neighbors it must have been a mistake, and no, nobody had to tell Shaw, when his brain caught up with what his eyes were seeing, and North stopped. Shaw was still walking, so he put his arm out, and Shaw bumped into him.

"What—"

North pointed to the bloody shoe print on the pavement in front of them. It hadn't dried, not completely, and the pavement was light-colored, which meant the shoe print was crisp even in the glow from the carriage house lanterns. North had seen Dalton Weber's cell. He remembered the pools of blood on the floor. He thought of the canvas slip-ons that were part of the inmate uniform. The blood would have dried, his brain said. But then he thought about the wet grass, the long walk across the lawn. By the time Philip Welch had reached this house, the blood could have been liquid enough to leave a print like this one.

Shaw drew in his breath like he might say something, but another sound registered at the periphery of North's consciousness, and he spun around.

The man was close to North's height but stockier, and he was dressed in what North thought of as church clothes—not nice stuff, but growing up in Lindenwood Park, North had seen a lot of working-class families in shirts and trousers from the Walmart collection. This guy had a round face and thinning blond hair so fair that at first, in the unsteady glimmer of the carriage house lanterns, North thought he was bald, and something about him looked familiar.

He was also holding a gun.

7

"Show me your hands," the man said, the gun pointed at Shaw.

It was a big gun, a Glock, what North would have called a doofus, baby-dick purchase, which Shaw knew was sexist and body-shaming but also, unfortunately, a little true. Under normal circumstances, Shaw would have suggested that the man undergo a thorough chakra cleansing, perhaps reach out to a sex surrogate, maybe even buy what North disparagingly—and unnecessarily—referred to as wang crystals. Citrine, maybe. Or carnelian.

Then North shifted his weight, and the man turned the gun on North, and a Sahara wind went through Shaw's mind, scouring everything else away.

"Hands!" the man barked.

North lifted his hands. Shaw copied him.

The man studied them. His pupils were wide, his cheeks flushed, and now that Shaw knew what to look for, he could see the faint tremor in the man's hand.

"You're doing a very good job," Shaw told him.

North made one of those quiet noises that was mostly in his throat.

"No talking," the man said.

Shaw nodded. He even mimed zipping his lips. North made that noise again.

"If I could say something, though," Shaw said.

There it was again. Like maybe North was practicing. Like maybe he was auditioning for a role in *Cats*, only he hadn't told Shaw because he wanted it to be a surprise and because he was desperate to be Grizabella, wait, no, Jellylorum, no, wait, probably Grizabella. And also on account of toxic masculinity.

"If I could say one tiny thing—" Shaw began.

"Shaw," North muttered.

"—I'd say you're doing an excellent job. Really excellent. The way you snuck up behind us. Oh, and the gun. And you even said 'Hands!' and it was really scary! But, you know, guns sometimes do the weirdest things, and so maybe, just possibly, as the tiniest note because you're doing such a great job, maybe you want to, um, not point it at us. Or at least not with your finger on the trigger. Just in case."

The man had one of those sour cream complexions that meant a lifetime of sunburned noses and cheeks and shoulders (like poor North with his delicate skin), and now a flush mottled his cheeks. But he lowered the gun. "Don't move," he told them. Then he fumbled in the pocket of the too-large blazer until he came up with a radio, and he said, "Uh, Pastor Jed, I've got kind of a situation."

"Is that a tattoo?" Shaw asked. It was, of course, clearly a neck tattoo, but Shaw had found that asking obvious questions was a way of facilitating introspection and self-discovery and, well, general chattiness. For example, you could ask your boyfriend if he was strong enough to lift all those weights, but then you had to spend a hot, sweaty hour in the garage while he lifted weights and put more weights on the bar thingy and you couldn't even look at your phone because he kept glancing over and he was so proud of himself. Other times it didn't work so well, though, like if you asked if someone not to be named really needed all that cheese on one cracker.

The tattoo in question was an elaborately done cross, with what looked like flowers twined around it. The shape of the flowers was suggestive of something, but before Shaw could pin it down, the radio crackled with another voice.

"I'm coming," a man said.

The front doors burst open, and a man stepped out. Shaw's first thought was that the man was drunk, but then he reconsidered. High, maybe. Or just...off. He was technically white, although in the carriage house lights, his spray-on tan looked orange, and he had rockabilly hair. The tracksuit didn't disguise the kind of build North would have called skinny fat: twiggy arms and legs, but a belly that hung over his waistband. A cross glinted at his neck, the gold catching the light; Shaw wasn't sure if there were standardized sizes for crosses, but to his mind, this one looked roughly the same size as his phone.

"What's going on?" the man shouted. "Who are you? What are you doing here?"

The guard—or whoever the man in the ill-fitting blazer was—sighed. "Gid, go back inside."

Instead, though, the man in the tracksuit came down the front steps. If he saw the bloody shoe prints, he didn't give any sign of it; he walked right over them, and Shaw felt more than saw North's wince. Closer, the man—Gid—gave off the reek of booze and weed, but Shaw figured something else was responsible for the glazed look in the man's eyes. This was beyond recreational, in Shaw's opinion. It looked more in the realm of heavy self-medication.

"Gid—" the guard tried again.

"Who are you?" Gid asked; his volume hadn't come down much, and his breath was a blast of alcohol-glazed halitosis. "I asked you a question. What are you doing here?"

"That's two questions," Shaw said in his most helpful tone. "And you actually asked us three questions because you also—" North shot him a sidelong look, and Shaw's voice grew smaller as Gid turned his attention on him. "—asked, 'What's going on?'"

"I already got Pastor Jed—" the guard tried.

"I'm here, aren't I?" Gid asked. "I can handle a couple of intruders."

"Are we intruders, North?" Shaw asked. "I thought we were more trespassers."

"Only if we're trapped in a fucking video game," North muttered.

"Pastor Jed's going to be right down—" the guard began.

"I said—" Gid fished a boxy pistol out of the tracksuit's waistband, giving them—if only for a moment—a glimpse of turquoise bikini briefs. Shaw considered whether now would be an appropriate time to tell Gid they made him look like he ought to tap into his mermaid tendencies. Merman tendencies. In a good way. "—I can handle it."

He motioned with the gun toward the front of the house and stepped aside, so North and Shaw could go first. North took the lead, and Shaw kept close to his side.

"Don't you fucking dare," North said in a low voice as they took the steps.

"What?" Shaw asked.

"You know what. You're thinking about that postcard from the Mermaid Society of Texas."

"Oh my God, North! I forgot about the postcard! And I can tell him they invited you, North McKinney, personally, to join them for their annual conference."

"Yeah, I wonder how I got on that particular brain-fuck of a mailing list."

Shaw kept his face perfectly smooth; it was more fun that way. "I wonder if I still have a picture of it on my phone."

"I swear to Jesus Christ, Shaw."

Inside, Shaw's first impression of the house was that it had too much masculine energy, which meant North was going to love it. His thought was confirmed when he saw North glancing around approvingly. Everything was hard lines, painted wood, and modernist glass. Through an opening ahead of them, Shaw glimpsed what he thought was the living room, with white damask sofas and leather accent chairs. Gid called out for them to turn to the right, though, and they passed a dining room, and then what Shaw suspected was called the butler's pantry or the catering pantry or the something pantry. A flight of stairs rose at the end of the hall, but Gid called for them to turn left, so they turned again, and he sent them through a door.

Into, it turned out, a laundry room.

"You have got to be fucking kidding me," North said, toeing a pile of clothes on the floor. "I'm about to get shot on top of some dude's raunchy trunks."

"All right," Gid said, shutting the door behind him. "Who are you?"

"It wouldn't be the first time," Shaw said, "you experienced, er, penetrative violence in less-than-surgical conditions."

For a moment, North's mouth worked soundlessly. Then he managed, "Look who's fucking talking."

"Hey," Gid said.

"Do you remember Ricky?" Shaw asked. "You hooked up with him for, like, half of sophomore year?"

North stabbed a finger at him. "I found another of those creepy Emery Hazards-with-the-macaroni-doodle under our bed, Shaw. Don't talk to me about Ricky Booth."

"It wasn't just that his room was filthy; it was the smell. You stank every time you came back."

"Hey!" Gid screamed. He waved the gun. "Listen to me. I'm talking and I have a gun, so you have to listen to me."

"What?" North snapped, rounding on Gid. "What's so fucking important we can't finish our conversation?"

Gid stared back at him. Whatever he'd taken, it was slowing him down, buffering his reactions. Finally he said, "Who are you?"

"Meals on wheels," North said.

"I think you've already used that one," Shaw said. "We're delegates from the Mermaid Society of Texas. Wait, he might check that. We're ~~representatives~~ official representatives—from the Mermaid Collective—"

He gave North a knowing look; North appeared to be trying to take calming breaths through his nose. "—of Missouri."

"Why in the fuck would they have a mermaid collective in Missouri? What the fuck even is a mermaid collective? Jesus Christ, Shaw, they don't even have an ocean. Where are the mermaids coming from? Are they humping their way up the interstate?"

"First of all, mermaids are very sexual beings, so in theory, they could hump their way wherever they wanted."

"I didn't mean—"

"And second of all, mermaids can live in lakes and rivers, North. It's a speciesist and oceanist stereotype to believe all mermaids—"

Gid screamed. When he finished, he waved the gun again, "Be quiet. Stop talking. Tell me your names."

Shaw considered pointing out the inherent difficulty in obeying both requests. He considered pointing out that Gid, like North, might have a tendency to repeat himself when he was excited.

"North McKinney," North said. "And Shaw Aldrich. We're private investigators working for the Wahredua Police Department, and you're currently committing false imprisonment and assault by forcing us in here with a fucking gun, you juvenile wad of fucks. Who the fuck are you?"

Before Gid could answer, the door behind him opened. Gid flinched as another man came into the room. He had to be Gid's brother; they shared a look, although the brother seemed to have his shit, to borrow a phrase from North's vernacular, much more together than Gid. He was around Gid's height, but thin to the point of lankiness, and his spray tan was so good it could almost pass for natural. Brushed-back hair and perfectly capped teeth. He made Shaw think of car salesmen and thirtysomething men who practiced smiling.

"What's going on here?" Then he saw the gun and barked, "Gideon!"

Gid slid the gun into his waistband and pulled the top of his tracksuit over it. His shoulders slumped. "I was asking them some questions," he told the pile of dirty clothes.

The guy with great teeth stared at him for a moment. Then he said, "We'll talk about this later." He looked at North and Shaw. His expression softened. His eyebrows went up. His brow even furrowed a little, which was a nice touch. "I'm so sorry; I'm not sure what my brother was thinking, but it's been a trying night. Are you all right?"

"Oh yeah," North said. "Peachy."

The guy smiled at that, giving them the teeth all the way in the back, the shiners. "Let's get you out of here."

He led them back through the enormous house and into the living room that Shaw had glimpsed earlier. It was an open concept plan, of course, flowing into a kitchen and a breakfast nook. French doors opened out onto a covered patio that Shaw guessed they called a veranda or a lanai or something equally expensive sounding. White wood. White damask upholstery. The chandeliers were minimalist and steel and geometric. Lines, lines, lines. Maybe it was a way to accent the crosses that hung on every wall.

"Can I get you a drink?" the man asked, stepping behind a bar. "I'm sorry again; we've all been through the wringer tonight, and—"

"Yeah," North said in the exact same tone he'd once used when Shaw had tried to explain his scientific process for making sweaters out of dryer lint. "Who are you?"

The man stopped in the middle of pouring himself what Shaw guessed was brandy. Then he gave them the shiners again. "I'm so sorry. I assumed you knew. Jedidiah Moss, but most people call me Pastor Jed."

"I'm not going to call you that," North said. "How's Jed sound?"

The shiners slipped a little. "That's all right."

"I'll call you Pastor Jed," Shaw said.

Jed blinked once, but then he picked right up again like he was reading off a teleprompter. "And who are you gentlemen?"

North repeated their introductions. Jed didn't flinch; his hand remained steady as he finished his pour, and nothing crossed his face. Maybe he'd been expecting them. That seemed like a possibility, and if so, it was an interesting one.

"I don't understand," Jed said, bringing his brandy with him as he rejoined them. Gid slunk into the room, but he kept his back pressed to the wall, and he wouldn't look any of them in the eye. "You said Wahredua? I know I've heard that name, but I don't think I could find it on a map." Then he smiled, and Shaw guessed it was the one that made the little old ladies reach for their pocketbooks. "Well, I suppose I could find it on my phone."

"That depends," North said drily. "Are you intellectually capable of finding the bottom of a paper bag?"

The shiners went away again. "I suppose I'm asking why you're here, gentlemen. I apologize again for my brother's behavior, but in his defense, one of our church deacons told me that he caught you trespassing. That doesn't sound like the behavior of someone employed by the Wahredua Police Department."

"Oh, that's easy," Shaw said. Jed turned that smile on him, and Shaw wondered if it was even better on television—some smiles were like that.

"We're trying to figure out how you and your family are connected to Philip Welch, the man who committed two murders tonight in the Dore County jail."

If Shaw had slapped Jed, he didn't think the reaction would have been much different. Jed's face went blank. And then red rushed into his cheeks, dusky under the orange tan.

"I don't know what you're talking about."

"Everyone tries that one first," North said. "Once, just once, I want someone to lead off with the mermaid convention."

"Philip Welch," Shaw said. "He's the one who crashed the sheriff's red Subaru into your fence. And then he walked—well, probably he ran—to the house. He's the one who left bloody footprints on the pavement. We took some pictures of those, by the way." That part was stretching the truth, but Shaw didn't want anybody rushing out with a scrub brush and a bottle of bleach. "Tiny guy, Black, he's got his head buzzed. Oh, you know what? You might remember him wearing an inmate's uniform, you know, the scrubs and the slip-on shoes."

Jed was silent too long. He must have realized it because the smile came back; that was his default setting, Shaw decided. Then he said, "You gentlemen are confused."

"They always try that one too," North said. "Here, try this: 'You've got your head packed full of shit.' At least that puts some variety into it."

"No one in our family has a connection to this man; I've never even heard his name before."

"Really?" North bared his teeth. "Maybe it's like Wahredua. I bet you could find it in your phone."

The smile shrank; the shiners disappeared. "No one—"

"Red paint on the fence," North said like he was reading items off a list. "Tire prints fucking up the lawn, and a lot of footprints—probably whoever you sent to get rid of the car. Shaw already told you about the bloody shoe prints. It's a fucking road map from two dead guys in a cell to your front door. Not to mention the fact that it's closing in on midnight, and the whole fucking lot of you are up and dressed and having a very civilized freak-out."

"You didn't let me finish," Jed said, and the television smile snapped off now. It was easier to see the similarities to Gid with the polish gone: the eyes, the mouth, the pinched look of the face. "No one has any connection with the man you're describing. But someone did break into our home tonight. That's why we have some of our brethren around, to help us keep an eye on things. And that's why Gid was so jumpy when you arrived."

But when Shaw glanced at Gid, jumpy wasn't the word he would have used to describe him. Sullen, maybe, because his big brother had swooped in and taken over. And scared. The fear was hiding under a chemical blanket, but it was there if you knew how to look for it.

"Someone broke in," North said.

"That's right."

"Jeez, what a coincidence."

"I didn't say it was a coincidence. It's obvious that man, the one you told us about, decided he needed money to continue his escape."

North nodded. "So, he drove a hundred miles to a church on the outskirts of a small town, and because he's a fugitive and he's looking for an easy mark, he plowed into a wrought-iron fence, ran a few hundred yards across open ground, and somehow knew that this big, beautiful house was lurking on the other side of that windbreak, even though he couldn't see it from the road. You know what? Maybe it was divine intervention. Maybe that's how he knew—maybe it was a miracle."

Jed threw back his brandy. Then he said, "I think it's time for you gentlemen to leave."

"No problem. We'll wait for the police." When Jed didn't say anything, North said, "You called the police, right? Because someone broke into your home? I'm sure they'll be interested to hear about our escaped killer."

For a moment, struggle showed in Jed's face.

But Gid spoke first, the words full of a petulant anger from where he skulked in the corner of the room: "Of course we called the police."

"Gideon!" Jed snapped.

"Great," North said, scanning the available seating. "We'll wait right here."

"What's going on here?" The voice was firm and clear. A woman's voice. The sound of shuffling steps came, and two people appeared in the opening to the entry hall. The woman was so white that at first, Shaw thought she was wearing powder, and combined with the bob of white hair parted on the side, she might have passed for Barbara Bush—or maybe Barbie's mother. Even at this hour, she wore a navy suit with a silk carnation pinned to the lapel, and it felt like a joke until Shaw looked in her eyes.

She was supporting a man who leaned heavily on a cane as he slowly moved into the room. He had to be Jed and Gid's father; the features were too similar for anything else. He was obviously old, but his face was curiously unlined—fleshy and soft. It gave Shaw the impression, strangely, of being damp, like something kept out of the sun. His silver ducktail was Brylcreemed in place, filling the air with the barbershop aroma. He wore a suit that matched the woman's perfectly, but something about it seemed…constrained. Shaw guessed that a girdle was involved.

"Mother," Jed said. And then, almost absently, "Father." He glanced at North and Shaw. "These are private detectives working for a police department somewhere else in the state. They say the man who broke in here is wanted for murder."

"Two murders, actually," North said. "And I'm curious why he came straight here."

"Gideon made a bad impression on them, you should know." It had the sound of childhood tattling, and when Shaw glanced over, the momentary rage on Gid's face was a child's rage. Jed continued, "I can't say I blame them after the scare he gave them."

"Oh, we weren't scared," Shaw said. "He would have had to take the safety off first."

For a moment, no one said anything. Then Jed barked a laugh and headed back to the bar. The woman—Mrs. Moss, presumably—helped her husband onto one of the damask sofas, where he started to tilt. She propped him up with some pillows and then sat and held his hand.

"My husband has to conserve his strength for his ministry," she said.

He looked, in Shaw's opinion, like he had to conserve his strength so he could keep breathing inside that girdle, but he decided now might not be the time to share that particular insight.

"I'm Lacey Stence Moss," she said. "I hope my boys offered you a seat and something to drink. You look like you've had a hard day and a long night."

"Mrs. Moss," North said, "I want to know why Philip Welch came here after killing a duly elected sheriff and a key witness in an ongoing investigation. I don't believe there was a break-in, and I think you should know that lying about what happened here tonight and about any connection your family or your church has to Welch is only going to make things worse. The truth is going to come out one way or another."

Lacey stared back at him, her face unreadable.

"Mother?" Jed said.

She ignored him; Shaw was distantly aware of Jed drifting behind the bar again. He checked, and Gid was still in the corner, face blotchy under the bad tan. But Lacey held his attention. It was something about the unyielding composure of her face. That, and the fact that right then, she was scary as hell, although Shaw couldn't put his finger on exactly why.

"I imagine my sons have already explained to you," she said in a quiet voice, "that we're a simple family trying to do the Lord's work."

"In a ten-thousand-square-foot home," North said.

She let the words drop away before she spoke again. "Nobody in this house knows a man called Philip Welch. Nobody had anything to do with those murders. My heart breaks for those men and their families, and I can assure you, my husband will pray for them tonight."

The pastor looked like he needed to spend all his energy praying not to fall face-first in his oatmeal; he smacked his lips at that moment and gave a huge yawn.

"But he came straight here," North said, "like there was a bullseye painted on this place."

"That's not surprising. My husband's ministry—and my sons'—has always been directed toward the less fortunate. Jesus says, 'I was in prison, and you came to me.'"

"In this case, I'd say the less fortunate were the men who got stabbed fifteen or twenty times and bled to death on the floor of a prison cell."

If the words shocked her, nothing appeared on her face. She was silent for a few moments, and when the pastor started to topple again, she caught him reflexively, without even seeming to think about it. "Our ministry is known for offering food, clothing, shelter. We ask no questions. I'm praying that what you've told me tonight is a strange twist of fate. But if that man didn't come here tonight to steal from us, perhaps he came because he knew our reputation."

North made a noise of understanding. "So, you have a history of aiding and abetting felons, helping escaped murderers, that kind of thing."

"Hey!" Gid shouted from the corner, but when North glanced at him, he took a quick step back and bumped a lamp. He caught it before it fell, but only barely.

"Mrs. Moss," Shaw said, "whatever else happened tonight, Philip Welch didn't come here as a burglar. I think there's something you and your sons aren't telling us."

Another of those long pauses came. In it, the sound of a sanctified air conditioning system whispered, and the sound made the hair on the back of Shaw's neck stand up.

"I'm sorry to hear that," Lacey said.

And that was when Shaw realized Jed had slipped out of the room at some point. How long had he been gone? Where had he gone? And why? He elbowed North, and North must have realized the same thing because he drew in a breath and sat up, head swiveling to take in the room.

"I'm sorry we weren't able to help you," Lacey said, steadying the pastor again. His jaw was slack, and a glistening strand of drool ran to the corner of his mouth. "But I'd like you to leave now."

"I don't think so," North said. "I think we're going to make a few calls and wait for the police to arrive. I'd like them to look at the footage from the security cameras I've seen all over this place. It'd sure be something if we saw Welch on them, wouldn't it? Maybe having a drink, chatting, right at home. Hell, what about kneeling in prayer? I think the police—"

"Son, today's your lucky day." Jonas Cassidy's hair was cropped short and almost white from the sun, and he had a smile that was just as bright. He met all the legal and technical specifications of a beefcake, which Shaw decided he would tell North the next time North made him spend a hot, sweaty afternoon in the garage "exercising" and "building strength." Cassidy had all his defined muscle on display in a uniform shirt he wore with a pair of ass-clutching jeans. The urge to point out, for everyone's illumination and benefit, that the Auburn chief of police shared his last name with North's middle name was strong, but Shaw managed to clamp down on it. For now. "Evening, Mrs. Moss; sorry these two are bothering you."

"Good evening, Chief. Do you know these men?"

"I've run into them a time or two. Heya, Gid. How's everything?"

Gid mumbled something, and Cassidy laughed and nodded like they were all having a great time.

"Here we go, boys," Cassidy said and hitched a thumb toward the front of the house. "On your feet."

"Sorry," North said, "I should have been clearer. We're waiting for the real police, not the Moss family's personal mall cop."

"Get on your feet." Cassidy waited a moment and added, "Son."

North opened his mouth. Shaw touched his wrist and gave a tiny shake of his head. It felt like a long time before North stood. Cassidy turned, gave a two-fingered salute to Mrs. Moss, and led them toward the entry hall. North and Shaw followed.

Outside, the heat closed around them like a fist, and the smell of bleach was overpowering. There was no sign of Jed, but someone had clearly gone to work scrubbing the bloody shoe prints that North had spotted earlier. Crickets called in the background. When Cassidy put one hand on his service weapon, the leather of his duty belt creaked.

"They probably didn't teach you this," North said, "when you got your junior police badge, but murdering people is technically against the law. And threatening to shoot a couple of private investigators on the front steps of a rich family, well, that's about the stupidest macho bullshit I've ever heard of. It's also a grade-A example of toxic masculinity. You want to watch out for that, because that shit will fuck you up."

But Cassidy didn't say anything. He didn't glare. He didn't huff. He was a good-looking guy, and he had a hint of a smirk. "Where's Emery?"

"Fuck off."

"Come on; he wouldn't let you two sniff around this neck of the woods by yourselves."

North smiled: big, bright. "Fuck off."

"Maybe I'll hang on to you. You think he'll come running? Hell, I might even give him a call."

"You can't hold us," Shaw said. "We were hired—"

"If I want to hear somebody talking out of a donkey's ass, son, they do a whole show like that in Branson. Don't speak again. Fuck, for that matter, don't look at me."

North's color was up, and his smile was bigger. "Say something to him again."

"North," Shaw said. "No."

"What'd you say? Say it again."

Cassidy shifted his weight. The belt creaked again, and the chorus of crickets swelled until the sound seemed to swallow everything else. His eyes cut away from North, and he seemed to be speaking past him when he said, "Here's how this is going to go: you're going to walk to that piece of shit you left parked on the side of the road, and you're going to leave. You're not ever going to come back to Auburn again. You're not going to bother the Mosses. As far as I'm concerned, you're going to cease to exist. Otherwise, I'm going to take you in. And we're going to go the long way back to the station. It might be a while before the twenty-four hours start counting down, and that's just how long I can hold you without charging you. Then, when the twenty-four hours are up, I'm going to slap you with trespassing, and we'll put you in a cruiser to county. You know what, though? You might get lost again. It might be Monday next week before you even stand in front of a judge, much less post bail. How do you feel about that?" The light from the carriage house lanterns turned his white-blond hair gold. Shadows filled the laugh lines of his smile. "We could get to know each other real well in a week."

North's breathing was fast and ragged.

Wrapping a hand around North's arm, Shaw said, "We're leaving."

Cassidy nodded, and Shaw towed North down the steps. The smell of bleach was thicker, cloying, an invisible cloud they had to fight their way through. North sounded like he was panting.

"I'll tell you what, son: put a bag over his face, and he wouldn't be half bad."

North made a wild sound and tried to turn, but Shaw yanked so hard that North staggered, and that must have shocked him or woken him or something, because he shook his head and let Shaw lead him into the night.

8

They found a truck stop on the outskirts of Auburn—convenience store hot dogs, energy drinks, dingy bathrooms—and then they went back. They parked behind a strip mall constructed of cinderblock and peeling white paint. It was just up the road from the Epiphany of Light campus, so they sat in the dark, with the GTO off and the windows down, and waited. The summer evening lay over them, a pall of dense air and sweat and the stink of rotting grass clippings. North's phone buzzed, but he kept his hands tight around the steering wheel, not trusting himself. The options were: stay completely still; break something; or say fuck it all and go for his emergency smokes. He was committed to option one, but option two and, particularly, option three were tempting.

"They were lying," Shaw said.

North let himself say it in his head: *No fucking shit.* But he reminded himself it wasn't Shaw's fault, and he finally managed to offer a neutral-ish grunt.

To his surprise, Shaw laughed quietly. He shifted around in his seat, and then his head came to rest on North's shoulder—a fresh patch of heat on a hot night, and the smell of his hair, his body. Then, for some reason, North felt all right again, and some of the ache in his jaw relaxed. He found Shaw's face and cupped his cheek.

"I don't care what he said about me," Shaw said.

"Fantastic."

"I don't want you to beat him up for me."

"Great."

"North Cassidy McKinney."

"What? I heard you."

"And you're still thinking vengeful thoughts."

"I'm thinking which bones I'm going to break and in which order. The order part is the most fun."

Shaw turned his head to kiss North's hand. Then he settled back, and the sound of their breathing mingled.

Their new position behind the strip mall offered a degree of concealment while still allowing them a line of sight down the main road in front of the Epiphany of Light campus. It was too dark—and they were too far—to make out details, but it would be impossible to miss a pair of headlights.

"Why?" Shaw said.

"Because nobody—and I mean nobody—talks about you like that. I don't care if he's chief of police or—or Elon fucking Musk—"

"Elon Musk?"

"I don't know," North mumbled. "I choked."

"I meant, why would Philip Welch go there?"

"Because the Mosses are tied up in this shit somehow. They're involved."

"Maybe. Ok, probably. But how? Or maybe the question is still why."

"Shaw, they're involved somehow. Welch came here like they had a homing beacon set up for him, and I don't care what bullshit story they gave us about a burglar, those people weren't frightened. They were angry and defensive and honestly a little bit nuts, but they weren't frightened."

"Gid was frightened."

North frowned and tried to think back. "Maybe. He was definitely high."

"The Cottonmouth Club?"

"Are you asking me if I think there's a connection?"

"I guess." Shaw shrugged against him. "I mean, Dalton was going to help identify the man he met there. Ambyr was another connection back to the club. And now they're dead, and Welch came straight here, and the Cottonmouth Club can't be more than a fifteen- or twenty-minute drive."

North finally settled on "I guess we're going to find out."

Twenty minutes and change went past before the distant rattle of the campus gate reached them and headlights appeared. The Auburn police cruiser passed them without slowing; Cassidy had power, and he clearly had great back and biceps days, but the man hadn't been near the front of the line when God had been handing out brains. North wished he'd said that last part out loud because he liked how it sounded.

"They're angry when an escaped killer shows up at their house," North said, "but they're not scared. They get rid of the sheriff's car—presumably, after swapping the plates, since it hasn't shown up on any traffic cameras. They scrub and bleach the hell out of the bloody shoe prints. They call in their bodyguard—that jackass in his Sunday clothes. And they've got the chief of police on a string, but they don't call him until we show up."

"Because they're more worried about us than they are about Welch," Shaw said.

North grunted. "What the fuck is going on?"

Another ten minutes passed before the gate rattled again. That was the problem with being a dumbass, North considered. Your estimation of your own abilities vastly exceeded reality. Which was why you waited barely ten minutes after the chief left before you tried to sneak out, headlights off, but you didn't consider the fact that the gate was loud enough to hear several blocks away. Because North knew what to look for, he caught the stray glimmers of light that gave away the sedan's position. It turned toward them, so he waited and watched.

Lights off, the sedan rolled past them. North could make out Gid's face behind the window.

"The whole bunch of them were near the back of the line the day God was handing out brains," North said.

Shaw twisted around to look at him.

"What?" North said.

"Were you saving that one?"

North jammed the key in the ignition and started the car. "What?"

Shaw burst out laughing. "Oh my God. Oh North. That's so cute!"

"I wasn't saving anything, you horse's ass."

"It was a really good one."

"God fucking damn it," North said as he pulled out.

It was hard to do a one-car tail—hard to do effectively, anyway, and hard to do without getting spotted—but after the first ten minutes, North stopped worrying about it. If Gid were concerned he was being followed, that was clearly near the bottom of the list. He didn't make sudden turns. He didn't take unnecessary detours and double back. He didn't even pick the kind of roads that lent themselves to spotting a tail. He did, however, have a lead foot; wherever Gid was going, he apparently felt the need for speed.

That was all right with North. Once they were on the highway, he opened up the GTO. He also—because he was a mature and responsible adult male with a healthy ego and developed sense of self-esteem and self-worth—ignored the fact that Shaw rolled his eyes.

They drove back to Wahredua. It was a minor surprise; North had been sure that something would happen if he waited outside the Epiphany of Light campus, but this hadn't been it. But as they drove, North decided it made a kind of sense. The murders had happened back in Wahredua; this was one more part of cleaning up the mess.

Inside the city limits, Gid led them north, away from the river. The city flowed and changed around them. Modest single-family homes shrank. Brick dissolved to clapboard and asbestos siding. Chain-link fences sprang up like weeds. The pavement and sidewalks buckled, or in places, opened up into potholes. A white woman with stringy hair sat on her stoop, rolling a spark for a joint. In another house, the gray flicker of television light gave a man a ballooning silhouette.

When Gid turned down the next street, North almost followed. At the last minute, though, he saw the NO OUTLET sign and let the GTO keep rolling to the end of the block. Then he killed the engine and put down the windows.

Night sounds filtered in: the movement of air, a noise like a tin can falling, a phone ringing on and on in a nearby house. What fucking year was it, North wanted to know. A landline? And hadn't they heard of an answering machine, never mind voicemail?

"Loop around on foot?" Shaw asked.

North opened his mouth to answer, but his phone buzzed. He checked it and saw a series of missed messages. The most recent one was from Tean: *Did you just drive by Bamford Place? Jem told me to call you asshats, but I didn't want to be rude.*

"We did," Shaw whispered with an unnecessary amount of excitement. "We did just drive by Bamford Place! That's the street Gid turned on."

North texted back: *Yes. Why?*

His phone buzzed with an incoming call from Tean. He answered on speaker.

"I saw that text message, and I know he didn't call you asshats," Jem said. "Also, since your method of private detecting involves driving a car that's literally noticeable from miles away, I was wondering if you'd ever considered adding one of those light-up signs on top. You know, like the Pizza Hut ones. It could say 'Private Detectives' or 'North and Shaw Are Right Here.'"

"That's a really good idea, North," Shaw said. "That could be really useful. Sometimes I don't know where you are. Like when it's time to trim the puppy's nails, but you need to run to the store for just one thing—"

"What do you want?" North asked.

"Well, I want you to help me trim the puppy's nails because last time he used that submission bite on me—"

"Not you!" It was slightly above a whisper, but North managed to put on the brakes. Barely.

On the other end of the call, Jem was laughing.

"I'm hanging up," North said.

The sound of laughter faded, and then Tean's voice came across the call. It sounded like he was speaking away from the phone as he said, "Enough already," and then his voice became clearer and he said, "We saw you drive past. We're staking out Adam Ezell's house."

North had to process that for a moment. "The missing deputy, huh. And let me guess, Gid went inside his house."

"Bingo bango bongo," Jem said in the background.

"I should start saying that," Shaw said.

"Don't you fucking dare," North told him. He tried to remember what he'd seen of the dead-end street and finally asked, "Where are you?"

"He tried to find us and couldn't," Jem said, apparently to Tean.

Tean shushed him. "Inside one of the houses. It was vacant—"

"How did you know it was vacant?" North interrupted.

"The grass in the backyard," Jem said, "plus the lockbox on the door, plus the Realtor sign that said For Rent—"

"Ok."

"—we looked in the windows—"

"I said ok!"

More laughter drifted across the call.

North decided to be mature and do mature things and react maturely. He tapped the screen, pulled up the keypad, and used his middle finger to hold down the asterisk. That was symbolic. The tone filled the call until it disconnected.

North refused to look at Shaw as he got out of the car. It was the mature thing to do.

They got their guns out of the lockboxes in the trunk of the GTO: North's CZ, and Shaw's Springfield. A quick glance at the backyards of the houses lining the dead-end street showed North the overgrown lawn and, therefore, the house where Tean and Jem were staked out. It was past one in the morning—closer to two, actually—and this part of the world had shut down for the night, so they started across the lawns. North did a wobbly vault to get over the chain-link fence, ignoring the fact that Shaw sprang over it like a fucking gazelle. At the next fence, the whole goddamn thing tipped and started to fall, and Shaw—already on the other side, of course—had to catch him.

"It's not your fault," Shaw whispered. "The psychic gravity of the masculine identity you've invested in those boots—"

"I. Will. Murder. You."

Shaw shut his mouth.

They reached the overgrown yard without further incident—barely. Jem grinned out at them from one of the windows, and he opened the back door as they came up the steps.

"Rookie mistake," North said as he stalked past Jem. "You're leaving fingerprints everywhere."

"Oh dang," Jem said, scratching his beard. "I knew I forgot something. In case I ever come back and murder someone here, I'll do some pre-cleaning first. Hey, Tean, did you know fences could go horizontal like that?"

The house was empty, and it had a musty, closed-up smell laced with a hint of animal urine. Empty houses were always a bit unsettling for North: the bare rooms, the undressed windows, the hint of past lives that hadn't been completely scrubbed away. He liked this one even less, with its big picture window looking out onto the dead-end street.

Tean sat on the floor to the side of the picture window, where he could look out at the street with relatively little risk of being seen himself. When North looked at him, Tean pointed to the house directly across the street.

The house was dark, but North could make out the details in the wash of the streetlights. It was a story-and-a-half bungalow with slumping windows and a big dormer window that reminded North of a cranky eye. He blamed that particular lunacy on too much time with Shaw, too much secondhand weed, and it being way too long since he'd had a decent night's sleep. The white board-and-batten needed freshening up, and the lava rock beds around the house were choked with weeds almost as tall as the overgrown lawn. Blinds hung in the windows, and from all North could tell, the house was dark.

"He's in there, huh?" North asked.

Tean nodded. "He walked around back, but we've seen a flashlight a couple of times. We were about to call John-Henry when Jem spotted your car."

"Spotted makes it sound like there was a chance of missing it," Jem said. "You don't spot a beached whale."

North glared at him, but Jem only grinned bigger, exposing two slightly crooked front teeth.

"Don't call John-Henry," North said. "Not yet."

"I don't know," Tean said. "We called him earlier, and he said we did the right thing—"

"If you call him, you're going to send Gid running, and we won't learn why he's here. What happened earlier? Why'd you call John-Henry?"

"Who's this guy anyway?" Jem asked. "I thought you were trying to track down that inmate."

"His name's Gid," Shaw said. "He has a gun! He made us go in a laundry room, and then North said something about dirty shorts—I wasn't really listening—and then Gid asked who we were, and I said—"

"He's got some connection to a megachurch." North caught a glimpse of the flashlight on the other side of Adam Ezell's blinds. "Welch, the inmate, drove straight there. We lost Welch, but we picked up Gid, and now he's poking around the house of a missing deputy. What the fuck do you think that's about?"

No one answered, but after a moment, Tean said, "You didn't put any of that in the group chat."

"Sorry, I was busy not getting shot, and then I was busy interviewing suspects, and then I was busy getting that bone-climber Cassidy off my ass, and then I was busy following Gid back here so he could do some very sus shit. Next time I take a crap, I'll try to update everyone. Is that ok with you?"

Out of the corner of his eye, North caught the change in Jem's expression: how it flattened, hardened, and in a way that left North slightly off-balance, looked nothing like the goof who had once worn a pair of Muppet Babies sleep pants to Waffle House. "Watch it—" Jem began.

But Tean gave a tiny shake of his head and said, "We're supposed to keep each other updated. You should have told us what was going on."

Shaw made an unhappy noise. "He's right, North. I'll do it right now."

"You didn't answer my question," North said. "What happened earlier?"

This time, Tean and Jem traded a long look.

"Another person went into Ezell's house," Tean said.

"It was in the group chat," Jem said, "but you didn't see that, of course."

North kept his attention on Tean. "And?"

"We tried to follow him, but we lost him—he took off like there was an emergency."

"What was he doing inside Ezell's house?"

Tean shook his head.

"You should have taken photos, or at least a physical description—"

"Oh damn," Jem said, "if only I hadn't had my head up my ass—oh wait, I didn't. Boom."

"Did you seriously just say boom?"

But Jem was too busy producing his phone and swiping through photos. When he presented the phone to North, the screen displayed a photo. North recognized the backdrop—he was looking at it through the window: Adam Ezell's house, and the stretch of sidewalk in front of it. The photo showed a man as he passed under a streetlight. North recognized him: it was the guy who'd been wearing his Sunday best when he'd pulled a gun on them, the one who'd been playing security guard at the Mosses' house. He was dressed in baggy mesh shorts and a white tee, but there was no mistaking that tattoo.

"He was here a few hours ago?"

Tean nodded. "We got here around nine, and it wasn't long after that."

"And then he took off in a hurry?"

More nodding. "We tried to follow—"

North grunted and showed the photo to Shaw.

Recognition filled Shaw's face. "The Mosses must have called him as soon as Welch showed up at their house. God, there were a lot of people driving between Wahredua and Auburn tonight."

"We think the tattoo might be significant—" Jem began.

"Huh," North said. A little too loud. A little too aggressively. But he was simultaneously tired and keyed up and, increasingly, on edge because none of this made sense.

In the dark, it was difficult to make out Jem's flush, but not impossible.

"No, go on," North said. "A tattoo might be identifying. Say more about that."

"North," Shaw said quietly.

Jem sent a strangely pleading look at Tean.

"Why don't we all calm down?" Tean said.

He said it kindly, and quietly, and with a kind of assurance that made North take a deep breath. He gave Jem a wary nod that was as close as he could come to an apology in that moment and said, "He's tied up with this church family. The cross in the tattoo, right? And that might be a letter E. Epiphany of Light is the name of the church."

Jem made a noise that could have meant anything.

"Good job with the photos," North said as he tossed the phone back to Jem. Then he crooked a grin. "For an amateur."

"Asshole," Jem muttered, but after a moment, he rolled his eyes and quirked a tiny smile back.

"Oh, that was so sweet," Shaw said. "Wasn't that sweet, Tean?"

Tean was suddenly very busy looking out the window, and his voice had a strangely tight quality, as though he were suppressing something as he said, "So sweet."

Before North could respond, movement outside the window drew his attention. The figure was dressed in black, and he looked shorter than average. He was wearing a mask, and he walked with a kind of easy confidence that was too genuine to be called swagger. The gun holstered on his hip might have had something to do with it. The matte-black sickle in his hand probably did too. A slight hitch to his movement suggested stiffness, maybe an injury. He cut down the side of Ezell's house and vanished into the shadows.

North's brain was still putting together the pieces—he had heard about the attack on Theo's house, about the man with the matte-black sickle and the matching knife—when Jem said, "Son of a bitch, it's him!" Before anyone could do anything, Jem threw the front door open and sprinted out of the house.

Tean was getting to his feet, panic emptying out his face.

"Stay here," North said. "Call John-Henry. Shaw—"

"I'll go around back," Shaw said.

They tore out of the house. There was no sign of either Jem or the man in black, and the only sound came from the buzz of the streetlights. North sprinted for the front of Ezell's house. He tried to tell if he could still see the flashlight moving on the other side of the blind, but the streetlights threw a glare on the windows. Shaw darted down the side of the house, disappearing into the shadows.

The first shot rang out. It came from inside the house, and even muffled by the walls, it was loud. Whoever the man in black was, he didn't care about noise. A man screamed, and North thought he recognized Gid's voice. North took the steps up to the front door and reached for the handle. If it was locked—

But the door flew inward, and the handle moved out of North's reach. His body followed it for a fraction of a second, an automatic reaction as he tried to catch hold. The movement sent him off balance. A moment later, Gid crashed into North. The impact knocked North off the stoop and into the bed of lava rocks along the foundation. Gid's footsteps clipped the sidewalk and faded down the street.

Another shot rang out.

Shaw was shouting.

North picked himself up, distantly aware of the scrapes and bangs from the fall, and scrambled up onto the stoop again. He plunged into the house. It was dark, with thin slats of gray light filtering through the blinds. The stink of gunpowder filled the air. His hand shook—he was shaking all over—and he tightened his grip around the CZ.

Luck and reflexes saved his life. Something moved in the silver face of a mirror, and North reared back. He couldn't see the blade; at first, all he felt was the flicker of something, the faint disturbance of air. Then his brain processed it, pulling up the image of that black sickle carving the darkness. He squeezed off a shot in what he hoped was the right direction. The muzzle flare burned off his night vision, and fear gripped him. He started to fire the next shot, but then he realized he didn't know if Jem and Shaw were in the house, and he managed to stop. He kept backing up until he slammed into a wall.

For the second time that night, luck and reflexes saved him. A whispering hiss alerted him, and he dropped as the sickle sliced through the air above him. Plaster popped and cracked as the blade tore along the wall. Where was Shaw? Where was Jem? North fired a second shot, and the muzzle flare blinded him again. His ears rang from the gunfire, making it impossible to hear anything.

As his vision began to adjust again, North made out the silhouette of a man in the doorway, framed by the glow of the streetlights. He had a gun pointed at North.

Then someone crashed into the man, and both bodies went tumbling out of the house. North got to his feet and stumbled after them. Shaw emerged from somewhere deeper in the house and sprinted past him, face painted with the weak light from the street, the Springfield coming up in his hand. By the time North reached the door, Shaw was already lining up a shot.

For a moment, the scene was surreal. On Adam Ezell's lawn, Jem and the man in black brawled like a couple of teenagers—grappling, rolling, flipping. Shaw hesitated; there was no clean shot, no way to fire without almost certainly hitting Jem too. After the thunder of the gunfire, the street's silence shimmered in North's ears. He clutched the doorjamb because he felt the floor sliding out from under him, and he wondered if he'd hit his head.

Then the man in black bucked Jem and sent him rolling toward the street. Shaw fired, and the man fired back. North grabbed Shaw and hauled him into the house. He waited for the next shot. For the screams.

But a heartbeat passed. And then another.

And then Jem called, "Motherfucking cowardly piece of shit!" In a weary voice, he added, "He's gone."

9

Apparently, North decided, shooting a gun in Wahredua was a bigger deal than in St. Louis, because they spent the rest of the night dealing with the fallout from the scene at Adam Ezell's house. They had to tell the whole story to the responding officers. Then they had to tell it to a sour-faced detective named Palomo. And then, eventually, they had to tell it to John-Henry again. In his office. With Emery glaring at them over John-Henry's shoulder.

When they'd finished, John-Henry rubbed his face, fighting a yawn. He was quiet for a moment. And then, in a controlled voice, he said, "I understand that our conversation earlier was rushed. I also understand that you're used to…to working independently."

"To doing our jobs," North said. "The jobs you hired us to do."

"To create a fucking shitstorm," Emery said. "Is that what you were hired to do?"

"We were hired to track down Welch," North shot back, "and we did."

"Really? Where is he? Was he in that private home on that residential street you shot up like it's the fucking Wild West?"

"We're following this case where it leads us, and it led us to that fucking church and to some sort of connection with that missing deputy. What the fuck have you been doing? Picking lint out of your ass?"

Emery opened his mouth, but John-Henry slapped the desk and barked, "Enough." In the wake of the shout, the buzz of the fluorescents was the only sound. "Ree, I'm handling this. North, knock it the fuck off."

Maybe it was the late night. Maybe it was the exhaustion. Maybe it was the powerlessness of watching death and chaos ripple through the town you were sworn to protect. Whatever it was, it was riding John-Henry like a devil, and North could see it in his face now: a man pushed to the edge.

With a grunt, North sat back and looked at Shaw. Shaw shrugged helplessly.

"Sorry," North muttered.

After a moment, John-Henry nodded. Emery leaned against the wall with an oddly satisfied look on his face.

"While you are working for the Wahredua PD," John-Henry said, the words clean and neutral, "I expect you to obey the law and conduct yourself in a way that will make whatever case we bring to trial airtight. Do you understand?"

The wait was like sandpaper on raw skin. Finally, North bit out, "Yes."

"And while you are working for the Wahredua PD, I expect regular updates about the progress of your investigation. You are not cowboys, to borrow Ree's metaphor. You're not on your own. You're part of a team, and I'm not just talking about Wahredua PD." Something in his voice yielded. "Either we're in this together, or we're not."

"We're in it together," Shaw said quietly.

North nodded.

Emery snorted.

"But also," North said, "fuck you, you big lump of fucks."

For some reason, that made John-Henry grin, and he looked younger.

"Have the Highway Patrol been any help?" Shaw asked.

The smile evaporated from John-Henry's face, but Emery was the one who spoke. "They're still processing the cells, taking an eternity so they can tell us what we already know: Philip Welch killed two men in there."

"They didn't catch Welch with the roadblock," John-Henry said, "but I think we've got an idea why—he was well past it by the time they put it into position."

"What are you going to do about that?" North asked. "The Moss family, the church."

"Cassidy," Emery said, that single word a dead sound.

Something flickered in John-Henry's expression, but when he spoke, he sounded tired. "It's going to be a jurisdictional nightmare. It already is, I suppose."

"And, as a result, we're going to spend as much time jerking each other off as we do actual police work, which is a vibrant reminder of why I purposefully left this bullshit behind."

"Also," North said, "they would have fired you anyway."

Emery turned a flat look on him.

"What about Gid?" Shaw asked.

"We're looking for him too," John-Henry said. "That shouldn't be as hard; I can't imagine the son of a preacher has the kind of skills and resources to lie low for an extended period of time. He'll swipe a credit card or pop up on a traffic camera."

"Of course, it would have been nice if you'd held on to him," Emery said.

North tried not to make a face about that, mostly because he agreed with Emery. Jem's all-clear had sent them venturing out onto Ezell's lawn, and by the time Shaw had remembered Gid, there was no sign of the man.

"We were a little busy," North said. "Fucking Jem. Rushing in there like a fucking amateur."

Emery raised his eyebrows.

Shaw made an unhappy noise.

"You know," John-Henry said, "there's a good chance Gid's still alive because Jem acted the way he did. This man in black, whoever he is, is a killer. And I don't like that he's carrying a gun now."

"No," Emery said, "it was so much better when he was a cross between Freddy Krueger and a ninja."

"Oh, he's not Freddy Krueger," Shaw said, "because Freddy Krueger had those hedge-trimming gloves."

"That was only in an episode of *The Simpsons*—" North tried.

"He's more like a cross between a ninja and...oh! A medieval peasant harvesting a cereal crop."

"John," Emery said.

"Or mowing hay."

John-Henry rubbed his eyes again. "Any idea what the son of a preacher was looking for in our missing deputy's house?"

North shook his head. "That's got to be enough for a warrant, though, right? We've got a clear trail that has Welch walking up to their front door, and a couple of hours later, Gid drives across the state to break into some random deputy's house? That's a connection."

"I'll see what I can do," John-Henry said through a yawn. "Right now, I'm hitting a wall."

North opened his mouth to say something—the phrase *weak sauce* was probably in there—when a yawn caught him too.

"We're sorry again, John-Henry," Shaw said. "Emery. We're really sorry. We'll do better."

Emery said nothing, amber eyes glittering as he studied them. John-Henry cracked a smile, though. "I'd appreciate it, if only so I don't lose my job." He was quiet a moment, and then he said, "Thank God you're all ok."

A false dawn turned the sky to pewter as North drove them back to their motel. They could have piled into the Hazard and Somerset household again—they'd done it before, on and off over the course of the last few insane weeks—but the house was already overcrowded, and, more importantly, every time North turned around, Colt was there. Literally. One time, he'd opened the refrigerator to get something to drink, and he'd hit the boy in the face with the door. Worse, Colt had apologized to him. Unless Shaw had been right, and he'd been apologizing to the refrigerator.

The Bridal Veil Motor Court was full of long shadows, and the glass-block accents winked as the headlights swept over them. North parked in front of their room—the motor court wasn't exactly burdened with an abundance of guests—and they went inside. They fumbled their clothes off in the pre-dawn gloom, and North pulled Shaw's back to his chest in bed. The mini-split couldn't keep up, and skin on skin was sticky, but he wanted him close. He wondered if what felt like the start of a raging boner was going to mean putting off sleep for another hour, and he was vaguely aware of his brain explaining the hormones still working their way through his body after a brush with death. And then he was asleep.

He woke to sunlight. Too much sun. And Shaw taking off his underwear.

"Guh," North muttered.

Shaw laughed quietly. He smelled like soap, and when he bent to kiss North, he tasted like toothpaste, and his hair was wet where it tickled North's chest and shoulder. North hardened quickly—first in Shaw's hand, then in his mouth. Shaw was already hard, of course, his dick brushing wet lines onto North's thigh. North heard his own uneven breaths, the sounds of Shaw's mouth, the rattle of the mini-split like coins tumbling in a dryer. Too much sun, his brain reminded him, and that's when he realized the curtains were only partially closed.

He was going to say something, and then Shaw pulled back, a lube-slick hand pumping North once before Shaw straddled him and seated himself. The first hot, gripping inches forced a noise out of North, and his hands bit into Shaw's thighs. Shaw whimpered as he settled himself slowly. Too slowly. And then he was there, all of him and all of North joined together. A flush ran across his thin chest. He was breathing in a way North recognized.

"Shit, baby," North muttered, and he manhandled Shaw until Shaw keened. "Already?"

Shaw nodded wildly and began to move, and North moved with him. It might have been thirty seconds, but North thanked God nobody had a stopwatch. Shaw first, then North, his hands tightening until he knew he'd leave bruises. When it was over, it was as though something had swept through North, hollowing his bones, scouring his insides. He felt light and empty and clean, and maybe it wasn't all that much sun, because as Shaw lay next to him, damp hair pillowing his head on North's chest, North realized he was about to fall asleep.

He woke the second time to "Oh shit, they're naked!"

And then a door slammed.

"Fuck me," North groaned.

Shaw laughed sleepily into his chest.

"Not like that," North said and slapped his ass.

"I wasn't trying to look, Theo." The voice was unmistakably Auggie's. "I'm just saying, I've never seen yours look all red and smushed like that. Well, I don't know, maybe because he's so white."

"How old is he?" North muttered. "Twelve? Is it legal to kill twelve-year-olds if they're complete and total twerps?"

"This seems like a good stopping point for our one and only conversation about North's dick," Theo said. Then he hammered on the door.

"Like Twinky Twerp," Shaw murmured. "That sounds like something Lars would say."

North pulled his hair until Shaw yelled, and then he sent him into the bathroom.

"They're definitely awake," Auggie said as he opened the door a crack. "I heard Shaw yell."

"I'm not saying they're not awake," Theo said, "I said let's not go in until we're sure—"

"For fuck's sake," North said, pulling the sheet over himself. "What the fuck is wrong with you two?"

"Are you, uh, decent?" Auggie asked.

"Decent. You already barged in here like a couple of cockhounds. I hope that was educational for you, Tiny-tot. In another ten or fifteen years, your body will go through some dramatic changes."

Auggie and Theo pressed into the room. Auggie wore a partial smirk, but the bandage couldn't dim his amusement. Theo's mouth was set in that tiny frown that was like crack for North. It was too easy to push the older man's buttons, especially when it came to Auggie. They were dressed like they had somewhere to go that involved a lot of bros slapping five and giving each other handies under the table—polos, slacks, shoes that were too nice to be called sneakers. Theo was carrying two paper cups, and

Auggie held a bag that, unless North's nose misled him, contained something remarkably delicious.

"Changes like what?" Auggie asked. "You know, I didn't realize your stomach could look like that while you were lying down."

"Make it through your twenties, dickbreath. Talk to me when your metabolism gives up the holy fucking ghost."

"Aren't you in your twenties?" Theo asked.

North gave him the bird. But he did sit up. And pulled the sheet higher.

"Theo's stomach definitely doesn't look like that," Auggie said.

"Yep, Grampsie is one in a million. Your lucky catch. What the fuck are you two doing here besides perving on us and getting your jollies?"

"Bringing you breakfast," Auggie said, hefting the bag.

"And coffee," Theo said.

"But if you'd rather us leave so you can continue, uh, exhibiting with the windows open..."

North made a gimme gesture, and Auggie's smirk grew as he handed over the bag. Theo set the coffees on the nightstand, and then they took the only chairs in the motel room. The bag held two enormous biscuit sandwiches, a clamshell container of home fries, and a hubcap-sized cinnamon roll.

"Holy Jesus," North said, "this is as big as your head, Strawberry Shortcake."

The nickname only made Auggie roll his eyes, but Theo's little frown came back. It was too easy, really.

North was cuffing the sandwich wrapper and opening his mouth when Shaw emerged from the bathroom, dripping wet and holding a washcloth in front of himself. Auggie's eyes got huge, and then he started to laugh into his hands. Theo didn't exactly make the sign of the cross, but he did look like a man seeking divine intercession.

"Hi, Auggie," Shaw said brightly. "Hi, Theo!"

"Put some pants on," North barked.

And then he realized his mistake.

Shaw's eyes fastened onto the breakfast sandwich. "No, North! Our diet!"

"No diet," North said and took the biggest bite his jaws were capable of. It was, admittedly, hard to swallow. And that made a voice in North's head perk up, the one that sounded like Shaw, that sounded like all those bad blowjob jokes, the ones about how he'd chewed the head off Nick's dick or whatever Shaw was always going on about. North powered through—there was that Shaw voice again, droning on about Nick—and managed to get the food down. The other day, at the park, Tean had been talking about geese not chewing their food, or maybe it had been ducks, and that memory came back vividly now.

"We're on a strict diet—" Shaw said, trying to climb across the bed—and, in the process, dropping the washcloth.

North elbowed him away. "Get off the bed. And get away from my sandwich. And get some fucking clothes on so you're not hanging dong in front of small fry; he's strictly PG-13."

"Oh God," Shaw said. "Sorry, Auggie."

"You know—" Theo began.

But Auggie squeezed his arm, laughing, and Theo grimaced and settled into his chair.

North finished the biscuit sandwich and half the coffee before he felt human again, and he entrusted Auggie with safeguarding the cinnamon roll because he knew if he left it to Shaw, the traitorous weasel would either eat it all himself or feed it to birds or summon an army of mice—God only knew, the list went on and on. He padded into the bathroom, and he chose to ignore—because he was an adult, and adults didn't argue with children—Auggie's final comment.

"Ok, I know you're going to think I'm joking, but is one cheek bigger than the other?"

The shower, added to the food and caffeine, went a long way toward completing that process of turning North back into a functioning person again. When he'd finished, he checked his stomach in the mirror and decided Auggie was full of shit. It was muscle. And mass. Then he checked his ass. It was hard to tell if there was a size difference. But there wasn't, because that wasn't a thing that happened to people. And it was this goddamn cheapass mirror, that was all.

Towel around his waist, he returned to the bedroom just in time. Shaw had the cinnamon roll in his lap, and when North threw a look at Auggie, Auggie sank down guiltily in his seat. Head thrown back, Shaw was saying, "And then sometimes he says—well, moans, really—'Yes, yes, Shaw, right there,' and he's talking about this spot—"

"What the fuck is wrong with you, bird brain?" North snapped as he snatched what remained of the cinnamon roll—less than half!—from Shaw and dropped onto the bed. "And you two, don't you have anything better to do?"

"Aside from bringing you breakfast?" Theo asked drily.

North scratched his cheek with his middle finger and attacked the cinnamon roll.

"Actually, we do have a reason for coming over," Auggie said.

"Wonder of wonders," North muttered, but the sarcasm was dampened by the mouthful of bread and icing.

"So, first of all, that guy Gid?" Auggie glanced from Shaw to North. "He's the one who chatted me up in the Cottonmouth Club a few days ago."

For what might have been the first time in his life, North forgot about a cinnamon roll. "You're shitting me."

Auggie shook his head. He held out his phone, displaying a publicity photo of the Moss family, and pointed to Gid. "Gideon Moss, right? He's the one who had you at gunpoint last night?"

Shaw nodded.

"When we were looking for those missing kids," Auggie said, "we went to the Cottonmouth Club."

"I remember," North said drily. "You couldn't stop talking about it after we kept your asses from getting capped in a parking lot."

"Jesus, North," Theo said under his breath.

"The point is," Auggie said, "a guy talked to me while I was in the club, and it was Gid. He even used the same name. I saw him get in a fight—well, an argument—with a couple of other guys, and then he was looking for a way to inflate his own ego, so he started talking to me—shooting his mouth off, really, because he wanted to brag, and in the process, saying a lot of stupid stuff."

"Like what?" Shaw asked.

"Like they did wild stuff there. Private stuff. Stuff you couldn't do anywhere else."

North waited, but when nothing more came, he said, "That's it? Shit, he could have been talking about playing Dungeons and Dragons in their jocks."

"He talked about getting Auggie a girl," Theo said.

"Seriously? Did he even look at the little wiener?"

Theo sat forward in his chair. "Knock it off."

Placing a hand on Theo's knee, Auggie said, "He didn't say anything super incriminating, no. But he talked about how the Cottonmouth Club was different, about how you could get a girl there and do whatever you wanted to her. That was the part he emphasized. And I think he realized he'd said too much to a stranger, because he left in a hurry. That was when I decided to get out of there, but as I was leaving, I spotted him talking to someone. He looked, well, worried."

North broke off another piece of cinnamon roll, but then he let it fall back into the box, and he wiped the icing from his thumb. "Ok," he finally said. "Welch takes us to Gid. Gid takes us to the Cottonmouth Club. And two of the three people who died last night, they were going to identify a man they'd met at the Cottonmouth Club."

Shaw tented his hands over his mouth and shook his head.

"Did you tell John-Henry about this?" North asked.

"Yeah, of course. As soon as Jem and Tean updated us—"

"Which wasn't their job," Theo said, "because we should have already been kept in the loop."

North scratched his cheek again.

"—I found that church's website, and boom, there was Gid."

"Auggie was up half the night doing research," Theo said.

"Theo was up all night," Auggie said. "When Jem and Tean left, he was in charge of keeping the kids safe."

Which, North had to admit, might explain why the grumpy teacher was a little grumpier than usual. So, he decided to forego the low-hanging fruit about *the kids*.

"Did you find out anything else about the church?" Shaw asked.

Auggie shrugged. "They must take in a lot of money. That huge campus, the one you saw last night? They've got a satellite campus in Joplin, and both campuses have fully equipped stages—lights, cameras, everything. They broadcast online, so there's no real distribution costs, and they've got a big audience. The guy who started it all, the dad—"

"We met him," North said. "He might as well be a piece of furniture; nobody's home."

Auggie nodded. "They talk about his advanced age and failing health, but nobody's come out and said that. The older son seems to be covering the responsibilities up here, and the satellite campus has somebody else running the show—not family, I mean. Kind of interesting, right, when you've got two sons and two campuses?"

"The brothers clearly didn't get along," Shaw said. "We saw that last night."

"But that's normal, right? Disagreements between brothers?" Theo asked. "Or what are we talking about?"

Shaw shook his head slowly. "I think this was more than that. The older brother, Jed, is clearly the more successful one. He's also clearly in charge. Gid was hopped up on something last night, and I doubt it was the first time. Add that to what Auggie told us, and it sounds like he's got substance abuse on top of already erratic behavior, plus the need for approval. That's what he was after with you, right, Auggie?"

Something like surprise flitted across Auggie's face, and he seemed to be considering Shaw anew. North recognized the look; it happened whenever someone got a glimpse of the real Shaw. "Uh, yeah," Auggie said. "That's exactly what he wanted."

"Anything that might explain why he went to that deputy's house last night?" North asked.

"Not really. That's what's so strange, I guess. Neither campus is located in Wahredua, and Jem and Tean said they didn't see anything inside Ezell's house that suggested a connection between him and the Epiphany of Light."

"Wait," Shaw said, "they went inside the deputy's house?"

"We're talking about Jem," Theo said with a half-smile.

Auggie glanced at each of them. "But the connection to the Cottonmouth Club, that's something, right?"

"And it's a connection that Emery and John-Henry are going to handle," Theo said.

"I know, I know," Auggie said. "But North and Shaw needed to hear about it, don't you think?"

Theo nodded, but the look on his face sent a mixed message.

"I guess you did your due diligence," North said, "although you could have put this in the group chat instead of playing peeping Tom. We'll see if we can run down—"

"That's not why we came over," Theo said. "Tell them, Auggie."

"I got us an appointment with Eric Brey."

"What?" And then, "Who?"

"Brey. He was one of Welch's visitors. Well, his only visitor, I guess." Auggie grinned. "And he's a state representative."

North honestly didn't know what to say for a moment. He finally said again, "You're shitting me."

"Nope. One guess where he's from."

"Auburn," Shaw said.

Auggie nodded.

"Jesus," North said. "What are we mucking around in?"

"Good question," Theo said.

North tried to run through what the connection meant, but the best he could come up with was the cold, hard reality: Welch's trail had gone cold at the Epiphany of Light, but Theo and Auggie had handed them a fresh trail to follow. Auggie was still grinning, obviously pleased with himself and just as obviously waiting for recognition.

"Good work, super squirt," North said.

Auggie rolled his eyes, but his grin got bigger.

"All right, if that's it, I'm going to get dressed. We've got work to do—"

"No, no, no," Auggie said. "I got the appointment for us. All of us."

North stared at him. Then he looked at Theo.

Theo held up both hands. "Oh no. I learned my lesson the hard way."

"Look," North said, "you did a good job—"

"I tracked him down," Auggie said. "I created the fake PAC. I built the damn website at three in the morning. And I'm the one who talked my way past his assistant and convinced Brey that he needed to see us today."

It was a long fifteen seconds before North gritted out, "Fine."

"And you should make him say sorry," Shaw said.

North turned on him so fast that Shaw fell off the bed. Auggie pulled his shirt up to cover a grin, and Theo rolled his eyes.

As North knelt next to his duffel and began rifling it for clothes, he said, "I'm not dressing like a penis in a collared shirt like the two of you. In case you were wondering."

Theo sighed. "No, North. I can honestly say nobody was wondering that."

"So?" North said as he threw a pair of jeans on the bed. "How'd you convince him to see us? Who are we, all that shit? Knock that look off your face; I'm not going to leave you behind. We'll get you all buckled into your car seat, and you can fall asleep on the nice long drive."

"You know what?" Auggie said. "I'm starting to get it."

North refused to ask what.

"This whole thing Shaw does. It makes more and more sense every day."

This time, North gave him a dirty look. "Talk, or you aren't going to get that pair of stilts for your birthday."

"We're 'Watchdogs for Information,'" Auggie said. "We're fighting the fake news media."

North thought about that. "God, that's a stupid name for a PAC."

In the tone of someone at the edge of his rope, Theo said, "North."

"What?" North said. "That's a compliment. They're all stupid."

"That was a compliment," Theo muttered.

Shaw, bare-assed and digging through his suitcase, suddenly straightened and looked over at them. "Oh my God, North, this is just like that dream I had. Except in that one, Theo was wearing those leather shorts."

10

Eric Brey, according to the articles Shaw read on the drive, was thirty-eight, and he was in his second term serving in the Missouri House of Representatives. He was a veteran—the Marines—and he now made his living owning a large farm and tractor supply store, although that was a family business, and from what Shaw gathered, it didn't sound like Brey had a passion for farm equipment. Although you never knew with people, which was one of Shaw's guiding principles, and one of the reasons he was clearly more open-minded than North.

Brey's political headquarters were located in a strip mall of muddy brick located on the north side of Auburn, sandwiched between a crab shack (not to be trusted, Shaw decided, this far from any ocean) and a place that, apparently, painted dogs' nails.

"Oh, we could—"

"No," North said.

The strip mall's lot was undergoing some sort of construction, and they had to drive over a steel plate. The borrowed Ford Focus came down on the other side hard enough to make Shaw's teeth click together.

"How the fuck does he drive this thing?" North said to himself. "It's like a fucking Cracker Jack box on wheels." He was silent for a moment as he steered them into a parking stall. "Maybe there was some kind of accident. He grew up on a farm, right? Maybe a thresher bit his dick off."

"In the first place, I'm very proud of you for taking Jem's feedback about the GTO and choosing a more sensible car."

"I didn't take his feedback. It was my idea, and the GTO is a sensible car—"

"And in the second place, it was very nice of Theo to let us use his car."

"Auggie makes fucking bank. And he'd do anything to keep daddy happy. For fuck's sake, all Theo has to do is hint that he'd like a decent car, and Auggie would probably die from spontaneous twink orgasm."

"Oh, I don't think so," Shaw said. "I'm not even sure Auggie is a twink anymore." He rolled down his window as Auggie and Theo pulled into the stall next to them, and Auggie buzzed his window down too. "Auggie, have you already experienced twink death?"

"Why did I roll my window down?" Auggie asked.

Theo said, "That was certainly a choice."

"Did you know that North used to drive a minivan?" Shaw asked.

"Roll your window back up," Theo said.

Auggie's eyebrows shot up. "Hold on, do you have photos? Because a lot of people would pay good money for that."

"Oh, I've got millions of photos. One time, he was waiting in line at McDonald's, and he bumped this other minivan in front of him, and she got out of her van and wanted North to get out of his van, only he wouldn't, so she kept asking if he was afraid—"

Then some sort of en-strangulation curse started to happen. It took Shaw an oxygen-deprived moment to realize North was twisting the collar of his shirt. A moment later, the passenger window hummed back up, cutting off the sound of Theo and Auggie's laughter.

North released Shaw, and Shaw gulped in air. "Thank God," Shaw said, "the strangulatus curse—"

"There was no curse, bird brain! Stop talking. And no more stories or explaining or questions or talking. Did I mention talking?"

Shaw nodded.

North looked like he was trying to let it go, but the words tore their way out of him. "She was pregnant, for fuck's sake. What did you want me to do?"

"She offered to give you a free punch."

North was making a high-pitched noise as he got out of the car.

By the time Shaw followed North onto the sidewalk, Theo and Auggie were already waiting at the door to Brey's office.

Theo was in the middle of saying, "—didn't think state representatives had offices."

"They do if they're going to run for Congress," Auggie said. "At least, this one does. You should have heard his assistant—you would have thought I'd called the White House. The vibe I'm getting is they all take themselves very seriously."

"We're doing the talking," North said. "You, try to look like you're under forty."

"I am under forty," Theo said.

"You, try to look like you're not expired goods."

"What's going on?" Auggie asked. "Is it my clothes? Is it my eyes, because I only get bags like this when I don't get enough sleep. When is twink death?"

"Honey," Shaw said, his voice full of sympathy. "If you have to ask."

Auggie's eyes got really wide, but before Shaw could explain all the opportunities that awaited him in his post-twink life, North opened the door, and they headed inside.

It was an office suite in an aging strip mall in a city called Auburn, Missouri, which was one way for Shaw to make sense of all the clashing shades of blue that had been used: navy blue carpet, royal blue paint on the walls, some sort of blue approaching teal for the chair rail. A curved desk sat immediately in front of the entrance, where a bright-eyed young woman was typing at a computer. Farther back, the office opened up: a central area with cubicles, presumably for volunteers, and then what appeared to be a suite of offices for Brey and his aides or assistants or whatever you wanted to call them. An enormous picture of the governor took up most of one wall, and everything else had been decorated with American flags.

"May I help you?" the young woman asked as Auggie and North stepped forward at the same time.

"Yeah—" North began.

"Hi, Marcy," Auggie said. He shook hands with her, smiling. "Paul. We spoke on the phone, the Watchdogs for Information meeting with Mr. Brey."

"Oh my gosh, Paul, yes." She was smiling right back. Shaw was smiling too because smiling was definitely contagious. North, he noticed, was not smiling. "I'll let Mr. Brey know you're here. Would you like anything while you wait? A water?"

"I thought we had an appointment," North said.

Marcy turned the smile down a few degrees and looked at North.

"We're fine, thanks," Auggie said. "We'll wait right here."

"What wait?" North muttered as Auggie herded him away from the desk. "What's the point of an appointment if you still have to wait?"

"He's cranky," Shaw said in answer to the unasked question on Auggie's face. "He's tired, and he either had too much sex and not enough cheese, or too much cheese and not enough sex. It's a tricky formula, getting the ratios right. Oh, and you're stealing his thunder. What I do when he's in a mood is sometimes I come up with a way for North to do something that I know will make him feel all manly and tough and proud, like maybe I'm just standing there and all of a sudden I say, 'Oh my God, my espadrille fell down this well,' and North says, 'We don't have a well, that's the storm drain,' and—"

"Does Marcy have any complimentary aspirin?" Theo asked.

"I don't have aspirin," Shaw said, patting himself down, "but sometimes I carry shredded willow bark—"

"It's your fault," North said to Auggie. "All this laughing. You're encouraging him. I'm going to have to bully him for six months straight to get him back to manageable levels."

To be fair, Auggie did look like he was trying not to laugh.

Fortunately, at that point Marcy said, "Mr. Brey will see you in the conference room." She pointed at an angle past the cubicles, and Auggie smoothed out his face, thanked her, and headed off in the lead. North power-walked to catch up with him.

"The male ego is a fragile, complicated thing," Shaw said to Theo. "It's nice that you have such a delicate touch with Auggie; he needs you, but he's getting too old to tell you he does. I really admire how you're able to meet those needs without ever making him feel like there's an imbalance in the relationship."

Theo opened his mouth like he might say something, but nothing came out, and then a strange, unreadable look came over his face as he studied Shaw more closely.

Like the rest of the office, the conference room was painted in multiple shades of blue, and the furniture was new and straddled the line between cheap and functional. Two men stood at the far end of the room, looking at a piece of paper. One of them, Shaw recognized from the camera stills that Deputy Weiss had pulled: square-jawed, his dark hair in a conservative cut, he was handsome in a way that suggested family values and strong Republican bloodlines. His suit was off the rack but good quality, and he'd clearly had it lightly tailored for a better fit. He glanced up, murmured something to the other man, and then stepped forward to shake Auggie's hand.

"Eric Brey," he said as the man he'd been talking to slipped out of the room. He repeated the introduction as he shook hands with the others. "I'm so glad we were able to make this meeting happen." He did a double take of Auggie's face. "You all right? That looks serious."

"Fine, thanks," Auggie said. "An accident. Thanks for taking the time to see us today, Mr. Brey. Do you mind if we sit down? This won't take long, but it's important."

Shaw took that opportunity to bump the door with his hip, and it shut quietly.

"I have to admit," Brey said as they took their seats around the table, "I'm not familiar with Watchdogs for Information, but your site is very impressive, and some of the numbers you were citing when you spoke to my assistant—"

"Yeah, that was bullshit," North said as he slapped a folder on the table. He opened it and took out the camera stills from the county jail. He slid them over to Brey. "We want to know why you visited Philip Welch and where he is now."

Brey's body language changed. It was subtle, masked by the suit, but still there: the man who had been in control of the situation was replaced by a man who sensed a threat. He held himself more tightly. His shoulders drew in—only barely, but still. He'd been a Marine, Shaw thought, or was a Marine, however you were supposed to say that. Had he seen combat?

Then Brey drew the pictures toward him. He studied them for a moment, looked up, and asked, "Who are you?"

"I'm North McKinney, and I'm a licensed investigator working for the Wahredua PD. I asked you a question, Mr. Brey."

But Brey's gaze settled on Shaw next, then Theo, and then, with disturbing intensity, on Auggie. Theo shifted in his seat, moving to the edge of the chair—preparing himself, Shaw recognized, to move fast. For a moment, it was like Shaw was seeing him for the first time, seeing what the mild manner and the quiet voice hid so well: the hard body, and inside, an even harder mind. When Theo moved, the polo tightened across his back, and Shaw could glimpse the muscles moving there. A capacity for violence, Shaw's brain suggested, and the image that floated at the edge of his subconscious, drifting in those dark, frozen waters, was of broken brown glass and ugly little pieces of stamped steel. And he wondered why he hadn't seen it before.

"What do you want?"

"Like I said." North's smile wasn't really a smile. "We'd like to know why you visited Philip Welch and where he is."

"He's in jail, that's where he is. What's wrong? Did something happen?"

"He killed two people," Auggie said. "And he's on the run."

Brey didn't respond. He stared at the photos again. After a few seconds, he looked up. "You'd better tell me as much as you can."

"That's all there is to tell," North said. "So, I'm going to ask you again: why did you visit Philip Welch, and where is he now?"

"I have no idea where he is," Brey said, and for the first time, his tone hardened. "And I don't appreciate the implication. I know Phil from a troubled teens program. I heard he'd gotten arrested again, so I went to check on him. He's a good kid, believe it or not." He stopped, as though he heard what he'd just said, and touched one of the pictures, pushing it away slightly. "You're sure he killed someone?"

"I'm going to ask you again," North said, "why you were visiting Philip Welch."

"I told you —"

"Wahredua is close to a hundred miles away. Try again."

Brey set his jaw. When he spoke, the words were clipped. "Phil's grandmother called me and told me he'd been arrested again. I told you, I have a relationship with him. When I had a chance, I went to check on him. We talked. I left. I was going to check on him again, just a phone call, but —" He pushed the rest of the photos away. "I got busy."

"What did you talk about when you visited him?" Shaw asked.

"Nothing. I mean, his grandma, life. We talked about making better choices. I'm sorry, I can't get over this — are you sure he killed those men?"

"Who said they were men?" North asked.

"I don't —" Brey stopped again. It was the total non-response that made Shaw wonder. It was possible someone might react to this kind of news by suppressing any sort of visible emotion. But it was also an excellent way to lie without actually lying. The silence dragged until Brey finally said, "I assumed. I don't know what you want from me."

"I told you what I want from you. I want to know what your relationship was with Philip Welch." North bared his teeth, and nobody reasonable could have called it a smile. "Remember?"

A disbelieving laugh. A shake of the head. But his hands were wrapped tight around the arms of his chair, visible in a brief moment when Brey rocked back in his seat. "I told you! He'd been in and out of the system. It was — it was a Big Brother program, for heaven's sake. You want to know what we talked about? Like, did we talk about how he was going to kill those m — people? Did he tell me his plans to escape? Do I really have to answer that?"

"You're asking a lot of questions, Mr. Brey," Shaw said. "I don't know if you noticed that."

A hint of color came into Brey's cheeks. "No, we didn't talk about anything like that. It was what I told you, we talked about his life, about how he was going to turn things around. And I already told you how I know Phil and why I went to visit him."

"Do you visit all the troubled teens you met through that program?" North traced an invisible line in the air. "A hundred miles between here and Wahredua. You keep that up, you won't have time to get yourself elected again."

"No, I don't do that with every teen. Phil and I connected. I don't know what you want me to say; I've never had to defend myself for volunteer work before."

"Get some practice. It'll pay off in that big political career you're planning."

"Where is Philip?" Shaw asked.

Brey's gaze snapped toward him, and he shut down again. Then he said, "How should I know?"

"You know him," Theo said. "You connected, isn't that what you told us?"

"Where has he gone before?" Auggie asked.

"I don't know; let me think. His grandmother's, I suppose. Did you already talk to her?"

"Where else?"

"He had a girlfriend, Maleah."

"Come on, Mr. Brey. I could have gotten this off his Instagram."

"I don't know." Brey glanced at his watch. "I'm sorry to hear about those deaths, I really am. And if I hear anything, I'll inform the authorities, of course."

"Of course," North said.

"What about the Cottonmouth Club?" Theo asked. "Would he go there?"

For a single moment, shock broke the wall of control. Then Brey shored his defenses up again, and he said, "Why would he go there?"

"You're familiar with the place?" Shaw asked.

"Familiar isn't the word I'd use. That cesspool is located in my district; I've heard stories."

"What kind of stories?"

"Drugs. And yes, I know Phil was convicted for possession. I suppose it's possible he went there, but to your point, Mr. McKinney, why would he drive a hundred miles? There are other places like the Cottonmouth Club, certainly ones closer to Wahredua."

"You know what?" Auggie said. "I'm starting to think there aren't."

"Mr. Brey, where were you last night?" North asked.

More color came into Brey's cheeks, and that stony silence met them again. "I was home. Alone, before you ask. I'm not married, and I don't have anyone who can testify I was there."

"Jeez, too bad."

"I don't know what you want me to say. I was home. I was alone. That's the truth."

North nodded slowly.

"And since I'd only planned on fifteen minutes for—" He shot Auggie a dirty look. "—a quick chat with a local PAC, I've got to wrap this up, gentlemen." Before they could say anything, he stood. "You can see yourselves out."

He strode past them, ignoring the way North smirked and Theo frowned, and disappeared through the doorway. A moment later, his voice came back to them as he said, "Marcy, have Parker throw them out if they don't leave."

Then the sound of the front door came, and North pushed back his chair.

"It's your turn," Shaw said.

"Rock, paper, scissors."

"No! It's your turn. I drove into those safety cones and spilled my ice cream, remember?"

"And I inspected those manholes—say something, pipsqueak, I dare you."

Auggie closed his mouth, but his grin was huge.

"Jesus," Theo muttered.

"Rock, paper, scissors," North said.

Shaw tried to cover North's fist. "No, it's your—"

"One, two, three, shoot—"

At the last minute, Shaw went with paper. North threw scissors.

"Two out of three," Shaw said.

"Go."

"North!"

"Come on, you can show off for Theo."

Shaw gave Theo a look. Theo did seem to be appropriately attentive, so Shaw sighed and said, "Fine. Theo, maybe you'd like to take notes or something. For posterity."

"Uh huh," Theo said. But he didn't reach for pen and paper, which wasn't, in Shaw's opinion, a good sign.

"You two," North said, "keep whoever comes in here busy. If they ask, we went to the bathroom."

"Together?" Auggie asked.

"Keep it up, pocket protector, and I'll take six more inches off."

Auggie rolled his eyes at that.

Shaw took the lead, and he left the conference room and followed the hallway that led deeper into the office.

A voice from behind stopped him: Marcy. "Excuse me?"

Shaw glanced back, smiled, waved. "It's ok. I'm just getting some water. I've got to take this pill because if I don't, North says I turn into a jackass, which isn't very nice, but it is a tiny bit true on account of a hex. Or maybe it was a curse. Or maybe an enchantment."

"It's an antifungal," North said, "because he picked up this weird skin thing from a donkey he was boinking—oh Christ Almighty!" He rubbed his ribs where Shaw had gotten in an elbow. "But he does have to take it."

Marcy frowned.

"It's fine," Shaw said, "I was watching this whole show about people who have to force feed their partners pills, you know, shoving it to the back of their throat and then holding their mouth shut, and then one person is choking and gagging, and sometimes they're kicking with their hind legs, and the other person is squeezing their snout and stroking their throat—"

"It was an infomercial," North said, "for those little treat pouches where you put pills for dogs, in case the 'snouts' and 'hind legs' didn't tip you off. Two AM and I want to sleep, and this jackanapes won't turn off his computer because he's high as giraffe balls. He thought he was witnessing domestic violence. The only good thing about it was he got Jay out of bed at half-past three and made him come over, the dumbass."

Marcy was staring at them.

North snapped his fingers. "Water, lady."

She startled. "We've got a staff kitchen—here, I'll show you."

"Don't get lost," North said sourly as Shaw followed. He did, unfortunately, manage to dodge the backwards kick that Shaw sent in his direction, and he was wearing an annoyingly self-satisfied expression.

"If you think about it," Shaw said as he followed Marcy across the office and into the kitchen, "it was a kind of domestic violence, on account of them living together, and I did see one lady kiss a cat's behind. And Jadon was very nice about it. He didn't even arrest me, not even for the weed. That's because we used to, um, do you know what rubbing weasels is?"

Marcy was fumbling with a stack of paper cups next to the water cooler. She had the same look on her face that North did when he said he didn't want to talk about Shaw's latest idea yet, even though the colon rake was going to revolutionize, well, everything. "I've really got to get back to—"

Shaw knocked a plastic fork onto the floor and said, "My donkey cure! I dropped it!"

Marcy let out a surprisingly frantic noise and, after a moment of fluttering indecision, set down the paper cup and said, "Ok, I'll help you look."

They looked for the pill with zero luck, which Shaw guessed might have something to do with the fact that he didn't actually have a donkey pill, although now he kind of wanted one, and he certainly hadn't dropped it. He let Marcy burrow into the crevice between the fridge and the cabinets, and he took the opportunity to move over to the water cooler.

"Did you know that if you leave your water out in sunlight too long, it becomes too acidic? Wait, or is it too alkaline? Anyway, you have to change it out frequently."

Marcy must have suspected something was up because she was trying to extricate herself from the crevice. "Wait, hold on, don't—"

Shaw picked up the five-gallon bottle, and water went everywhere.

Marcy screamed.

Shaw dropped the bottle, and it made a surprisingly loud crack when it hit the floor. More water rushed out.

"Wow," Shaw said. "That is a lot of water!"

Marcy, a total trooper, had taken the brunt of it because she was still on her hands and knees. "Get out!" she screamed.

Shaw splashed out of the kitchen.

He found North in the office that clearly belonged to Brey: the picture of Brey at the swearing-in ceremony was a good clue. Nothing looked particularly out of the ordinary: particleboard desk and cabinets, steel filing cabinets, a few more pictures of Brey, these showing him fishing and kayaking. Papers covered the desk in neat stacks around a laptop, and North was flipping through one.

"You made her cry?" North asked and tilted his head in the direction of the kitchen, where it did sound like, possibly, Marcy might be crying.

"It's all the water," Shaw said as he moved over to the phone on Brey's desk. "It's very good for blocked emotions. What's going on with Theo and Auggie?"

"Who knows? Maybe Super Dad and Wundertwink are actually being useful for once, but I wouldn't bet on it."

Shaw picked up the receiver, pressed the redial button on the phone's base, and listened. After a moment, a woman said, "Representative McCarthy's office, how may I direct your call?" Shaw hung up.

"He's not going to call his accomplices on his office landline," North said.

"Worth a shot."

North grunted. He was still flipping through the papers as Shaw settled at the desk. The laptop woke when Shaw tapped the touchpad, but the screen was locked.

"That's private property," a man said, "and you have no right to be in here. I'm calling the police—North?"

Shaw recognized the note in the man's voice. He didn't even have to look up from the laptop to know what it meant; he'd been hearing that note on and off since freshman year, and although—thankfully—their run-ins with North's former fuck toys and friends with benefits had dwindled since they'd left Chouteau College, Shaw would never forget the sound of a Chouteau boy North had lined up and knocked down. Sometimes, knocked down multiple times.

The man in the doorway had the kind of slim-hipped, broad-shouldered athleticism that made Shaw think of swimmers, and layered over the natural good looks—the short, dark hair; the hazel eyes (not unlike his own, Shaw thought with a flash of—what?); the bone structure that had doubtless sent pretty boys to sob in a corner—was the sheen of money and breeding and class that had always been like crack to North.

"Park?" North said. And then, a beat too late, "Parker?"

Confusion battled a smile on Parker's face. "Oh my God, I can't believe—what are you doing here?" And then reality seemed to settle in, and he said in a different tone, "What are you doing here?"

North shot Shaw a look rife with too many emotions for Shaw to parse. Then he said, "Park, close the door, would you?" Parker was already shaking his head, but North said, "Please. Two minutes, that's all I'm asking."

Parker shut the door. And then he said, "I can't believe I'm doing this." He studied them. "I guess I should say you're looking good."

"But I actually look like shit?" North said with a grin.

Parker shrugged.

"A few rough nights. You look fantastic."

"I know," Parker said.

Shaw coughed. Loudly.

"This is Shaw," North said. "Shaw, this is Parker Rhodes."

If the name had ever meant something to Shaw, he'd forgotten it. And anyway, the immediate problems were too pressing for him to comb through his memory—the immediate problems being that Parker looked like he wanted to eat North alive, and North looked like he was eighteen again, sticking his chest out like a fucking rooster, that Chouteau-boy-devouring smirk cocked at the corner of his mouth.

Shaw coughed again.

"Oh," North said. "Right. Shaw's my partner."

Parker made a dismissive noise and looked back at North. "Not that I'm not happy to see you, but why are you here? I mean—is this one of those candid camera shows? What in the world is going on?"

"Why are you here?" Shaw asked.

"I work here. I'm Mr. Brey's aide. Wait, I remember you. You're the one who got stabbed."

Heat rippled through Shaw's body, and he opened his mouth to reply, but North said hurriedly, "Park, there is something seriously wrong here. I don't know what it is, but we're looking into a double murder, and I think your boss is tied up in it somehow."

"That's ridiculous," Park said. "Eric wouldn't kill anyone."

North took a deep breath and glanced at Shaw. Shaw shrugged.

"What do you mean?" Park asked. "You're serious? But he wouldn't..." Park didn't finish the sentence, though, and a strange look crossed his face.

"What?" North asked. "What is it?"

"I mean—ok, it's not like this was my dream, right, to be closing in on thirty and doing what's basically an intern's job for a guy who's to the right of Bush, Jr. But my parents threw a lot of money at Eric, and they're convinced I need some 'real world experience'—" He drew the air quotes with his fingers. "—and so when they asked Eric to find me a spot, he couldn't exactly say no. So, here I am. For the time being, I guess. Anyway, that's a long way to tell you when I got here, I wasn't exactly thrilled. I talked shit with the girls, you know, normal girl stuff."

"That sounds sexist," Shaw said. "And maybe like internalized homophobia."

Parker looked at him like some new bug had crawled out from under the desk. "It's a joke, it's just a way of talking—"

"And what?" North said. "Did someone say something?"

"This girl was here; she's gone now, Lindsey something. She said she hooked up with Eric once. And she said it got...weird. Like, bondage, that kind of thing."

"That's called kink-shaming." Shaw laughed, but the sound felt hollow in his chest. "Boy, you really shouldn't kink-shame."

"Weird how?" North asked. "Because of the BDSM stuff?"

"I don't know. I don't think so; she seemed...scared. And then she was gone."

"What do you mean, gone? Dead?"

"God, no. She quit. She didn't come back." Parker smoothed his trousers over his hips. "But then you said murder, and my first thought was, Oh God, he killed some hookers. That happens, you know. These conservative guys, all that stuff builds up in their system, they're all repressed, and one day they blow."

"They're called sex workers," Shaw said. "Hookers is an offensive term. Jeez, you're not North's type at all."

North blinked like that one had caught him upside the head. Parker's expression shifted to confused and then, a moment later, to a kind of amused bewilderment.

"Wait, you two—"

"Do you think Eric's like that?" North asked.

"I don't know. It was only that one time; I've never heard anything else like that. But you can't forget that kind of thing either, you know?" He smoothed his palms down his trousers again. "This feels crazy. You're here, and I'm saying this stuff, and—"

"Do you know where he was last night?" North said. "Or what he's got scheduled today? Chunks of time he's got blocked off with no explanation? Anything that doesn't make sense?"

"This is crazy," Parker said again, but something on North's face must have convinced him. "North, that's—I mean, it's unethical at the least, and it's probably illegal—"

"If he didn't do anything wrong, then nobody will ever know. If he did, then you're helping solve two murders, and maybe a lot more."

Indecision spiderwebbed across Parker's face. "He was home last night."

"He said he didn't have an alibi." Then North's expression screwed up. "Park, don't tell me—"

"No," Parker said with a little laugh. "Why? Jealous?" Before the question could do more than land, he was speaking again. "I was going to drop off some paperwork he needed to sign, but when I got there, I saw that he had, uh, company."

"What kind of company?"

"The kind that doesn't require any clothes." Parker shrugged. "The lights were on. I mean, certain body parts make a pretty clear silhouette, you know?"

"What time was this?" Shaw asked.

"Seven? Eight? I don't know. Probably closer to eight; I was mad because I'd been here late, and he was off fucking around. Literally."

"You're sure he was home at eight last night?" North asked.

"I mean, I didn't see his face, but his car was there, and one of the people I saw was a man." Parker hesitated. "What you said about his schedule? About him disappearing and stuff?"

"Has that happened? Anything, even if it's only a little strange—"

"It's happening right now." The words rushed out of him. "He's supposed to be in the office all day today. He's got calls, video conferences, even a couple of in-person meetings like the one you had. He just canceled two calls, pretty important ones, and rushed out of here. Didn't say where he was going. He said he had a family emergency, that's all."

There was more in his face—more he wanted to say, even though something was holding him back. "But you know where he's going," Shaw said. "Don't you?"

Parker directed a pleading look at North.

"Do you?" North asked.

"I...I might know his password. To his computer. He needed me to send him a file one time, and he never changed the password." A hint of heat smoldered in his cheeks. "I checked."

"Park, you're amazing."

For a moment, Park smiled—mostly, a watery kind of relief, but a hint of genuine pleasure too. He scooted past Shaw to reach the laptop, typed quickly, and stepped back as the screen unlocked.

Shaw grabbed the laptop and began clicking. Brey had closed his browser, which was smart. But he hadn't cleared his browser history, which was less smart. The second most recent tab was a map, and when Shaw restored it, it showed a place called Eldoria Hot Springs. It was located right about halfway between Auburn and Wahredua.

"Fucking A," North said, clapping Parker on the shoulder.

"I was the one who—" Shaw began.

"Park, that was fantastic." North dug out a business card. "If he calls, if you hear anything—Shaw, let's go—let us know, all right? And don't tell him about any of this. If he's dangerous—"

North didn't finish the sentence because he was already halfway out the room, and Shaw had to jog after him to keep up.

11

Shaw's phone began to buzz as North merged onto the state highway. "It's Theo and Auggie."

"Tell them to search Brey's house," North said as he accelerated. The Focus's engine whined. "Jesus Christ, this car. I'm not exaggerating: I might as well be driving a fucking cracker box."

"Hi, Auggie," Shaw said as he answered on speakerphone. "Sorry—"

"Did you guys seriously race out of here and not tell us where you were going?"

"Well, the thing is—"

"Because that's what it looked like."

"Pint size," North said, "you and Poo-paw get your asses over to Brey's house and see what you can find. The place should be empty, but don't take any risks."

"What the hell happened—" Auggie began.

"What happened is we're working," North said. "Do what I told you."

"I got us that interview. Me. And if you'd let me get a word in—no, Theo, I don't need you to handle this for me. If you'd listened to me, I'd have told you when I saw Brey—"

Shaw's phone began to buzz with another call, and North said, "Gotta run, sweet cheeks. Go toss Brey's house."

He tapped the screen to switch calls.

"Hello?" The voice was a woman's, elderly, and a hint of the delivery suggested she was Black. "Is this the Treasury?"

Shaw said, "Yes, hello, Asset Recovery. How may I help you?"

"Well, yes. Hello. My name is Carly Welch, and I received a message asking me to call this number. It's about money."

"All right, Mrs. Welch," Shaw said. "Let me see here. I don't have anything listed for a Carly Welch. I'm sorry, did they—"

"No, no, no, it was for my grandson. Philip."

Another call began to come in—from Auggie again. Shaw dismissed it. "Ok, well, I can only release that information to Mr. Welch."

"But he's not here, see. That's the problem."

"That's not what I have in my records," Shaw said. He read out Carly Welch's number. "That's the contact information I have for Mr. Welch."

"He was in jail, and now he's not. The police were here today asking me about it. So, what I need to know is if this is time sensitive, see? If it's time sensitive, maybe I can handle it. That's why I'm calling you."

The phone buzzed—Auggie again. Shaw dismissed this call too.

"Well, that's not our usual procedure," he said. "Do you have a phone number? A way for me to contact Mr. Welch?"

"Honey, he's run away. Nobody can find him. You ought to call the jail and tell them that you're with the government. They'll tell you all about it."

"All right, Mrs. Welch. Thank you so much for your help. Do you want me to update Mr. Welch's contact information in our system."

"No, no," she said. "But if it's time sensitive, I need to know what I can do. If it's his money, he ought to get it, don't you think?"

Shaw managed to get off the call after a few more reassurances, then he flopped back against the seat.

"Either she's a cunning mastermind," North said, "or she actually might not know where her grandson is."

"He definitely didn't show up at her house. There's no way she would have called back if she was helping him hide."

"Cross her off the list," North said. "What about the other two?"

Shaw tried his prerecorded message on the cousin, Melvin. This time, a man interrupted him, his voice harsh and loud.

"I don't know where he is," Melvin Welch said, "and I don't want to know. Don't call me again. You want to know where he is, talk to the police."

"Not suspicious at all," North said after the call disconnected.

"It's the same thing, though," Shaw said. "If the Highway Patrol already talked to him, why would he answer?"

North made a noncommittal noise.

Shaw tried Maleah Donaldson, presumably the girlfriend, and got voicemail again.

"We might need to talk to her face to face," he said. "Maybe she's not calling back because she thinks it's a scam. Or maybe it's like you said, maybe she's hiding him."

North nodded. His face was intent, his focus directed on trying to pass what appeared to be a mother and four children in a mammoth Kia.

"Momma is really hauling ass," North muttered as the Ford's engine whined again. "Does this thing top out at sixty? For fuck's sake."

"Should I call Auggie back?"

"No, he already knows this car is a piece of shit."

"No, I mean—he sounded angry."

"He's fine."

"He's not wrong. We did run out of there. We just…left them."

"Shaw, he's fine. He's a grown-ass man, appearances to the contrary, and he's got Big Papa Pump with him. We're not attached at the hip."

"Yeah, but—"

"And we need someone to take a look at Brey's house. We can't do it, I mean, we're not supposed to because John-Henry wants to keep his nose clean. That leaves Jem and Tean or Auggie and Theo, and Jem and Tean are an hour and a half away."

"I don't think they're upset about the job—"

"Jesus Christ, lady, it's not a fucking race!"

North undermined his point, though, by dropping his foot on the accelerator again.

Their Maps app directed them to an unremarkable turnoff that carried them into a forest. Even though Shaw was a city boy, he knew enough to recognize the mix of hardwood and pine, with a surprisingly thick understory. Old trees, or old enough. Shadows dappled the car, running over the hood like a river.

At the next turn, county road maintenance must have ended: they traded asphalt for a mix of dirt and gravel. Stones pinged against the Focus's undercarriage, and clouds of dust billowed in their wake. The smell of the dust filtered into the car, and even with the stones ringing out against metal, the world felt quiet now, and close.

"Great," North muttered. "This is a great way to sneak up on somebody. All this fucking dust, we might as well be sending smoke signals."

"What would be better," Shaw said, "would be if we were in a classic muscle car that was all grumbly and growly and sometimes you don't shift very cleanly, and it makes that really loud noise."

"I shift just fucking fine, thank you," North snapped. "And at least the GTO has a legit engine in it. This thing's got four hamsters running in a cage."

Shaw tried not to say it, but the words slipped out anyway. "I bet Parker would love the GTO."

"Nah, Park was never into cars."

"Oh? Really? What was he into?"

"Running, and he loved those cooking shows, and —" North must have sensed the trap too late because his head came up and his body stiffened. He looked slowly over at Shaw.

"Go on."

"Jesus Christ, Shaw."

"No, please. What else does Parker like? And not like? It's good that you know the things he doesn't like too."

"Are you for real right now?"

"Oh, Park, you're amazing."

"He helped us! What did you want me to say?"

"This is my amazing and ultra-sexually-endowed boyfriend who puts up with all my bullshit like the time I played Speed Racer with a mom in a crossover!"

"She was going sixty fucking miles an hour, Shaw, and every time I tried to pass her, she sped up! What the fuck did you want me to do? She's lucky I didn't run her off the fucking road!"

"He didn't even know we were a couple!"

"Who the fuck cares what he thinks? I'm in love with you!" The shout echoed inside the sedan. North moved around in his seat, restless, his face twisting. Then he slapped the dash. Hard.

The sound made Shaw startle. His face was tingling, and he buzzed down the window. The air had the kind of dense, low-boil heat that was August in the Midwest, and it smelled like loam and sumac and a hint of their exhaust.

"I realize it's kind of a mixed message when I say it like that," North said in a low voice.

Shaw nodded. The hot, humid air did nothing to help with the tears in his eyes.

"Come on," North said. "I haven't seen him in how many years, and then boom, there he is, while we're in the middle of searching his boss's office."

Shaw ran his arm over his eyes. "Was it serious?"

"Shaw."

"I can ask."

"Did you know me in college?"

In spite of everything, that made Shaw smile.

"Ok, I wasn't that bad," North grumbled.

"We had to keep a line. Ok, sir, go on in. It's your turn."

"Jesus Christ."

"You were the pre-fuckboy fuckboy."

"Yeah, I broke a lot of barriers."

"I seem to remember you telling Percy you were 'up to your dick in Chouteau boys' at one point. Then you said, 'I mean standing up, like, height-wise, not balls deep.'"

North laughed, and the sound was both startled and genuine. "So, I was a colossal asshole. Not a lot has changed."

Shaw glanced at him. North looked back. He was very fair, and when he blushed, the color rode high and clear in his cheeks.

"You weren't an asshole," Shaw said. "Well, maybe sometimes. Like when you threw out my sociology experiment."

"Porn."

"And my biology experiment."

"Also porn."

"And my literary masterpiece."

"The porniest of porn." North shifted around again, hands running along the steering wheel. "Park and I screwed around for a while, and then it was over. I'm sorry. I guess I assumed—I'll call him."

Shaw stared. "What is wrong with you?"

"You wanted me to—"

"Oh my God."

"Well, how am I supposed to tell him?"

"Stop. Right now."

North was silent as the Focus rocked over the ruts in the old road. Then, in a tight voice, he said, "You are making this really fucking hard."

Sitting back, Shaw considered that and finally said, "Good."

North probably didn't want him to notice, but that made him smile. Just a little.

"And that mom was driving a respectable speed—"

"Don't you fucking dare," North growled, but a few minutes later, the smile was a tiny bit bigger.

Their first sign that they were in the right place was the peeling, mid-century sign poking out of a massive growth of honeysuckle. ELDORIA HOT SPRINGS, it said, and then a jaunty, Space Race arrow and the words THIS WAY! After another hundred yards, the road widened into what at some point had been a parking lot. Nature was slowly reclaiming the space; enough gravel remained to suggest the outline of the space, but weeds grew tall and, in places, thick. Trees and brush crowded the edges, making it impossible to see anything beyond the lot. At least one vehicle had been here before them, its tracks visible where the weeds had been flattened, but if the vehicle were still present, Shaw didn't see it. North did a three-point turn and parked the Focus facing the way they had come.

"One way out," North said. "That's fucking fantastic." Craning to look over his shoulder, he said, "I don't want to drive any closer; someone might hear us. Hell, if someone's listening, they probably heard us a while ago, but no point making it any easier for them."

Shaw nodded. When they'd switched cars, they'd transferred some of their equipment to the Focus's trunk, so they retrieved their pepper gel and their guns. North grabbed a flashlight, and Shaw decided that was a good idea, so he grabbed one too. Then they headed toward the far end of the lot.

When they reached the wall of trees and brush, Shaw spotted what he'd missed before: a chain-link fence that was hidden by the vegetation. Faded signs warned, POSTED—NO TRESPASSING and DANGER—DO NOT ENTER. Spray-painted penises of all shapes, colors, and sizes suggested how effective the warnings had been.

"It's very inclusive," Shaw said.

North gave him the stink eye.

"What?" Shaw said. "Sometimes I like to see a little doodle. It's invigorating. So much possibility."

"I changed my mind. It was serious with Park. Very serious. I'm reconsidering everything."

Shaw tried to pepper spray him, but North was laughing that low, quiet laugh, and he managed to keep pulling Shaw's finger off the trigger right before Shaw unleashed a blast. Finally, Shaw decided a nice, quiet, domestic smothering would be more pleasant for both of them, and he gave up.

"Give me a boost," North said.

Shaw did. The chain-link rattled and chimed, and North grunted and swore as he hauled himself up.

"We'll have to be quiet," he managed to say, his breaths becoming more and more explosive as he neared the top. The fence was practically singing at this point. "Don't know—what—waiting—"

It was more of a fall than a jump. It might, technically, have been considered a drop, but a graceless one. The thud of the landing almost covered up North's *uhfff*.

"Christ," North wheezed as he got to his feet. "That fence has got to be, like, thirty feet high."

Ten, Shaw thought, but maybe those heavy boots made it feel taller.

"You're remarkably sweaty," Shaw said. "When was the last time you did a full-body pore purge?"

"Oh, that's easy, it was the twenty-first of Go Fuck That Bullshit. Come on, get your skinny ass up there."

Shaw pulled back the loose section of fencing and slipped through the gap.

North was staring at him. And breathing. Loudly.

"Is your face that red from the climb or—"

That was when North pushed him into the fence. A couple of times, actually, taking advantage of the chain-link's natural springiness to throw Show around.

Shaw was still giggling when North stalked off, and he had to run after him to catch up.

When they pressed through the rest of the new growth, the remains of the resort came into view. It must have been impressive sixty or seventy years ago: arcs and fins and curving walls of concrete, faded reds and yellows, everything channeling a dated futurism that also had a dash of *The Jetsons.*

In the decades since, generations of local kids—and God only knew who else—had trashed the place. Sheets of plywood that had been fastened over the doors and windows had been broken or torn free and were now swollen and disintegrating from years of rain and humidity. A heart-shaped mattress floated in the murky rain-trap of an old swimming pool. Shards of glass—from the windows, yes, but also, Shaw could tell even at a distance, mirrors too—lay everywhere. And, of course, the graffiti. Some of it was the graffiti artist's stock in trade: boobs, dicks, and bubble letters that said FART. Someone possessed of unshakeable confidence had tagged a concrete fin with the proclamation BEST BALLS IN TOWN, and someone else had done what Shaw thought might be a hippo but with a threatening case of…engorgement.

No sign, though, of Eric Brey or whoever he might be meeting here.

"This is why I don't go in for that psychic bullshit," North said as he started toward the closest building. "You go see a psychic—"

"I'm a psychic."

"No, you're not. You go see a psychic, and the first thing they say is, 'You're going to die in an abandoned hot springs resort.'"

"I'm a psychic."

"And then you've got to live with that shit for the rest of your life. Which, in my case, probably isn't going to be much longer."

"North, I'm a psychic."

"Ok."

"I am."

"Baby, come on. Level five?"

"No! I'm—" Shaw hesitated because on his last visit to Master Hermes, there had been some talk about advancing to a higher plane and reaching a new stage of consciousness and, of course, something about the manipulation of ferrets. But they'd both been pretty high by that point, and Shaw couldn't remember if he'd already made the appropriate donation, which meant maybe he didn't have any right to claim—he wanted to say level twenty?

"It's ok," North said with that syrupy, placating tone Shaw recognized as specifically meant to chap his ass. "At level five you're allowed to fuck goats or something, right? That's pretty good."

Shaw tried to shove him off the path, but sometimes North had surprisingly good reflexes.

They fell silent as they moved into the resort. The concrete walls gave back strange echoes, and both men slowed, trying to minimize the sound of their steps. Even North, in those ridiculous boots, managed it. Most of the time. The smell of rust and mold shifted with the air, rising with the occasional reek of stagnant water. Flattened plastic two-liters of Vess had tumbled into available corners. Needles glittered between the cracks in the pavement, but then the sky darkened, and everything became flat and matte. A stronger breeze pulled at Shaw's hair, stirring the loose ends of his bun. The underbelly of the cloud wall moving towards them was purple.

More of those Jetsons-style signs met them at an intersection, where the boarded-up eyes of half a dozen buildings stared down at them. POOLS, one said. And SPA. And NATURE WALK. North studied the signage for a moment. Shaw touched the one for the pools; the metal was gritty, and he pulled his hand back.

They followed the path in the direction the sign had indicated. The ground sloped down, following the curve of the land as they left behind the cluster of blinded, gap-mouthed buildings. As they moved lower, the stench of moldering textiles and rotting wood thinned, and something else took its place. Something…stronger. Shaw's first whiff made him think of eggs, and then he caught it again and recognized it: sulfur. The hot springs.

Voices drifted up to them, and North put out a hand to stop Shaw. The words were indistinct, warped by distance and, Shaw thought, perhaps by more than that. But he thought the voices belonged to men. And if he had to put money on it, he would have guessed one was Eric Brey.

After a moment, North started forward again.

The curve of the path brought them around the side of a steep hill, and when they reached the bottom, Shaw saw why. In the face of the hillside, visible even behind the prairie grasses and sedge that had grown almost to Shaw's chest, was the mouth of a cave.

North shook his head, his mouth compressed into a thin line. He eased the CZ from behind his waistband, motioned for Shaw to stay back, and started toward the limestone opening. The voices were clearer now, and one was definitely Eric's, although Shaw still wasn't able to make out the words. The clouds continued to push in. Shadows thickened, and the weight of the sun eased; the day almost felt cool. Then they reached the mouth of the cave. The gloom of the storm wall meant that Shaw's eyes only had to adjust a little to the darkness of the cave's interior.

Philip Welch was even smaller than he'd looked in the photos, but his face was a hardened mask, the kind he had learned, Shaw guessed, to wear young. He'd lost the prison scrubs somewhere along the way, and now he wore a dark tee and baggy jeans. In one hand was a gun. The edge in his voice made the words carry, and Shaw caught the end of the sentence: "—get in his fucking house and find it!"

Eric Brey was still in his suit, and for an instant, that fact alone made Shaw want to roll his eyes. Brey opened his mouth to say something, and then he saw North and Shaw. Shock blitzed across his face.

Welch turned to follow his gaze. His eyes widened, and he spun back toward Brey, shouting, "You piece of shit!"

His voice was high. That was Shaw's last thought before Welch fired.

The muzzle flash lit up the cave, and for a moment, light and color popped into existence. Then it was dark again, and the thunder of the shot echoed back from the limestone. Brey was shouting. Welch was shouting. In the aftermath of the flash, Shaw could only make out their shapes, both men separating. Welch fired again, and the flash was like a lightning strike. For a moment, Welch was there, painted against the cave wall by his own gunfire. And then North grabbed Shaw and yanked, and Shaw tumbled with him into the prairie grass.

It scratched at his neck and face, and the smell of freshly broken earth filled his lungs as he hit the ground. North lay half on top of him. Brey was still shouting, but his voice sounded closer. Shaw twisted. North growled in protest, but let Shaw slide out from under him.

Through the broken line they'd made in the grass, Shaw had a narrow view of the cave's mouth. Brey appeared there. He was gray in the thin light of the coming storm, but he didn't appear to have been shot. As he started to step out of the cave, the rock next to his head exploded.

Brey screamed and fell back, arm raised to shield his face, and he disappeared inside the cave again. Wrong. That was Shaw's first thought.

That shot had been wrong, it had been impossible because Welch was on the other side of the cave and there was no way he could have fired a shot at that angle—

"Sniper," North said into Shaw's ear. His free hand gripped Shaw's nape, and the gesture was half-possessive and half-reassuring. "Someone's out there, and they're trying to clean house."

Shaw pictured the man in black, the one who had followed Gid into Adam Ezell's house. The one who had almost killed Jem and Theo. And, the night before, North.

"We've got to get out of here," North said. Another shot rang out. It whizzed through the grass, and Shaw flinched. He felt North's body contract next to him, and then, more a noise in his chest than a word, North's single "Fuck." They both lay still for a moment, and then North said, "We're sitting ducks out here. The angle of that shot—"

"He's in a tree. He can see us."

"He can't see us, or we'd be dead, but he doesn't have to be a genius to figure out where we are and get a lucky shot. Shit, shit, shit!"

Shaw's window through the grass showed him the dark of the cave. "If we can get—"

"Yeah," North said. "On the count of three."

Horror came on like a lightbulb inside Shaw. "North, don't you dare—"

"One."

"—try to stay behind—"

"Two."

"—I'm serious—"

"Thr—"

Before North could finish the word, though, a familiar voice shouted, "Hey! Hey, up here!"

They both looked up.

At the top of the hill, Auggie was backlit against the purple bellies of the clouds.

"Auggie," Shaw screamed, "run!"

Maybe it was because he was young, but Auggie had good reflexes. He turned and ran, and at the same moment, a spray of gunfire tore open the hillside, throwing up clumps of earth where Auggie had stood a moment before.

North sprang to his feet, and Shaw copied him, the Springfield heavy and solid in his hand. No muzzle flashes. Nothing to give the shooter away except—

A branch that hung too low in an old, leafed-out oak.

Shaw fired, and North must have seen the same incongruity, because he fired too. Or maybe he was just following Shaw's line. It didn't really matter; their shots were, at best, a distraction. At that distance, anything he hit with the Springfield would be pure luck. Even as Shaw had the thought, North grabbed his arm, and together, they stumbled backward toward the mouth of the cave.

Cool air on fevered cheeks. The taste of damp stone, the stink of sulfur, the hot, grainy smoke of gunfire. His back pressing into the rough surface of the cave wall. Darkness tightened around them, and the low, flat light of the coming storm made a tarnished coin in the mouth of the cave. Next to him, North panted, hands unsteady as he shifted them around the CZ.

No more shots came.

Slowly, Shaw's eyes adjusted to the gloom.

No Welch.

No Brey.

"I am going to kiss that little shit right on the mouth," North said as he sagged against the stone. One arm looped around Shaw's neck; North was all sweaty, but Shaw decided to let that pass without comment. This time. But only because he was having a hard time finding his words. Everything that had happened was now happening again, happening faster, all the loose threads of potential catastrophes spinning off it. "And then I'm going to fucking murder him," North added. He bumped heads with Shaw, and he made shushing noises and held him closer until they heard the sirens.

12

North had been here before, more than once actually, the little one-story cinderblock building with white paint and black, stenciled-on letters that said AUBURN POLICE DEPARTMENT. It fronted a small harbor on the lake, not far from the reservoir, and people who drove past it probably got a little goose of civic pride, looking at this unassuming bastion of law and order.

Inside, it was cramped, harshly lit by fluorescents, and it made North think of a rummage sale run by a hoarder. Lots of shit—lots of paper, lots of ancient desktops, lots of desks, all of it in too little space. And nobody was allowed to take any of it, clean things out, get rid of the junk, even though that was the whole purpose of a rummage sale. The reek of cigarette smoke battled some sort of piney-fresh cleaner, and the air was like glue. A little window unit had plastic streamers on it, fluttering as it puffed out what was supposed to be cool air. So you knew it was working, North guessed.

Shaw was using his handcuff like a maraca and humming.

A Black deputy—her nametag said Bonilla—watched them from her desk.

"Knock it off," North said. It had been hours. Hours lost at that fucking resort, waiting with local law enforcement before they were turned over to the Auburn Police Department and Chief Cassidy. When North had asked why they were going to Auburn, nobody had bothered to answer him. And then hours here, handcuffed to this fucking chair and needing to pee like a mother. Hours while nothing happened, and that raised the hair on the back of North's neck, because he thought it meant, most likely, that Cassidy was waiting for someone to tell him what to do. Hours of listening to Shaw try to transpose "Escape (The Piña Colada Song)." Grimacing, he said, "I'm serious."

Shaw broke off the humming long enough to say, "I've almost got it. The whole problem was the harmony, but I solved that because I realized if it's an atonal composition, I no longer need harmony as the primary structural element."

"What you need is a bullet to the head. How about it, Deputy Bonilla?" She stared back at him.

North smiled. "Then how about one for me? A mercy killing?"

Nothing. Not even a glimmer. Maybe she was deaf. Maybe that was why she hadn't killed Shaw already.

A door at the back of the station opened, and Chief Cassidy stepped out. North tried to decide if Cassidy was more of a human-sized pimple or a human-sized genital wart—probably the wart. Today, in an Auburn PD polo and jeans, the clothes making sure everyone knew his body was made up of hard lines and sharp vees and, in the right places, swells and curves, Cassidy looked more like what he probably was: a frat boy who'd never grown up, with gym time and lake time competing equally for his limited brain cells.

"You were a frat bro too," Shaw whispered. When North glanced at him, unable to help himself, he added, "See? I am psychic. And not just for the goat-fucking."

That, at least, got a reaction from Bonilla. Her eyes widened. So, maybe she wasn't deaf.

Cassidy came over to them and stood there, hands on hips, looking down at them. North's eyes were about crotch level. He sat back and stared. Then, when he felt like he'd made his point, he cut his eyes up to Cassidy's and smirked. "See, most guys make the same mistake when they pad their junk—they go too big. Roll up a tube sock and stuff it down there, and nobody's going to believe it. The trick is to start small. Tape a roll of quarters to your thigh, try that."

"You're an expert, huh?"

"You betcha."

"He really is an expert," Shaw said. "One time, back when North was in his fuckboy phase—well, pretty much all his phases have been fuckboy phases, except when we got moon-bound, so now he's a fuckboy for one man only, and that's me—but back when North was in his prime—"

"Excuse me?"

"—he stuffed one of the spring snakes, um, down there—you know what I'm talking about, the ones that are in a can of nuts, and then you open them and they jump out at you, and your aunt says, 'I can't do this, Phoebe,

I can't do this with Shaw anymore,' and you're not allowed to wrap Christmas presents after that—"

North rolled a finger. "Finish the story, bird brain."

"—and that's why we don't celebrate Christmas with my family!"

"Jesus Christ." North rubbed his forehead. Then he pointed. "Padding his tiny dick?"

"Oh! Right! He had one of those spring snakes in his, uh, pleasure pocket, and Bentley Dunn was going to go down on him, only North didn't like Bentley because one time Bentley said I was too faggy, and so Bentley got a snake in the face." Shaw laughed. "Only not the snake he wanted, if you know what I mean. He was all screaming and shouting, 'My tooth, my tooth.' It was hilarious." Shaw seemed to take in his stone-faced audience, and in a quieter voice, he added, "I guess you had to be there."

Cassidy studied them for another long moment. Then he said, "Gentlemen, in case it wasn't clear from the handcuffs, I'm taking you into custody."

"Great," North said. "What are you charging us with?"

"Well, I'm not sure yet."

"That's going to be perfect when we haul your ass to court. Can you say it a little louder? Deputy Bonilla, did you hear my habeas corpus getting fucked wide open?"

"I don't think you can say it like that, like, 'my habeas corpus,'" Shaw said.

"Good point. Let's call a lawyer and find out."

"You guys are a riot," Cassidy said. "I'm taking you into custody because there was a shooting and because nobody's exactly sure what happened yet. I'd be remiss in my duties if I let a couple of strangers wander out of here, without even trying to figure out if they were who they said they were, if their guns had been used in any previous crimes, that kind of thing. Now, don't get your feathers ruffled; I'm sure we can sort it all out in a day or so, and if you're clear, we'll send you on your way." He waited a beat. And then he smiled.

Because, North knew, they wouldn't be clear. An eyewitness to an old crime would miraculously appear and identify them. Or their guns would yield a ballistics match to an old case. Or, easiest of all, a pound of coke would be discovered inside the Focus. Twenty-four hours was a lot of time for a piece of shit like Cassidy to work.

"Now, we're going to take you back to the cells," Cassidy said, his smile growing. "And then maybe we can have a talk. A nice, long one. See, you know one of my old pals, and I'd love to hear what you can tell me about Emery."

"Imagine an asshole with its own center of gravity," North said, "and then give him a perfect life—this great guy for a husband, a couple of kickass kids, beautiful house, good job. You ask yourself, 'What'd that asshole do in another existence to get all this stuff?'"

"He saved my life," Shaw said. "But that was in a different lifetime, when we were both temple prostitutes in Corinth."

Nobody said anything to that, but Deputy Bonilla did look a little wide eyed again.

"Oh wait," Shaw said with a laugh. "He saved my life in this lifetime too! Remember, North? You were playing grab-ass, and Emery had to tackle me to—"

"I was not—" North began.

Before he could finish, though, the door to the station opened, and Emery stepped into the room. He looked exhausted, his already pale face washed out, amber eyes bruised with fatigue. He was still in the jeans and tee North had seen him wearing—when? Sometime the night before? John-Henry entered a moment later. He'd lost the uniform and wore a Wahredua PD polo not too different from Cassidy's, and he looked, if possible, even more worn out than Emery—his golden complexion gray, his eyes bloodshot, a hint of blond stubble. Both men looked at North and Shaw and then at Cassidy. It reminded North of elementary school, his mom and dad showing up after North had gotten caught scrapping on the playground.

"You've got to be kidding me," North breathed as he sank into the seat, fighting the urge to cover his eyes.

"Let them go," Emery said.

"Emery," Cassidy said. He'd slapped on a smile, but it didn't look right, and his eyes kept moving around the tiny station. "I didn't expect you—"

"Chief Cassidy," John-Henry said, "these men are currently employed by the Wahredua PD. I understand there was an incident. I'd love for you to debrief me, and then I've got to get these men back to work. We're dealing with two high-profile murders, and I know you understand how valuable every minute is at the beginning of an investigation."

His eyes shot to North again, and North heard the rest of it, what was left unsaid: *Time I've lost driving an hour and a half across the state to pull your asses off the coals.*

"Well, I don't know—" Cassidy began.

"Then I'll explain it to you," Emery said with the ghost of a smile.

"Then I'll call Lieutenant Mendez in the Highway Patrol," John-Henry said firmly, "and you can tell him why you're jamming me up."

Cassidy's gaze swung from one man to the other. His expression soured.

"All right," he said as he yanked on North's cuff. He unlocked it and let the bracelet fall away, then he repeated the move with Shaw. "Here you go. They're persons of interest in a shooting, but that's no big deal, I guess. Not for a couple of bigwigs like you."

"And their vehicle," Emery said when Cassidy stepped back.

"And our guns," North said.

Emery shot him a look, but then he turned back to Cassidy and nodded.

"Those guns are potential evidence, but what do I know? You want 'em? Sure, have 'em. Leah, you're seeing this, right?"

Deputy Bonilla didn't say anything.

Cassidy returned with their guns, which Emery collected. He tossed the keys for the Focus at North, who snagged them out of the air.

"Anything else?" Cassidy asked. "Suppose they killed someone out there, and we haven't found the bodies yet. You want me to bury them for you?"

Emery snorted as he inspected the guns and passed them back to North and Shaw.

"I'm curious to know if Eldoria PD has any idea who might have been shooting from the trees," John-Henry said.

"Why don't you ask them yourself?"

"I'm asking you."

"I don't know, Chief." Cassidy offered a crooked grin. "Why don't you and Emery roll into Eldoria and see if you can solve it for them? Traveling detectives. Just like you did here."

Emery snorted again. "Has anyone made contact with Brey? Is it possible he was taken by Welch?"

"Brey's fine. Talked to him five minutes ago."

"You talked to him on the phone?" Emery said. "Jesus, Jonas."

"He needs to be in a station house giving his statement," John-Henry said. "Where is he?"

Cassidy's crooked smile was back. "He's recovering from a traumatic shock. I'm going to take his statement personally once he's calmed down."

"Fantastic. I'll join you."

"What? No—"

"Me or Lieutenant Mendez, your pick. Eric Brey was in contact with Welch after the murders, after Welch escaped from jail. He lied about it to my investigators. And then he almost got three people killed when his meeting with Welch turned into an ambush. I'd like to know what he has to say for himself." He glanced at his watch. "Get on the phone with Brey and let him know he needs to be here in the next hour."

Cassidy stared at them for several long seconds. He marched into his office and slammed the door.

"Do you think—" Emery began.

John-Henry shook his head and glanced at Bonilla, and then he motioned for the others to follow him outside.

The late afternoon shadows made pockets in the copper-colored light that filled the street and spilled out into the harbor. A few cars tootled along, but otherwise Auburn was empty. Except, of course, for the black Audi idling at the curb, where Theo's and Auggie's profiles were visible. One of them must have been watching because the Audi's engine cut out and the two men got out of the car.

"Nice to see you too," North said, examining the twin dirty looks directed at him and Shaw. "You're welcome, by the way."

"You're welcome?" Auggie repeated.

"What the hell was that stunt—" Theo began.

"You jackasses ran off without telling us anything!" Auggie shouted.

Red slashed Theo's cheekbones. "You almost got Auggie killed!"

"I got you that fucking interview, and you turned around and ditched us!"

"Walking into a fucking ambush like a couple of fucking imbeciles!"

"What the fuck is your problem?"

"What the fuck is wrong with you?"

Auggie wiped sweat from his forehead. He held North's gaze for another moment and then looked away, shaking his head. Theo's chest was heaving, and he didn't look away.

"Get it all out of your system?" North asked.

Shaw made an unhappy noise.

"Fuck you," Theo said.

"Sure, Pop-Pop. Call me in thirty minutes when the Viagra kicks in."

"Jesus Christ, North," Auggie said. And then, with a kind of parceled out delivery, like he wanted to make sure every beat of the insult landed, Auggie said, "If you'd picked up the phone, jackass, I would have told you I'd seen Brey before. He was in the Cottonmouth Club the night I was there. He was arguing with Gid."

The words erupted from North before he could stop them: "And you couldn't take five fucking seconds to tell us that?"

For a moment, something ugly rose in Theo's face until it lay just under the surface of his usual calm. Then, bit by bit, he must have forced it back down, because he took a deep breath, caught Auggie's arm, and said, "We're going."

"You're welcome Shaw kept your twinky ass alive," North called after them. "That's what you're welcome for."

Auggie looked like he tried to turn back, but Theo said something too low for North to hear and kept a tight grip on him. A minute later, the Audi was pulling away.

As the rush of the shouting match faded, the prickle of a flush worked its way across North's chest, up his neck. Emery and John-Henry were staring at him. Worse, so was Shaw.

"Those dumbasses shouldn't have followed—"

"You're lucky they did," Emery said. "You're lucky Auggie followed you, and you're lucky he saw that you were pinned down. You're lucky he had the brains to understand what it meant and acted quickly to help you. You're lucky that he had the guts to do something like that for a couple of assholes who screwed him over. You're lucky he bought you an opportunity to move to a more defensible position after you walked into an ambush like a couple of amateurs."

"Hold on—"

"But it shouldn't have been an ambush," Shaw said. "It doesn't make any sense—"

"What doesn't make any sense," John-Henry said, and his voice was raw, "is why two of my investigators would meet with a state representative without telling the chief of police. Do you understand that this is my job? That I have people I report to? It's not a two-bit detective agency operating out of a strip mall. I'm working two murders. I'm already down a detective, and I've got the Highway Patrol breathing down my neck, and believe it or not, I'd like a couple of hours of sleep. Instead, I've got to spend three hours out of the first forty-eight driving halfway across the state to keep you two out of jail. And you know what really gets me? You could have gotten Auggie killed because you two wanted to play Lone Ranger instead of picking up the fucking phone!"

The shout echoed down the empty street.

"Nobody asked you to—" North began.

Shaw's voice was sharp and pitchy: "North!"

Even Emery, one hand on John-Henry's shoulder, stared at him with a kind of wide-eyed disbelief, like he'd never seen this particular degree of idiocy before.

It took some doing, but North shut his mouth.

"I can't deal with them right now," John-Henry said.

Emery nodded. "See what you can get out of Brey, and then come home."

John-Henry headed into the Auburn station again. A hot wind stirred, pushing on North, pushing on everything: kicking up eddies of dust, riffling the copper-colored water in the harbor, sweeping an old Drumstick wrapper under one of the Focus's back tires.

Emery held out his hand.

North gave him the keys, and they started back to Wahredua.

13

Somehow, Shaw slept.

It had seemed impossible at first, the heat trapped inside the small room of the motor court, the mini-split struggling and failing to keep up. Even after a cold shower to sluice away the dirt and sweat and stink of gunpowder, even lying naked on the bed as he dried, Shaw had known he was too hot to sleep. And then, later, he had felt the bed shifting, awareness rising like something swimming up from that deep place inside him, and North had said, "Go back to sleep." So, he had.

When he woke the next time, North lay next to him, and the room was dark. It was starting to acquire what Shaw, after years of experience with hotels and motels and motor courts and little hot-pillow joints, thought of as motel funk—the smell of damp towels that never fully dried, mixed with day-old clothes and air that didn't circulate properly.

North lay on his side, breathing the deep, measured breaths of sleep. The weak light softened his face, smoothing the hard edges of cheek and jaw, erasing the strain of always trying so hard to protect himself—and Shaw, of course. He looked younger like this, in the weak, refracted glow of the security lights that filtered through the curtains. Not like the boy Shaw had seen standing in their dorm all those years ago, not really. Maybe younger wasn't the right word. But something like that. Like something he carried every day had been, for a few hours, lifted.

North slid a hand across the mattress and rested it on Shaw's belly. Then he scooted closer until his face was pressed into Shaw's side.

"You're supposed to be sleeping," Shaw whispered.

"Can't sleep," North mumbled into his side. "Horny."

Shaw laughed and tickled the back of North's neck. "Oh yeah?"

But North didn't move. Didn't roll onto his back, didn't do any fiddling or fooling or fumbling, and he was good at all three. Shaw ran a hand down the line of North's spine, and North arched slightly into the touch.

"Jesus Christ," North said, still speaking into Shaw's side. "What the fuck is wrong with me?"

"Nothing's wrong with you."

"Why am I such an asshole?"

"You're not. The last couple weeks have been a lot."

"I fucked the whole thing up."

"You didn't fuck anything up. We should have told John-Henry we were going to see Brey, but honestly, I kind of thought Auggie had told him. And—" Shaw had to plunge into the next words. "And we should have called Auggie, or answered his call. Whatever. You know what I mean. They don't work for us, and it's not fair to expect them to do what we tell them to do."

North shifted slightly, exposing more of his face, and he rolled his eyes. "Christ on a cracker, how was I supposed to know he had something useful to tell us?"

Laughing again, Shaw scritched his fingers through North's messy blond thatch. "That's kind of the whole problem, you know."

North grunted and pressed his face into Shaw's side again.

"So," Shaw said, "are you still, um, feeling amorous?"

"No. And don't call it that."

"Really? Because—"

"I'm sulking."

"—if you were interested, I could be persuaded—"

"I'm not. I'm depressed."

"You wouldn't even have to do anything," Shaw said. "I mean, not too much, anyway. If you put your hand right here—"

But North snatched his hand away and rolled off the bed. "John-Henry didn't fire us." He grabbed a fresh tee and pulled it on. "That means we're still working this investigation. That means we've still got work to do."

"Yes, but you realize we could be fast and have a physically and emotionally satisfying intimate moment and then work—"

"Move, Shaw."

"I feel like I'm getting mixed messages because you're at, uh, three-quarters mast."

North threw a towel at him and ducked into the bathroom.

Shaw dressed—nothing too lovely, on account of it was nighttime and, therefore, sneakery was probably afoot. The leisure suit was a gray so dark it was almost black, and it was summer weight, so it was surprisingly comfortable. Especially because Shaw decided that a shirt under the jacket was optional.

He was just pulling on his jackboots when North emerged from the bathroom—three-quarters mast had deflated to about half-mast—and said, "No."

"But they're black!"

"Absolutely not." He rooted around in one of Shaw's suitcases and pitched first one black sneaker and then another.

"But these are my orthotics! For the nursing home!"

"That thing is going to make hamburger out of your nipples, you know."

Sometimes, the only way to deal with North was to be haughty, so Shaw raised his chin and said, "My nipples will be fine."

But later, in the bathroom, he did put on the little nipple chafing covers he'd started buying in bulk.

North, of course, was in jeans and the Red Wings again.

"Have you ever considered—"

"No."

"But would you—"

"No."

"For the sake of your ass—"

He didn't even get to finish that one because, it turned out, you could apparently give someone a vicious wedgie even if they were wearing nothing but a leisure suit, and the squeaking noise he made didn't qualify as words.

By the time Shaw had recovered, they were in the GTO, the engine purring as North eased them out of the motor court's parking lot.

"Adam Ezell?" Shaw asked as he soothed his ravaged nethers. "That's who they had to be talking about, right? What Welch was saying about looking for something in his house."

North grunted.

"You realize this is polyester, right? You realize it's like rug burn, and you effectively ravaged my—"

"Say 'nethers,' Shaw. Say it and see what happens."

There was a certain dignity, Shaw decided, in silence.

When they drove past the dead-end street on the north side of town, Adam Ezell's house looked dark. North found a spot on the next block and parked. Then he took out his phone.

"Who are you texting?" Shaw asked.

North displayed the message he'd sent to Jem and Tean. *Are you watching Ezell's house?*

Tean answered: *No.*

Then a second message came through immediately. *Jem says to wait for us. We're on our way.*

"Jesus Christ," North said and threw his head back. It bounced off the seat. "Why don't they bring Evie too? Why don't they bring the whole daycare?"

"Well, it's almost nine o'clock at night, so the daycare is probably closed." That had seemed like a trenchant observation, but something about the way North looked at Shaw made him ask, "What?"

North got out of the car, muttering to himself as he stalked down the block.

They cut through backyards to approach Ezell's house from the rear. It didn't look much better from this side—the board-and-batten siding with its dingy paint, the weeds growing in the lava-rock beds, the blinds that hung closed in every window. The lawn was at least a week past needing mowing, and what might, years ago, have been a raised garden bed was now a crumbling spill of earth and wood.

"Well, that's fucking inconsiderate," North said, crouching to examine the back door. "What kind of fuckery is this?"

"It's a lock," Shaw said.

"I know it's a lock. I'm trying to decide how I want to open it." He was quiet for a moment and added, "My fucking luck. Last night, every fucking Sally for a hundred miles was walking through this door, and now it's locked."

Shaw considered the lock. It did look different from some of the other locks he'd seen. "Usually you do it—wait, we've talked about this. You do it the same way you do sex. You stick it in and wiggle it around."

"One fucking time," North muttered. "I make one mistake, and there goes the rest of my fucking life. I could probably kick it in—"

Before he could finish, the deadbolt slid back. North scrambled upright, putting distance between himself and the door as it swung open.

"Pay up," Jem said from where he leaned against the doorjamb.

"That's not really fair," Tean said from deeper inside the house. "Mostly because I never agreed to the bet."

"It took less than five minutes for North to want to kick something with those huge-ass boots. That means you owe me twenty bucks."

"Also, on a related note, you already have all my money."

"We watched one race," Jem told North and Shaw. "I cleaned him out. You'd think a veterinarian would be able to pick the ponies."

"Believe it or not, horse gambling was not something we learned about in veterinary school. Also, I think you cheated, but I don't know how."

"Yeah," Jem said. "Obviously."

"How stupid are you?" North said. "I could have shot you."

"With your invisible gun," Jem said, grinning as his gaze raked North up and down. "Sweet."

North glared at him. He didn't seem to know what to do with his hands. He put them on his hips, finally, and for some reason that made Jem break up laughing. Growling, North pushed past him. He was gentler with Tean, hands on Tean's shoulders, easing him out of the way, but that went about as well as could be expected because Tean immediately got flustered, and his feet tangled with North's, and they both almost went down. By that point, Jem was laughing so hard that he just kind of staggered into Tean, and Tean had to hold him up as North moved deeper into the house.

"You're making him feel bad," Tean said in a quiet voice as he tried to keep Jem from falling.

Jem swallowed some more laughter, but his eyes were bright when he looked at Shaw.

"He's very sensitive," Shaw whispered.

"Oh, yeah, everybody can tell that." Jem shrugged. "But does he know he's a sweetheart?"

"I am not a fucking sweetheart!" North shouted back.

"How did you guys get here so fast?" Shaw asked.

"We were across the street, watching the house," Tean said. It was hard to tell in the low light, but it looked like he was blushing.

"We lied," Jem said.

"Technically, I lied," Tean said. "And it's not even ethically defensible because I wasn't under duress."

"But it was funny, and that's ethical."

"No, not even close."

They moved into the house, flicking on lights as they went. Adam Ezell seemed to have paid the interior of the house the same level of care and attention as the outside. The walls were a sandy yellow that, Shaw guessed, hadn't been touched up in twenty years. For the ceiling, he'd apparently gone with water stains as the chief decorative element. In the living room, where they found North, the low-pile carpet was the color of dog food, and maybe there'd been a package deal or a combo or a set on offer, because the Naugahyde recliner and the loveseat were the exact same color. Someone had clearly been through here before them: cushions had been slashed open, the dust covers ripped away, a framed poster of a sexualized fish—Shaw wanted to say it was a trout—torn from the wall. The obligatory Big Masculine TV lay overturned on the floor, and North was looking at it with something approaching lust.

"You know on Black Friday, you can get one this size for a few hundred bucks," North said.

"No," Shaw said.

"They're all smart TVs. They've got OLED."

"You don't even know what OLED is, and besides, we're going on a TV fast once we get home, so you don't need a bigger TV."

"Sometimes they give you a toaster," North said, his eyes distant. "Or an electric griddle."

"You should definitely get the free griddle," Jem said. "That's the best way to make a grilled cheese."

"North thinks the best way to make one is with a clothes iron," Shaw said.

"It was one time," North snapped, his focus locking onto Shaw again. "And it was on a BuzzFeed list, and—you know what? I don't have to explain myself to you. It's not my fault this motherfucker won't let it go."

"Didn't the cheese get in all the steam holes?" Jem asked.

"Oh my God, he had to use a toothpick—" Shaw began.

"Could we please get to work?" North put his hands on his hips again, seemed to remember how well that had worked before, and stalked out of the room. "Could the professionals please be allowed to work, and the amateurs go back to jacking each other off in an abandoned house?"

"That sounds like a very good plan," Jem said to Tean.

"Go help him, please," Tean said.

"You heard him: the best way we can help is—"

Tean had to use both hands to push him out of the room, and Jem was laughing the whole way.

Shaw decided the best place to start was right there, in the living room. He drew a pair of disposable gloves from his pocket. Then he glanced at Tean, who was already pulling on his own pair. Shaw's eyebrows went up.

"Please don't," Tean murmured. "He's a very bad influence."

They moved through the room. If there had been something easily hidden, it was gone now—whoever had torn this place apart, they'd worked hard and fast and hit all the obvious spots. But Shaw took his time: pulling back the baseboards, removing the poster from its frame, examining each leg in the loveseat and the recliner. Tean trailed after him until Shaw started giving him assignments; to Shaw's surprise, the vet produced a multitool from one pocket of his khakis and had no problem unscrewing the back of the TV.

"I don't understand," Shaw said, sitting back on his heels and surveying the room again. "Who did this? Gid wasn't in here long enough, not for something like this. The man in black wasn't either. What about the bodyguard from the church?"

Tean nodded. "Same thing: he came through here pretty quickly. Otherwise, we probably would have been able to hold on to him until the police got here."

"Did you check the baseboards?" Jem called.

Tean opened his mouth to answer, but it was North who shouted back, "Of course I checked the fucking baseboards. This isn't my first fucking time."

"Oh," Jem shouted back with way too much enthusiasm. "Good."

The best way to describe North's answering silence was…big.

"I should tell him not to antagonize North," Tean said.

"It's actually good for North," Shaw said absently as he looked around the room. "It's like acupuncture or ice plunges or saunas. It gets the blood flowing."

"I'm not sure that's how acupuncture—"

"What kind of animal would be best at searching for hidden treasures?"

"Uh."

"Non-mythical, of course."

"Of course."

"I'm basically a level ten psychic, which means I can broadcast on UHF; I just need the certificate. And you're a wildlife vet. I was thinking a magpie. Or an otter! Or a stoat!"

"With our powers combined," Jem said from the next room.

"For God's sake," North said, "don't encourage him."

"Exactly! With our powers combined, we could probably make a magpie search this room, and then we could spend more time—have you ever spanked a horse?"

Maybe it was just those huge, adorable glasses, but sometimes Tean's eyes looked really big. "You know, maybe I'll work on the kitchen."

"That's a great idea," Shaw said as he followed Tean out of the living room.

"No, I meant—you could stay in the living room and put the back of the TV on, and—"

"Great idea," North said from what sounded like the bathroom. "Give him a knife."

"I'm very responsible," Shaw said. "I even paid all the bill."

"Bills," North said. "With an s. And he didn't pay them, he put them in the mailbox with Power Rangers stickers all over them. We didn't have electricity for a week and a half."

"Here's a tip," Jem called from the bedroom. "Fake books."

"That's not a tip. It's not even a sentence."

"I meant people hide stuff in fake books. That's another place you should put on your Super-Duper Private Investigator List, patent pending."

North was making a sound like the time he'd found the puppy trying to eat one of his boots.

"Let's just scoot into the kitchen," Shaw said. "Sometimes North gets in a mood, and he can be a real pills." He made extra sure to pronounce the s.

Tean probably didn't search a lot of houses; Shaw could tell from his breathing that he was excited. It was nice, Shaw thought, that people could still be happy about the little things.

The kitchen had suffered the same fate as the rest of the house. Cabinet doors stood open, plates and dishes shoved aside or broken, food dumped out on the floor: dried pasta, pancake mix, rice, bricks of ramen, at least six different types of breakfast cereal, the scree of bag after bag of potato chips. Jars and bottles had been emptied into the sink, presumably, and now stood on the table and countertop: two-liters of Coke, shelf-stable soup, ketchup and mustard and barbecue sauce, even a jug of iced tea.

When Shaw opened the refrigerator, it wasn't much better. The disorder suggested someone had gone through it as part of the same frenzied search. Individually wrapped slices of American cheese lay fanned out on one shelf. Half of a frozen pizza had been knocked off its plate. Chicken nuggets under a pathetic skin of shrink wrap were shoved into a corner.

"We haven't been watching this place twenty-four-seven," Tean said as he toed a small mountain of dried macaroni. "We've been trying to find Adam, but we haven't been here all day, every day."

"Of course not," Shaw said. "No one expects you to."

"Sure," North said from the next room. "Sit on your thumbs, hit the malt shop, flirt with boys. The rest of us are just busy working."

"I actually do love a chocolate malt," Jem said. "But Tean won't let me flirt with any boys because he says Scipio has a jealousy complex."

Tean looked like he was trying to adjust his glasses. "I never said—"

"Oh my God," Shaw said, "the puppy has a jealousy complex!"

North was making that noise again.

"We've tried all the normal ways to find him," Tean said in a rush. "We tried talking to his family, but there's only the brother, and he's never home and only picked up the phone once. We tried his social media. We even tried his credit cards—"

"You did?" North's voice took on fresh interest. "How?"

"Uh," Tean managed a smile that looked shockingly guilty. "Nothing illegal?"

North snorted.

"Brain stroke," Jem said, "I've got another place you should look—"

"Brainstorm," North said, "and so help me God, I've been working as a fucking private detective for—Shaw, how many years?"

"Fake pipes. Check it out. Maybe he's got a fake pipe!"

"Like for smoking?" Shaw asked. "Or, like, house pipes?"

"Will you for once in your life," North called, "please not fucking do this?"

"God," Jem said with a laugh. "I didn't even think about a pipe you can smoke. We should check for those too."

"You're a scientist," Shaw said, and he opened the fridge to grab one of the American singles. "What kind of advances has medical science made towards testing for a bovine genetic component?"

The sound of feet came surprisingly quickly, and a red-cheeked North appeared in the doorway. He stabbed a finger at Tean and said, "Do not answer that."

"North is willing to be a test subject."

"No, I surely fucking am not."

Tean opened his mouth.

"It's his love of cheese," Shaw said. "That could be an indicator, right? Further testing warranted?"

"Everybody loves cheese." North swatted the single out of Shaw's hand. "What in the fuck do you think—"

Jem appeared behind him, a shit-eating grin on his face as he proclaimed, "Hang rods."

A tic started at the corner of North's eye.

"Seriously, guys, did you ever think about checking hang rods? You should definitely add that to your list."

"Mother of Christ—" North began in what Shaw thought of as his murdering tone.

"Maybe we should split up again," Tean suggested, eyeing North. "Like, really split up. Like Jem and I will go back to—"

"Fivers," Jem said.

"No—"

North opened his mouth.

"If there's anything in this house," Shaw said, "it's probably in that box of shredded wheat."

North looked at him.

Jem looked at him.

Tean looked at him.

Shaw glanced over his shoulder in case he'd missed something.

North was the first one to move, stomping through the food debris on the floor to pick up the box of shredded wheat. He turned it upside down and nothing came out, but a look of horror was forming on his face.

"I found it with my—"

"No," North tried.

"—psychic abilities."

"Found what?" Tean said.

Jem's brow furrowed.

"He found it," North said like someone trying to climb a mountain, "because all the other food in this house is shit and because there's one box of unsweetened shredded wheat, and that doesn't make sense."

Jem let out a tiny laugh. "You should definitely add that to your list."

"Found what?" Tean asked again.

North shook his head, a man wrestling with something larger than himself. Then he tore the flap at the bottom of the box, where the cardboard overlapped and was glued together.

An SD card fell into his hand.

"It's just not fair," North said to no one in particular. And then, "Fuck me."

"We can talk about it," Jem said, "but I'd really like you to be nicer to me first."

14

The next morning, North and Shaw waited with Emery in the Wahredua police station. The room was dark, a concession to the one-way mirror that let them observe the attached interview room. On the other side of the glass, Gideon Moss waited with his lawyer, a severe woman with a helmet-like bob. The air was close and warm and smelled faintly like old, engrained body odor, and North felt like a million bucks.

Part of that, he was sure, had to do with getting ten hours of sleep and catching Shaw in the shower, with enough hot water left to get handsy. The other part was that they had Gid on the hook now, and North could feel it, call it whatever you wanted: electricity, energy, a charge. The investigation had legs again, and they were making progress. Plus he'd had about eight cups of coffee.

After discovering the SD card, they'd taken it to Auggie and Theo, who had been both delighted (Auggie) and grumpy (Theo) at their unannounced and late-ish arrival. Auggie, of course, had immediately found the right adapter and connected the SD card to his laptop. The card held only a single video. It was footage from a security camera, and it showed Gid in one of the jail's private interview rooms, where he proceeded to have sex with a young woman in inmate scrubs. The video ended once the two separated.

No corrections officers had appeared on camera. No deputies. Nobody besides Gid and the unnamed woman. But Adam Ezell was a deputy sheriff, and he'd worked at the county jail, and the SD card had been in his house. And now Ezell was missing, and two men were dead.

On the other side of the glass, Gid shifted in his seat. He hadn't been charged, not yet, which meant no cuffs and, more importantly, none of the systemic apparatus designed to break you down, to scare the shit out of you in a way that made you compliant and eager to please. The lawyer with the helmet bob looked like four hundred dollars an hour of being a pain in the ass. All of that was the bad stuff.

The good stuff, though, was that Gid looked like shit. He'd dressed for the occasion—a dark suit, a white shirt, a red tie. His rockabilly hair, though, was greasy and lank, and his eyes had that cartoonish look people got sometimes, when fatigue made them big and droopy. Even under the spray-on tan, his color was bad. He'd kept the cross, and every time he moved in his seat, it swung around his neck like a car air freshener. And Gid must have been having a hard time staying still, because he was moving in his seat a lot.

The door to the observation room opened, and John-Henry stepped into the room. He was in uniform again, and he looked better for having caught some sleep and some food and a shower. North didn't miss the way Emery's eyes immediately scanned the blond man. It was clearly automatic, some sort of reflexive assessment. Whatever part of Emery was a cyborg (North put the percentage somewhere between fifty and eighty) was clearly doing a biometric scan or some Terminator-level bullshit like that, and it was equal parts cute and annoying. Not that anything Emery did was cute. Not that North would ever—ever—say any of this where Shaw could hear. And it was equally cute and annoying that John-Henry registered it, that he gave back a tiny smile in response, and that it all happened between the two of them like some sort of secret language that nine out of ten people in the world missed completely.

And meanwhile, the love of North's life had gotten caught inside his own shirt again.

"For the love of God," North said as he yanked the shirt down, forcing Shaw's head through the opening. The fabric was some kind of rustling, silvery nonsense that was probably ridiculously expensive. It buttoned up the side, and the aesthetic seemed to land somewhere between technocop and astronaut's whorehouse. North had never seen it before, and he was one hundred percent sure it hadn't been in Shaw's suitcase when they'd left St. Louis. "Quit trying to bite the tag; there's got to be a hundred pairs of scissors in this place if you want it off so bad."

"But—" Shaw began.

"John," Emery said. "Please."

"Really quick before I go in there," John-Henry said, "I wanted to tell you again this was fantastic work. Really, really good. I spent the rest of yesterday having Eric Brey's attorney feed me bullshit by the spoonful, so when you told me you found this—" He grinned. "It definitely turned my day around."

"And you brought it to John instead of stepping all over your own dicks," Emery said drily, "which was an unexpected improvement."

"What did Brey tell you?" North asked.

"Nothing, unfortunately. I mean, he and his attorney had clearly cooked up the statement together. Eric is a passionate supporter of troubled teen intervention programs, he's forged many lifelong bonds with the teens he's helped, he hoped that by meeting privately with Welch he could convince him to turn himself in, he understands he made a mistake, and he is, of course, willing to do everything in his power to make things right. On and on like that."

"You should have slapped him with aiding and abetting," Emery said sourly. John-Henry looked at him, and Emery straightened up and mumbled, "But, of course, your best judgment—"

"Uh huh," John-Henry said. To North and Shaw, he said, "I'm going to interview Gid. Let me know if you see anything I miss. And guys? That was A-plus work. I knew bringing you on was the right thing to do."

As soon as the door closed behind him, Shaw said, "We should get tattoos. Matching tattoos. The four of us."

"Jesus Christ," North muttered. "Why don't you work on that tag some more?"

When John-Henry stepped into the interview room, he was carrying a laptop under one arm. The lawyer with the helmet bob sat up straight and began her spiel: Mr. Moss was only here because he was a good citizen, because he wanted to do whatever he could to help law enforcement, and because of his moral obligations as a Christian. She talked around that point a number of times actually. North had to give her credit; she never actually came out and said, *He's got a shitload of money from Daddy's megachurch*, but she did a fantastic job of painting it into the subtext.

Finally, she left enough of an opening for John-Henry to ask, "Gideon, how long have you been having sex with inmates at the county jail?"

Confusion muddled Gid's features. Then, for only an instant, North would have sworn Gid looked relieved. He sputtered, "That's—I didn't—I never—" His lawyer laid a hand on his arm, and he cut off.

"That's a serious—and offensive—allegation, Chief Somerset."

John-Henry placed the laptop on the table and opened it. The video was already cued up, and he played it. The lawyer had a good poker face. Gid, on the other hand, did not. His jaw loosened. Sweat beaded along that rockabilly hairline. He glanced around the small room as though someone might have installed an escape hatch.

"How long have you been having sex with inmates at the county jail?" John-Henry asked again.

Gid opened his mouth, but his lawyer said, "Don't answer that."

"That's a mistake," John-Henry said. "I've got video evidence, and before you start spinning me a story, let me remind you that sexual activity is not permitted between inmates and visitors at the Dore County Correctional Center. On top of that, it's a violation of the city's public indecency ordinance."

The lawyer was quiet for several long moments. "Are you charging my client?"

"Was Adam Ezell blackmailing you?" John-Henry asked.

"Don't answer that," the lawyer said again. "This interview—"

"Is this what you were looking for when you broke into Adam Ezell's house two nights ago?"

Gid's color had dropped even more, and the spray-on tan looked like what it was: a bad paint job.

"We're leaving," the lawyer said, taking Gid's arm.

"Why did you arrange the murders of Dalton Weber and Sheriff Engels?"

"I didn't!" Gid looked like he was going to pass out. "I didn't have anything to do with that!"

"Stop talking," the lawyer said.

"What was your arrangement with Philip Welch?"

"Nothing! I don't even know him!"

"Really? Why did Welch drive directly to your home after committing double homicide? And why did you, only a few hours later, drive to Adam Ezell's house to recover this blackmail?"

"That's not what happened!"

"What is the connection between you, Eric Brey, Philip Welch, and the Cottonmouth Club?"

"Nothing, there's nothing—"

"For God's sake, Gideon," the lawyer snapped, "shut up!"

Gid stared at John-Henry, panic lighting up his face. Then he spun away from the table and vomited on the floor. The lawyer let out a noise of disgust and scooted backwards. John-Henry got to his feet and moved to the door to call for a cleanup.

"Unless you're arresting my client," the lawyer said, her gaze moving from the vomit to a trembling Gid to John-Henry, "we're finished here."

"You can help yourself right now," John-Henry said to Gid. "But if you wait until I'm bricking you in with this case, it's going to be too late."

Gid wiped his mouth with the back of his hand. He looked like he was about to cry.

The lawyer dragged him toward the door, and then they were gone.

John-Henry collected the laptop, and he passed a man with a mop and bucket on his way out of the room. A moment later, he joined North and Shaw and Emery. He was buzzing with energy that felt like a mix of excitement and caffeine and the dregs of adrenaline. The smile he cocked at Emery reminded North that, his whole life, John-Henry had known he was hot shit.

"If he hadn't had the lawyer," Emery said with disgust and shook his head.

"I know, I know. But that was something, right? He was falling apart, and all I did was poke him."

"You're lucky it was puke," North said. "He looked like he was about to shit himself."

"Did you see him when I showed him the video? Jesus, that was satisfying."

North thought about the strange moment when, for a heartbeat, he'd thought Gid had been relieved. But before he could say anything, Emery spoke again.

"You could have held him on the public indecency charge."

"And he would have bailed out before I closed the cell door," John-Henry said. "I want that hanging over his head."

"Have you tracked her down yet?" Shaw asked.

"The woman in the video?" John-Henry shook his head. "We've got a name, and Emery's working on finding her. We're going to have to interview everybody in that jail a second time. Jesus, the hours on this are going to bankrupt us. But if he did it once…"

"He didn't just do it once," Emery said. "And he definitely didn't like it when you brought Welch into the equation."

"I wish we had something more solid on him, but until we talk to that woman—"

"Assuming you can find her."

"—I'm going to start by telling his lawyer he's lost visiting privileges at the jail." John-Henry shook his head. "It got me thinking about Brey, though. He and his lawyer had cooked up some serious bull about the shooting at the hot springs. I thought maybe the smokescreen was to cover the fact that Brey had lured Welch out to kill him."

"And almost got his own ass capped," North said. "Welch was pissed. If we hadn't shown up, he would have plugged Brey and walked away."

"The sniper," Shaw said.

John-Henry nodded. "Exactly. I thought maybe Brey had a buddy out there, somebody to take care of Welch once Brey got him in the open. But after what I saw in there with Gid, I'm starting to think things are more complicated than they seemed."

"You mean somebody else was cleaning house," North said, "and Brey got caught in the crossfire."

"Technically, you got caught in the crossfire."

North scratched his temple with his middle finger. "I get that Ezell was blackmailing Gid; that's pretty clear. But why was Gid at the jail in the first place? He wasn't on any of the records."

"He does a ministry," John-Henry said. "Once a week, conducts a service."

"And gets laid," Emery said. "We've got the pieces: Gideon Moss is a regular at the Cottonmouth Club. So is Brey. Dalton Weber can identify Moss as the man who hired an underage teen to perform sex acts. He's preying on female inmates at the county jail and, in the process, manages to make an arrangement with Welch to kill a witness and a troublesome deputy."

"You think Ezell's dead?" North asked.

"I think if I were Gid and I'd contracted one killing to cover my ass, I wouldn't stop there. What I don't like is the coincidence, Gid happening to meet someone during his ministry who's willing to do murder for hire. In supermax, ok. In a county jail, a kid picked up for possession? And he just happens to be in the isolation unit where a key witness is being kept? And Brey knows him?"

Shaw opened his mouth, but before he could speak, his phone buzzed. North followed him out of the observation room as he took the call on speakerphone.

A woman spoke. "Someone said you've got money for Philip Welch."

"And with whom am I speaking?"

The speaker hesitated. Then she said, "Maleah Donaldson."

"I'm so sorry, Ms. Donaldson. I need to speak to Mr. Welch or someone with his power of attorney —"

"What if he owes me money?"

"I'm sorry?"

"He owes me money. A lot of money. And I can prove it. So, I want to know why I can't have that money, since he owes me."

Shaw went for doubtful. "Well, we'd need to see documentation…"

"I've got documentation. I've got anything you want to see. I've got IOUs, I've got this letter he sent me when he was in jail—"

"I'm sorry, did you say he was in jail?"

"That's another thing. I bet you didn't know he's in jail. You can't give him that money, can you? Not like that."

Shaw let the pause draw out. "I'm so sorry. I need to talk to my supervisor—"

"Why? You told me you needed to see documentation. I've got the documentation. I told you I've got it. Where do I bring it?" And then some of the eagerness slid into her voice. "How much are we talking, anyway?"

"I'm afraid I can't discuss that without establishing protocol."

Whatever that meant, North thought as Shaw gave him a shit-eater grin.

"If you could provide an address and times when you're generally available, I can have a treasury representative visit you to see about your case."

He'd barely finished speaking when Maleah rattled off an address and told him she'd be available every day after four.

"Well?" North asked.

"It's better than nothing," Shaw said.

When they returned to the observation room, Emery shot them a questioning look.

"We think we've got a line on Maleah Donaldson," Shaw said. "The potential girlfriend. She wants to know if she can collect the money, seeing as Welch is in jail and, more importantly, owes her money."

"She didn't know he escaped?"

"It didn't seem like it, but she sure seemed like she wanted to talk."

Emery made an interested noise.

North grinned. "How pissed is that fuck Cassidy going to be when we stomp all over his backyard again?"

15

At four o'clock, a silver Chevy the size of a teacup pulled into the driveway of the house Shaw and North were watching. Shaw resisted the urge to sit up for a closer look; that was the kind of thing—sudden movement, in this case—that got you noticed. Instead, he said, "She's here."

As he spoke the words, a Black woman in a pencil skirt and a lightweight cardigan emerged from the Chevy. She went up the steps, unlocked the door of the duplex on the right, and went inside.

So far, so good.

They'd been watching the two-unit brick building for a little over an hour. Emery and John-Henry had been preoccupied with moving forward with the investigation into Gideon. North and Shaw, meanwhile, had spent the day tracking down the missing deputy. Trying to, anyway. If Adam Ezell was still alive, he was doing a damn good job of hiding. Tean and Jem hadn't been lying about the dead ends. North and Shaw tried to locate his family, but the closest they got was the same brother Tean and Jem had already told them about—Kingston Ezell. His phone number went straight to voicemail, and his address left them at a run-down apartment building on the outskirts of Wahredua. An online search for assets didn't turn up anything interesting either—neither Adam nor his brother owned a conveniently out-of-the-way cabin or hunting lodge or, for that matter, so much as an RV. Adam Ezell didn't have outrageous debts, and there was no sign that he'd been anything but what Deputy Weiss had originally told them: a mediocre deputy who had, somehow, vanished during his shift. By then, it had been time to start the drive to Auburn, and now, true to her word, Maleah Donaldson had arrived home right on time.

"Here we go," North said as he got out of the car.

When they knocked on the porch, Maleah opened the door on a chain. She looked out at them from the narrow opening, scanning first North, then Shaw.

"I like it because it makes me feel like a cosmonaut." He plucked at the silver silk. "Plus it's super comfy when it's hot."

"Can I help you?" she asked.

"North McKinney. This is Shaw Aldrich. We're private investigators working with the Wahredua Police Department." When Maleah didn't say anything, he continued, "We'd like to talk to you about Philip Welch."

"What do you mean, private investigators?"

"Ms. Donaldson, this is important."

Her breathing changed. She let out a taut, scornful little laugh. "There's no money."

"No, I'm afraid not."

"How do I know you are who you say you are? Do you have badges?"

North showed her his ID and his private investigator license.

"I'm going to call the police and ask them."

"The Wahredua PD," North said. "That's who you've got to call."

She nodded and shut the door. The bolt went home.

"Does that seem a little...excessive?" Shaw asked.

"I don't know. If I were a single woman living alone and someone dressed like a silver scrotum showed up on my doorstep, I'd probably call the police too."

Shaw considered that. "It does kind of look like a scrote, doesn't it? Right here where it's all wrinkly?"

North glared at him.

"What?"

"You know perfectly fucking well." He was silent for a second and then, because he was North, he burst out, "You can't let me have one fucking thing, can you?"

Shaw kept his smile on the inside.

Almost ten minutes passed before Maleah opened the door, this time without the chain. She handed back North's ID and license, and then she said, "I'm sorry about that."

"Let me guess," North said. "Somebody remembered him?"

A tiny smile appeared on Maleah's face. "I think there was a comment about the Tin Man."

"I didn't even think about the Tin Man," Shaw said.

This time, Maleah laughed. "Come on in."

The living room was furnished with what Shaw guessed was secondhand furniture—a chintz sofa, its upholstery once fine but baggy and growing dingy; wicker armchairs that looked like they'd moved households one too many times; a coffee table with a few scars. A faux-fur throw was folded over the back of the sofa, and cheery cushions padded the chairs. The candle on the coffee table was the big, fat kind that Shaw loved and that North had a disturbing tendency to try to light, even though Shaw had explained a dozen times they were only for decoration. An opening at the back connected with a kitchen, and two closed doors suggested a bedroom and bathroom.

"I've never talked to private detectives before. Do you want to sit down?"

They sat. She smiled at North, but her gaze kept coming back to Shaw.

"You're the one I talked to on the phone."

"Sorry about that," Shaw said. "You wouldn't believe it, but sometimes people lie to us."

That made her laugh. "I was...worked up when we talked. I'm not usually like that, but I was so mad. I feel bad—the police have come by twice, and I won't answer the door because I don't want to talk about Phil. But I called you back for the money. What does that say about me?"

Shaw nodded. "It says you're mad. That's ok; sometimes it's good to be mad."

"It doesn't feel good. It feels like I'm sick."

She was pretty, Shaw decided. Not beautiful, but put together and healthy and intelligent. She was wearing something light, a floral body spray. She swallowed and looked like she was about to cry.

"How do you know Philip Welch?" North asked.

A tear slid free, and she wiped it away. "We met at a party."

"He was nice," Shaw said.

She looked startled and nodded. "He was. He was really sweet, actually. Not like a lot of guys I meet. Especially not a lot of guys around here. He wanted to talk. A lot of guys, they pretend they're listening, but Phil actually listened. When the party started going, he said maybe we should go somewhere quieter, but I didn't want to do that, and he said I was smart." More tears began to run. When she ran her hands over her cheeks, she left a glistening smear of drying salt. "God, I was such an idiot."

"What happened?" North asked.

"Nothing out of the ordinary, even though I knew, right from the beginning, he was trouble. He was cute, and he was funny, but I was pretty sure he was using. It was the way he acted. He'd seem...manic sometimes.

And then he'd crash. Other times, he smelled like weed, and then he'd be totally different. You know how it is. He always needed money, and at first, I said yes. I didn't like it; I'm not stupid, and I know a lot of girls who get themselves into situations like that. Their boyfriends never work, their boyfriends always need a loan, their boyfriends get kicked out of their apartment, and the next thing you know, their boyfriends are moving in, the girl gets pregnant, and that's that. If she's lucky, maybe they get married. I guess I should say if she's lucky, the jerk stays. Usually he stays unless he finds an even bigger sucker. I've got a lady I work with—sweet, smart, can whip a room full of kindergartners into shape in thirty seconds—and her boyfriend hasn't worked since he 'hurt his back' in the '90s."

When she paused for a breath, Shaw said, "You have IOUs?"

Nodding, Maleah rose. She went into the bedroom and came back with a manila folder, which she passed over to Shaw. It held only a few pieces of paper. Several were handwritten, with Welch's name signed in tiny, schoolboy letters. Two were typed but had the same signature at the bottom. The individual amounts weren't substantial, but all together, the total came to just over two thousand dollars.

"What happened when you asked him to pay you back?" North asked.

"He made excuses. I knew where this was going, but—but it's different when it's you, right? Because I'd make excuses for him too, in my head. I'd say I was jumping to conclusions. I'd say he was having a rough patch. He was so sweet, and you don't know how hard it is…" Her small smile looked too old for her face, full of self-mockery. "I know what you're thinking. The drugs. The fact that he didn't work. How desperate could she be for a man?"

"My husband screwed everything that moved," North said, his voice rough. "And he beat the shit out of me. For years. You want to talk about twisting yourself into a pretzel to explain things away? I'm your guy."

Maleah looked at him—not with surprise, not exactly, but with a kind of new, more intense interest. Then she nodded. "He paid me back, eventually. The first note. And I thought, ok, things are starting to turn around. But then it got even worse. He always needed money. And I'm not—I'm a teacher, for heaven's sake. I have a tight budget."

"What happened when you started saying no?"

"He got angry. He shouted. We fought. And then he came back, a day later, and apologized. But it happened again. And then again."

Shaw could hear it in her voice: the turning point, the sharp curve on a dark road, and they were all going too fast to stop now.

"And then," Maleah said, "One night, I invited him over for dinner, and he put something in my drink."

Shaw shook his head and looked down. Blood whooshed in his ears, and he was distantly aware of the springs in the sofa creaking as Maleah shifted position, of the rasp of fabric as she smoothed her skirt with both hands. Then, because she was a person and deserved that much, he looked up again and forced himself to meet her eyes.

"I woke up the next day, and he was gone. I wasn't sure what had happened. I thought maybe I'd had too much to drink, but...but part of me knew that was wrong. Knew something was wrong. I had bruises. I..." Her hand hovered above her midsection. "I hurt. I had some bleeding. And I couldn't even think about it, couldn't even ask the question, even though part of me was already asking it, I suppose. There was this gap in the night, and that was fine. I wanted to fall into that gap, forget about all of it, pretend it hadn't happened. Then—" Her voice broke. Her chest hitched, and the hand that had been hovering turned into a fist, and she pressed it between her breasts. "He texted me that afternoon. A picture."

North nodded. Shaw nodded too, but he was only distantly aware of the movement. Inside, he could feel the labyrinth opening. The forking paths. His mind took him through his imagination's most vivid reconstruction of what that awful day must have been like. Unregulated empathy, Dr. Farr called it. He could feel what it must have been like for her, waking up, head aching, a part of you hurting in a way that you knew wasn't right. No, go back. The blurry minutes of drugged semiconsciousness, hands on you, hands, your legs being forced apart. No, go back. A stumbling, assisted walk to the bedroom, your fumbling attempt at resistance, pain as your hair was pulled and whatever was fogging your brain made it easier to surrender than keep fighting. No, go back—

North's hand bit into Shaw's thigh. Shaw drew in a sharp breath; the pain was a lifeline, and Shaw followed it, swimming up from that place inside his head.

"—wanted money again," Maleah said. "I said no. I was going to the police. Then he said fine, he'd put those pictures everywhere. Online. At my school." She glanced at a bag leaning against the coffee table, worksheets covered in children's handwriting that were poking out of the top.

North squeezed Shaw's leg again—digging his fingers into sensitive flesh, the grip brutal and unyielding. It made Shaw open his mouth as he fought a cry of pain. Then North relented, and Shaw forced himself to form words: "What—what grade do you teach?"

"Third." She smiled reflexively. "Fourth; I've got to stop saying third. We had a teacher quit, and—" Another on-off smile like someone was running it from a switchboard. "You don't care about that."

"My fourth-grade teacher was Mrs. Willows," Shaw said. "She smelled like lavender, and she taught us all the state capitals, and she loved to say, 'Ten-four'. That was the first time I ever heard someone say that."

Maleah began to cry in earnest, hands covering her face. Shaw moved to sit next to her. He didn't touch her; he wasn't sure she wanted that, not after whatever she'd been through.

"It was one dumb decision," she finally managed to say through the tears. "Why should I have to pay for it the rest of my life?"

"It wasn't a dumb decision," North said. "He took advantage of your trust; you didn't do anything wrong. What happened to you was terrible and evil, and I'm sorry."

Maleah excused herself and came back with a wad of tissues. She sat next to Shaw again, wiping her face, staring into a place where she was alone. "I don't know if you understand what it's like. Being a teacher. Being a teacher in a small town. Being a teacher who's young and Black and a woman in a small town where ninety-five percent of the population is white. If I had gone to the police, they might have found him. They might have arrested him. I kept telling myself I had to do it so that this didn't happen to some other girl. But I didn't do it, because I knew once he posted those pictures, it wouldn't matter that I was the victim. I'd lose my job. And I'd never work again, not as a teacher." She was still staring off into that alone place, her face dead, as she said, "They're not just nudes. He tied me up. There were...toys."

North met Shaw's eyes. His jaw tightened; his cheeks looked hectic, and his eyes were hooded with rage as he shook his head and looked away again.

"Do you still have the picture?" Shaw asked.

Maleah shredded a tissue on her lap. "I want him to leave me alone."

Shaw took a deep breath. "How long did it go on? After that night, I mean."

"A few months. Then he got arrested. I guess he wasn't dumb enough to try anything from there; they record your calls, don't they? Or something like that? I knew he wasn't going to be gone forever, but it felt like—it felt like magic. Like someone had swooped in and touched everything with a magic wand and given me my life back. It was a few weeks after he got picked up that I had my first real night's sleep."

"And then?" North asked.

She stared down at the strips of tissue. Her breathing was rapid and shallow. Shaw had spent enough time at this point watching anime together with North—you could technically call it *together* if you were hiding behind the couch and he was sitting on the couch and everything was fine because North didn't need to know you were watching anime together, but then the puppy bit your ankle—that some of the visual language had become a reference point for him. And what he was seeing on Maleah right then was what he thought of as dead eyes, blank circles where the eyes should have been. When a character shut down. When a character couldn't take it anymore—and *it* meant everything, anything, the experience of being alive in a bad world.

"Why did you call Philip?" Shaw asked.

A tear escaped, and Maleah blotted it with the tissue. She held her hand there. She was trembling, and the confetti-strip ends of the torn tissue trembled with her. "I heard him."

"Philip—" North began.

She shook her head, and North stopped. Her breathing came faster and faster. "I was at Walmart. And I heard him, in the next aisle over. His laugh. I recognized his laugh, and all of a sudden, it was like flashbulbs going off: these pictures, these moments. Oh my God."

It couldn't have been more than a minute or two that she cried again, and this time, when she leaned against Shaw, he put his arm around her. He concentrated on the feeling of bone and muscle jarred by sobs, of the solidity of her body, like a kind of thunder against him. He anchored himself there, and when he looked up, when he saw the worry in North's eyes, he nodded. The worry stayed, though, and North's lips parted like he might say what he couldn't help himself from saying, over and over again: *maybe you should step outside* or *I can handle this.* But he couldn't, of course. Not without Shaw.

Before North could speak, though, Maleah dried her eyes and sat up. She smiled a watery thank-you to Shaw, mopped her face with the tissues, and blew her nose. "I'm sorry. It's—it's still a lot, and I try not to think about it."

"You remembered something from the night Philip drugged you."

She nodded. "It was so strange; I've never had anything like that happen to me before. But I heard that laugh, and I knew I'd heard it before, and then it was like all these other fragments of memories surfaced. Things they did." She stopped and shook her head.

"That's a common trauma response," Shaw said. "Even drugged, your body was locking those memories in place. It's not unusual for a stimulus to trigger you to recall the episode—that's pretty much textbook, actually."

Maleah had those dead eyes again, and Shaw wasn't sure she'd heard him. "I thought I was going to pee myself. I was standing there in Walmart, holding a jar of bread-and-butter pickles, and I honestly thought I was going to mess myself. As soon as I saw him, I knew who he was."

"Who?" North asked.

But Shaw already knew. It had been swimming in that dark place inside him, and now, as she spoke, the answer rose to meet her words.

"He's a state representative." She gave a disbelieving laugh. "I didn't vote for him, thank God."

"Eric Brey," Shaw said.

She gave him a startled look. "You know him?"

"Did you approach Brey?" Shaw asked, but he already knew the answer.

Maleah shook her head. "Wait, how did you know?"

"We've heard a similar story," North said. He looked at Shaw, and he didn't have to say what he was thinking: that Brey must have gotten scared after his intern left, must have worried she'd talk, and so he'd escalated. He'd started looking for girls who wouldn't tell. Who couldn't tell.

"Oh God. He did it to someone else?"

North nodded. "Maleah, what did you say when you called Philip?"

"I had to leave a message, you know; you can't call them direct. I told him to leave me alone. I told him I knew who his friend was, the one he'd brought to my house, and if he ever bothered me again, I'd tell everyone." She looked from North to Shaw. "What? Did I do something wrong?"

"No," Shaw said, "but you might be in danger. Do you have somewhere you can go for a while?"

"I can't leave; school just started. What do you mean in danger?"

"Philip Welch escaped from jail," North said. "I'm going to call John-Henry."

"He can't do anything for her in Auburn," Shaw said.

"What do you mean he escaped?" Then she moaned, wrapping her arms around herself. "Oh God, what do you mean he escaped?"

"I know he can't do anything here," North said. "But he still needs to know, and I don't want him snapping my balls off because we didn't tell him as soon as we heard."

"Oh my God," Maleah said. "Oh my God, oh my God."

Shaw waved for North to go, and North let himself out onto the stoop, and the door clicked shut behind him. Catching Maleah's shoulders, Shaw said, "Maleah, listen to me: everything's going to be fine. But right now, you need to pack a bag, and then you need to go stay with a family member or a friend. Somewhere away from Auburn. Just for a few days."

Maleah moaned again, the sound long and wordless and vibrating through her body, but then, with what must have taken an immense effort, she dragged herself upright. She wet her lips. Her eyes shone like she might start crying again, and she wiped the tears before they could fall, and then she nodded.

"Don't worry about school," Shaw said, "and don't worry about anything else. Where are you going?"

"I—I have an aunt in St. Louis."

"Great. We live in St. Louis. We've got some friends who can check on you, and if you need anything you can give them a call."

She nodded, but Shaw wasn't sure she'd heard him. "I have to pack. I have to—he could come here. He could come here right now."

"He's not coming here right now. He's got bigger things to worry about. He's on the run, and there are a lot of people looking for him, people who are good at their jobs and who are going to make sure he doesn't hurt anyone else. But right now, I need you to help us. Can you do that?"

"I don't know."

"Sure, you can. You're going to take a deep breath, and then another, and then another. And then you can do anything."

She took a few breaths. They weren't all that deep, but some color came back into her lips and cheeks, and the glassiness left her eyes.

"I need you to think of anywhere Philip might be, or anyone who might know where he is."

"I don't know. I don't know where he could be. I mean, we only ever went here or back to his place, and I liked here better."

"The police have already checked his grandmother's house; he's not staying there." An idea occurred to Shaw. "Did you have any kind of relationship with his grandmother? Would she talk to you?"

"His grandmother? I never met his grandmother."

Shaw opened his mouth to ask, and then he stopped.

Maleah must have heard the question anyway; confusion was scrawled over the fear in her face. "We never went to his grandmother's."

He chose his words carefully. "That's the address on his license. That's the address on all the records—the police, the jail."

Maleah shook her head. "Maybe he put her address on official paperwork, but when I knew him, Philip never lived with his grandma. He lived out at the park-and-store."

16

It took time to coordinate across three different law enforcement agencies. Time for everyone to put in their opinion. Time for everyone to argue. Time for everyone to feel important. And time for everyone to actually get their asses out of their chairs and do what they were supposed to do.

"He probably died of old age by now," North muttered inside the GTO.

It was dark, the afternoon and evening eaten up by bureaucracy. Even with the sun down, the air was hot and sticky, and a mosquito had gotten inside the GTO and whined in North's ear intermittently. They were parked a quarter mile from Al's RV Park and Self-Store, on a country road outside Auburn. They'd been sitting there for half an hour, waiting for the go-ahead from Chief Cassidy. In that time, the only traffic had been a horse-drawn buggy. The horses looked long in the tooth and tired, and the guy driving them hadn't been much better, his face pinched and sunburned under a newsboy cap and beard. Amish, North guessed; they still had a few communities around here. He figured if the guy was secretly working with Welch and spying on them, they still had a hundred and some odd years before he reached the park-and-store.

Ahead of them, John-Henry and Emery sat in the Mustang; they were waiting. And ahead of them sat an Auburn PD cruiser. And ahead of the Auburn PD's finest were a couple of Highway Patrol boners. Everybody waiting. Because all hell would break loose if someone actually, you know, did anything. North considered flashing his headlights. He could picture Emery's face, and that would have been something at least. But he didn't. He stayed in line, dick in his hand, and waited too.

"We did this the right way," Shaw said. He had changed, thank God, into a black tee and black jeans purchased at the Auburn Walmart, and there was nary a cosmonaut in sight. "We called John-Henry like we were supposed to. We did it exactly right."

"That's going to be a tremendous fucking comfort when we find out Welch rabbited as soon as he saw this fucking parade of idiocy. Bad enough Brey lawyered up; now they're going to blow our only other lead."

"I thought Welch died of old age."

North tried to slam Shaw's head into the dash, but Shaw was slippery—and always stronger than North remembered.

Another half hour crawled past.

"Fuck this," North said. "We could have gone in there and hauled his ass out before dinner and not waited while this jabroni called that jabroni so they could swing their dicks and piss all over each other about jurisdiction. I mean, this is a joke. John-Henry's not even in charge anymore, and we had to include fucking Cassidy?"

"That's not what John-Henry hired us to do."

"Did he hire us to sit on our fucking thumbs?"

"If he did, I would definitely get paid more."

He tried to slam Shaw into the dash again, but Shaw was such a fucking eel.

North's phone buzzed, and he answered it on speaker.

"What the fuck is going on back there?"

"Don't answer him," Shaw said. "Someone might be listening. We'll have to use code. I-ay hate-ay—wait, how do you do pig Latin again?"

"This is why I said you should fire them," Emery said.

"Don't listen to Shaw," North said. "Those horse-spies left a long time ago."

John-Henry laughed quietly.

"I asked you," Emery said, breaking each word out of the sentence like he was talking to someone particularly stupid, "what was going on back there."

"I got a flat and decided to change the tire," North said.

"We're playing bucking bronco," Shaw said, "and I'm the bronco."

"No, we're playing hopscotch, but Hinkelbaan rules."

It seemed impossible, but North thought he could hear Emery grinding his teeth.

"Oh, we're working on our gymnastics routine," Shaw said. "But no peeking because that's going to be your birthday present."

"Actually, a mosquito bit my dick," North said, swatting at the insect as it hummed by his ear again. "We were just performing lifesaving first aid."

"Because it was engorged," Shaw said. "Because of all the blood flow."

On the other end of the call, Emery was saying, "Keep making those calming noises, John, and see how very fucking calm I become."

John-Henry said, "I'm going to disconnect—" Then he stopped, and a moment later, his voice came back with an edge. "Here we go."

Ahead of them, the Highway Patrol guys rolled out, then the Auburn PD, then the Mustang with John-Henry and Emery, and then North and Shaw.

Al's RV Park and Self-Store was located behind a line · of old cottonwoods, and the drive was nothing more than washboard gravel. Behind the trees, the drive snaked past an office building and a pavilion toward the RV lots, and farther back was the self-store facility. North had been to trailer parks and mobile home communities once or twice, and it reminded him of a similar layout: pull-throughs and back-ins with concrete slabs and utility hookups, each lot separated from its neighbor by what looked like overgrown strands of honeysuckle. It was, in official police terms, a walking knob-fuck of a tactical setup. The honeysuckle meant lots of places to hide, which was a hell of a lot of fun when you were looking for an escaped convict who'd already killed two men.

North scanned the pads, trying to spot anything that might suggest where Welch was hiding. Some of the RVs, you could tell, weren't planning on being there long. Those had nothing more than a few camping chairs set up, maybe a sign that said THE JOHNSONS, the kind that you could stake in the ground and pull up the next day. But others were clearly here for the long haul, maybe even permanently. An aluminum Airstream, for example, had chili pepper lights strung across its awning. Window boxes with tiny, frosted spruce trees decorated a Roadtrek. In front of a mammoth Winnebago, an inflatable Rudolph's red nose was on the fritz, flashing rapidly and then going dark for long stretches. At first North thought they'd been here since December. Then he caught the sign next to the manager's office announcing JOIN US FOR CHRISTMAS IN JULY.

By the time North parked behind the Mustang, one of the Highway Patrol brass was already directing officers to begin their search. John-Henry moved to join him, while Emery stayed near the car, arms folded and a glower on his face. North started toward the Highway Patrol officer, and Emery said, "You stay here."

"Nah," North said, ignoring Shaw's worried look. "Thanks, though."

The Highway Patrol guy had to be in his forties, and he had that special asshole look that some cops seemed to think was a badge of honor. As North approached, the officer broke off whatever he'd been saying to John-Henry and said, "Wait by your car, sir."

"Chief Somerset," North said, "I think we could help—"

"Go back to your car," the Highway Patrol guy said. "I'll let you know if we need you for anything."

"I'm asking Chief Somerset a question," North said. "If I want somebody to wipe my ass, I'll give you a holler."

"What if we—" Shaw began.

Gravel crunched under the Highway Patrol guy's feet as he shifted his weight and spoke over Shaw. "I don't have time for this. Where's—Eaton!" A chinless redhead in an Auburn PD uniform jerked to attention. "Escort these men back to their car. If they give you any trouble, arrest them."

"These men are contracted to the Wahredua PD," John-Henry said, and although his tone was mild, there was iron behind the words. "I'll handle this."

"Get them out of here."

John-Henry waved North and Shaw ahead of him, and they moved back to the cars. Emery was scowling, his gaze fixed on the Highway Patrol officer, who was back to issuing orders.

"I need you to wait with Emery," John-Henry said.

"As I told you," Emery said, still glaring past them.

"We broke this open," North said. "It's bullshit to stick us in the corner now."

"North, this is a complicated situation—"

"What's complicated about it? I can knock on doors. Believe it or not, Shaw can too."

"I can," Shaw said. "And you need as many bodies as you can get."

"I appreciate that," John-Henry said, "but as you can see, there are a lot of factors in play right now. For now, please wait here."

"Again," Emery said sourly, "as I told you."

North made an understanding sound. "Ok. Gotcha."

"Thank you," John-Henry said.

"Just one question: did it hurt when that guy turned you into his personal ass puppet?"

John-Henry breathed out slowly.

"Because that's what I figure happened," North said. "He shoved his hand right up your ass, and now your mouth is moving, but I'm hearing his bullshit."

"North," Shaw said. And then, "John-Henry, that isn't—"

Emery rounded on North, but before he could say anything, John-Henry held up a hand. When he spoke, the words were clipped. "Stay here."

Then he left.

"This is fucking bullshit," North called after him. "It's our break, and you guys have been sitting around, scratching each other's hemorrhoids while our first good lead goes cold."

John-Henry kept walking and didn't look back. North thought about going after him, but the chinless uniform must have taken the Highway Patrol guy's order literally, because he stood a few yards away, hand on his cuffs like he might have to spring into action at any moment. So, instead, North stood there, wrestling down the need to shout or swear or kick something.

"You know what?" Emery said. The security lights were distant, and shadows lay over Emery's face. His eyes glinted with a hint of that frozen amber. "You are a real asshole."

"Takes one to know one, I guess." North shook off Shaw's hand, the words boiling up. "And you want to know something? You're a fucking hypocrite, because if it had been anybody else except John-Henry, you'd have lost your mind at this bullshit. You've got this big act about how you don't eat shit, and then John-Henry smiles at you, and you sit down with a fucking spoon."

"North," Shaw said, his voice sharp.

Emery shook his head, the movement barely more than a sketch in the darkness. Then he started toward the road, checking North with his shoulder as he passed him. North stumbled, caught himself, and spun to go after him. Shaw was faster, though, catching North's wrist in an iron grip.

"Sir—" the uniformed officer, Eaton, tried.

Emery kept walking.

North was trying to twist free of Shaw's grip.

"Knock it off," Shaw whispered fiercely. "You're frustrated, and you're angry, and I understand that. I'm frustrated too. But you're treating people you care about poorly, and you need to cut it out right now." North turned his arm, trying to break Shaw's hold, and Shaw gave him a shake. "North!"

It was like a tide running out. All of a sudden, North felt tired, his head hollow and throbbing. He couldn't meet Shaw's eye as he nodded. Shaw held him for another moment. Then his hand relaxed, and he stroked North's arm. Even at this hour, in the dark, the heat coiled around them, the air like school paste, making skin stick to skin as Shaw trailed his fingers up and down. The breeze turned, and the stink of old charcoal fires and smoke and rancid fat drifted in. The cemented-in park grills, a distant part of North thought. That's what he was smelling. He tried to fix his gaze on a yellow caution sign that said CAREFUL—CHILDREN. It had been shot to hell with a BB gun. His stomach turned, and he was surprised at the flop sweat on his nape and chest.

Lights were coming on across the park. Voices mingled with the noise that spilled out of open RV doors: televisions and radios and an infant screaming. The whole park was coming alive, and North wanted to shake his head, but all he could do was stand there.

"This is how they do things," Shaw said. "It's their case. We're just helping them."

North wanted to say that it was more than a police case. That this was real, this was happening now, that someone was doing everything they could to cover up whatever was happening at the Cottonmouth Club, and that included trying to kill Jem and Tean and Theo and Auggie, and by this point, probably the rest of them as well. He wanted to say that the bad guys were winning, and that every time they turned around, another door slammed shut. But he didn't say anything. One of the RV televisions must have been tuned to a game show, because everybody was cheering.

Maybe Shaw heard some of it anyway, though, because he let out an unhappy sound and pressed his face to North's shoulder. He stood there, watching and running his hand over Shaw's auburn hair. A Wahredua PD officer came back and said something to John-Henry, and then John-Henry followed him deeper into the park, disappearing into the clean-cut geometry of shadows created by competing lights. At one of the closer lots, a woman emerged, pushing past the man who was talking to the Highway Patrol trooper in the doorway. She was carrying a screaming baby over her shoulder, patting the infant's back as she paced. A few pads down, the exterior lights of a Keystone came on, and the door flew open, and five children spilled out, shouting with excitement as they began doing what North took to be an impromptu karate performance—all with the occasional, excited pause to see if a police officer was watching.

Shaw laughed into North's shoulder, and in spite of himself, North felt a grin stretch his cheeks. "This is a total shitshow."

"Yep," Shaw said.

"God damn it," North said, but he couldn't bring any heat to the words.

"Can you imagine if this was how you had to do the job all the time?"

"Sure," North said. "I'd get a job as a mall cop instead. Then I'd shoot myself."

Shaw laughed again. "If Welch didn't know we were here before, I don't know how he could miss it now."

"Christ, I don't know how he could—" North began. Then he stopped as he heard himself. He finished more slowly, "I don't know how he could have hidden here in the first place."

Shaw raised his head. "I know we were being optimistic. I mean, Maleah never told us he was definitely here, only that he used to bring her here. You're right: there's no reason he'd come back—"

"No," North said. "That's not what I—Shaw, say you're Philip Welch. You like to party. You deal some drugs. You definitely use from your own supply. You always need money. Is this where you're going to set up shop?"

Darkness hid Shaw's expression, but his hesitation was an answer. "Lots of trailer parks have a high incidence of drug use, drug dealing, that kind of thing. And in the privacy of an RV—"

"But this isn't a trailer park; it's an RV park. Does Welch strike you as the kind of guy who owns an RV? And look at this place—look at the storm of shit just because a few police officers started knocking on doors. People are always coming and going at a place like this. Families coming and going. High traffic. Vigilant parents. These are the kind of people who celebrate Christmas in July and pack plastic reindeer and chili pepper lights."

"You know where they should go? They should go to Santaland, where it's Christmas all year—" Shaw squeaked when North got one of his nips. He pulled free and rubbed his chest, directing a dirty look at North. "Ok, ok, I see your point. But if we're wasting our time...well, it's not like we have another option."

"We're not wasting our time. Maleah didn't say Welch had an RV here. She said he brought her to the park-and-store." And then North shifted his gaze to the chain-link fence and, behind it, the corrugated steel walls of the self-store building.

Shaw made a soft sound of understanding.

North started toward Officer Eaton. The chinless kid went for his handcuffs again, so North held up both hands. "Hey, buddy, I need to talk to whoever's in charge."

"Take a step back, sir."

"I've got to talk to him. It'll take two minutes."

"Sir, go back to your car."

North eyed the kid. In the shadows, it was difficult to make out more than his outline, but his shoulders were hunched, and his breathing sounded rapid. "What about Chief Somerset?"

"Chief Somerset is busy, sir. You need to wait with your vehicle."

"What about Chief Cassidy?" North was trying to remember if he'd seen the Auburn jackhole. "Did he bother to show up for his own party?"

"Sir, I'm going to ask you to step back right now and return to your car."

"They sure train them good at the academy, huh?"

The kid didn't answer.

"Come on," Shaw whispered.

"Your tax dollars at work," North said.

Still nothing.

Shaw tugged at North's arm.

"Can I get a soda?" North asked, jerking his head at the manager's office. "It'd be nice to have a cold drink while I stick my thumb up my ass."

"I'm not sure about drinking during ass play," Shaw said to the kid, "but actually, any kind of temperature play does add a new element to the sexual experience."

The kid shifted. His gun belt must have been brand new because it squeaked. "Just don't come over here where they're working."

Security lights mounted around the manager's office shattered the darkness, and as North and Shaw approached the building, North took the opportunity to study Shaw.

"Did you know that kid was going to freak out at the mention of ass play? Or was that a lucky coincidence?"

"I have no idea what you're talking about," Shaw said.

"What were you going to say next?"

"I don't plan my conversations; I believe in letting a dialogue flow organically."

"I bet you do."

The ghost of a smile fluttered across Shaw's mouth. "It might have been flowing toward those frozen butt plugs and the possibility of internal frostbite."

North laughed in spite of himself.

"But sadly," Shaw said, "we'll never know."

Rapping on the front of the illuminated Coke machine, North glanced at the uniformed kid. Eaton was still watching them. "Buy me a Coke?"

"Oh, I don't have any quarters," Shaw said. "I experienced a psychic katabasis and had to change all my quarters into obols."

"No, you didn't."

"Plus these pants don't have pockets."

"Interesting, because you were playing pocket pool in the car earlier."

"I was getting to know my own body, for your information, which is an important part of an awakened sexuality—"

"Quarters. Now."

"I had to give them to Jem because he bet me I couldn't stand on one foot while I was standing next to the wall, but of course, in my past life, I was a lady flamingo, so I knew I could—"

"Jesus Christ. Never mind. I was going to share."

Shaw patted himself down. "You know what? I think some of those obols might have magically transmuted themselves back into quarters now that my autosexual pilgrimage is over."

"I thought it was a psychic katabasis."

Shaw went for haughty. "It can be two things."

The Coke was cold enough to make North's throat tighten, the fizz and the sugar and the caffeine all a pleasantly painful overload. Shaw was literally unable to hold still as he pressed against North, eyes on the can.

"Don't spot your shorts," North muttered as he held out the can. "Slowly."

Shaw nodded agreement, snatched the can, and began to guzzle it.

"Hey!"

With something like a whimper, Shaw pulled the can away from his mouth. The green in his hazel eyes looked electric, and he grinned as he said, "It's cold."

"This is sad. You know that, right?"

"And my tongue tastes like a battery."

"Jesus Christ. I wonder if they have Al-Anon but for, well, this. Private investigators whose life partners are cola freaks."

Shaw made a noise that was probably meant to suggest he was listening, but his eyes glittered as he stared at the can. "Oh my God, North, you know what we never did? We never got the puppy baptized. Oh! And we never got the puppy enrolled in preschool. Oh! And we never got the puppy godparents. Oh! And I bet I could run straight up this wall. Here, take a video!"

Eaton wasn't looking at them anymore, so North twisted Shaw's collar into an improvised handhold and steered him away from the manager's office. They drifted into the darkness beyond the perimeter of lights, and the sounds of the RV park faded. The slosh of the Coke can and Shaw's swallowing suggested the soda was already almost gone, and then a moment later, Shaw smacked his lips and let out a regretful sigh. He started to turn, saying, "I think I forgot my phone—"

"Unh-uh," North said and hauled him back by the collar.

Shaw whined and pulled and spun as North manhandled him toward the chain-link fence, but he quieted when North gave him a little shake.

"Up and over," North said, pointing to the fence. "Then wait. If you're good, I'll let you raid John-Henry's Pepsi."

A flood of words poured out of Shaw. "That's not fair because Pepsi isn't the same—"

"You want to argue? You want me to take Colt out for a Coke instead?"

"North!"

"Up and over, and then wait."

Shaw made a distressed noise, but then he spun and launched himself at the chain-link fence. It rattled, the metal chiming softly as Shaw climbed. He cleared the fence so quickly North thought he might have broken the sound barrier. Maybe there was a genetic component, North wondered. Maybe they could sell this shit to the Army. Super-soldiers fueled by Coke and pony princesses. Profiles in courage and all that.

It took North longer, and by the time he dropped on the other side of the fence, Shaw was sprinting in short bursts and doing flying kicks. It reminded North of the karate shows the kids had been putting on for the officers, only a little more...manic. North glanced back, but no one was looking in their direction. Maybe he should have brought a brass band, hired a drum line. The next time one of the kicks brought Shaw within range, North caught his collar again and yanked him around a few times. Then he held a finger to his lips and pointed toward the self-storage building.

They walked a circuit of it, and Shaw, panting with excitement, was the one who found the open door. To a casual glance, it would have appeared closed and presumably locked, but when North tugged on it, it opened easily, and he could see where the latch had been taped back to keep it from locking when it fell shut.

Inside, the building was a maze of corrugated steel panels and roll-up doors. Emergency lights pushed back enough of the darkness for North to lead them deeper into the building, but shadows pooled between the spaced-out lights, and more than once North stopped, his heart speeding up as he squinted and listened, trying to decide if something lurked in the darkness ahead. Shaw appeared to have channeled his Coke-head energy into something useful for once because he moved silently behind North, the only sign of the buzz his restless scanning of the space around them.

A whiff of cheap weed made North stop. Shaw breathed deeply a few times and whispered, "He's here."

"Or the night clerk is having a toke."

Shaw didn't answer. He took more of those deep breaths and started walking toward the next intersection, and when North followed, the fug grew stronger. Someone was here, or had been here recently, and the last time North had seen Philip Welch, he'd been trying to shoot Eric Brey. It had been an ambush, and Brey had walked right into it. North wanted to reach for his waistband, but that was pointless; the CZ was still locked up in the trunk of the GTO. Maybe if they went back, North could explain that he wanted to do some target practice. Hell, maybe Eaton would think that was why he'd wanted the Coke in the first place, like he and Shaw were lining up cans on fence posts like a couple of good old boys.

North spotted light behind one of the roll-up doors. He caught Shaw's arm to stop him and pointed. Under North's touch, Shaw was vibrating with caffeine and adrenaline. Thirty seconds passed, and nothing happened. Then a minute. Then two. North tried to make a map of the building in his head. They were near the back, about as far from the RV park as you could get, and the unit was located at the end of the corridor. For a moment, North considered climbing—or, more realistically, sending Shaw up. The interior of the building was divided up by more of the corrugated paneling, but the walls ended a couple of feet below the ceiling. North guessed that, like other storage units he'd been in, the tops of the units were closed off by some kind of mesh paneling—it allowed for air flow through the units, and, of course, for the fire sprinklers. But North dismissed the idea almost as quickly as it came; up there, Shaw would be a sitting duck.

Still nothing. The silence inside the building grew in North's ears like a kind of white noise.

"Maybe he's not here," Shaw whispered.

North shook his head. "No lock. He's here."

"Should we go get John-Henry and Emery?"

North shook his head again. He considered the unit. The light around the door was barely anything—if the rest of the building hadn't been so dark, he probably wouldn't have been able to see it at all. The weed smell was stronger, but there was something else too—a stink that made North's hackles rise, and a hint of something else, something like rubbing alcohol.

"I'm going to check," Shaw said. When North opened his mouth, Shaw said, "I'll be careful."

North fought the same fight he always had with himself and, as usual, lost. He squeezed Shaw's arm once, and Shaw crept forward.

In the dark clothes, he was quickly swallowed up by the shadows. His sneakers made no noise on the concrete slab. A moment later, North caught a glimpse of Shaw silhouetted against the light bleeding out from around the roll-up door. Shaw was motionless for a minute. Then his silhouette passed in front of the light again, and after several long heartbeats, he emerged from the gloom to stand in front of North.

"He's not in there."

"You're fucking with me."

"I could see between the tracks and the panel. There's a little battery-powered lantern, and there are some clothes and a camp cot. I think he ran while we were sitting out there, like you said, and he was in such a hurry he forgot to turn off the lantern."

North weighed his options. Then he said, "Keep an eye out."

His mind went back to the missing padlock. In North's opinion, it was another sign of a hasty flight; Welch must have torn out of there as soon as he caught wind of them. More likely, the same person who was letting him stay here had also tipped him off. North guessed the manager was going to be having some long, painful conversations with law enforcement sooner rather than later. North raised the door. Metal screeched against metal as it slid up its track, and he winced and stopped.

Shaw's silence was a condemnation.

"How the fuck was I supposed to know?" North whispered furiously.

More silence. But, of course, now it was simply amused.

He ducked under the partially raised door. As Shaw had described, the furnishings were simple: the cot, with a sleeping bag pushed to one end; clothes strewn across the floor; the battery-powered lantern. North found a box of Blazer 9mm, with enough cartridges missing for him to guess this was what Welch had been firing at the hot springs. He crouched to pick through the clothes—they looked like they'd come from a resale shop or a from a box in somebody's basement, but when he got closer, he saw the bloodstains—when he heard a sound from the corridor. It took him a moment to identify it as rubber soles slapping concrete. Shaw, of course. Probably practicing his parkour or channeling his inner cat or doing ballet—

Movement behind North made him turn. Shaw slipped under the roll-up door, and North opened his mouth to say something about keeping watch, but the mixture of fear and anger on Shaw's face stopped him.

Then he saw the second pair of legs standing out in the hall, and North had long enough to remember that the last time anyone had seen Welch, it had been a trap.

The roll-up door screeched down, and the slide lock hammered home.

17

The sound of the slide lock registered only distantly for Shaw. Fury—fury directed at himself, plain and simple—blended with the chaos of the caffeine and adrenaline, and his brain felt like what you saw in movies sometimes, when someone cut a power cord and sparks started to fly, and the cord twisted and snaked and shot out more sparks.

One moment, he'd been standing there, keeping an eye out. The next, Welch had rolled over the side of one of the storage units and landed next to Shaw. He'd already had the gun ready and everything. Because, of course, this had been planned.

"Don't do anything stupid," Welch said from the other side of the roll-up door.

"A little late for that," North said. "Jesus Christ, you left the fucking light on for us."

"You cool?" Welch asked. "Everybody's got to stay cool. You start shouting, and we're done."

North caught Shaw's eye, and Shaw struggled to shut down that live wire of rage. He focused on his body, on the way his heart pounded, the feel of his pulse in his fingertips, his still-drying sweat and the cool of the air conditioning. He thought about the roll-up door, the panels. A fraction of an inch thick, all of them. Maybe if they squeezed behind one of the support columns like cartoon characters, they'd have a chance; otherwise, they were fish in a barrel.

"We're some chill-ass cucumbers," North said.

Seconds ticked past. Shaw's shirt, bunched with sweat under his arms, was starting to itch, and he was aware again of a sour stink that lay under the smell of the weed, and even fainter, the hint of something cold and antiseptic. Somewhere in the building, metal boomed, and Shaw flinched. North did too, and then he let out a shaky breath.

Welch's laugh sounded nervous. "That's the AC coming on. Every couple of hours. Wasn't like that before. You can't sleep in this place."

"What's the deal, Philip?" North asked as Shaw worked his phone out of his pocket. North nodded in approval as Shaw began typing out a message to Emery and John-Henry: *In storage. Back of building. Welch here with a gun.* He made sure his phone was on silent and sent the message. At the same time, North was speaking to Welch again. "You've got us where you wanted, I guess. So, what's next?"

"Where I wanted. Man, I didn't want any of this. This is some bad shit, you know?"

"Oh yeah? What happened?"

"What happened? The whole thing, man. It was bad from the start."

"What's that mean?" North asked. "Somebody set you up?"

"You're goddamn right."

"You didn't kill Dalton Weber and Sheriff Engels?"

Welch hesitated. "You want me to tell you about that, you got to get me out of here."

"How am I supposed to do that?"

"Man, I don't know. Figure it the fuck out!"

The panic in his voice sounded like a thing unraveling.

Shaw said, "It went wrong, didn't it?"

Welch made a noise that seemed like a yes. Rubber squeaked on concrete. And then more words poured out of him. "It wasn't supposed to be the sheriff. It was supposed to be Ezell."

"What happened?" North asked.

"I don't know!"

"Why don't you walk us through—"

"No, no, no! You listen to me now, ok?" He paused like someone trying to corral his thoughts. "These motherfuckers, they're trying to kill me. They want Ezell. So, I figure I give them Ezell, and they let me walk. How about that?"

"I don't know," North said. "You've got to tell me more than that."

"He's at this lake. Bolmer Lake. There's some old shop, that's where he's hiding."

"How do you know where he is?" Shaw asked.

"Man, I followed him. I went out to that church first thing, right? And they didn't want nothing to do with me. So, I left. But then I started thinking maybe I shouldn't have left, so I went back. I just sat down the block for a while, watching, and then you two showed up. And then, a little later, I was still watching that place when they kicked you out. And then that jackass

Gid rabbited, and you followed him, and I followed you. And when we got to that little house where Gid wanted to poke around, you know who I saw? Just pure chance, the headlights shining right on his face."

"Ezell."

"Fucking Deputy Ezell, watching his own house. Course, I didn't know what he was watching then, but I knew they wanted him. So, when he ran, I went after him."

"Why didn't you kill him right then?" North asked. "That would have solved your problem, right? Hell, for that matter, why haven't you cleared out of here?"

Welch laughed, but the sound wasn't amused. "Man, I wish I had."

The words swam up to Shaw out of that dark place: the bloody clothes, the strange smells. "You got shot."

Only silence came from the hallway.

"How bad is it?" North asked.

The silence lasted longer this time. "It's not great."

"When? At the hot springs?"

"Came out of nowhere." Welch hissed, and the sound of metal flexing came from one of the walls. Shaw could picture Welch slumping against it. "God damn, I'm tired."

"You want Ezell dead," North said, "you're going to have to kill him yourself."

"Fuck that, man. I want to be done with this. You get Ezell. Give these fuckers something else to worry about besides me."

"What does that mean?" Shaw asked.

"Brey wants Ezell's phone. You know what that means? It means he's got something, and they want it. So, go find out what it is, and I'm going to find some nice Mex doctor, some nice brown girl with big brown titties to take care of me."

"Jesus," North said. "You're a class act."

A nice brown girl. And Shaw thought of Maleah, thought of those hours wrapped in a chemical haze, thought of waking up, the hurt of a body that was no longer your own. He thought of the way she had cried, how she had leaned into him. He thought of the worksheets covered in children's scribbles poking out of her bag, the way she had said third grade and then fourth. When he spoke, it was without thinking—the words came from that frozen, bottomless well. "Like Maleah?"

North gave him a sharp look and jerked his head.

Welch didn't say anything.

"Is that what you mean?" Shaw said. "Find a pretty girl like Maleah to take care of you?"

"Man," Welch said.

"Is this where you brought her?"

"Shaw," North said in a tight whisper.

"Not the last time," Shaw said. "That was at her house. Remember that? When you drugged her?"

"Shaw, not now."

"When you let Brey do whatever he wanted to her."

"That fucking cunt," Welch said with a pained noise that might have been a laugh. "Guess I got to make a stop before I go out of town, huh?"

"Go ahead," Shaw said. He'd done polar plunges. He'd gone skinny dipping on a spring morning at the lake, when the water was like glass, and the first dive was like going through a window, a thousand shards cutting you a thousand different ways. This was like that now, the warning from his body that registered like heat, and the unmistakable cold. "Stop by Maleah's. I'll know right where to find you."

Five seconds passed. Ten. Then Welch said, "Shit," like a man who's had yet another door slam in his face.

North grabbed Shaw and dragged him down.

The first shot came, and Shaw's thought was that it had sounded curiously distant. A metal panel warped as something heavy hit it, and Shaw thought of Welch staggering, his body colliding with the wall. Then a voice called, "Stop! Police!" and another shot rang out. It echoed through the steel cavern of the storage building, shaking itself out like thunder, and the stink of gunfire drifted into the unit where Shaw huddled under North.

The panel made another sound as the weight lifted from it and the metal relaxed. Then something heavy hit the floor. A body, Shaw thought. Welch's body.

Steps moved toward them. The jingle of cuffs. The creak of leather.

Ignoring North's grappling attempts to stop him, Shaw slithered across the floor until he could see between the wall panel and the door track. A distant emergency light allowed him to make out the shape of Welch's fallen body, but not more than that. Then another figure stepped into view. Only a silhouette, but Shaw registered the details: a muscular build, the shape of the shirt collar suggesting a polo, white-blond hair that caught the light like flax. The man stooped over the body. Then something clicked, the sound of a polymer frame against concrete. Welch's gun, Shaw thought. The man straightened and turned toward the storage unit.

"Somebody in there?" Cassidy asked. "This is Chief Cassidy with the Auburn Police."

His gaze seemed to home in on Shaw. It should have been impossible, but Shaw was convinced, in that moment, Cassidy had spotted him—that somehow he had located Shaw and was staring directly at him. Cassidy's next breath sounded satisfied. He was nothing more than an outline, but it was enough to see his arm move.

Cassidy fired. At the same moment, North grabbed Shaw's ankle and hauled him away from the panel. The weak light of the lantern seemed too bright for a moment, and then Shaw's eyes adjusted. Where Shaw had been a moment before, the bullet had punched out a chunk of the corrugated metal. The clap of the shot was still ringing in Shaw's ears. A second shot came, tearing another hole in the panel. North was shouting something, but Shaw couldn't hear him. The whole storage unit seemed to be shaking, the metal rippling like a struck bell as shot after shot came. One bullet struck the floor inches from Shaw, and chips of concrete stung his face.

North yanked Shaw toward him again, and now the words he'd been shouting penetrated: "Come on! Come on!"

The whole storage unit had been shaking, Shaw realized. It hadn't been a trick of his imagination, fear skewing his perceptions. It had been North, and he'd been kicking the rear panel loose. North was half-scooting, half-squirming through the narrow opening he'd forced between the panel and the support post, and he was trying to drag Shaw with him as he went. Shaw slid on his belly after North.

A moment later, they were on their feet in another darkened corridor. Alone. Shots continued to ring out, but they were coming from the next aisle over. North spun, trying to orient himself, but Shaw recognized the corridor. He grabbed North's tee, hauled him away from the gunfire, and ran.

18

What came next had the quality of a nightmare—one of those hyperreal unrealities that North occasionally dreamed, where the rules of logic and reason no longer applied, where everything had been turned on its head.

The first panicked minutes after their escape, North had been convinced that all he had to do was reach Emery and John-Henry, and everything would be fine. But that hadn't turned out to be true because the gunshots had called every available officer away from the search of the RV park. North and Shaw had barely avoided being mown down by nervous cops who were preparing to rush into the storage building. They'd been ordered to the ground, then cuffed, and then roughly searched while men screamed down at them. John-Henry had waded into the scrum, shouting orders and pushing men aside, but the Highway Patrol asshole had been there too, and he'd been louder. There had barely been enough time for North to tell Shaw not to say anything about what Welch had told them or what had happened with Cassidy, and then North and Shaw had been placed in separate Highway Patrol cruisers.

Inside the cruiser the silence had a compacted quality, like something that had been packed tight around North. So tight, in fact, that sometimes it was hard to breathe, like there was something heavy on his chest and he couldn't get enough air. Like being buried alive, he thought, and he felt dizzy. He tried to focus on the silent drama playing out under the RV park's security lights: John-Henry and the Highway Patrol asshole in each other's faces, mouths moving in shouts North couldn't hear. Emery was there too, at the edge of the shadows, amber eyes slitted with rage.

And Cassidy, of course. The hero of the hour. He sat on the back of an ambulance but refused a blanket, and he spoke in short snatches with men who approached him to offer a word. He was good at what he did; North had to give him that. The grace to look exhausted after a shoot-out, after gunning down a man. But also, a kind of resolve, a fortitude. He'd done what he had to do. It was a grade-A performance; North bet he'd get a hell of a Christmas bonus. In his mind, North played back the events: the first shot, and then the shout of *Stop! Police!* after Welch had been good and dead, and then Cassidy picking up Welch's gun to fire at them.

The interview came next: hours under the buzz of fluorescent lights at the Auburn police station, while the Highway Patrol asshole—his name was Lieutenant Mendez—stared at North and asked the same questions again and again. *Tell me what happened. Why did you believe Welch was hiding inside the storage building? Why didn't you inform an officer? Why didn't you return and report when you believed you'd discovered Welch's location? Did Welch say anything before attempting to kill you?* And then, of course, the classic: *Let's go over it again from the beginning.*

No, Welch hadn't said anything. No, he hadn't been able to see what happened between Chief Cassidy and Welch. No, he didn't know if Welch had attempted to shoot Cassidy first. He forgot, once, that in this version of events, Welch had been the one shooting at them inside the storage unit, and Cassidy had arrived in time to save them. That stupid fucking text message they'd sent—*In storage. Back of building. Welch here with a gun*—only seemed to bear out the story. By the time Mendez let him go, North had a headache throbbing between his eyes.

It didn't help that he found Shaw sitting on the station's stoop, eating ice cream out of a paper cup. It looked like chocolate. Maybe chocolate brownie. Shaw looked up, beamed, and said, "Leah bought me ice cream."

"Sure," North said as he sat. "Why the fuck not?"

It was close to one in the morning, and the little city of Auburn was still. Sluggish curtains of air moved in a fitful breeze, and in the tiny harbor, under the blanching cone of a security light, the water moved sluggishly too. The concrete still held a hint of the day's heat under him, and he could smell Shaw's sweat and, more distantly, the garbage-water smell from the dock. Shaw offered him a spoonful of ice cream. Cold, chocolate, and sugar rushed through him. He let his head rest on Shaw's shoulder, and Shaw riffled his hair.

"Let's go back to the motor court," he said quietly. "I can drive."

North shook his head against Shaw's shoulder.

"I'm a very good driver," Shaw said. "You said so yourself."

"John-Henry?"

"He was waiting to talk to Lieutenant Mendez."

"Emery?"

"I don't know. Do you want me to call him?"

North shook his head again. What he wanted was for the world to make sense again. To be home—his home—with Shaw and the puppy, and to go to work and listen to Pari and Shaw scream at each other about a missing almond croissant, and then do some shouting himself about how he was going to start his own agency and nobody would be allowed to bring any fucking almond croissants to work. He wanted to do good, solid work to build Borealis. He wanted the occasional night off in front of the TV. He wanted to grill on Sunday and, when he passed Jadon to grab another beer from the house, give the dumbass a dead-arm. What he didn't want was to be here, in this upside-down universe, where Shaw had almost gotten killed. Again.

Shaw's fingers combed his hair. "I know," he whispered. "But it's almost over."

"Is it?" North asked. But he sat up and rubbed his eyes and said, before Shaw could answer, "My guess is they're going to try to shut this down. They've got Welch. That's two murders wrapped up. They'll let John-Henry try to find Ezell if he can, but this is the end of it."

Shaw wrapped both hands around the paper cup of melting ice cream, his silence dense and unhappy. Finally he said, "Why didn't we tell them what Welch said?"

"Because," North said, getting to his feet. He held out a hand to help Shaw. "We played by the rules with Welch, and look how well that turned out. If we go in there and tell them what really happened, Shaw, how do you think it's going to play out? These guys can't find their ass with both hands. We'll lose our last lead."

"But John-Henry—"

"John-Henry isn't calling the shots anymore." North tried to soften his voice. "We'll call him as soon as we've got Ezell in a pair of cuffs. Come on."

"North, he's trusting us—"

"And no ice cream in my car. Throw that away."

"North!"

"You know the rules."

"You literally ate ice cream in it last week. You kept pretending to hump it because you said it was so good."

"Rules just changed."

"That's not fair!"

"My car, my rules."

19

When the GPS said they were a quarter mile out, North killed the lights and slowed the GTO. The car's distinctive rumble made him wonder, for a moment, if Jem might have been on to something. But then, he also considered that Jem owned and wore a shocking number of Teenage Mutant Ninja Turtles t-shirts, which yes, was dope, but also made it hard to take him seriously about, well, everything.

According to the Maps app, there was only one Bolmer Lake, and it was a good couple of hours north of Wahredua. North and Shaw had stopped for fuel, and now, with the caffeine from a couple of energy drinks ricocheting along his bloodstream, North felt wide eyed and alert, even though the clock read half-past three. The gravel road led them over and around a string of low hills. And then he saw it below them, a hint of an opening in the graphite landscape revealed by moonlight: the lake. When he cracked the window, he could smell water lapping against the shore.

North parked and turned the car off. When he touched Shaw's leg, Shaw jerked upright with a drooly "Muh?" and wiped his mouth. He looked blankly at North for a moment, then blinked, glanced around. "What's that?"

He was pointing at an old building: plywood siding, a flat roof, windows boarded up. A concrete island suggested that at one point, gas pumps had been a feature. "Some kind of convenience store," North said. "Maybe at some point, enough people were coming here for it to make sense."

Shaw made a noise like he was considering that. "I don't see a car."

"If I were Ezell, I'd park it behind that building."

"I don't see any light."

"If he's smart," North said, "he's camping. If he's not intellectually gifted, he's probably holed up in that convenience store."

"You told me you'd rather be fucked with broken glass than go camping."

"Yeah, well, I wasn't on the run and suspected of aiding and abetting a murderer. Besides, the Cardinals were playing. Here we go."

North was quiet about opening the trunk, unlocking the gun safe, and closing the trunk again. They each carried pepper gel and a flashlight as well, but it was the gun that North wanted. After everything that had happened that day, the weight of the CZ was grounding. No running, this time. No scurrying around inside a metal box, praying they wouldn't get shot. Shaw touched his arm, and North startled. He couldn't make out Shaw's expression in the dark, but the touch came again, rubbing lightly up to the swell of his biceps. North felt, now, the tightness in his own jaw, the way the jet fuel of the energy drinks was making his skin tight, making his head feel like a drum. He let out a breath slowly, took in another, and nodded. He sensed, more than saw, Shaw's answering nod.

Their first few steps, gravel crunched underfoot. Then they reached the shoulder of the road, moving into the weeds and tall grasses. North went first, breaking trail, trampling thistles with the Red Wings so that Shaw wouldn't get caught on them. He scanned the area around them, but even with the relative brightness of the moon tonight, he couldn't make out more than general details. Someone could have been five feet away, lying flat on the ground, and North would have walked right past them. Or someone could be in those trees along the lake. He thought of the hot springs. He thought of night-vision scopes, how he and Shaw would stand out like signal flares.

But he couldn't see anything, so he listened. Blood hissed in his ears. The lake, the restlessness of the water. Farther off, a branch creaked. And then the snap and rustle of movement through vegetation. His pulse ratcheted up again. Were those normal sounds? Animals moving in the night? Or were those sounds all wrong? He had the sudden, gut-clenching wish that Emery were here, or John-Henry, or Theo, or hell, even the vet. He'd have taken any of them, anybody who hadn't grown up in a city, spent his whole life in a city, and sure as hell wished he were in a city right then.

No gunshots came. No bear charged at them out of the woods. North had a vague idea about water moccasins dropping out of trees, but so far, he and Shaw were in the clear. Slowly and steadily — and, more importantly, quietly — they made their way down the hill. When they reached the convenience store, they found the lot overgrown with weeds. Close up, North could see that the walls were papered over with old advertisements for beer and cigarettes and Pepsi products. The ads were bleached from the sun, so damaged by water and exposure that in places they had disintegrated. An earthy odor met him, kind of like the smell of button mushrooms before they'd been cleaned. Dry rot. It was a miracle the shack hadn't collapsed yet.

Behind the store, they found Ezell's F-150. The license plates didn't match, but that actually made sense—Ezell worked in law enforcement, and he must have known he could be tracked that way, so he'd switched them. North took a couple of photos.

When he finished, he found Shaw standing by a door at the back of the building. Shaw pointed to the hasp, with padlock still attached, that had been pried away from the doorjamb. When Shaw applied pressure, the door rocked slightly and then stopped. Blocked by something on the other side. Probably Ezell's security measure while he slept.

North motioned Shaw back, and they moved away from the door. He picked up a handful of gravel and slung it against the side of the building. Stones rattled against plywood, and he shouted, "Ezell, wake the fuck up!"

The sound of wood jarring against wood came from inside the store. Then silence.

North gathered more gravel and threw it. "We know you're in there. We're working for the Wahredua PD, so think really carefully about what you do next."

More silence.

Now North threw the stones one by one, pinging them against the side of the building. "Come on, Ezell, we can do this the easy way or the hard way. The easy way is you come with us, and you get to tell your side of the story. The hard way is we get every cop in a hundred miles out here, and you can play like it's the Alamo."

The sound of movement came again. North watched the boarded-up windows. He'd chosen a spot where a direct line of fire would be difficult for the fugitive deputy; put somebody in a corner, and they're liable to do some stupid shit. But he still watched the windows in case Ezell was trickier than he thought.

"I'm not stupid," Ezell called from inside. His voice wavered. "I know who you are. Fuck off, or I'll shoot."

"We're working for Wahredua PD—" Shaw tried.

"I'm not an idiot! I'm going to count from ten!"

"Dumbass," North shouted back, "if I wanted you dead, I wouldn't have woken you up to have this cozy little chat. You'd be dead. End of story."

Ezell tried for a laugh. "Not gonna work. You want me to come out there. Ten!"

"If we wanted to get you out of the building," Shaw said, "we would have waited until you needed to pee, or you needed water, or you wanted to stretch your legs."

"Nine!"

"Or we would have just set the store on fire," Shaw said. "You would have woken up, panicked, and rushed out. Bang. The end."

The silence from inside the store had a horrified quality.

"That's some dark shit," North said.

Shaw shrugged. "Shadow work."

"How about this?" North said. "You give us a little credit because we didn't set this shitheap on fire and/or murder you in your sleep. And, if you want a little more reinforcement, call the station on your burner and ask about the private investigators working for Chief Somerset."

Thirty seconds. Then a minute. "Don't try anything funny."

"Why do they always say that?" North asked. "What am I going to do?"

"Blow a clown?" Shaw suggested.

"That's not what they mean—"

"It's funny on lots of levels. First, it's a clown, so that's always funny."

"No, clowns are creepy."

"And second, it's you, so there's this whole intellectual humor."

North opened his mouth. Then he managed to say, "No. Nope. Unh-uh."

"Because—"

"I didn't ask, Shaw."

"—you're so bad at BJs—"

"Excuse me?"

"—and because you know, you're supposed to be gay—"

"What the fuck does that mean, supposed to be?"

"—and, of course, your history with Nick." Shaw coughed delicately. "Your incisors? Remember? All that blood?"

"Listen to me, you aged-out, flat-assed, patchouli-funked expired excuse for a twink—"

"Ok," Ezell called from inside the building, "I want to see some ID—"

"—if I'm so fucking terrible at blow jobs, then you don't have anything to worry about—"

"Hey! Did you hear me?"

"—because I will never, ever, ever be giving you one again—"

"North, no!" It was hard to tell in the dark, but it sounded like Shaw was close to giggling. "Don't give up on your dreams!"

"Are you listening to me? I said—"

"What the fuck is wrong with you?" North shouted toward the store. "Are you blind? Are you deaf? Do you have zero fucking awareness that I'm in the middle of something?"

A handful of seconds trickled past, and Ezell said, "Uh, sorry?"

North rubbed his forehead; a vein was throbbing in his temple. Maybe that would be a good way to go. Something bursts in your brain, and then it's over. Short and sweet. It sounded especially good compared to the possibility of growing old with—

"I think it's admirable that you've never given up," Shaw said, "not even after the lawsuits, the injunctions, the court orders, the skin grafts."

"Jesus, take me now," North said as he stalked toward the back door.

"It's inspirational, North. You're an inspiration. You could inspire, uh, dozens of gaybros to keep fighting for their dreams of one day being able to—what's the gentlemanly version of swinging on a knob? Oh, you could do speaking tours!"

When North reached the door, he said, "Do you have a gun?"

Ezell said, "Um."

"Great. Shoot this motherfucker, and I'll let you go."

The most disappointing part, North thought distantly, was that the only response was silence.

"Open the fuck up," North said.

"Your IDs—"

"Get the fuck out of here about the IDs. Do you hear the kind of shit I have to put up with? Open the fucking door, turn on the fucking lights, and then step out here with your fucking hands where I can see them, or this is going to be the fastest murder-suicide on record."

"Interesting fact," Shaw said, "the previous record holder was—what was the name of the guy who looked like Rasputin, only not quite as sexy, and he liked ladies to hit him with their shoes?"

"Never mind," North said, "it's just going to be a suicide."

Something squeaked as it was dragged across the floorboards, and the door inched open. A moment later, warm yellow light spilled out into the night.

"I'm coming out," Ezell said.

"Nice and slow," North said.

"Don't shoot."

After the most recent spate of bullshit, North didn't exactly like the fact that he and Shaw rolled their eyes at exactly the same time. But he couldn't help but appreciate it.

Ezell stepped out of the store, and North's first thought was that his hands were empty. North's second thought was that, strangely, he looked familiar. He had a moon face and red cheeks, and his thin blond hair was slicked back tight against his skull. Average height, stocky build, tattoo on the inside of his arm, lots of gothic swirls with what might have been a sword or a gun—it was too dark to tell. He wore jeans and a t-shirt that said YOU LOOK LIKE I NEED A DRINK. He was the kind of person North would have wanted to punch on general principle.

"Where's the gun?" North asked.

"Inside."

"Shaw."

Shaw slipped past Ezell, and a moment later, he said, "Got it."

"Go on," North said. "Remember: we're still moving nice and slow."

He followed Ezell inside and put the deputy up against the wall, patted him down, and stepped back once he was satisfied Ezell wasn't carrying anything else. Then he got a look at the space.

They were in some kind of backroom, and a single Coleman lantern hissed quietly as it shed light. The walls were lined with shelves empty aside from scraps and junk: broken Styrofoam containers, dusty reels, a spool of green fishing line, a tackle box turned on its side. Someone had used fingernail polish to paint ROD'S TACKLE on the lid. What appeared to be a refrigerated bait case sat near the door—presumably what Ezell had used to barricade himself inside. The earthy, fungal smell was stronger now, but mixed with an old fishiness that turned North's stomach.

A single door, its bottom ruined by water damage, opened into what appeared to be the front of the shop. In there, North found a long counter covered in more ads for cigarettes and beer and spinner rods, an ancient mechanical till with its SALE flag perpetually raised, empty aisles formed by gondola shelves and drink coolers that were dusty and full of dead bugs. A pair of doors suggested restrooms, and a quick check revealed both were empty. When North moved back toward the storage room, he spotted what he'd missed on his first sweep: a cluster of cans of what turned out to be spaghetti rings, a half-empty jug of water, another Coleman lantern. The lingering hint of body odor hung in the air, and he spotted the sleeping bag on the floor behind the till.

In the storage room, Shaw was holding his Springfield in one hand, and Ezell's doughy face was covered in fine drops of sweat.

"He was thinking about being naughty," Shaw informed him. "So, I told him I'd shoot his balls off."

"That sounds about right," North muttered. He leaned against the refrigerated bait case, crossed his arms, and said, "Talk."

Ezell shook his head. "You don't understand, man. These people, they're going to kill me."

"Or Shaw's going to shoot your balls off. You have what I believe is called a classic dilemma."

"He just learned that phrase," Shaw told Ezell. "Emery—Emery's my best friend—Emery said it to him the other day when we were arguing about whether North should eat all the Parmigiano-Reggiano with crackers or save it for his salad. We had to hear the whole mental process, all the pros and cons."

"It was a difficult decision," North snapped, "and you motherfuckers weren't any help."

"Notice that eating some of the cheese and saving some for his salad wasn't an option."

"Great. Here we go."

"And sharing with everyone else definitely wasn't—"

"I asked! Before I went to the store, I asked if anyone wanted anything, and—no, you know what? I'm not doing this, not again." He pointed a finger at Ezell, who was staring at them, slack jawed. "Who paid you to kill Dalton Weber?"

"I didn't kill anyone," Ezell mumbled.

"No, you let Welch do the actual killing. But you were involved." North waited a beat and said, "All right. We can finish this conversation at the station, and maybe a night in the county jail will soften you up. You'll have to be in the isolation unit because you were a cop. How about that? All by yourself, nice and safe in one of those little cells."

"You can't! They'll kill me! You've got to—I can tell you. And then you let me go, and I won't be a problem. I didn't hurt anyone!"

The last few words were delivered in a wail, and tears spilled from Ezell's eyes. With his round face and his fine blond hair slick against his skull, he looked like a giant baby. A giant baby, North reminded himself, who had helped arrange murder for hire.

"Who hired you?" North asked.

"All I was supposed to do was turn off the cameras, put the girl in the laundry, and leave the cells unlocked."

"Then you ran," Shaw said.

"I knew they wanted it to look like an accident, like Welch got me by surprise and overpowered me. But I'm not stupid. I started thinking about it, and the more I thought about it, the more I realized they weren't going to leave it like that." He stopped. Then he blurted, "They were going to kill me."

"Probably," North said.

Shaw cocked his head as though hearing something, and a tiny crease appeared between his eyebrows, but all he said was "What did you do?"

"I told the sheriff I was sick. I had plenty of leave, and it was a quiet night. He said he'd stay. As soon as I was out of there, I called that son of a bitch and told him he'd better pay up, or I was going to make sure everybody knew what he'd done. I've got proof." Ezell's face crumpled. "Only it all went to shit. The little bastard turned on me."

"Names—" North began.

Then he heard it, the sound that Shaw must have noticed a moment before. It was rumbling, metallic, uneven. It took a moment for his mind to fill in the blanks: wheels, something heavy on an uneven surface.

"North," Shaw said.

He followed Shaw's gaze through the doorway. The dirty windows at the front of the store made it impossible to make out details, but it looked like a fireball was rolling down the hill, headed straight toward them. Fast.

Lurching away from the cooler, North moved toward the front of the store. The fireball was racing toward him now, and a small, sickened part of him knew what he was looking at, what it had to be, even though the rest of his brain was still trying to process that knowledge into words. He was aware of movement at his shoulder, and then Shaw saying, "What—"

Then Shaw made a weird, breathy noise and lurched into North. North stumbled. Ezell hammered at his neck, his fist connecting with the base of North's skull, and the world went Technicolor. Distantly, North was aware of the weight of the CZ leaving his waistband, of Ezell shoving Shaw into him again. No longer in control of his own body, North was still moving forward, under the combined force of Ezell's blows and Shaw's weight.

The fireball hurtled toward them. It bucked over the concrete island where the gas pumps had once been, and then it hopped the curb again when it reached the store itself. For a moment, even through the filthy glass, the flames illuminated a familiar outline. North tried to turn his movement into a controlled fall, and he and Shaw went down together as the GTO crashed through the front of the store.

Metal screeched. Glass shattered. Wood snapped. The GTO kept coming, all that mass pressing forward with the power generated as it had rolled down the hill. Gondola shelves flew into the air. The car hit a drink cooler like a pool ball, and it slammed into the back wall of the store hard enough to punch halfway through it. North rolled toward the counter, thought of Shaw, stopped.

And by then, it was over.

Dust hung in the air. A stink enveloped North: gasoline, melting synthetics, particleboard on fire. He scrambled to his feet, looked for Shaw, and found him. The GTO had tipped over one of the gondola shelves, pinning Shaw beneath it. All North could see was where Shaw's legs stuck out, the black jeans, the black sneakers.

A fuse blew in North's brain, and the world went dark.

He didn't remember crossing the space to Shaw. He was only distantly aware of the heat of the fire, of the blaze spreading from the car to the cheap shelving and broken plywood. The fact that it was the GTO registered only at the edge of consciousness, in the same way that a part of him knew Ezell was escaping. None of it mattered.

North crouched, grabbed Shaw's calf, and called, "Shaw! Shaw!"

Shaw's leg moved, and he shouted something back. But over the roar of the flames and his pulse rushing in his ears, he couldn't make out Shaw's words.

Get him out, North thought. Got to get him out. He got his fingers under the shelving and lifted. Muscles in his arms corded. His biceps strained. Nothing. The fucker didn't shift. North swallowed a scream, adjusted his position and tried again. The flames beat against the side of his face, and he thought maybe something was wrong with his vision, maybe he'd hit his head, because the world rippled under waves of light and shadow. This time, he felt the strain through his arms, down his back, gathering at his spine like something spiked. He knew he was being stupid; he knew this was a bad lift, and if he kept it up, he was more likely to hurt himself than anything else. But it didn't matter. What mattered was getting Shaw free.

Somewhere far off, Shaw was shouting.

Finally, North released the shelves. He slumped over them for a minute, and the hammer strokes of his heartbeat blacked out everything else for a moment. He tried again, and fuzz moved into his vision. "Move," he grunted. "Move! Move, you bitch! You fucking piece of shit, move!" The last was a scream, and then he couldn't anymore, and he dropped onto his ass, kicking wildly at the shelving, lost in a frenzy fueled by terror. The flames were growing hotter. When they flared up, it felt like a slap on the cheek.

Maybe it was the fact that his body couldn't help him, and so he had to try something else. Maybe it was the fact that, sooner or later, no matter how much of a dumbass you are, your brain comes online again. Whatever the reason, enough of his vision cleared for North to make out the problem: the GTO had collapsed part of the gondola shelves beneath it. North wasn't just trying to lift the shelving unit; he was trying to lift the whole car. He scrambled over to the burning wreckage, set his shoulder to the front, ignoring the hot-brand steel that seared through his shirt, and pushed. For a moment, nothing. Then the GTO rocked backward.

That was when the first gunshot rang out.

Shaw shouted something, and the tone wasn't panic or pleading—it was an order, and it sounded like, "Go! Go!"

Another shot rang out. Closer.

North gave the GTO another shove, and then he got to his feet. His gun. His gun—then memory returned, Ezell shoving Shaw into him, taking North's gun. Shaw had been in possession of Ezell's gun and his own, but he was trapped under the debris of the shelves. North checked himself, but he'd lost his pepper gel in the fall. He grabbed his flashlight from where it had rolled up against the counter and scanned the room for another weapon.

The back door flew open, and Ezell staggered inside. He'd fallen in mud, and the left leg of his jeans was soaked. Not mud, North realized an instant later. Blood. His already pale face was colorless now, and his eyes were wide and unseeing, settling on North the way he might have looked at anything else—the old reels, the bait cooler, the tackle box. "Help me," Ezell said. "You've got to help—"

Then the man in black stepped through the doorway. He was the same man North had seen outside Ezell's house, he was sure of it. And he thought odds were good this was the same man Theo and Jem had fought. On his hips, still sheathed, he carried a sickle and a big fucker of a knife. In one hand, he held a pistol, and he raised it and shot Ezell: once in the back, once in the head. Ezell's body gave a little dance-step twist, and his momentum carried him another pace before he fell.

North was already moving. He grabbed the first can of spaghetti rings and hurled it. All those summers of Chouteau-boy softball came back to him, and the can pegged the man in black in the face. The mask muffled the sound, but the man cried out. North hurled the lantern next. This time, it was a body blow, and the man in black let out a sharp noise and staggered back. Another shot went off, and chips of wood sprayed from the wall. The man was off balance now, one hand moving toward his ribs. Jem had stabbed him in the side the first time they'd met, North remembered. That explained the way the man held himself, the slight stiffness of his movements. Another shot rang out, and the tackle box flipped over. How many was that? More importantly, how many did he have in the magazine? Before the man could recover his balance, North hooked the half-empty water jug and sprinted forward. He timed it so that the jug left his hand at the same time the man began to steady himself. It was a bad throw, but then, North didn't have much practice throwing jugs. It hit the man in the midsection. Not hard enough to hurt anybody else, but this guy grunted and staggered back—if only for a moment.

A moment was all North needed. By then, he'd closed the distance, and he brought the flashlight—with its steel body and the weight of its batteries—down in a savage swing. He aimed for the head, and it was the kind of blow that should have incapacitated the man, maybe even killed him. But this guy was fast, and he was coordinated, and he rotated in place, taking the blow on his shoulder instead of the head. The crunch of metal on bone transmitted itself up through the steel and into North's hand, and the man screamed. The gun fell from his nerveless hand and hit the floor. North went for it.

And almost got killed. The sickle came at him in a black blur, and only luck and a lifetime of jackassing with Shaw let him dodge in time. The blade moved through the air, missing North by a fraction of an inch, and a clinical part of his brain noted that it didn't sound like a whistle, the way sometimes people said. This thing, at least, hissed—barely a noise at all, but low and furious. He threw himself sideways, and the sickle missed him again. It had come close enough, this time, to tug at his shirt.

North hit the floor, flipped over, and kicked the bait cooler into the man's path. The man kicked it back, and North kicked it again, hard, sending it straight into the man's legs. The man grunted. He hip-checked the cooler out of his path this time, away from North, and took another step. One hand hung empty at this side—his injured arm. In the other, he held the sickle. But not by the handle, North saw. He'd adjusted his grip to a strap at the end of the weapon. North scrambled to get upright. His back hit the shelves. Run, his brain said. When it's you against a guy with a knife—hell, when it's you against a guy with a fucking sickle—run.

But Shaw.

The man in black moved his good hand, swinging the sickle by its strap, and the blade blurred. North hadn't ever seen anything like it—it was some martial arts shit, the kind of thing that would have looked badass and hokey all at the same time in a movie. In real life, it made North's bowels loosen, made his legs feel like water. The sound. It sounded like a machine, something moving with tremendous power and speed, but barely making more than a hiss as it came toward him. North shifted his grip on the flashlight. He tried to think. Stay out of his range. Block with the flashlight if you have to. Wait for your opening, because he's going to fuck up sooner or later.

Would he, though? This guy, whoever he was, was good. He'd taken on Jem and Theo at the same time, and for all intents and purposes, he'd won. He'd dodged a blow that ought to have broken his skull, and even without the use of one arm, he'd still gotten North on the defensive. And, unless North missed his guess, he stood pretty good odds of killing North in the next fifteen seconds.

As though hearing the thought, the man in black stepped forward. The sickle seemed to be a hundred places at once, spinning at the end of the strap. North slid along the shelves, trying to find space to move. The roar of the fire was so much bigger now, and the superheated air, with its stink, full of the smoke of manmade materials scorched and smoldering, made it impossible to breathe. He could feel the shallow, panting breaths he was taking. His whole body burned for one good, clean breath. The man in black darted forward.

A shot rang, and the man in black threw himself sideways. Shaw stood in the doorway to the burning front of the shop, blood matting his auburn hair, and gumming one eye shut. But his hand was steady as he lined up another shot. The man in black ducked toward Ezell's body. Shaw fired again, and splinters exploded from the floorboards. The man in black grabbed something, and too late, North realized what it was: Ezell's phone.

Shaw fired a third time, and the man darted out into the night and was gone.

20

It was sometime near dawn, and in the emergency room cubicle, Shaw was having trouble keeping his eyes open. This little room was full of the usual hospital smells: the slightly stinging scent of a disinfectant, too many bodies, the cleaner they used on the floors. It smelled like fire, too, and greasy smoke. When Shaw moved, the paper on the examination table rustled.

North, in the chair he'd pulled next to the table, had his eyes closed, and he looked paler than usual, but his voice was its familiar hard smolder when he said, "You're supposed to be resting."

"You're supposed to be resting too."

"Huh," North said. "I wonder what keeps interrupting me."

Shaw wriggled around some more until he lay on his side, facing North, and the paper rustled and pulled and finally split along the edge. North opened his eyes to slits. They looked like sunlight, Shaw always thought. The way sunlight would look the moment it caught a sheet of ice. A blue so pale it speared through him, every day, every time, ever since that first day when he'd seen him in the dorms.

"I feel fine," Shaw said.

North grunted.

"I don't even have a concussion. The doctor said so."

Nothing came from North this time, but those blue eyes were still slitted open. A pair of men walked past the cubicle, voices drifting with the lazy meter of people without a care. "It's fine if you can get past that ninth hole; the rest of it plays like a dream."

"I'm not talking about the course. The guy with the carts acts like he's doing me a favor every time I give him my credit card. Give me a break; I can take my money somewhere else."

One part about being in a relationship with someone was that, even after years and years, they could still surprise you. For example, Shaw hadn't known until right then that North could roll his eyes when they were barely open.

"They sound nice," Shaw whispered.

"They sound like that guy we caught humping his putter."

"They could be your friends. We need more friends."

"We need more friends like I need a hole in the head." He put on what Shaw thought of as his Chouteau accent and said, "The ninth hole is a dream."

Fighting a giggle, Shaw shook his head. "No, the ninth hole is the whole problem. Weren't you listening? This is why we can't ever make any new friends."

North looked like he was trying not to smile. Then the expression guttered and went out, and something dark and collapsed was all that remained. He reached out, brushing that spot of Shaw's hair he loved to touch, the one he always went back to, even though Shaw couldn't see anything different about it. He swallowed, and his fingers trembled. "Jesus Christ. I thought—"

"What the fuck were you thinking?" Emery asked as he blew into the cubicle. The curtain billowed in his wake, and John-Henry had to catch it and pull it shut behind him as he joined them. Emery continued, "I'm perfectly well aware that you do a lot of stupid shit, but this is a new order of magnitude for you."

North surged up from his seat, his face hardening as he crowded Emery back. "I was doing my fucking job, which is a hell of a lot more than I can say for you."

"Both of you—" John-Henry began.

"Please—" Shaw tried.

"You had a lead," Emery said, "and instead of bringing it to us—which is the definition of your job, since you seem to have forgotten—you had to hare off and be Pecos fucking Bill. And now our last lead on our case is dead because as usual, you can't do the one simple thing that's been asked of you."

"It's not your case! Did you forget about that? Here, I'll remind you: you're not a cop. Not anymore. You're a fucking nobody just like the rest of us. You can play with your balls and fantasize about the good old days and sniff around after him, but don't give me that bullshit about 'our case.' You're in the same position we're in, and if it'd been you, you would have done the exact same thing."

"I would have told John, and we would have brought Ezell in without getting him shot to death in the process! But that's apparently too much for you—"

"Emery, enough," John-Henry said.

"Too much for me?" North asked.

"North," Shaw said, "Emery, please, we're friends. We love each other."

"What's too much is having to watch while the little circle jerk you've put together fucks up everything I hand them. I turn over Gid and the Moss family, and what comes up? Crackerjacks. I turn over Brey and Maleah, and what do I get? Zilch. I give you Welch on a silver fucking platter, even though nobody else could find him, and it's like watching a clown college do a fucking search. He's sitting there right under your noses, and you still wouldn't have found him if we hadn't done your job for you. Again."

Emery opened his mouth, but before he could speak, John-Henry caught his arm and wheeled him toward the curtained opening. He made a furious sound, but John-Henry said, "Get out in the hall, and don't come in here again." The curtain flapped once, and Emery's heavy steps pounded the linoleum, and then he was gone.

Something seemed to break inside North. He didn't seem to be able to stand up straight, and he had one hand pressed low against his belly as he breathed raggedly. "Finally," he managed to say. "Thank you—"

"Stop talking," John-Henry said. Even the golden tan couldn't hide his exhaustion, as though the fluorescent lights had peeled everything back. The lines at the corner of his mouth were white with pressure. One hand was a fist, and he kept moving the fingers as though he wanted to loosen them but couldn't. Finally, in a voice that didn't sound very much like John-Henry, he asked, "Are you all right?"

North nodded.

"We're ok," Shaw said, and the words sounded small. "We know Emery's upset—"

North made a sharp gesture with one hand, and Shaw subsided.

Quick steps hurried past, and the curtain fluttered on its rings. Shaw could hear his heartbeat inside his head. His face felt hot, and his eyes stung. North was still taking those terrible breaths.

"Fine," John-Henry said. "I mean, good. That's good." Then he stopped again. "You've done some good work on this case. You found Welch; thank you for that. I think this is the appropriate time to close out your part in the investigation. If you'll submit an invoice, I'll see that you get paid as quickly as possible."

North made a noise that might have been a laugh.

Shaw opened his mouth, but nothing came. Finally, he managed, "John-Henry."

"I've got a uniformed officer waiting to give you a ride back to the motor court," John-Henry said.

"But we're not done," Shaw said. "You don't have to pay us, that's fine, but this isn't done. We don't know who hired Ezell. We don't know if Brey was behind it or Gid or someone else entirely. There are still links to the Cottonmouth Club, and we need to follow them back, find a way to get someone to talk. Otherwise, they'll keep getting away with it."

John-Henry gave him a look that might have been pitying. All he said was "Officer Foley will get you back to the motor court, and Auggie offered to drive you back to St. Louis." He caught the curtain with one hand, his back to them now, and said, "I'm sorry this is how things worked out."

The curtain fluttered behind him.

North slapped a plastic pamphlet holder off the countertop. It cracked against the wall, and pamphlets went everywhere. He shouted, "Fuck!" and kicked a stool, and its casters screeched as it spun away.

A nurse yanked the curtain back—fortyish, Black, with either a great ponytail or an even better weave. "What's going on in here?"

North was taking those awful breaths again. It was the way something hurt breathed, Shaw realized. Something hurting so much it couldn't get all the air it needed. He glared at the nurse, but it didn't seem to faze her.

"Nothing," Shaw said, slipping off the exam table. He took North's hand. "We're leaving."

21

North didn't sleep that night (morning, whatever it was), or not anything that felt like sleep, anyway. He woke again and again with the heat of the fire on his face, confused by the darkness, the smell of damp cotton, with the echoes of gunshots fading in his ears. He saw Emery's face, the fury animating it, and played their conversation a hundred different ways, saying all the things he should have said.

He didn't wake until noon, and Shaw was still asleep. He showered, dried himself off, checked himself out in the mirror. Some circles around the eyes. Some bruises that were starting to stiffen him up. Nothing a few days wouldn't sort out. He'd had worse, on plenty of occasions, after a bad night with Tucker.

After dressing as quietly as he could, he began repacking their bags. He'd text Auggie. Wouldn't that be the cherry on top of all this fucking mess, having one of the Super Friends drive them home because the GTO was nothing but a slagheap? Shaw wouldn't mind, of course; he and Auggie would probably watch TikTok the whole way, and North would have to drive, and while the Audi wasn't a bad car, he could actually feel his balls getting smaller.

When the bags were packed, he knelt there, and he thought, It's over. He recognized what he was feeling, that sense of detachment, the distance from himself and from that river running through him. He had felt this way before. He hadn't died from it. Sleep, he thought. And food.

Food sounded good, so he checked Shaw once more—still asleep, some of that auburn hair curling across his cheek, the occasional snore slipping out of him—and let himself out into the blistering sunlight. Summer hung on him like one of Shaw's cloaks, sticky and heavy and clinging. He checked his phone as he went down the exterior steps. There had to be a place close enough for him to walk and grab something for them to eat. Shaw would be starving, maybe even hungry enough not to drag North over the coals if North picked up some shakes to go with the—

The buzz of a window made him look up, and it wasn't until that moment that he registered the sound of an engine running. A Honda Odyssey was parked in one of the stalls, and Emery sat there, drumming his fingers on the wheel. It might have been a full minute, the sun like a hand pushing down on North, that he stood there trading stares with Emery. Then he gave Emery the finger. The tension in Emery's shoulders eased, and he tilted his head toward the empty passenger seat.

North climbed into the minivan as Emery buzzed the window up again, and a wall of air conditioning met him. The van had the usual parental clutter—abandoned cups, a pair of shoes that must have belonged to Evie, toys, stray French fries. A couple of paper bags were stashed between the front seats, and a heavenly smell drifted up.

"Breakfast," Emery said. "Although I suppose it's lunch by now. And it's either a peace offering or a bribe. Both, I guess."

North let his gaze slide up. Today, Emery was dressed in what North thought of as his usual outfit: tactical boots, jeans, a t-shirt. The t-shirt was Death Cab for Cutie, and it looked a little too small for him, and washed within an inch of its life. It was obvious Emery had showered, but he still looked like a wreck.

"You know, I was just thinking about my balls shriveling up," North said, reaching for the bag, "and then I saw you sitting in this van." He opened one of the containers and was met with a cheesy, sausage-y, and most importantly cheesy croissant. It tasted—

"God," Emery muttered. "Now I'm going to have that sound in my head for the rest of my life."

North managed to stifle additional noises, but he took another bite, and then another. Then he paused and said, "It's still hot."

"Adults swallow their food before speaking." Then Emery must have remembered this was an apology-slash-bribe meal, and he gestured to the cup holders. "I assume Shaw wants the unicorn latte. I got you one too, but if you'd like to pretend that you prefer your coffee black, I also bought you a decoy cup."

North chewed the next bite more slowly, studying Emery. After he swallowed, he said, "You're a lot."

To his surprise, Emery laughed quietly. "I think that's the consensus."

"It's hot."

Emery's eyes widened, and North gave him a crooked grin and held up the croissant.

"Don't do that," Emery said with a weirdly breathy laugh. "John has this insane theory about us—" He stopped whatever he'd been about to say. "It wouldn't be much of an apology if it were cold."

"I thought it was a bribe."

"That too."

"And you've been out here since…?"

"Ten." A wry smile creased the corner of his mouth. "I think the delivery people are getting sick of me."

That pulled a laugh from North. He ate some more. And then—because his balls had not shriveled up, not entirely, anyway, and because he was a man, and because he could do this, regardless of what Shaw thought, and definitely not because of those creepy fix-your-relationship VHS tapes Shaw had bought in bulk at an estate sale and then forced North to watch when it was his night to pick something on TV—North said, "I fucked up. I'm sorry."

Emery nodded. "I fucked up too. And you don't need to apologize to me. I, on the other hand, definitely need to apologize to you." He looked out the windshield, and his hands wrapped around the steering wheel again. "John has been under tremendous pressure. First, those kids. Then Dalton and the sheriff. I know that this is personal for you, but I don't think you can understand."

"It's different," North said. "I get that. The sheriff was your friend. This is your home. John-Henry's in the spotlight." He wrestled for a moment with the next bit. "I'm not blaming John-Henry. Sometimes leads don't pan out; I get that. The Moss family is going to keep their secrets, and Eric Brey's got a lawyer, and he knows how to terrorize women into being quiet. But that search at the RV park was a cock-up, and it almost got me and Shaw killed. You're good at what you do, I know that. John-Henry too. But last night, half of those guys didn't know their ass from their elbow. And then Cassidy—"

"What happened with Cassidy?"

North gave himself a mental kick. And then he told him.

Instead of exploding, Emery said, "I wish you would have told us."

"That's it?"

Emery blinked. "Pardon me?"

"Colt told me a story about you punching a tree because a branch almost fell on him."

"I didn't punch it, I—" Emery stopped, and that tiny smile flickered again. "I'm not surprised Jonas killed Welch in the way you described. Or, frankly, that he tried to kill you. Jonas is concerned primarily with Jonas, and when it comes to protecting himself, he'll do whatever he has to." He was silent for a moment. "It'll be impossible to use as leverage, unfortunately. It's your word against his, and you were inside a storage unit. He already admitted to moving Welch's gun, so there's an explanation for his prints on it. No, I don't think there's anything we can do with it. But it's good to know. We suspected he was involved; now we know he is, at some level. Even if he doesn't have a connection back to the Cottonmouth Club, he's tied up with the Mosses and Brey, and he can't be trusted."

North waited for more. "That's it?"

"I assume that your experience with Jonas and your frustration with the search at the RV park explain why you acted independently when going after Ezell."

"Uh, yeah."

"Perhaps you could tell John that."

"What?"

"John is almost unbelievably willing to forgive. He did what he did—"

"Fired our asses."

"—because he felt like he had to."

"After we unpacked this entire fucking case for you."

"You did, yes. But North, be reasonable. You are, if I'm being honest, a terrible employee. Tell me, is this how you conduct your own investigations? When you're working independently, just you and a client?"

North considered the question. "Pretty much."

"Don't be ridiculous; of course it's not. You write reports. You provide updates. You work within the parameters the client has established. This case is different, and I understand that. Our window of time is compressed, and there's not a chance for you to write up your findings and submit them and wait for further instructions. But there's always been time for you to make phone calls. I thought, for a while, you understood and were doing better. It seems that wasn't the case. You put John in a terrible position. He has to explain not only why you acted the way you did, which resulted in the death of two people key to this investigation, but he has to tell the whole world that he had no idea you were even doing it—that the people he trusted kept him in the dark."

The croissant was gone. North went for one of the unicorn lattes, ignoring the way Emery raised an eyebrow. It was sweet, and the caffeine kicked like a mule—well, a unicorn—and it did nothing to help with the sloshing feeling in North's stomach. Finally, he muttered, "Ok, well, yeah, I'm an asshole."

"You do that a surprising amount, you know."

More coffee. The sloshing only got worse. "Do what?"

"Parade your...combativeness, as though that were its own kind of excuse. Perform self-awareness as a way of distancing yourself from your behavior. It's a defense mechanism, I believe. It's one of your standard maneuvers. That, and picking on someone. Usually, Auggie, which on general principle is probably fine; God knows he needs it."

"I don't pick on—" But North stopped and stared into the mountain of whipped cream and rainbow sprinkles. He wanted to say that's what he did with Shaw, and it was true. Because he loved Shaw. And messing around with him was fun. Especially because Shaw loved it, and because later, he had plenty of time and opportunity to show Shaw how he really felt. But had he had that opportunity with Auggie? Or Theo? Or Jem? Or, for that matter, Emery? He put the coffee back and said, "Remember how I told you that you're a lot?"

Emery laughed again. When he quieted, though, his tone was serious. "I do not always remember you being this abrasive, however."

The sting in North's eyes surprised him. He closed them briefly, barely more than a blink. "Yeah, well, I guess you've got me all figured out."

Something crossed Emery's face. His eyebrows drew together, and his hands loosened around the steering wheel.

"You know, it's not like the last couple weeks have been easy. You get that, right?" North tried to stop there. He tried to think of what he ought to be saying—something light, something with an edge. He'd spent years of his life perfecting it, the dry ironic distance that kept the Chouteau boys on one side of the wall, and him always on the other. Everyone except Shaw, as it turned out, who had the insanely fucking annoying habit of jumping over the wall no matter how high North built it. Maybe it was the exhaustion. Maybe it was the reality of the last few days, everything finally soaking in. "You know, Shaw could have died last night. We both could have, but Shaw—" He had to stop again, his throat tightening. "And that asshole just kept coming. It didn't matter what I did; I couldn't stop him. He had that fucking sickle, and he—he just wouldn't stop." The sun caught in the glass blocks of the motor court, and he had to close his eyes again. He gave up on what it felt like, on trying to make the words into some kind of sense. Opening his eyes, he shook his head. "John-Henry was right to fire me. Fucking useless, that's what I was." He pushed open the door, and the heat was a tidal wave. "Thanks for breakfast."

Emery's hand on his shoulder stopped North, as much from the surprise as the actual contact. North wasn't sure Emery had ever touched him before—nothing beyond a handshake, maybe some incidental contact somewhere along the line. Not like this: the touch purposeful, firm, unhesitating. It was, in its own way, a demand, and North's eyes rose to Emery's in spite of his best efforts.

The gold-glitter of amber looked surprisingly soft right then. Maybe not even amber at all. "North, for a long time now we've been drifting in and out of each other's lives. My husband is convinced that it's somehow meaningful that I have you on speed dial. My son worships the ground you walk on. And if there's one thing I've learned from John and Colt, it's that nobody can control who comes into your life. Chaos or chance or the universe, call it what you will—it brings people into your orbit, and you can't control it, can't change it, can't stop it. But at some point, you can't keep drifting. You either take hold, or you let go." He paused. "You've been an ally to me. In some bizarre, twisted way, you've been a mentor. You've certainly been a pain in the ass. I'd like you to be my friend."

"Do I have to?" The words popped out, more as a way for North to deal with the rush that stung his eyes, but he didn't miss the way Emery's brow wrinkled with annoyance. "Sorry; bad habit."

Emery made a sound that could have meant anything.

"Do we have to braid each other's hair now?"

"I believe you were leaving."

"Shaw would say we should kiss, but no tongue."

"This is very good. This is all the proof I'll need when I tell John—again—that I was right and he was wrong."

"Fine. Yes." North couldn't actually look Emery in the eye, but he managed to mumble, "We should be friends. We are friends." He couldn't help adding, "I guess."

"Remind me again: you're how old? And in some clownery version of a committed relationship?"

"Well, fuck you," North said. "I don't go around squirting my feelings every time things get bad. I'm so fucking sorry."

The smile was tiny. Barely even there.

"Yeah, yeah," North said. "I hear it; I'm an asshole." He slid out of the van, grabbed the remaining breakfast sandwich and the unicorn latte, and said, "This has got to be a secret. If you tell Shaw about this, he might literally kill me."

"Hm."

"I'm not joking. When you asked Tean for his opinion about those two weird documentaries, he went into the garage and tore up a bunch of old newspaper and screamed."

"I was saving those newspapers."

North stared at him. Then, to himself, he said, "What the fuck did I get myself into?"

When he moved to shut the door, Emery said, "North, I still believe John did the right thing, ending your contract with the department. But I hope you'll remember that the breakfast, it was a bribe too. Don't leave." North wasn't sure how much it cost Emery to add, "Please. This isn't over."

"What are friends for," North said sourly and then, because things were getting real grab-assy, he slammed the door.

Upstairs, Shaw was pretending to sleep.

"How much did you hear?" North asked as he shut the door.

A yawn. An elaborate stretch. "Hm? Oh, where'd you—"

"Cut it out, or I'll drink this unicorn latte your best friend got you."

"No!"

With a roll of his eyes, North delivered the food and then dropped into a chair to take off the Red Wings. Shaw tore into the breakfast sandwich—it reminded North of some of those animal shows Tean occasionally put on TV, the ones where John-Henry always had to say, "No, that deer is fine, it's just sleeping," before ushering Evie and Lana out of the room. Throughout the process, though, Shaw somehow managed to keep his eyes locked on North.

Finally, North said, "What?"

Shaw kept eating. And looking.

"It's not a big deal." But Shaw was still staring at him, and North found himself fidgeting in his seat. "He wanted to talk. He...he made some good points about, uh, the stuff with John-Henry. He doesn't want us to go home. He practically begged me."

"And?"

North shrugged. "That's it. I'm ok with staying, I guess. For a little longer. If you are."

"I don't care about that. I want to hear the good part."

"I don't know what you're talking about."

"When he asked you to be his friend!"

It wasn't exactly a surprise; Shaw was a born snoop, and the whole sham sleep meant North already suspected Shaw had heard some of it. But the friend revelation made him think of a lot of screaming and a lot—like, seriously, an overwhelming amount—of shredded newspaper. A part of North's brain felt a moment of dismay as he thought, What the hell was he saving them for?

"Uh, he asked me to be his friend."

"And you said yes!" Shaw practically sang the words. He kicked back the covers, tossed aside the now-empty sandwich wrapper, and clambered over to North. The tone was confusing, but North was pretty sure Shaw would go for his eyes, so he was unprepared when Shaw climbed on top of him and wrapped him in a hug.

"What's happening?" North asked. "Are we fighting?"

"Of course we're not fighting."

"Is this a trick?"

"Of course it's not a trick."

"I don't even want to be his friend. Is that why this is ok? Is that why — well, we don't have any newspaper."

Shaw hugged him tighter. He kissed North on the temple, and North was surprised to feel tears on Shaw's face.

"What's wrong? Hey, it doesn't mean anything. He just said it because he knew I was pissed —"

"Of course he didn't! Oh North, I'm so happy for you!" More kisses. And definitely tears.

"Well —" North wasn't sure what to say, so he went with "I'm not!"

Shaw ignored that. He made more of those crooning, contented noises, and he planted a lot of kisses — so many, in fact, that North finally had to shove him away a few times. They ended up with Shaw sitting sideways on his lap, one of North's arms around his waist. Shaw was beaming and blinking his eyes, still trying to clear them.

"Ok, I was sure I was going to have to tell you in a padded room. Or one of those rooms where they let you break everything. Or maybe first one then the other."

"What? Why?" Then Shaw laughed. "Oh my God, North, I'm not jealous. I mean, it's cute that you have a friend. Finally. After, like — wait, how long have I known you? And I'm glad it's Emery. See, Emery and I are soulmates, so it would make sense that he'd also be attracted to your — is grumpishness a word?"

North wasn't sure about grumpishness, but he did know that their current position meant Shaw was basically in prime position for a sack tap. While Shaw was still groaning, he dumped him on the floor, crawled across the bed, and helped himself to the second unicorn latte. Shaw whined and moaned and made a pathetic display of dragging himself onto the bed, but a few sips of the unicorn latte proved to be restorative, and not too long after, they were cuddled up on the bed together. The mini-split chugged, trying to cool the room. The sun had climbed above the window, filling the room with shadows. Outside, a car accelerated, and then the sound faded into the distance.

"I'm very happy you have a friend," Shaw whispered.

North grunted.

"Did you hug?" Shaw asked.

"Are you out of your fucking mind?"

For some reason, that made Shaw giggle into North's side, and North stroked his hair. When Shaw had recovered, he propped his chin on North's shoulder and stared at him.

"What?" North asked. And he thought maybe grumpishness was a real word. Maybe.

"I want to know what you're feeling."

"I'm not feeling anything."

"North!"

"Jesus Christ." He wrestled with that one for a while and finally said, "It's fine, I guess. Holy shit!"

He rubbed the spot where Shaw had pinched him as Shaw said, "Emery and I are not going to be friends with you—"

"God damn it, am I going to have to hear that for the rest of my life?"

"—if you act like this."

"Great. Fantastic. I'll watch whatever I want on TV, and nobody will scratch me with their fucking toenails at night, and I'll stop getting calls at six in the morning because some asshole across the state wants to argue about the best model of telephoto lens."

That made Shaw giggle again, and North stroked his hair some more. He could feel something loosening, his muscles relaxing, his hand slowing against the silk of Shaw's hair.

"I know you have friends," Shaw whispered. "But everyone from college is in such a different phase in their life, and you've got Jadon and Zion and Truck and Pari—"

"Yeah, Pari."

Shaw punched him and continued, "—but it's different because of work. And it's different with us because we're, well, us now. And I want you to have people you can be yourself with, and be happy with, and know that they love you."

"All of that sounds like the fucking worst." But Shaw's silence dragged more words out of North, and he heard himself talking. "Apparently I'm a royal asshole. Some of the stuff Emery said." He tried to stop there. "Do I really pick on Auggie? I mean, I know I give him shit."

"Oh yes," Shaw said.

"What the hell, Shaw?"

"Does it help that he likes it?"

"Are you serious right now? Oh my God. Even my partner thinks I'm an asshole."

Laughing quietly, Shaw bent to kiss his shoulder. "You're not an asshole. Well, you are, but you do it on purpose, and that's different."

"Now I have to be nice to all those motherfuckers."

Shaw made a skeptical noise.

"I will. I'm going to be nice to them. I can be nice." That got nothing from Shaw, so North said, "Say something, dumbass!"

"I'm sure you can be very nice."

"Jesus Christ. No wonder I'm such an asshole. This is the kind of support I get."

"You're going to be the nicest. You're going to be so nice. Even to Theo."

"Fuck me, I forgot about Theo."

That made Shaw laugh again.

It took North a while to find a way to speak again, and when he did, he was surprised at how hesitant he felt. Almost timid, and he didn't think he'd felt timid in a long time, maybe not since he'd been a child. "Emery said some stuff about me. About how I make jokes, about defense mechanisms. About giving people shit—I guess that was part of it too."

Shaw was quiet for a while. He traced one finger across North's chest and asked, "How do you feel about that?"

"I don't know. Shitty."

"North—"

"I mean, he's not wrong. He's Emery fucking Hazard; when is he ever wrong?"

"I bet John-Henry keeps a list."

But the joke slid past North. "He's not wrong, not really. Growing up, and then at Chouteau." It was hard, he wanted to say, but he couldn't quite summon the words. It was hard to be the queer kid in Lindenwood Park. It was hard to be the guy paying his own way when everybody else had trust funds. It was hard when you were afraid because you knew the person you loved most in the world kept getting hurt over and over again, and you couldn't do anything about it. And it was hard when you'd grown up being told never to show fear—never to show anything. What he wanted to say was that it was hard when you'd never been allowed to be gentle, not until you met a certain doofus who wouldn't take no for an answer. And so it was easier to be an asshole, but a funny one, because it kept everybody at arm's length. But he couldn't bring himself to say it, so he said, "He's not wrong."

An old man in a custodial uniform passed their window, pushing a cart that bumped along the uneven floor. Then silence. Then a bird. And then silence again.

"God," North said, and he tried to laugh, but he wasn't sure what to call the sound that came out. "Do they all hate me?"

"No! No, no, no." Shaw stretched up to kiss him.

North shook his head.

"They don't hate you," Shaw said. "They're our friends."

North shook his head again.

"They are," Shaw said firmly.

"Ok."

"North."

"I said ok."

Shaw was silent for what felt like a long time. "You won Emery over, didn't you?"

"Yeah," North said.

Another of those pauses came. Shaw made an unhappy noise. "North, I don't want you to be sad."

North touched that coppery patch of Shaw's hair and forced himself to smile. "I'm not sad, baby. I've got you."

22

Voices pulled North from his bed.

He and Shaw had spent the day relaxing, after what felt like endless days and nights of work. They'd taken their dirty clothes to the laundromat, and while the clothes washed, they'd walked up and down Market Street so Shaw could check out the shops. Then, after switching the clothes to dry, they'd gotten a very late lunch—halfway to dinner, really—at a cop bar called St. Taffy's. They'd brought their clothes back to the motor court, and while Shaw meditated (napped), North flipped channels.

Until, that was, he heard men talking outside their room.

He stood at the door and listened.

"Because—" That voice was definitely Jem's. "You're the only one he won't yell at."

"That's an assumption." The second voice was clearly Tean's. "You're assuming he won't yell at me because he hasn't yelled at me yet, but that doesn't necessarily mean—"

"It's because of your beautiful eyes."

Silence.

"Probably," Jem added.

"Probably? Jem, he doesn't care about my eyes—"

"That's what you should do if you get into trouble. If he looks like he's getting mad, or like you're bothering him—"

"I don't want to bother him. I don't even want to be here."

"—you just take off your glasses and—ok, try batting your eyelashes. No, you're staring at me. Batting your eyelashes is more like blinking but— do you have any mascara?"

"Why don't you go talk to him?" Tean asked.

"I already told you: you're his favorite."

"I'm not his favorite. One time he put a blanket on me and then later I heard him tell Shaw he didn't see me sitting on the couch."

"See? You've already got your meet-cute."

"Jem!"

"Please?"

North had heard that tone before, and he knew that Teancum Leon, wildlife vet, had lost the battle.

After a moment, Tean snapped, "Fine."

"Thank you."

"But if anything goes wrong, I'm not batting my eyelashes."

"No, not without mascara."

"I'm going to say, 'Boy, it's so hot out here.' No, that doesn't sound natural. I'm going to say, 'It's really hot out here.' And then you come charging up the stairs and save me."

"I don't know if me charging up the stairs—"

"This is why I have a husband!"

"Ok, ok. I'll come charging up the stairs. As soon as I hear you use your safe word."

Jem grunted, and the sound suggested he'd been punched. Probably not hard enough. Steps rang out on the concrete, and when the sound drew closer, North threw open the door.

"What?" he demanded.

Tean stared at him, his hair wild, his eyebrows crazy. He did have beautiful eyes, North thought. Jem hadn't been wrong about that.

"Boy," Tean said in an unnaturally loud voice, "it's hot out here."

What sounded suspiciously like laughter came from the bottom of the stairs.

North stared at the vet.

Big drops of sweat were breaking out on Tean's forehead, and North was willing to bet they were only partially connected to the simmering evening heat. Tean stammered, "We were wondering—"

"I," Jem prompted from the bottom of the stairs.

Tean shot a furious look toward the voice, but he started over. "I was wondering if you and Shaw would, um, want to get a drink. With me. At a bar."

"You don't drink," North told him.

Tean stared at him for a heartbeat. "It is really hot out here."

Jem sounded like he was about to pee himself.

"Oh my Christ," North muttered. "Shaw, wake up. We're going to get a drink with Tean." He pitched his voice louder. "And Jem."

"'mwake," Shaw snorted as he sat up. Then, blinking, he added muzzily, "Hi, Tean. Is it morning already?"

"Morning," North said as he pulled on the Red Wings. And then, a little louder than necessary, "I thought you were meditating."

"I was meditating, but then I went on a vision quest—"

North pitched a pair of lime-colored capris at Shaw, followed by some sort of creamy silk tunic thing, and then his Chacos. Shaw struggled into the clothes—literally.

"Ok, this tunic is definitely cursed because the neck hole keeps changing into the arm holes—" He was, as a matter of fact, stuck inside one of the arm holes in question when he pushed back some of the fabric, peered out, and said, "Hi, Jem!"

"I think this bar has a rule about pants," Jem said from where he'd moved to the landing.

"He's going to wear—" North stopped the shout. No shouting. Not anymore. No snapping, either. No barking. No growling. Maybe, in a few years, he could work his way up to yipping, like the puppy. In a calmer voice, "He's going to wear pants, Jem." North was feeling quite proud of himself because he even managed not to say, *Obviously*.

"Commando?" Jem asked.

North had to leave the room.

He was down in the parking lot, contemplating the possibility of a quick smoke—better not, he decided; Jem had an uncanny way of showing up where he wasn't supposed to be—when the other three joined him. They rode in the rental Jetta across town, and North focused on Tean's remarkable obedience to traffic lights so that he wouldn't comment on what their choice of rental car—a base-model Jetta, for Christ's sake? And white?—said about them as human beings. He did almost lose it the third time Tean stopped at a green light—not red, not even yellow—but he managed to swallow the comment.

A little noise must have escaped him, though, because Tean mumbled, "It looked like it was about to turn yellow."

North didn't say anything to that either. He even managed a noise that, under the right conditions, might have sounded like acknowledgment.

When they got to the Pretty Pretty, the club was doing steady traffic without being busy. North had driven past the club; he recognized the industrial-chic exterior, and he knew it was Wahredua's only gay bar. He'd never been inside, so once the bouncer waved them through, he was only partially prepared for the contrast: mirrors, colored lights, the blast of dance music, the heat of bodies making the mixture of body sprays and colognes steam in the air. He'd been in plenty of clubs—gay and straight—before, and the Pretty Pretty struck a nice balance between over-the-top campiness and unexpectedly comfortable.

The other guys were already at the bar. A chorus of greetings met North and Shaw as they joined them, and North found himself on a stool with Auggie on one side and Jem on the other. The bartender was pretty and dark haired, and he kept glancing at Emery with the kind of wariness that suggested the possibility he'd been punched at least once. North asked about the beers on tap and was trying to decide when he caught a fragment of the conversation next to him.

"Colt is spending the night at Ashley's house," Emery was saying, "and Evie and Lana are with Foley—he's got a million fucking kids to wear them out. Are you ok there?"

"Fine," Auggie said. "It's a little bit of a stretch. My toes can touch the floor if I scoot all the way to the edge."

No, North thought, and he threw up a mental wall. No comments. No jabs. No jokes. No picking on anyone, not even Auggie, not even when he deserved it. North asked for an IPA, nodded at whatever the bartender said back, and tried to focus on the music.

That, of course, was when Theo said, "Darn it, I forgot my cheaters."

For a moment, the unfairness of it all washed over North. Not just his reading glasses. Hell, not even just *my cheaters*. He'd said *Darn it*. Right out loud. In public. And North couldn't say anything about it because—

Because he was going to be nice. He was going to be a decent human being. He could—and would—make friends. Even if it killed him.

"I know it's lush," Jem was shouting over the music, running both hands over his beard as he spoke to Shaw. "But do you think it's too lush? Or does it need to be lusher? More lush? Like Theo's?"

That one almost got North; the words were right there on the tip of his tongue, something about Gramps and Brylcreem, or maybe Vitalis—but at the last moment, he hit the brakes.

One thing, he argued with himself. One tiny thing. Because Jem could go on for hours about his stupid beard.

No, he told himself. Not tonight. Not ever. Never again.

His beer came, and he lifted the glass and was about to take a sip when he caught a glimpse of Emery's face. The pulsing lights and shadows made it hard to tell if it was only North's imagination, but he would have sworn Emery was smiling.

And then Auggie giggled, of course.

"What the fuck?" North demanded.

Theo put a hand over his mouth. Jem was cracking up.

"No," North said. "No. No. What the actual fuck?"

"Would you guys be nice to him, please?" John-Henry said. "He's trying so hard, and all you want to do is bait him."

"In their defense," Emery said, "he does make it easy."

North stared. His jaw slackened for a moment. And then he said, "Y'all are a box of dicks."

That broke them all up. Even Tean was taking a suspiciously long time to wipe his mouth with a napkin.

"Fuck you," North said, "and you, and you—fuck all y'all, and you can fuck yourselves with a big old multipack of dildos."

"Don't be mad," Auggie said through a grin. "Jem texted us about the green lights, and it was just too funny."

"You were in on it too?" North demanded of Tean.

Tean managed a not-quite-convincing, "Um, yes?"

"You make it too easy," Jem said.

"I was trying to be nice, you collective fuckstain!" North did hear, in the wake of that comment, the mixed message. He pointed at Theo. "And you, Paw-paw! You're supposed to be a fucking adult. Senior citizen card revoked. AARP membership canceled. Turn in the keys to your golf cart."

It was, as far as North knew, the first time he'd seen Theo laugh hard—not a chuckle, not quiet amusement, but the laughter welling up and spilling over. Auggie leaned into him, the two of them practically crying.

John-Henry put a hand on North's shoulder, squeezed once, and leaned in to whisper, "One thing you should know about your friends? They live for this stuff." Then, moving back, he called out, "I'm the designated driver tonight, so everybody else needs to get a drink and start relaxing."

They got drinks—North, Jem, Theo, and Auggie with beers, Emery insisting on a Guinness, Tean with a cider that Jem picked for him, and Shaw and John-Henry with Cokes. They moved to one of the booths, and food started arriving—it was only bar food, wings and toasted ravioli, but North was surprised he was hungry, and surprised again by how much fun it was to sit around, beer in hand, shooting the shit. Plus, he'd be lying if he said it wasn't nice to be able to yell at these dillholes again.

He wasn't sure how it happened. He threw a French fry at Auggie to make a point—he couldn't remember what, exactly—and Auggie the wundertwink snatched it out of the air without missing a beat. A cheer went up around the table.

"Luck," North said. He threw the next fry like a javelin, and Auggie caught that one too. More cheers went up, and Auggie pretended to bow.

"How do you think I get him to eat his vegetables?" Theo asked.

Everyone burst out laughing, and North could hear his own, scandalized, "Gramps!" ring out as Auggie blushed and shouldered into Theo and then started laughing too.

"Oh my God," Jem said, "we should play darts!"

"Nice try," North said. "But I like my money."

Everyone else declined until, of all people, Emery said yes. And then it was something they couldn't walk away from. They had to wait while the bartender—Chase, North heard Emery call him—rummaged around until he found the dartboard (clearly not a regular feature at the Pretty Pretty). But he hung it for them near the bar, and he had a full set of darts, and Emery and Jem started their game.

It went pretty much how North had expected. Jem yammered and chattered and pranced around—acted like Jem, in other words—while he slaughtered Emery in the game. Emery grew flustered, to the point that once, when he went for his drink after a bad throw, he crashed into Jem, and Jem had a shocked look on his face as they separated. But after a couple of drinks, Emery seemed back to usual, making his little comments, offering his tiny smile, and whatever the blip had been, it was over.

When the game was over, their group did a little cheer for Jem, and he bowed and clapped Emery on the shoulder and grinned. "Good thing we weren't playing for money, right?"

"Good thing indeed," Emery said. Then he did this thing with his eyebrows that was annoying, and North decided to tell him how annoying it was, but when he opened his mouth, he stopped. Because Emery was holding up Jem's wallet.

Jem's mouth opened in an O.

"Holy shit," Auggie crowed.

"You didn't," Jem said, but he was already laughing.

Emery shrugged and passed back the wallet, and Jem wrapped him in a hug, and everybody had to cheer again.

More drinks. More food. It was, it turned out, karaoke night, and as the club staff set up the equipment on a temporary stage, someone in their group ordered shots—that part was hazy—and Theo came back with a roll of quarters.

"You're shitting me," North said.

"In college, North always beat everybody at quarters," Shaw said, hanging from North's neck. He was talking at approximately the speed of light, and North tried to make a mental note to cut off his Coke the next time he had a chance. "North always beats everyone at quarters!"

Auggie said something to Theo that made Theo grin, and then they started to play. Tean, Shaw, and John-Henry opted out, but the rest of the guys were in. They set up the goal cups and the penalty drink, and they started to play. North managed to get his quarter in—barely. Emery didn't, and he had to drink. Auggie drank too. Jem got his quarter in with a smirk.

But so did Theo. And something about the way Theo grinned—a tiny expression, only for himself—made North worried.

He messed up the next round and had to drink, and Emery—after a lot of swearing—drank as well and then said, "I'm out." Auggie had to do a shot, and then, with a surprisingly guilty look at Theo, said, "Me too."

Jem made his next shot, and Theo.

North didn't. He ripped another shot.

After that, he knew he was fighting an uphill battle. He couldn't prove it, but he was pretty sure Jem was cheating somehow—although what that might look like in a game of quarters, North had no idea, and he wasn't in any condition to consider it more carefully. Theo, on the other hand, was just a machine, and he destroyed North.

Finally, North had to surrender. "I give up! I give up!"

Theo laughed, and Jem slapped him five, and somehow North was grinning as big as anyone else at the table.

That was when the music started, and a familiar voice came over the speakers. Shaw had gotten on the stage somehow without North noticing, and next to him, of all people, was John-Henry, grinning.

"This song goes out to my soulmate—" Shaw began.

"Take it off!" someone from the crowd shouted.

John-Henry grinned and patted the air for quiet.

"We want to see the duct tape!" another man screamed.

Whatever that meant, it made John-Henry burst out laughing. Even Emery laughed, and North felt a moment of remote surprise when he realized Emery Hazard was drunk. And I'm drunk, he thought, although that was less clear to him. We're all drunk.

"—North McKinney," Shaw concluded.

Maybe it was the beer. Ok, it was definitely the beer. But North felt himself tearing up.

The song was "Save a Horse (Ride a Cowboy)," by Big & Rich, and an enormous cheer went up from the crowd. North already knew Shaw had a nice voice, but he was surprised—and then not—that John-Henry did too. Because of course John-Henry did. Because he was John-Henry. The best part was that they both got into it, and when the chorus came, Shaw dropped down to all fours, and John-Henry stood astride him and pretended to twirl a lasso. If that wasn't a panty-drop moment, North decided, he didn't know what one was.

That was why he almost missed Tean and Theo's private contest. The two men were sitting in the booth, faces screwed up as they stared at each other, and for one unsteady moment, North thought they were shitting themselves. Then Tean reached into his mouth and pulled out a cherry stem that he'd tied into a knot. With his tongue.

"Oh my God," Auggie hammered on the table. "The doc!"

Tean blushed, but he was smiling, and Theo grinned wryly as he pulled the cherry stem from his mouth—untied, North noticed.

"That is my man!" Jem shouted as he crawled down the booth to pin Tean against the wall and start what looked like a serious make-out session.

Everything was less clear from that point. North had a vague recollection of Tean (once he'd wriggled free from Jem) and John-Henry trying to balance coasters on their noses. And he remembered Emery and Shaw doing barstool races, spinning and then running and then spinning again until they couldn't stand up straight and had to lean against each other, laughing. And then, of course, the dance-off.

He couldn't remember how it started, only that he found himself at the edge of a clearing on the dance floor as Jem made his way to the center of the circle. The music changed, and when the beat dropped, Jem started break dancing. North knew enough to recognize top rock, and Jem was doing some quality footwork. Then, when the bass hammered in, Jem went down. He started with the flare, his body supported on one arm as he swung his lower body around in a circle. Then he flipped over, and North had no idea what the next move was called, only that it was some kind of transition into the windmill. Jem rolled and spun, only his shoulders and arms making contact with the floor. The music swelled, and all of a sudden Jem was doing a one-handed handstand—a freeze, North thought it was called. And then it was over.

North was surprised to hear himself screaming along with everybody else as Jem got to his feet, grinning. Tean collided with him, and Jem staggered as the two of them moved out of the circle. Auggie was laughing as Theo whispered in his ear, and then he slipped out onto the dance floor. He looked so serious for a moment that North had to fight the giggles. Then the beat dropped, and Auggie started to move.

It was pop-and-lock, and maybe it was the beer, and maybe it was the long night of surprises, and maybe it was the fact that Auggie was just such a wiener, but North actually couldn't believe how good the kid was. Maybe, a distant part of his brain suggested, it was all that fucking TikTok. Auggie started with forearm hits, then added in the isolations. A body roll. And, of course, locking. But when the beat changed, and the song accelerated toward its end, Auggie turned everything up. All of a sudden, he was shirtless, and he chest-popped his way over to Theo and, with apparently zero inhibitions, stuck his tongue down Theo's throat. And Gramps—well, North could say one thing for Gramps, and it was that he was clearly a hell of a kisser. Auggie broke the kiss, grinning goofily, and as the song ended, did a standing backflip.

And then, because he was a little shit, he did another.

More cheers went up. Jem lurched out onto the dance floor, crashed into Auggie, and for a moment, the two of them looked like they'd go down. But they steadied each other, laughing, as the crowd roared.

North remembered apologizing to John-Henry, the words pouring out of him as John-Henry patted his back and told him it was ok. But he definitely didn't remember getting loaded into the minivan.

"We're not going to Waffle House," John-Henry was saying, and he had the tone of someone who was sick of repeating himself, so maybe this had already come up before. "North, seat belt. Shaw, seat belt. Auggie, don't you dare puke in my minivan."

"It's my minivan," Emery said from the passenger seat. "I drive a fucking minivan!" And then he whooped drunkenly.

"Good Lord," John-Henry said.

"We can't go home," Jem was saying in the back seat. "Guys, we can't go home. Guys, we can't—did you see Auggie do a backflip?"

"Auggie can do anything," Theo said. And then, his tone darkening, "If you think Auggie can't do anything, I will fight you!"

"Nobody's fighting anyone," John-Henry said. "Theo, cool it."

"Jem's right," Emery said, "we can't go home."

"We should go to the moon," Shaw said with jittery energy. "I designed a rocket that's powered by Coke, and by my calculations, we could get to the moon in—North, where are my napkins?"

"We should go camping," Tean said. "You guys are my best friends, and I want to go camping with you."

"Camping is dope," Emery said.

"Dope," John-Henry muttered. "Does anyone have a camera?"

It turned out everyone did, and they all told John-Henry about it until he was shouting, "Stop talking! Everybody stop talking! Bunch of lousy drunks, that's what you all are!"

That was when Jem shouted, "Think fast!"

He hurled a football toward the front of the minivan. North blinked blearily. He was vaguely aware that the football had to have come from somewhere, and he thought tracking that down might be a good thing for a detective to do. He was also vaguely aware of John-Henry laughing and swearing, the van lurching, everyone swaying around him.

"Did you see that?" Jem asked. "Tean, did you see that? Guys, did you see me throw that football? I've got a fucking rocket on this arm!"

"Theo can—" Auggie tried to say, but then he made a dangerous noise and leaned against the glass.

"That was nothing," Emery was saying in the front seat. "That was nothing! You should see John throw. John has a trophy!"

"Oh my God," Tean said. "We've got to see the trophy."

"We're not going to see—" John-Henry began.

"Trophy!" Shaw shouted.

"Tro-phy," Theo said, and he split the word. "Tro-phy!"

North picked it up. "Tro-phy! Tro-phy!"

Emery joined in. "Tro-phy! Tro-phy!"

The chant grew. Jem, then Tean. Even poor Auggie, who was definitely looking greenish.

"Oh my God," John-Henry said, laughing. "Fine, fine." Shaw was trying to do some sort of spider-monkey hold on John-Henry from behind, and John-Henry laughed harder as he said, "You're going to make me drive off the road!"

Somehow, they made it to the high school. The night was still and surprisingly cool. The sky was clear. As soon as Jem was out of the car, he struck a Heisman pose, the football tucked up against his chest. Then he sprinted across the lot toward the football field. Laughing, North took off after him, and he could hear the other guys behind him.

The field lights were off, but the ambient light from the city around them, combined with moonlight and starlight, turned the field into sketched-out sections of turf mixed with thick shadows. North wasn't sure how it began; the pick-up game just seemed to happen. At one point, he had the ball, and then Theo was on him, riding him down to the ground. The turf felt like ice against North's hot cheeks. Dew soaked his shirt. When he rolled over, Auggie (remarkably recovered after some noisy puking) and Shaw had turned the lower bleacher into a stage and were doing a cheer.

Later, and after another chant, John-Henry took them inside the school. He did a trick, jumping up to slap the corner of a fire door, and it made the door pop open. Which was pretty badass, even though Theo had a key to the building. North remembered standing in a dimly lit hallway, looking at the trophies, smelling floor wax and dry erase markers and thinking that schools never changed. He caught a glimpse of something, Emery with his arms around John-Henry, both of them staring at the trophies like they meant something else, something only for them.

And much later, they were sitting on the bleachers. Auggie fit in the vee of Theo's legs, and Jem was asleep with his head in Tean's lap. Emery and John-Henry huddled together. The morning was so cool it was almost cold, and the sky was a gray thinning to white. North tucked Shaw under his arm, and his head rested on Shaw's, and he could feel Shaw breathing, the slow, full easiness of it all. The sun came up, light spilling across the field, climbing the bleachers, bronze riding the edge of the turned aluminum. It caught that coppery patch in Shaw's hair, and North felt something rising inside himself to meet it, and he realized, with something like wonder, that it was morning.

23

The keening note of a tuning fork filled their room at the motor court, and North realized he was dying.

The hangover wasn't actually all that bad—at least, North refused to let it be that bad, since it had been one night, and he was still young, and he could handle his booze. He had a faint memory, at one point the night before, of Theo ordering another round of shots after North had tried to slide under the table, but he was confident (pretty sure, anyway) he was remembering that wrong.

What he was not remembering wrong—because it was currently happening—was how that fucking tuning fork made his head want to split in half. A noise grew in his throat as he pulled a pillow over his face.

"It's cleansing," Shaw announced with the kind of chipperness that inspired murders and torture dungeons and decades of unrepentant bullying. "You just hit it like this—" The note came again, like an icepick going into North's ear. "—and it drives off all the bad vibrations and unclean energy. You're going to feel better in no time."

Under the pillow, North squeezed his eyes shut and managed to rasp, "I'll feel better after I sleep."

"Did you know Leonardo da Vinci only slept twelve minutes every year? And that was before anybody invented Coke! Oh, and North, you know what else is amazing about a tuning fork?" The fork's high-pitched note rang out again, and North moaned in spite of himself. "It doesn't run out of uses! I can hit it again and again and—"

North managed to flop his way to the bathroom before he started puking. Barely.

By the time he'd finished, he was pretty sure he'd lost a layer of stomach lining and his skin was starting to crack like an exoskeleton. He crawled back to bed.

"Please," he whispered.

"See?" Shaw said brightly, throwing open the curtains. "It worked like a charm."

Shuddering, North squirmed under the covers and pulled the pillow over him again.

"Your body is full of toxins," Shaw announced. The clatter of plastic came, and then the click of glass. Water ran. North tried to think what could be happening, but all he could imagine was that Shaw had perfected some other, even greater torture, and now that he'd gotten bored with the tuning fork, he was moving on to the next step of his plan—the goal of which was, clearly, to kill North while he was in a weakened condition. "Not only the alcohol—although, this is why I always tell you that cannabis is much, much healthier for you, not only because it's natural, but because your aging body—"

North found the TV remote blindly and chucked it in the direction of the voice.

"Oh no," Shaw said. "You were way off. Kind of like last night when you threw that pass to Emery, and then Jem caught it, and you tried to tackle Jem, only you didn't tackle him because you fell on the ground again, and you made that noise like the time I had a hurdy-gurdy—"

Another moan was rising in North.

"Yes! Exactly like that!"

Shaw kept talking, but between the pounding headache and the focus required to keep his stomach from shedding another layer of lining, North couldn't really keep track of it. He only knew one thing: when he recovered—if he recovered—he was never, ever, ever allowing Shaw to touch a Coke. Not ever again.

After a while, a smell like hot grass filled the room, and a few minutes later, the mattress sank as Shaw sat next to North.

"Drink this," Shaw said, peeling the pillow away.

North squinted against the light. "Is it poison?"

"It's a healing tea Master Hermes taught me to make. It's especially for hangovers."

"What's in it?"

"Oh, um. Plants?"

Maybe it was poison, North thought. Maybe it would make everything better. He took a swallow, and his stomach heaved. "Holy fuck, it tastes like butt grass."

"You have to drink all of it, or it won't work," Shaw said and then proceeded to force North to drink the rest of the tea

When North had finished, he was still alive, which meant it was, at best, a slow-acting poison. Shaw rolled him onto his stomach, and then came the sound of a tin being opened, and a moment later, Shaw's hands were pressing against North's shoulders, rubbing. Well, rubbing sounded pleasant. Digging in. Biting. When, North wanted to know, had Shaw's fingers gotten so strong? There was something on Shaw's hands, something that made his touch glide over North's bare skin, and the smell of eucalyptus and cumin and clove drifted up to North.

"I'm going to die smelling like a spice rack fell on me," he mumbled.

"It's a healing salve," Shaw whispered. "And it'll only take away ten percent of your virility."

North had something to say about that, but the tea, strangely, had settled his stomach, and the pressure of Shaw's fingers had changed into something almost pleasant, and the smell of the salve—

When he woke, the light had shifted, and he realized, with something like wonder, that he wasn't going to die. His headache had dwindled to a tiny pulse. His skin no longer felt like it was about to split. His stomach, by some miracle, was back to normal. The motel room was quiet, and when North cracked an eye, he saw that Shaw had left.

For a while, he lay there, enjoying the rare luxury of waking slowly, of riding the cusp of sleep and waking, his body loose and relaxed. His mind wandered, playing back fragments of the last few days. At first, it was the chaos of it all, as some part of him still tried to integrate what had happened into something cohesive: the shock of learning of the murders at the prison; the sniper at the hot springs; the cold-blooded killing of Welch at the self-storage facility; the man in black, and the attack at the old bait shop. He drifted through snippets of the arguments with Theo and Auggie and Jem and Tean and Emery and John-Henry, all the ugly little squabbles from the last few days, everything escalating until John-Henry had fired North and Shaw.

And then he found himself thinking about the day before. Not just Emery showing up unannounced, and the extreme awkwardness (in true Emery fashion) of the offer of friendship. Not even the night at the Pretty Pretty—getting slaughtered at quarters by Theo, or watching Shaw and Emery laughing helplessly as they did their barstool race, or Auggie and Jem's dance-off. It wasn't even what came after, those fragmented hours at the high school, when they'd all been kids again. It was...what? North wasn't sure he had a name for it. He'd had friends before. He'd never had a brother, much less six of them, whose asses he wanted to kick pretty much every day.

A memory swam up at him from the previous night, and North cringed: his arm around Auggie's neck, with the kind of close, drunken talking that had seemed perfectly appropriate at the time. Telling each other they were going to get tattoos. We should get tattoos because we're brothers. They'd been talking about being Sigma Sigma brothers, but in a way, North thought, all of those guys—

It was like something snapping into place, and he sat up so fast that his head spun.

The tattoo.

Outside, a key rattled, and the door opened. Shaw stepped inside with a takeout bag, and he smiled and hoisted it, the smell of seared meat and grilled onions filling the room. "I thought burgers—"

"Adam Ezell," North said. "Did he have a tattoo?"

"What?"

"Did he have a tattoo? Did you see a tattoo?"

"North, are you feeling all right? I didn't exactly follow Master Hermes's recipe for that tea—"

"I know we only saw him for a few minutes, but I swear to God he had a tattoo on his arm. Do you think John-Henry would let us look at the body? Christ, where is the body? Did they leave it—God, what county were we in?"

"North—"

"I'm fine, Shaw. You boiled your old stockings in grass water, and I'm healed. Magic. This is important: I need you to look up the name of the county where we found Adam, and I'm going to call John-Henry—"

"Or we could ask somebody who knew Adam," Shaw said. "One of the other deputies."

North stumbled out of bed, kissed Shaw on the forehead, and said, "You're a genius."

"If you're fully recovered due to my magic, would you mind giving me an idea of the state of your, um, virility? Because I'm appreciating the view, and also, last night, there was something about that time you tackled Jem—"

Grabbing his phone, North searched for the number of the sheriff's station.

"—like, I know it was probably a trick of the light, but I could have sworn you had his head between your thighs—"

"That never happened," North said as he placed the call.

"Right, of course, but you understand how it might have prompted certain needs, um, that might not have been addressed—"

When a woman answered, North said into the phone, "Yes, I need to talk to Deputy Weiss."

Shaw was looking at him pitifully.

Taking the bag from him, North swatted him on the ass and said, "Rub one out in the bathroom, baby. Good job with the burgers."

"But I—"

The call clicked, and Weiss's voice came on the line. "This is Deputy Weiss."

"Did Adam Ezell have a tattoo?"

The silence lasted a beat.

"This is North McKinney," he said. "We met at the jail. Did he have a tattoo?"

Another beat. Then Weiss said, "I think he did. Hold on." The line went silent for a moment, and when Weiss came back, she said, "He had a tattoo on his arm. Why? Is there some question about identifying the body—"

"What was it? The tattoo, I mean."

"A cross, I think. It had the letter E on it. For Ezell."

North squeezed the phone and thought, Fuck yeah. Fucking yes. He said, "Thanks."

"What—" Weiss began, but he disconnected.

"What's the deal with—" Shaw began.

"Adam Ezell had a tattoo with a cross and the letter E."

Shaw opened his mouth, stopped, and then said, "That man at the Mosses' home, the one who was playing security guard, he had a tattoo with a cross and the letter E."

"And because I'm a fucking genius," North said, "I thought the E was for the church—Epiphany of Light. But what if it wasn't? What if it was like Adam's? The E is for Ezell?"

The sharp symmetry of Shaw's face flickered with thought. "That would explain a lot. We didn't have a direct connection between Gid and Adam, not unless you count that blackmail video. That's one of the things that bothered me—it's one thing for Gid to bribe a deputy and get some alone time with the women in the jail, but why Wahredua? That's the part that didn't make any sense. But if Adam's brother is a member of the Mosses' congregation—"

"Then it's easy to connect the dots. Gid knows the brother. The brother puts him in touch with Adam. Adam arranges Gid's playtime at the jail, under the guise of his ministry, or whatever the fuck they called it."

Shaw dropped onto the bed. "Jem and Tean told us about the man they saw going into Adam's house, remember? They said he had a tattoo."

"And I assumed it was the Mosses up to some dirty shit." North paused in the middle of opening a takeout container. "Fuck me. I am a fucking idiot."

"That's not fair. We couldn't have—"

"We should have listened to them. We should have asked questions. We should have treated Jem and Tean like what they are: competent, intelligent adults."

"I'm hearing a lot of 'we' talk, but if you'll recall—"

"You were there too, jackass. You're supposed to keep my head on straight." North tore a bite from the burger, and as he chewed, added, "This is your fault too."

Shaw made an outraged noise. "I want you to apologize right now, or I'm going to tell Jem everything you said."

North chewed slowly. "You know, I think I could beat him up."

"What? Who?"

"Jem. Especially if he doesn't have his little toys. He's got some mass, and he fights dirty, but I still think I could take him."

For a moment, Shaw stared at him. "He's our friend."

"Right. I know. I'm just saying, in theory." North took another big bite. "How good do you think he is at wrestling?"

"What is happening?"

"You wouldn't get it," North said. "It's a brother thing."

24

When Shaw placed the call, it went to voicemail, and John-Henry's voice told him that if it was an emergency, to call 911.

"I guess he gets a lot of calls from the community," Shaw said.

North swore as he braked. Their rental was a twenty-year-old Chrysler Sebring the color of used chewing gum, the top permanently down, with no AC. It had been the only option, and it was still costing them almost a hundred dollars a day—Shaw knew because North had repeated these facts, intermingled with a lot of swearing, for the last ten minutes. "Another reason," North said, "I'd blow my brains out if I were John-Henry."

"I'm going to try the station," Shaw said.

"The other reason is being married to Emery."

"Emery is your friend."

"Yeah," North said. "Duh."

"I'm sorry." The voice belonged to a female officer, and Shaw had the sneaking suspicion that in a previous incarnation, the woman had hit her stride as one of those animals that lie around all day waiting to pick fights with other animals. Tean would know. Maybe a cuttlefish. "Chief Somerset is in a meeting with Lieutenant Mendez, and he can't be disturbed."

"But it's an emergency—"

"If it's an emergency," she said, "call 911."

"It's like they train them," Shaw said, staring at the phone in his hand. "It's like that's the only thing they know how to say."

"Call Emery," North said. "Oh, and tell him that zinger."

Shaw blinked. "That you'd blow your brains out if you were married to him?"

With a frown, North tapped his thumbs on the steering wheel. "You're right. I should save that one for when I can see his face."

"This is the problem," Shaw said. "You realize that, right?"

"Dumbass, they like me to be mean to them. That was the whole point of last night."

"No, the whole point of last night was that they love you in spite of —"

"Fine, I'll call him."

"No!" Shaw placed the call before North could dig out his phone. Sometimes, Shaw had to admit, he wondered what it would be like to be in a relationship with another adult, but then, he also had to admit he didn't mind being the mature one.

The problem was that Emery didn't answer either. Shaw left a message explaining that this was an emergency, a real one, not like the other seven emergencies he'd called about at various points, including the one when he'd gotten trapped in a phone booth. But after a minute, and then another, when he tried again, he still got nothing.

"We'll talk to him," North said. "That's all."

Shaw nodded, but he thought, And look how well that turned out last time.

They drove across Wahredua to a run-down apartment complex on the outskirts of town. The building had been done in brownish-white stucco with a red roof that was supposed to suggest clay tile. Algae stained the walls in long vertical blooms, and in more than one place, the uppermost layer of textured stucco had flaked away, leaving the walls looking scabby and picked at. North parked the Sebring, which gave an ominous wheeze as the engine died, and they headed in search of Kingston Ezell.

Apartment 1G was a garden unit, and the stairs down looked perpetually damp, the concrete cracked to allow some sort of prickly weed to grow. When North knocked, no answer came. Shaw padded around the building, but there was no sign Kingston might be fleeing. He made his way back and shook his head in answer to North's unasked question.

"We might have to try the Mosses," North said as he pounded on the door again. "Maybe the main campus of the Epiphany of Light. If he's not there —"

The door swung open, and North's hand swung through empty air. Kingston Ezell stood in the doorway. He was the same man Shaw remembered from the night this had all started, when they'd followed Welch all the way to Auburn and the Mosses' home. Like his brother, he had a round face, and his hair was blond. But in this part of the world, there were lots of men with round faces and blond hair, and beyond those basic features, the men resembled each other only distantly. Kingston looked older, with his thinning hair cut so short he might have passed for bald. And in the brief time that Shaw had spent with Adam, he'd sensed a different energy—at least in part, Shaw judged, because Adam had been one of those guys who liked wearing a badge.

Kingston still hadn't said anything.

"Remember us?" North said.

Somewhere above them, in one of the open corridors, a child was singing something from *Moana*, and then a woman started to harmonize. Shaw took in more details: the dark circles under Kingston's eyes, the slight unsteadiness to how he held himself, as though he could barely keep himself on his feet.

"I'm sorry about Adam," Shaw said quietly.

Kingston blinked rapidly and nodded.

"We need to talk," North said.

Clutching the doorjamb, Kingston seemed to consider it. Then he stepped back and let them inside.

It was about what Shaw had expected; his work with North regularly took them to places like Kingston Ezell's apartment. Brown carpet that was flattened in tracks, where decades of feet had walked from the door to the kitchen, from the kitchen to the couch, from the couch to the bedroom. Dingy linoleum. Half-buried windows that let in a squinting light. There were always differences, of course. Someone, at some point, had painted the walls an olive color that had faded over the years. Maybe it had been Kingston, because the color seemed perfectly coordinated with a lamp with peacock feathers. The only other decorations were poster-sized art prints of Bible stories—everyone with big, ruddy, Germanic features, everybody looking like in between whatever they were doing in the Holy Land, they made streusel and schnitzel and drank a lot of beer.

Kingston directed them to a sofa in cream-colored polyester, and he took the matching loveseat. He looked worse in the apartment's low light— yellow and wrinkled and old. When the old sofa set's springs had stopped squeaking, quiet crept in. If the girl was still singing *Moana*, Shaw couldn't hear her anymore.

"You helped Gideon Moss kill those people," North said. "That makes you an accessory. And in case you're wondering, that makes you responsible for your brother's death."

Kingston shook his head, but he started to cry and covered his eyes.

North opened his mouth, but Shaw shook his head. "Kingston, what happened?"

Big shoulders shook. His breath had that raspy, struggling quality Shaw associated with a man trying to hold himself together and failing. After what felt like a long time, Kingston wiped his face.

"I didn't know, ok?" The words sounded petulant, almost childish, and Shaw wondered about a man who spent all his time doing odd jobs for his pastor's family, who drove an hour and a half to church, who had chosen — or made a series of choices, anyway — to live like this. "He wanted to talk to Adam. That's all."

"And you put them in contact," North said.

"I didn't know what he was going to do!"

"Who—" Shaw tried.

"He's a good man, ok? He works so hard. He helps so many people. It's — it's a privilege to help him. To be part of that. I had no idea what he was going to ask. I still wouldn't believe it, except — well, except for Adam."

North glanced over; Shaw caught the look. He felt it too; whatever undercurrent they'd missed, it was swirling around beneath them, and Shaw didn't like that at all.

"Go back to the beginning," North said. "When did Gid ask you to put him in contact with Adam?"

Kingston's slight hesitation suggested confusion, as though North had changed the subject unexpectedly. "You mean the prison ministry? I don't know. Couple of years, I guess. That's Gid's pet project, ok? It keeps him out of Pastor Moss's hair, and that's about all anyone can ask with Gid."

North was silent for so long that Shaw wondered if he might have to speak, but finally North said, "Keep going."

Another of those confused pauses came. "He just said he wanted to talk to Adam. He said it was important. 'Crucial to the ministry,' that's what he said. I figured it had something to do with the prison ministry, ok? Maybe they were going to expand. I figure maybe Gid did something right for once, and wouldn't that make Pastor Moss happy. He—"

"Who?"

This time, Kingston blinked. "Pastor Moss. The young one."

Jed, Shaw thought.

"Jed came to you," North said, "and he wanted to talk to Adam?"

"Well, yeah."

"When?"

No more than a few days ago, Shaw thought. As soon as the people in charge realized Dalton Weber had been arrested and, worse, was going to talk. As soon as they realized they were vulnerable.

But Kingston said, "Oh, a few months ago, I guess. More than that. Easter, I think. They still had the Easter stuff all over the sanctuary."

North moved in his seat. He didn't glance over at Shaw this time, but Shaw felt it, the connection as they both thought some variation of the same thing: *What the fuck?*

"He said he wanted to talk to Adam, ok? So, I said sure. And I thought that was it."

"But?" North asked.

"Monday night, he called me. Pastor Moss doesn't get flustered. You should see him up there, when he's preaching, and the Holy Spirit comes upon him. It's something." Kingston paused as though savoring the thought. "But Monday, he sounded like he was at the end of his rope. 'Where's Adam?' he said. Not hello or how are you or anything. I told him I didn't know, and that's the first time I ever heard him use the Lord's name in vain. He told me to find him. So, I called Adam, went over to his house, couldn't find him. I called Pastor Moss back and told him."

"What did you think when you couldn't find Adam?" Shaw asked.

Kingston shrugged. "I thought maybe he was working, and he told me not to bother him at work."

"Were you worried?"

After a slow breath, Kingston said, "He worked nights sometimes. It was normal."

Which wasn't really an answer, but Shaw decided not to press it.

"What did Pastor Moss say when you called him back?" North asked.

"He didn't say anything for a while, and then he told me to get out there. No please or anything. So, I drove out there. They were all scared because of the break-in, and I can't say I blamed them. Pastor Moss asked me some more about Adam, where he might be, what he might be doing, if he was hanging out with some friends. I told him Adam had to be at work or he'd answer the phone, and I swear, I thought Pastor Moss was going to blow his stack. Then he calmed down, kind of, and asked me to hang around. For security, he said. They'd had that break-in."

"And then?"

"I was there that night. And the next day, before I went home, he asked me about Adam again. Where is he? If he was in trouble, where would he go? That kind of thing. I asked him what was going on, and he said Adam had made some bad decisions and needed help, and then he asked me again. But I didn't know where Adam was. That's what I kept telling him, and that was the truth. I didn't—I didn't learn about the stuff at the jail 'til I went home."

"Were you ever able to contact Adam?" North asked.

Kingston's eyes went to an apple-cheeked Jesus on the wall; he looked like he was water-skiing, and although Shaw had to admit he wasn't an expert on the Bible, he didn't remember that part. He thought he might have liked it more if he had. "He called me. I didn't recognize the number, so I didn't answer at first, but then he sent me a text. He had a burner phone. And he said I couldn't tell anybody where he was." His voice broke, and he rubbed his jaw. The faint sound suggested stubble so blond it was all but invisible. He dried his other hand on his trousers. "He said he was all right, but he was going to send me something. If anything happened to him, I was supposed to take it to the police." His eyes screwed up, and he started to cry again. "I didn't know."

That, more than anything else, confirmed what Shaw had suspected. "When did you tell Pastor Moss where Adam was?"

For a few moments, the only answer was the sound of thick, snotty breathing, interrupted by little bleats of distress. "He was so worried. He told me things had changed. He told me they had to talk to Adam, please. It was the ministry, now. There were bad men involved, dangerous men who wanted to destroy Pastor Moss's work. And if I could help him find Adam, it could save the ministry."

Bad men, Shaw thought. Boogeymen. Jed hadn't needed to be more specific—there were always dark powers fighting against the forces of light, and for Kingston, that had been enough.

"You knew where Adam was," North said.

"There's a place," Kingston said. "A lake. Our dad used to take us there, but nobody goes out there now. Nothing around it for miles."

North sat back and rubbed his eyes. To Shaw, the chain of events was also clear: Kingston spilled the beans, Jed—or someone else in the Moss family—sent someone out to clean up the mess, and Adam Ezell got gunned down in an abandoned bait shop. Never mind that North and Shaw had almost gotten killed too.

"Why didn't you take the video to the police?" Shaw asked.

Kingston started to cry again—softer, this time, but in some ways, harder to watch. Grief cleaved his face, and Shaw knew this was more than the loss of a brother.

"Did you watch the video?" North asked.

"Someone came and told me about Adam." He was crying harder now, and the words emerged in fragments. "A deputy."

"What was on the video?"

"It was my fault."

"Kingston, what's on the video?"

He dried his face with his sleeve, fumbled in his pocket, and produced a phone. He tapped the screen a few times and passed it over. It was a smartphone, but only barely—slow to respond, the screen still black as it loaded the video. Shaw didn't recognize the brand, TCL. Then the video began, and he forgot about the phone.

The scene was familiar: one of the interview rooms at the jail, with nothing more than a table and a few chairs. Shaw had seen this before—the same room, the same table, the same chairs. The same camera angle, even. Because this looked exactly like the video they'd found in Adam's house, the one where Gid had sex with a female inmate. Probably not, Shaw thought, the first full-service ministry in the history of the world.

This video was different, though. Gid was fully clothed, as was the woman. And it only took Shaw a moment to recognize Ambyr Hobbs. She was the woman Auggie and Theo had tracked down. She was the other potential witness, the one who could have identified someone at the Cottonmouth Club. And she had hanged herself in the prison laundry.

Or that's what they'd been told.

Now, Shaw watched as Gid strangled the woman to death. He used some sort of improvised noose—a bedsheet, it looked like. The video seemed to go on for a long time: the struggle, Ambyr flailing, clawing, drumming her heels against the floor. A part of Shaw was already going down to the labyrinth, to those forking paths. What had she been thinking in those final moments? What had she felt before, as she was ushered into the room? Had she known Gid? Had she seen his face and understood she was about to die? What had she felt on the long walk from her cell—

North took the phone. His fingers bit into Shaw's thigh, the pain like a red gravity that settled Shaw—for the moment, anyway. The last thing Shaw saw before North angled the phone away from him was Ambyr's body going limp. She'd lost one shoe, and Shaw thought with unreal clarity, Where'd her shoe go?

Kingston was crying harder now, and from that distant place—from the labyrinth—Shaw could appreciate, in a clinical way, his distress. He'd given himself to the Moss family, and they'd repaid him by turning around and shattering his faith: one brother a blackmailer (since there was no doubt in Shaw's mind that was why Jed had approached Adam), the other a sexual predator, taking advantage of helpless women in prison, and then the brothers working together to murder Adam Ezell.

But all of that registered like something Shaw had read in a book somewhere. In his mind, he was still following those branching footpaths, trapped in the high walls of that place inside himself, where each turn brought him to the sound of Ambyr's body as she bucked, the squeak of the table legs over bare concrete, Gid's breathy grunts as he struggled with her.

"Enough," North said in a voice meant just for Shaw, and his fingers dug in harder.

Tears sprang to Shaw's eyes, but he wasn't crying. The tears were fresh and stinging, and like North's fingers, the pain helped. He breathed. He let the weight of the pain settle through him, giving his body heaviness, solidity. When he felt like he could, he nodded.

If Kingston had noticed, he gave no sign of it. He was still wrapped up in his own tragedy.

"We're going to take this," North said.

Kingston nodded and wiped his face.

"I'll send a copy to Chief Somerset, but you should go to the station and make a statement."

"Yeah, ok."

North stood, pulling Shaw to his feet as well, and the hardness in his face eased as he considered Kingston. "I'm sorry about your brother."

"They said it was for the ministry," Kingston said, running his arm across his face again. "What was I supposed to do?"

25

North pressed the Sebring as hard as he dared, but something was definitely wrong with the engine—it was straining, the RPMs way too high, and every once in a while, there was the faintest sensation like a shudder. Like a buck, his brain said, and then he saw again the way Ambyr Hobbs had bucked, her back arching in that last, final struggle.

He shut that thought down and focused on the wind raking them. With the top down, pressing sixty, the noise was tremendous, and strands of Shaw's hair, loose from their bun, whipped wildly behind him. Shaw, though, said nothing. His face was pale, his features frozen. It wasn't as bad as it could get—North had seen how bad it could get—but it wasn't good either. And all the usual tactics, all the ways he tried to help, wouldn't work when you couldn't talk because of the wind, when you couldn't stop, couldn't hold him, couldn't even hold his hand because this fucking wildebeest of a car kept threatening to lock up at sixty miles an hour.

But North had to do something.

He freed one hand from the steering wheel, just for a moment, and pulled Shaw's hair until Shaw shouted and slapped him away. Then, fighting with the wind, North bellowed, "Call John-Henry!"

Scowling, Shaw massaged his scalp. But some of the color had come back into his face, and he took out his phone. After a minute, he placed another call. Then he shook his head.

"They're not answering, neither of them."

Of course they weren't, North thought. Because for this whole investigation, from the minute North and Shaw had signed on, Emery and John-Henry had been riding their asses. And now, when it was important, the two were probably duck-fucking each other in a station-house closet.

The problem was that Kingston Ezell was clearly feeling pretty torn up about getting his brother killed. But at the same time, he hadn't gone to the police with the video, had he? And so North thought it was even odds whether Kingston went to the police, the way North had instructed, or panicked and called his beloved Pastor Moss. And if Kingston was going to make that phone call, he'd make it soon—which meant North and Shaw didn't have time to wait until they could get in touch with Emery and John-Henry.

When North glanced over, he saw the same resolve in Shaw's face. It was a good change; some of the lost horror in his expression had faded, and maybe, if God were good, it wouldn't come back. This time.

The drive carried them through central Missouri, the air hot and ripping at them, humidity and bugs and the roar of their passage. Shafts of sunlight poked through the clouds, spotlighting fields of—well, as far as North knew, they could have been anything from corn to magic beans. Then the clouds began to shred, and more and more sky became visible. It was like someone raising the light on a dimmer switch. It was hot.

The outskirts of Auburn looked pretty much as North remembered them: the quiet two-lanes, the strip malls, the fast-food chains and convenience stores. When they reached the Epiphany of Light campus, the gates stood open. No guard. They rolled through—well, as much as the Sebring could roll anywhere, with those ominous hitchings and wheezings—and drove past the main building. They turned at the sanctuary, and a few moments later, they were pulling across the wide arc of pavement in front of the Mosses' home.

In late afternoon, the house looked dark and empty. North took the stairs two at a time and rapped on the front door. No Kingston Ezell-wannabe popped out to take them captive again. Nobody came at all, in fact. What day was it? He tried to do the math. Could it be Sunday? Then he checked his phone. Friday. That seemed impossible. He knocked again, and still nobody came.

"Want to get inside?" Shaw said. "Take a look around?"

North shook his head. "With this video, John-Henry can get a warrant to toss this place."

"And we'd just fuck everything up." Frustration twisted his words. "I should have thought of that."

"We're both tired."

Shaw nodded, but he rubbed his eyes. "The church?"

So, they got back in the Sebring, and the car took them back down the drive toward the Epiphany of Light building. By the time they parked, the Sebring was rattling so hard it felt like it was going to fall apart.

"Somebody's here," North said, scanning the lot. A few trucks, a handful of sedans, most of the vehicles domestic, most of them low- or mid-trim models. Nothing flashy. Nothing one of the Mosses might drive, North was fairly sure.

Then Shaw pointed to a patch of shade along the side of the building. Golf carts were parked there, and on the back of each one, silver letters suggested the owner: *Pastor Moss* and *Pastor Moss*, which must have meant the older and the younger, and *Brother Moss*, which must have been Gid. Of course, North thought. They lived on the fucking campus—why not drive a golf cart the hundred yards from your house? Hell, they probably thought they were being humble. Jesus probably drove a golf cart.

When they tried the front doors, they were unlocked. The lobby was vast and cool and a pool of shadows, and the building had the unnatural silence of a space that was meant to be noisy and full of bodies. It didn't look like any church lobby North had ever seen. He wasn't a church expert, but he'd seen enough to know some of it was standard fare—a cluster of seating, faith-promoting pamphlets, religious artwork that had the distinction of being both sentimental and banal at the same time. In most of them, Our Lord and Savior looked like he'd be better off running a MyFans. Why was it so important to show that the Redeemer of the World had abs?

That was where similarities ended. The lobby also had a coffee shop, with a roll-up counter door that was currently closed, and a blackboard listing expensive iced drinks for worshippers to enjoy while having their souls saved. There was a popcorn machine, dark and empty and clean. A rock-climbing wall dominated one side of the lobby, apparently in case someone felt the need for a burst of high-adrenaline rappelling in the middle of a sermon. North even spotted a religiously themed pinball machine, and the way it was set up, it looked like you were shooting the pinballs right at the Lamb of the World's nuggets.

No one came to see what they wanted. No outraged guards with assault rifles burst through the doors. Nobody even asked for a donation, and North thought they were missing their opportunity because if he were going to become religious, and Shaw didn't make him become a witch or a warlock or high priestess of whatever-whatever (there were probably hats involved), this would be the church for him. He'd recommend one of those arcade games they had in bars, the one where you were hunting a deer, and the little plastic rifle was mounted on a swivel. Maybe they could change it up. Maybe instead of deer, you could be hunting liberals.

Hallways opened on the left and right, and North gave each a quick look. A few doors stood open, lights on, and they appeared to be offices. It probably took a good number of people to keep an operation like this running smoothly. Instead of trying one of the halls, though, he crossed to the wall of doors at the far end of the lobby—eight pairs of steel doors. Lots of doors for moving lots of people.

On the other side, he looked into a space that seemed like a combination of a sports arena and a TV production studio. Stadium seating rose on three sides of the stage, and North wondered how many people might be able to fit in the room—in the thousands, he guessed, and that was probably a conservative estimate. The stage itself was framed with equipment: lighting rigs, cameras, a sound board. The pulpit looked like it had previously done service on the Starship Enterprise. An enormous metal cross hung on the wall behind the stage, but LED screens mounted everywhere dominated the space, ensuring everyone had a good view of Pastor Moss.

All of those details registered in the first moments that North scanned the room. Then his attention fixed on the handful of people gathered near the stage: Gid and his brother Jed, their mother, and the old Pastor Moss.

The Mosses didn't seem to have noticed North and Shaw yet. Gid slouched in a director's chair. Mrs. Moss sat next to her husband in the lowest row of the stadium seating. Old Pastor Moss's head hung to the side, and his eyes stared unblinkingly into the dimly lit expanse of the sanctuary. Jed was the only one who seemed alive in that moment: he held a sheaf of papers and was pacing back and forth in front of the stage.

"If it's going to be a cruise," Jed was saying, "don't we need to tie that in somehow?" He took a pen from behind his ear, held the pages against his leg, and crossed something out. "Walking the Waves with Jesus? Something like that?"

"People respond better when there's a catchy name," Mrs. Moss agreed. "We saw a sixteen percent jump after we transitioned the food pantry to Peter's Pantry."

"Ride the Wave of Faith," Jed said, mostly to himself. "Ride Your Personal Wave of Faith. Riding Your Wave of Faith to Jesus." He made a noise and shook his head.

"Gideon?" Mrs. Moss said. "What do you think?"

If Gideon had been cast in a faith-promoting movie, North thought— perhaps *Cowabunga!: Riding Your Faith to Jesus 2, The Curse of the Shaka Wave*—he would have been playing the part of Sulky Rebellious Teenager. He slouched in the director's chair, not making eye contact with anyone, and he waited long enough after his mother's question for the pause to become an insult. Then he said, "I think it was my idea. And you said I was going to give the sermon this week, and you said I could tell people about it—"

"Yes," Mrs. Moss said, in that church lady voice, "and that was before you fucked everything up. Jed, let's go with Walking the Waves with Jesus."

Jed scribbled on the page again, muttering to himself, and Gid shrank further into his seat. Sullen, yes, North thought as he started the voice recorder on his phone and walked toward the stage. But something more. Angry, maybe. They were about to find out.

They were halfway to the stage when Mrs. Moss turned and looked at them.

"Sorry to interrupt," North said. "We just wanted a word with Gid."

Gid scrambled around to face them. Jed looked up from his notes. Old Pastor Moss wheezed and started to fall sideways before Mrs. Moss caught him. The movement seemed reflexive; she didn't even have to look.

"You need to leave," Mrs. Moss said. "Right now. As of this moment, you're trespassing, and I won't ask you again."

"Do you want me to—" Jed began.

Mrs. Moss cut her hand through the air, and Jed stopped.

"Gid," Shaw said, "you can either talk to us, or you can talk to the police. It's going to be better if you talk to us."

Gid swallowed, and although his gaze didn't move to his mom, it did shift a little in her direction. He didn't look good: his rockabilly hair was flat, his eyes were baggy, and the rumpled tracksuit looked like it was stained with food. Even under all that spray-on orange, he paled.

"Did you hear my mother?" Jed began.

Mrs. Moss moved her hand again, and Jed fell silent.

"Gideon's not going to talk to you," Mrs. Moss said. "And he's certainly not going to talk to the police. Chief Somerset can contact our lawyer if he'd like to talk with Gideon, and then our lawyer will advise the best course of action."

"The best course of action." North snorted. "The best course of action would be to tie these two in a sack, drop them in the river, and start over."

Jed gasped. Gid's eyes got huge. But Mrs. Moss, steadying her husband again, only watched North. She was so white; he was struck by it again. And the bob of white hair. And the white daisy pinned to the lapel of her gray jacket.

"Sorry, Jed," Shaw said with a shrug. "But you two are kind of duds."

"Where the hell do you get off?" Jed shouted.

"Watch your language," Mrs. Moss said, and Jed flinched. "Call for security."

Glaring, Jed reached into his suit jacket and pulled out a walkie-talkie.

"Go ahead," North said. "It'll be good to have an audience for this video."

Whatever color still remained under Gideon's spray-on tan drained out of him now. Jed's tan was better, but he froze, the walkie halfway to his mouth.

Mrs. Moss only watched. The silence had a sound to it—the almost imperceptible hiss of an enormous HVAC system circulating air quietly and efficiently.

"He's talking about the videos you paid Adam Ezell to get for you," Shaw said, directing the words to Jed. "The ones you were going to use to blackmail your brother into leaving the ministry."

Gid stood up so fast the director's chair toppled over. "What?"

Mrs. Moss took a deep breath and said, "Call Chief Cassidy."

"What the fuck are they talking about?" He spun toward Jed, and he must have seen the guilt on his brother's face—it was pretty clear to North, anyway. Jed gaped at Gid, still clutching the walkie. "Are you fucking kidding me?"

"Watch your mouth, Gideon," Mrs. Moss snapped. "Jedidiah, call Chief Cassidy right now. Tell him to be discreet."

"You?" Gid shouted at Jed. "You were going to blackmail me?"

Jed seemed to have recovered. As he traded the walkie for a cellphone, he shook his head. "Give me a break, Gid."

"I get half! That was always what Dad said!"

"Jesus."

"I get half!" The scream rang out in the sanctuary. "I earned it! It's mine!"

"It's yours," Jed said, and he seemed to forget the phone as he turned his attention on Gid again. "You earned it. What the fuck did you do to earn it? Jack off and smoke meth and pay for pussy because you can't get it on your own?"

"Jedidiah—" Mrs. Moss began.

"He was dipping it in the girls at that jail, Mom. You didn't ever wonder about that? Why he had to drive halfway across the goddamn state for that stupid prison ministry?"

The shock on Mrs. Moss's face, at least, seemed genuine.

"Oh, we were going to—" Shaw said. "I mean, that was actually kind of our big reveal. One of them anyway. So, you know, if you could say, 'Spoiler alert' next time or—"

Mrs. Moss rounded on Gid. "How stupid are you?"

But Gid was still fixed on Jed. "What about the time you got that Maddox girl pregnant, huh? What about that? Who got her that fucking abortion?"

"You don't show up for services," Jed was saying back, his volume competing with Gid's. "When you do, you're drunk. You can't be bothered to prepare anything, so when we put you on stage, you mumble and ramble and nobody has any idea what the hell you're saying—"

"Boys!" Mrs. Moss clapped her hands, and maybe for the first time in her life, it didn't work. North wondered if next she might bring out the wooden spoon.

"You piece of shit!" Gid's shout echoed through the sanctuary. "What the fuck is wrong with you?"

"Wrong with me?" Jed laughed. "You know what, Gid? You're a joke. Out of your head on that damn pipe and then jamming pills down your gullet to keep your heart from exploding in your chest. Half the time you're gone to that club, and we're all supposed to pretend we don't know what you're doing, what goes on there." His voice softened to weary familiarity. "Come on, Gid. You hate doing the preacher bit. You've always hated it. I was doing you a favor."

Gid swung. It was a wild blow, and it went wide. Jed scrambled back, eyes huge, his own hands coming up like he might ward Gid off. But Gid didn't go after him. He stood there, panting, his face that awful, bleached white.

A laugh slipped free from Jed. It was a crazy sound, like something with its tail cut off. He rubbed a hand over his hair. But he turned away from Gid, obviously having decided that his brother wasn't going to press the attack. To North and Shaw, he said, "You guys can go on and blow. Gid's not going anywhere, and he's certainly not talking to you. If the police want to talk to our lawyer, they can, but it'll be a waste of time. He had sex with those women, that's all. What are they going to do? Tell him he can't go back?"

"It might be a bit more serious than that," Shaw said. "Sexual relationships with inmates are illegal because inmates can't give consent. I think once Chief Somerset has time to interview some of those women, they'll tell a different story about what happened to them, and Gid will probably be looking at sexual assault charges."

"But that's the least he has to worry about." North kept the voice recorder running on his phone, but he opened the video from Kingston. "Funny you should mention the Cottonmouth Club. That place is a fucking cesspool. Every time I turn around, I'm stepping in that shit. We're not here about those girls. We're here about one girl. Remember Ambyr, Gid?"

He played the video. The screen was tiny, and even at full volume, the phone's speaker couldn't fill the vast space of the sanctuary. But it was enough. Gid's breathing became labored, and he rocked unsteadily, hands clutching the lapels of his jacket. Jed watched, his expression shifting from incomprehension to shock. Only Mrs. Moss seemed unaffected. If anything, she grew whiter, colder, a frozen statue of herself. On the hand she was using to keep Pastor Moss upright, the bones stood out in pale lines under her skin.

When the video ended, no one spoke. The sibilant movement of air continued in the background. North thought he could even feel it, like the darkness of the sanctuary was moving too, brushing his cheek, and he couldn't tell if it was his imagination. He thought, for a moment, of the man in black, the way he had moved.

"What the fuck did you do?" Jed demanded.

Gid started to cry.

"You need to come with us now," North said. "You killed Ambyr. You arranged with Philip Welch to kill Dalton Weber. Because of you, Sheriff Engels is dead, and Adam Ezell is dead, and Philip Welch is dead. Time to go, Gid."

But Gid stood there, struggling to get his breath as silent sobs wracked him. Mrs. Moss was still staring at them. Pastor Moss began to tip; he looked like he was about to slide right out of his suit jacket.

Jed recovered first. "This is ridiculous." He fumbled the walkie to his mouth and said, "Security to the sanctuary right now."

Gid stood up straight. His breathing slowed. His face relaxed, and with one hand, he dried his face.

Jed stepped toward North and Shaw, saying, "I don't know what that video is or how you made it look like that, but you can believe Chief Cassidy will get to the bottom of this, and when he does, the truth will come out—"

He was mid-shout when Gid pulled out a gun and shot him in the back of the head.

A mist of blood—North only allowed himself to think of the blood—touched North's face. It was already cool by the time it reached him, and so fine that he couldn't see it. Just the sensation of cold. It made him think of a ride in an amusement park. A haunted house, maybe. Some dumb trick on set.

Shaw made a horrible noise.

Jed was still walking. Not really, North's brain tried to inform him. Because he was dead. But for a moment, the movement of his body continued the illusion. What looked like another energetic step toward them became a fall. The sound of his body hitting the carpet was swallowed up by the vast space of the sanctuary.

Another, even softer thud came a moment later. Mrs. Moss had lost her grip. She was staring white-faced at Jed, and Pastor Moss looked like a rummage sale heap on the floor at her feet.

Gid was taking those huge, deep breaths as he swung the gun toward North and Shaw. North showed him his hands, holding nothing but the phone. Next to him, Shaw's breathing was so quick and light that it made North think of the sound of skates cutting ice. He wanted to look. He needed to look, to see Shaw's face. But Gid was staring down the length of the gun, using one arm to clean the gore from his cheek.

"You need to slow down and think—" North began.

"Jed!" Mrs. Moss said. It wasn't a shout, not really, and her voice quavered on the single syllable. Then North understood the sound. A call. Like she was calling upstairs because he'd overslept. "Jed!"

"They made me kill her," Gid said.

His momentary calm seemed to have deserted him, and his chest heaved. The gun wobbled, the muzzle drifting towards Shaw and then yanking back to North again. Shaw was still doing that horrible ice-skating breath. A vast, black sound—that rushing noise of air moving through darkness—blew through North's head, and he couldn't find words, couldn't think of anything. There was the gun. There was Shaw. And he was paralyzed.

"Because I ran my mouth," Gid said, as though that explained anything. "Because it was all my fault. And then Adam called, and he was going to tell everyone, and I knew I'd fucked up. So, I called him. I told him he had to help me make it go away." He stopped. His mouth hung open, his breath rasping unevenly. "I didn't want anybody to get hurt."

"Nobody has to get hurt," North said. A part of him couldn't even believe he managed the words. His tongue was dry and stiff inside his mouth. That rushing noise was like a high wind, carrying everything away.

"Jed," Mrs. Moss said, her voice breaking this time. She stood and took a step toward her fallen son, but it carried her into her fallen husband. Pastor Moss was tangled around her feet, and Mrs. Moss went down. She screamed, the sound furious and frustrated and helpless, and began to kick at the old man.

"I didn't want anybody to get hurt," Gid said again, and his eyes were pleading, focused on North with an intensity that demanded a response.

"Put the gun down." North tried to swallow. "Put the gun down, and we'll figure this out. Nobody has to get hurt."

Gid's hand steadied. The gun steadied. He smiled, sad and tired and disbelieving. And shook his head. Tiny drops of blood fanned up across his temple and into the rockabilly hair. "You have no idea what they're going to do to you," he said. "You haven't seen anything yet."

And then he put the gun to his head and pulled the trigger.

26

North woke in darkness and listened.

Shaw's breathing was flat, even, regular. Close. In the tiny motel bed, he must have only been inches from North. And awake. Awake in the dark. And alone. And not close at all. Lightyears away from North. That was the gap, the amount of time it took light to cross darkness.

The Auburn police had come. The Wahredua police had come. The Highway Patrol had come. North had told his story so many times he'd gotten lost in it, his throat hurting, his head hurting, every inch of him stinking with flop sweat and gun smoke and the faint hint of violence done to bodies.

And Shaw had said only one thing, at the beginning. "He must have been so scared." Then he'd been gone, lost in that place inside himself where North couldn't go, where all the best parts of Shaw turned their knives on him and set to work.

Eventually, the police had released them. Jem and Tean had shown up to drive North and Shaw back to the motor court. Somewhere out in the parking lot, North guessed, Jem was jackassing around, and Tean was telling him to stop, and the whole world was normal and spinning along the way it always did.

He had to get up from the bed quickly, move into the tiny bathroom, shut the door before he turned on the light. He sat on the closed toilet seat and twisted a washcloth between his hands, telling himself no, no, no. And then, when no wasn't enough, he bit the corner of the washcloth and cried as quietly as he could. For himself, mostly. Self-pity was an old friend. But for Shaw, too. For a world that never let up, and for Shaw, who, no matter how many times he was hurt, never grew the calluses everyone else took for granted.

After a while, he grew sick of the taste of washcloth and self-pity, and he turned off the light and let himself out into their room. He wasn't an idiot; Shaw must have heard something, must have suspected. When he stretched out in the bed next to Shaw, he heard that same measured breathing. Then Shaw's hand came to rest on North's belly, startlingly warm and heavy.

"I'm ok," Shaw said. But he didn't sound like Shaw. He sounded like someone speaking out of a Valium bath. "I'm fine, North."

"I know."

"It was just a lot. First Maleah, what she told us, those horrible things that happened to her. And then Philip and Adam. And Gid." He paused. His fingers twitched against North's bare skin. "Ambyr."

"Don't think about it," North said, like that had ever worked. "Try not to think about it."

"I'm not."

He found Shaw's face in the dark, felt the tears there.

"I'm fine," Shaw whispered, and then he moved his hand in an arc, a sweep of warmth across North's belly and chest. "Go back to sleep."

"We both need to sleep," North said.

"I'm falling asleep right now," Shaw said with a little laugh that wasn't Shaw.

North closed his eyes. In the morning, they would call Dr. Farr. Shaw could FaceTime with her, and then, later this week, they'd have an in-person session. And it would be fine. It was always fine. They always came out of this, made their way through it. He ran through the plan again and again. And, at some point, he fell asleep.

The fighting started in the morning.

"Because I don't want to!"

That was Shaw's only explanation for why he refused to FaceTime Dr. Farr. The argument had escalated slowly over the course of the morning. At first, when Shaw had made excuses, or put off the call, North had said nothing. Well, he'd tried to say nothing. Shaw was tired, after all. Exhausted. Hurting. North told himself that an extra hour wouldn't hurt. Maybe after some food. Maybe once they'd both had a chance to clean up.

But when he'd raised the issue again, Shaw had said, simply, "No."

"What do you mean, no?"

"I mean no."

North stared at him. The best he came up with was "Why not?"

"Because I don't want to."

At first, it had been confusion more than anything else as North asked and questioned and tried to get a better answer. Shaw's responses had become stiff. Curt. And then North had dug in his heels. He'd started insisting. He'd tried ordering. Shaw had begun to shout. He stalked away from North—in a moment so ludicrous it would have been laughable (if North hadn't been in a murderous rage by that point), even going so far as to climb over the bed to get away from him. At one point, Shaw even tried to throw the hair dryer at him, which ended up being ineffective because it was one of the wall-mounted varieties and the cord wasn't all that long.

The whole shitshow reached its climax when Shaw shut himself up inside the bathroom, slamming the door so hard that the sound ran through the tiny motel room like a gunshot.

North, in one of his finer moments, jiggled the handle and screamed through the hollow-core. "I will kick this fucking door down and drag you by the fucking hair to her office, do you understand me? Open this fucking door!"

"No!" Only it wasn't even really a word; it was a shriek of defiance.

Stepping back, North lined himself up. It was a shitty door in a shitty motel, and one good kick would probably pop the latch free of the strike plate. He was readying himself when the motel room door swung open.

Theo stood there, with Auggie behind him. "That's why I was saying you should open it with your ass," Auggie was saying. "Remember? Like that one time?"

"I remember something," Theo said. "Wasn't that when I was still single?"

"Fuck off," North growled.

In the bathroom, Shaw was crying.

Something North couldn't decipher crossed Theo's face. Then Theo glanced over his shoulder, sharing a look with Auggie, and both men stepped into the room.

"Did you hear me?" North asked. "Get the fuck out of here."

They came around the bed. Auggie moved toward the bathroom door.

"Get away from there," North said as he moved to stop him.

But Theo caught North's arm.

North let out a sound that was supposed to be a laugh. "Bad move, Pop-pop."

"You've been through a lot," Theo said. "And I understand you're upset, and you're worried about Shaw. But you need to walk outside with me right now."

"Like fuck."

"Then the next people who come through that door are going to be police officers, North. The motor court staff called in a complaint."

Auggie crouched at the bathroom door, and he was saying something too quietly for North to make out. Shaw said something back, and Auggie turned and gave Theo a nod. When Auggie's gaze skated over North's, it was full of a kindness that only added fuel to North's fire.

Theo tugged, and North let himself be led out of the room.

The day was warm, already spilling over into hot, with the sun climbing and thinning the shadows in the parking lot. The smell of tar softening in the summer day rose, mixed with the faint bleachiness of the motor court's laundry. North shook off Theo's hold, but then he felt lightheaded. He moved over to the railing that looked down into the lot and grabbed the steel to steady himself.

Theo stepped up next to him.

"Say something," North said.

Theo propped himself on his elbows. After a few seconds of silence, North decided that even in profile he looked like a grizzled old dick.

"Even in profile you look like a grizzled old dick," North told him.

Theo made a noise that could have meant anything.

"I thought I should tell you. One of those dicks that's—have you ever seen a garden hose that's so stretched out it's about to burst?"

"You lead an interesting life, North," Theo said without looking over at him. "One day, you'll have to tell me why and where you've been up close and personal with so many ancient penises."

When North glanced over his shoulder, he could see into the motel room through the window. Shaw and Auggie sat crisscross on the floor, with Shaw's suitcase open between them. A pile of clothing suggested they were looking through outfits. At the moment, Shaw was displaying a full-body, spangled Spandex suit that he described as "Catwoman, but if she were a gay man and fabulous." Which actually wasn't far off, North had tried to argue, from the regular Catwoman, but apparently involved more sequins.

"He's going to be fine," Theo said, although he hadn't bothered to look. "Auggie's good at this kind of thing."

"Great," North said. "The most important person in my life, and you put Tiny-tot in charge of him."

Something made him check Theo's expression, and North could have sworn he'd seen a smile before it flickered away. When North turned his gaze back to the window, Shaw's hair was out of its bun, and Auggie sat behind him on the bed, slowly running a comb through it. Shaw's whole body drooped, as though he could barely hold himself up. He's tired, North thought. He's devastated. Even though the people he was grieving were, for the most part, pieces of shit. Because that was who Shaw was. And North knew he'd made it worse, forcing Shaw into an argument, taking them both to the breaking point. North's eyes stung.

"Don't beat yourself up about it," Theo said quietly.

The tears started to run, so North walked toward the stairs.

"North?"

His voice was thick, and it wasn't his best delivery, and there was, overall, room for improvement. But North was still pretty proud of himself when he managed to say, "Fuck off, Pappy Van Winkle."

It did undercut it, a bit, that he was fairly sure he heard Theo laughing.

For a while, North paced in the parking lot. The sun baked him as it rose. Sweat bunched his shirt under his arms and made the cotton ride up his back. Theo stood where North had left him, watching. He didn't even have the decency to read on his phone or be like other old people and drift off unexpectedly and then pretend he hadn't been napping. When North couldn't stand it anymore, he left the motor court and walked a few blocks to the closest convenience store—a classy joint called a Kum & Go. They didn't have American Spirits, so, because he was feeling particularly vengeful toward himself, he bought a pack of Pall Malls and walked back to the motor court. He found a patch of shade out of sight and sat and lit up. The first cigarette was absolute shit. So was the second.

The sound of a step alerted him. His head came up, and he moved to stub out the cigarette. But Theo was already standing there, and North froze. To North's surprise, Theo lowered himself to the ground to sit next to him. Then he plucked the cigarette from North's hand, tilted his head back, and took a deep drag. He coughed once, held the smoke, and then released it slowly. He had little tears in his eyes as he shook his head.

"Holy shit, North," he wheezed. "You know they make cigarettes that don't taste like you're sucking on a decomposing ashtray, right?"

Approximately a thousand things North wanted to say—no, needed to say—swirled through his head. All that came out, though, was a startled laugh.

Theo drew hard on the cigarette again, closing his eyes, moving his head slightly to lift the flow of strawberry-blond hair from his neck. He didn't cough this time, but when he blew out, he still made a face. Then he opened his eyes and offered the cigarette back.

"You have got to be shitting me," North said.

Theo's eyes crinkled in amusement. "Don't tell Auggie."

"Don't tell Shaw."

The crinkles got a little bigger, and North was surprised to find himself grinning as he took the cigarette. For a while, they sat in silence, sharing the rest of the cigarette. North wasn't sure the last time he'd shared one. High school, he guessed.

When Theo scrubbed the butt under one heel, he said, "I haven't smoked since—jeez, since before I met Ian, I guess. I wasn't ever really serious about it, but just about everyone around me smoked, and it was hard not to pick it up as a social habit."

"A social habit," North said. "Must have been fucking nice."

Theo smiled. Neither of them spoke, and cars ran back and forth on the road, the sound of tires rising and falling. Kind of like water, North thought after a while. Kind of like waves.

"Maybe you ought to go up there," Theo finally said.

North thought about that. Then he nodded. His face heated as he said, "It's not—I was worried about him."

"I know."

"It's not like—" He stopped. "I know I shouldn't have let things get out of hand like that."

Theo laughed and scratched his beard. "You're talking to the master of letting things get out of hand. It's not ideal, but it happens. You've both had some time to cool off. That tends to happen too."

A white lady with a Great Dane jogged past. The Great Dane didn't look like he was particularly enjoying the experience—the white lady kept having to tug on the leash and say, "Yadi, hurry up!"

"Good fucking Lord," North muttered.

Theo shook his head, but he was grinning.

Maybe it was simply the fact that Theo was there, and North needed to talk to somebody. Maybe it was more than that. Maybe it was the annoyingly unescapable reality that, in spite of North's best efforts, Theo was pretty much unflappable—always calm, always kind. North had grown up with a very different kind of father, but it was hard to ignore the fact that Theo had some seriously good dad energy. Which was, North considered in a moment of clarity, probably why North's knee-jerk reaction was to see what it would take to get Theo to lose control.

Whatever the reason, North heard himself talking before he realized he was going to say anything.

"We did this before." He stared at the Pall Malls, rattled them in their pack. "In college."

Theo tucked his hair behind his ears and watched him.

"Does Auggie ever want to punch you in the face?"

A tiny smile creased the corner of Theo's mouth. "What happened in college?"

"He...Shaw got attacked. By this psycho with a knife. And things just got worse. Every day was worse. Until finally he wasn't leaving the apartment anymore, and then he wasn't leaving his room anymore, and — and I knew where he was going. Knew what was happening." His thumb pressed down hard enough to dimple the pack. "So, I kicked down the door and took him out of there. I took him home. His parents hadn't known how bad it had gotten. And I stayed there with him." North almost said, *Until he was better*. But that wasn't right, was it?

"Then Shaw's lucky to know you." Theo straightened his leg and massaged his knee, which deserved some sort of crack about arthritis and old joints, but North didn't have it in him. "Of course, I think anyone who watches the two of you for more than a minute knows that."

North looked up. The sun was so bright he had to squint, which was a good cover for blinking his eyes. "Yeah, well." He had to count to ten. "It doesn't feel like that."

Theo was silent, and the passing cars dwindled until the only sound was the rustle of fabric as Theo massaged his knee through his jeans. When he spoke, his voice had an unfamiliar note, and North was surprised, when he recognized it, to realize it was pain.

"Did you know Auggie was eighteen when we met?" Theo's smile was more of a grimace. "And my student."

"I saw this episode of *To Catch a Predator*."

That startled a laugh out of Theo. "That's what it felt like, honestly. I was in a bad place, and Auggie was...Auggie."

Alive, North thought. It was the first word for Auggie; maybe not the best word, but the first. Vibrantly alive. And happy. Funny and fun. "A hot little pocket rocket."

The smile seemed wry this time. "That too, which didn't help my situation. We ended up becoming entangled in each other's lives. And then, after a couple of years, we started dating."

"Did he have one of those terminal diseases and then, against all odds, he was cured, and by then it was too late for him to back out?"

"And it was easy, actually. Surprisingly easy. Because I loved him. And because I wanted him. And it was easy right up until it wasn't. We don't fight much, but when we do... We were in the middle of one of those awful fights, and he said something to me like 'It's never going to change, is it?' I can't remember the exact words, but it was something like that. 'We're never going to be equals.' And, of course, that was throwing oil on the fire because he was right. As usual. It had been easy because we hadn't been equals, and because I hadn't been interested in changing that. So, after I cooled down, I realized that we'd both changed from where we'd been when we met, and if we were going to stay together, if we were going to make it work, our relationship had to change with us."

"Get to the part where you kept him tied up in your basement, Grampsie."

Theo gave him a look. "Am I making my point clear?"

"Yeah, yeah," North muttered.

"I couldn't hear that."

"For the love of fuck, yes," North snapped.

"You are not the same person you were in college. Shaw isn't the same person."

"Jesus Christ, is this what you're like in a classroom? I said I get it."

Theo pushed his hair back again, studying North with that look that seemed to demand an answer.

"And for the record, I think I'm starting to get it."

"Get what?" Theo asked.

"This whole daddy thing. It's working for me."

"Ok," Theo said with a sigh. "We're done here."

"What's the runt's policy on loaning you out?"

"Goodbye, North."

"Like, are the spankings mandatory? Those aren't a hard no for me, but I want to know in advance."

Theo moved like he might get up, but North caught his arm. He let go almost immediately, but Theo sank back down. They sat there again. A breeze washed them in the hot, syrupy air, and Theo moved the hair off his neck again. North fanned himself with his shirt.

Then he let his head thunk back against the bricks. "Growing up fucking sucks."

"Is it any consolation if I tell you that you aren't particularly grown-up?"

North flipped him the middle finger. But he couldn't quite meet Theo's eye when he asked, "Do I have to apologize or something?"

"Now why," Theo said with a giant smile, "would you go and ruin everything by doing that?"

North opened his mouth—he had something in mind about Theo fucking himself on his own cane—but before he could, an urgent whisper came from around the corner of the building.

"Now hug!"

Theo let out a tiny groan.

North's hand tightened around the Pall Malls, panic needling his gut at the sound of Shaw's voice. Theo must have spotted the reaction; he made a gimme gesture, palmed the pack from North, and stuffed it into the back pocket of his jeans.

"Yeah," Auggie whisper-called, "you should definitely hug."

"He didn't know he was supposed to hug Emery," Shaw explained, now at full volume. "Sometimes you have to tell him even the most basic things."

"Scram, dumbasses," North called.

"Don't get me started," Auggie said. "Do you realize one time I showed up on Theo's porch, nips out, and he still didn't realize what he was supposed to do?"

"The adults are talking," Theo said mildly.

"Hug! Hug! Hug!"

After a few seconds of listening to them chant, Theo said, "They're not going to give up."

"Give up?" North said. "Shaw's going to escalate."

"Kiss!" Shaw shouted.

"Uh," Auggie said.

It was, perhaps, the most awkward hug on record. But only at first. And then North could feel how tense his own body was, and how long it had been since someone who wasn't Shaw had shown him affection, and how some of the tightness in his muscles relaxed. When Theo patted him on the back, they separated, and both of them cleared their throats and stared at the ground. Theo even kicked a rock.

"That was the sweetest thing I've ever seen," Shaw announced as he emerged from around the corner of the building. He was wearing the gay Catwoman suit and, of course, no shoes, and Auggie had done something with Shaw's hair so that it hung down his back. "Now you're best friends."

"I'm not sure—" Theo said.

"No," North said. "We're not."

"Also, point of clarification," Auggie said, "I didn't actually have eyes on the hug, so—not that I care—but, like, was there a kiss?"

When Theo looked at him, Auggie grinned, but there was also a hint of a blush.

"I think we're going to take off," Theo said. He made the end of it a question, and when he looked at North, North nodded. To North's surprise, Shaw hugged Auggie and whispered something in his ear. When he let the smaller man go, Auggie was smirking and, unless North was imagining it, avoiding eye contact with North.

"What?" North said.

"Nothing," Shaw said.

"What did you say to him? Short Round, what did he say to you?"

"Get some rest," Theo said as he steered a now laughing Auggie toward their car. "You need it."

Auggie whispered something to Theo, and Theo belted out a laugh.

North gave Shaw the crook eye.

Shaw smiled uncertainly. Then, with a backward glance over his shoulder, he padded across the hot asphalt and took the stairs up to their room.

When North stepped out of the sun, the room smelled like weed, which certainly explained some of the Shaw and Auggie Happy Hour, with a hint of soap and the cool, damp air of the mini-split. He shut the door. His eyes were adjusting to the relative darkness of the room as he sat on the bed, so he couldn't make out the expression on Shaw's face, all the way across the room where Shaw sat on a chair.

Voices rose in the motor court's parking lot, the sound of a man and woman calling, "Anthony! Anthony!" and a little boy's laughter. The lines of Shaw's face emerged from the gloom. The uncertainty there.

So, North went with tried and true. "What are you doing over there?"

Shaw shrugged.

"Get over here."

A long moment passed, and North wondered if this, too, was one of those things that had changed without him realizing it. But then Shaw slunk over to the bed.

North made a dissatisfied noise.

Shaw wriggled across the mattress toward him. He lay there, stretched out in that ridiculous goddamn Catwoman suit, face pressed against North's thigh. North ran his hand across Shaw's head.

"What the fuck did he do to your hair?"

"It's called a braid."

"I know what it is. Does he think you're twelve years old?"

Shaw pulled away. "I like it. Plus Auggie said he only knows how to do one braid and hair clips, and we didn't have any hair clips."

"So much for wundertwink," North muttered. But now Shaw was looking at him, and North's hand was less steady as he ran it over Shaw's hair again. "It looks good, I guess."

Shaw's eyes were half-closed, and even in the indirect light that made its way through the window, tears glimmered there.

"I'm sorry," North said.

"No, I'm sorry."

"Well, perfect, look at that. We're as good at making up as we are at everything else."

Shaw smiled and dashed tears away. He pressed his face into North's thigh again.

North let his hand slide down to follow the familiar contours of Shaw's body: the ridge of shoulder, the ripple of spine. "Theo said—" He wrestled with the question, and then it got free of him. "Are we different?"

"What?" Shaw raised his head. "Different how?"

"Did we change? Did you grow up and I didn't realize it, and now we're not a good fit anymore? I don't know. Something has been different. And I know part of it is me. I get it, I promise. The college shit, that doesn't fly anymore—being an asshole and expecting people to shrug it off, keeping everybody at arm's length. But us—" He tried and failed to lock down his voice. "I thought we were solid."

"We are." Shaw sat up and gathered North's hand in his. "We are solid. I love you."

"I love you." North pinched tears away. "So, what the fuck happened today?"

"North," Shaw whispered.

"I was such a fucking asshole, I know, but Shaw, you were scaring me."

He let himself be drawn down by Shaw until his head rested against Shaw's chest. They stayed like that for a while, Shaw's chest rising and falling slowly as North mastered himself. Then, somehow, they ended up lying on the bed, North's arm pulling Shaw against his side. His eyes itched, and his cheeks had the sticky tightness of drying tears.

"I think Theo's right," Shaw said, his voice soft in the stillness of the motel room. "I think maybe things are different. We're different. And we can't—we can't pretend things are the same. We're not kids anymore, North. You saved me. And I will always love you for saving me. But—but we're older now, and we both know life is never that simple."

"Not as simple as kicking down a door, huh?"

In profile, a smile curved Shaw's lips. He rubbed North's belly. "My white knight."

"Jesus."

"I mean it. I'm so grateful for you, for everything about you. For the fact that you want to save me. But you can't, North. Not from this. You can't kick down a door and make me better."

"I don't want you to be better." North's voice failed him again, and he struggled through the tightness. "I want you to be happy. I want you to be ok."

"I'll be ok."

North dried his eyes on his arm.

"I will, North. I promise. I just—there's a lot of stuff I'm dealing with right now. And I—I don't want to talk to Dr. Farr about it. Not all of it. So, I want some time. And then, when I'm ready, I'll talk to her." His voice was almost a whisper as he rubbed slow circles into North's belly again. "I'll be ok."

Nodding, North hugged Shaw against him. They lay for a while, neither of them speaking. And then North said, "I will kick down every fucking door in this universe if I have to."

Shaw let out a tiny giggle.

"I'm serious. You want to talk about how I'm half-mule or I was raised by a mule or I've got mule energy or I'm channeling Gladys the Groovy Mule, fine, great, fucking fantastic. But I am serious, Shaw. I'll find you. And I'll bring you back." He took a deep breath. "But I'll try, you know, giving you some space first."

For a long time, Shaw said nothing. Then he whispered, "Thank you."

Outside, the sky was a blue so bright that it was almost a blaze, and when North closed his eyes, he thought he could still see the intensity of the expanse. He breathed slowly, under the comfort of Shaw's weight, the warmth of another body. And, as soon as he let his guard down, all the frustration and disappointment of the last few days crowded in again.

As usual, Shaw's mind ran along the same tracks. "It's over, isn't it?" He was so quiet they were barely even words. "They're going to get away with it."

North opened his eyes. The cracked plaster of the ceiling stared down at them. Finally, he said, "I guess so."

27

"It's a two-hour car ride," Emery said, "not the Met Gala. Close your suitcase so I can put it in the fucking car."

Three days later, everyone was going home. Everyone, in this case, being North and Shaw and Jem and Tean. They had waited for a new development, some break in the investigation that might give them an angle on the organization operating out of the Cottonmouth Club. But nothing came. And, if North were being brutally honest with himself, maybe they had spent enough time chasing their tails.

"This is why I said you didn't need to come say goodbye," North said as he yanked the zipper shut.

Shaw, meanwhile, was completely ignoring Emery by pulling what had to have been the third Renaissance Faire tunic out of his suitcase and saying, "But I just don't have the right breechclout."

Emery started to growl.

"Why don't we step outside?" John-Henry said, touching Emery's arm.

"Because, John, I'm helping."

John-Henry sighed.

"You know what you could do?" Auggie was saying from where he sat on the motel bed. "You could sew your own breechclout. That way, you could pick out the right fabric and everything."

Shaw's head came up with excitement.

"Don't these places provide a pack-and-play?" North said.

At the same moment, Emery said, "Isn't there some sort of institutional daycare—" He cut off, glowering at North, of all people, and went back to haranguing Shaw.

"Or we could go on another dream-quest," Auggie said.

"All right," Theo said quietly.

From the way Auggie smirked, he must have gotten what he wanted.

One flight suit, two pairs of clogs, and a near-life-ending encounter with a scarf later, Shaw was packed, and Emery headed for the stairs with the bag.

"What the fuck do you have in here?"

"My bronze dildo collection," Shaw said, hurrying after him. "Be careful, they're antiques. Oh, let me tell you about them. The first one I found at a garage sale, only it was a witch's garage sale, and—no, wait, it was a harem—"

"I changed my mind," North said as he grabbed his bag. "I'm staying."

"Does he really have a bronze dildo collection?" Auggie asked.

"How the fuck should I know? A little help here, sweet cheeks?"

Auggie grinned and grabbed North's bag, and his steps rang out on the stairs as he called after Shaw.

North did one last sweep of the motel room. John-Henry lounged against the mini-split, in a lightweight, long-sleeved tee that covered the tats, athleisure shorts, and flip-flops. He looked like he'd finally had a decent night's sleep and deserved a few more. Theo, in shorts and a tee, had propped himself against the door, arms folded like he was doing bouncer duty.

Hands on hips, North said, "I guess this is it."

Theo's face was hard.

John-Henry said, "I'm sorry."

North shook his head. "Not your fault."

A grin skewed John-Henry's good features. "Yeah? It sure as hell feels like it is."

But it wasn't his fault. It wasn't anyone's fault, North knew. Sometimes a case just went belly up, and there was nothing you could do about it. Everything had ended with Adam's death and Gid's suicide. Welch's escape, and the murders of Dalton Weber and Sheriff Engels, had been blamed on a corrupt deputy. Gid's suicide tied up Ambyr's death. Sure, there were still questions—what were the odds, for example, that Welch would be forced to kill not only the sheriff but also another inmate during his escape? But aside from John-Henry, no one seemed interested in answering those questions. And even if they had, what were they going to do? All the leads had gone cold.

"I'm going to watch Brey like a hawk," John-Henry said. "He might be a state rep, but I'm going to camp out on his ass, and the first time he fucks up, we'll have him. Same goes for Cassidy."

North nodded. "I guess you've got Maleah, too. That might go somewhere."

John-Henry gave an unhappy shrug. "Maybe."

He thought about that for a moment. Thought about how nothing had happened yet. And then he let out a tired "Fuck me."

"It's not over, North."

North nodded.

"I promise, I'm not going to let Brey—or anybody else—get away with this."

"I know, man." North surprised himself by squeezing John-Henry's shoulder. "I know."

John-Henry shook his head.

"Come on," Theo said. "They're waiting."

Waiting might have been a loose definition, in North's opinion, but the other guys were gathered around Jem and Tean's rented Jetta. Shaw and Auggie and Jem were laughing and showing each other things on their phones, but it had a forced quality, like they were trying too hard. Emery and Tean stood in the shade, faces dour.

"I'm sorry," Tean said when North reached them. "We've got to go back. The girls need us, and work—"

"Don't apologize," Emery said. "You've got your own life to live."

"And you've done so much," Auggie said as he led Jem and Shaw over. "We wouldn't be here without you."

"In this mess, he means," North said, but his grin felt tired.

"Or alive," Jem said, and it might have been a joke, but Theo nodded emphatically.

"This is for the best," John-Henry said. "Jem's been a target from the beginning. We should have sent you away sooner."

No one said anything to that.

"I'm sorry," Tean said again, and his voice was very small.

"No more saying sorry," North said. "We did the best we could. Sometimes, you just get fucked."

Shaw started to cry. Not big tears, not sobbing. But he wiped steadily at his face. For a moment, no one seemed to know what to do; they all stood there. Then Emery crossed the circle and hugged Shaw.

Everyone moved then. Hugs and handshakes, clapping each other on the back, weak attempts at jokes that everyone laughed too hard at. And then it was over, and North and Shaw climbed into the Jetta with Tean and Jem, and they drove away from the motor court. It was another shining day, swimmy with heat, like all the others. North settled into his seat. It was all right, he thought. They'd done what they could. And now everyone had to get on with their lives. He and Shaw would go back to St. Louis, and Tean and Jem would fly home to Utah, and the rest of them would pick up where they'd left off—doing their jobs, living their lives. And the world would keep spinning. The world always kept spinning.

And then, because he couldn't help himself, North looked over his shoulder. The four men made a ragged line, and at that distance, they were nothing more than outlines against the sun-bright brick of the motor court. And he thought, with breaking clarity, We're leaving them behind.

The Evening Wolves

Keep reading for a sneak preview of *The Evening Wolves,* the final book of Iron on Iron.

1

A broken jaw of Christmas lights sagged ahead of Emery Hazard, and he stepped gingerly over a fallen strand. Leaves, wet and slimy, made the sidewalk treacherous underfoot. A siren in the distance. A door slamming. The wind a wolf at his heels. Not a night for a private detective to be out in the cold, much less a nineteen-year-old girl.

Ahead, the dark funnel of the street ran until it dissolved. It was barely half past six, and he was in a city with millions. But it was winter, and on this street, half of the streetlights were dead. Maybe one house in three showed a scrap of light where curtains failed to seal a window adequately. It was late for this kind of work, which was better done in the daylight — among other reasons, people in the camps tended to go to sleep once the sun went down. But he wanted to finish the job and go home, and so he kept walking. Not for the first time, he checked the revolver holstered under his arm.

The homeless encampment took shape gradually: a jumbled geometry of shadows at first, and then, by degrees, discrete shapes. A pallet leaning at a drunken angle. Plastic tarps rustling when a winter wind moved through them and made them billow. Armchairs lashed together with bungee cords. One improvised wall had been made from a pair of bifold doors. Cardboard, of course — flattened boxes bending with moisture.

Encampment was a grandiose word, Emery decided, for a space that couldn't have held more than a dozen people. The camp was on an empty lot in one of the inner Kansas City neighborhoods. On the next street, strip malls held massage parlors and tattoo artists and payday loan stores. Go a block in the other direction and you'd find tire yards and a Dollar General and a walk-in clinic with security grating over the windows and about a million signs that said WE DO NOT HAVE OPIOIDS. A hundred years ago, the Italianate brick homes here, with their mansard roofs and redbrick walls, had held the city's well-to-do. Fifty years ago, they'd been less desirable as people with money fled to subdivisions and developments farther out. Thirty years ago, they'd been slated for urban renovation, only the money had mysteriously disappeared. Emery stepped over a used condom and thought maybe they should just clear everyone out and light a match. At least then people would be warm.

Huddled amidst the makeshift structures of the camp were a few tents, and at the curb, a Ford Airstream, thirty years old minimum with powder blue stripes and flat tires. Many of the camps Emery had visited over the day had been similar—a mixture of types of shelter. Like everyone else, people who were homeless had a pecking order. He ignored the van for now and turned toward the cluster of tents and shanties.

Pushing back his coat, he cleared the Blackhawk under his arm. The cold pressed against his chest. He called in a low voice, "Deanna?"

In some ways, Deanna Vance might have been considered lucky—or, at least, luckier than many people. She was alive, for one reason. For another, she had family who cared for her. Parents who, until recently, sent her money. The last time, to a Western Union fifteen blocks from here. They'd known about her drug use. They hadn't known where she was staying. When Emery had asked, her mother had said, *With a friend*, the way some people talked about Santa Claus.

As he moved into the encampment, he left the sidewalk behind. Instead of leaves, he now had to navigate a path trampled into the snow, which had melted and frozen again, and he moved slowly to keep his balance. The stink of smoke met him—an acrid, unclean smell that suggested whatever they'd been burning had been soaked in chemicals. Pressure-treated lumber, maybe. Or some sort of synthetic. When the breeze bellied the tarps again, plastic rustling, he caught a whiff of soiled bodies, a hint of shit. Among the shanties, the darkness thickened, and he worked a flashlight out of his pocket and turned it on. "Deanna?"

"Fuck off!" a man's voice barked back at him from a jumble of fruit crates.

Emery kept moving. The beam from his flashlight showed him the garbage littering the snow: flattened foam cups, an airplane bottle of Fireball, an empty pack of USA Gold, its cellophane unspooling to catch the light. Someone was moving, nylon whispering, their steps heavy and uneven.

The wind picked up again. Emery's ears stung. The tip of his nose. He blinked his eyes clear. How cold was it? The weather had predicted in the 20s for tonight, but when the wind picked up…

"Deanna," he called as he stepped over a lone, detached bicycle wheel.

The sound of a zipper came, and Emery shot his light in that direction. A man poked his head out of a tent. He had to be in his fifties, his face lined and puffy under graying stubble, and unless Emery missed his guess, his glasses were bifocals. He wore a Bass Pro hat, and then a hood pulled up over the hat. He stared at Emery for a long moment. Then he pointed in the direction Emery had been going and said, "She's at the end."

Emery nodded.

The man stared a little longer. Maybe it was a threat or a warning. Maybe it was simply curiosity. Maybe he'd been hitting his substance of choice.

When nothing more came, Emery continued in the direction he'd been walking. He glanced back once and, even in the dark, could make out the man's head as a silhouette against the dark.

The tent at the end of the row was striped red and gray, and the beam of the flashlight penetrated the thin shell enough to suggest shadows on the other side. A two-tier shopping cart was tied to one tentpole, the top basket filled with a carry-on roller bag, the lower basket jammed with loose clothing. Plastic totes were stacked next to the cart; the topmost's lid was broken, and inside lay what appeared to be nothing more than junk: wadded-up newspaper, a clear vinyl toiletry bag, a coaxial cable, more bungee cords.

Emery stood to one side of the tent's flap and asked, "Deanna?"

No reply.

He shifted a little farther to the side and called again. After thirty seconds, he gripped one of the poles and jostled the tent. In a louder voice, he said, "I'm looking for Deanna Vance."

"Shut up," the first man called from far off, "or I'm going to shut you up!"

Emery counted to thirty again. He unzipped the tent, and the sound of the zipper seemed unnaturally loud in the stillness. He braced himself for sudden movement, for outraged shouts, for drug-fueled confusion and rage. But nothing came.

She was too pale, dirty hair spilling over one cloudy eye, blueness at her lips. Then he registered the dirty water bottles piled around her, the improvised pallet of clothing, a sleeping bag twisted around her waist. The smell of loose bowels was stronger here, enough to make him rear back, draw in a lungful of the relatively cleaner air, the sharpness of it catching in his throat.

Before anything else, he drew on a pair of disposable gloves. Then he checked her pulse. Nothing. She was cold, and rigor had set in. Or perhaps, in this weather, her body was literally frozen. He would leave that to a forensic pathologist.

He found her purse, a glossy black thing that reminded him of patent leather shoes his mother had bought for him when he'd been a child. For church. It was split on one side, and the clasp had broken. No license. No ID of any kind. No cash. A tampon, a clump of dirty tissues, a stub of lipstick that, if she had used it, she hadn't been wearing when she died. A nearly empty bottle of hand sanitizer. He returned it all to the purse and set it next to her. Scabs marked one side of her face. No bruising that he could see. No visible wounds. No petechiae to indicate strangulation, although again, that would be a decision for the pathologist. No needles, no empty baggies. She was nineteen, and he thought she had died from the cold, alone, in the dark. He noticed distantly that the sirens had stopped.

The sound of a zipper came from behind Emery, then heavy breathing, footsteps. When he turned, it was the man in the Bass Pro hat. Over the hoodie, he wore a satin Royals jacket, and where his jeans rode up, Emery saw at least two layers of socks. He looked past Emery into the tent and shivered, his shoulders riding up.

"Did you know her?" Emery asked.

The man shrugged.

"Did you hear anything tonight? See anything?"

The man shook his head.

Emery nodded and took out his phone to call emergency services.

"You the friend?" the man asked.

As Emery raised the phone to his ear, one of the streetlights sparked and went out. "She didn't have any friends."

Acknowledgments

My deepest thanks go out to the following people (in alphabetical order):

Jolanta Benal, for fixing so many of my unnecessary AND missing hyphens, for queue vs. cue among other things, and for her excellent point about Tean (even though it didn't make it into the book).

Savannah Cordle, for catching missing endmarks, for spotting characters who traded names, and most of all for making me smile with her reactions to this book (and for reminding these guys that THERE'S STILL ONE MORE BOOK!).

Fritz, for catching so many of my typos (Cassiday), for suggesting clarifications (for examples, North's interrupted speech!), and for forgiving me for the GTO!

Austin Gwin, for pointing out missed opportunities for Shaw jokes, for helping nail the characterization details, and (as always) catching all the car things I didn't think about.

Marie Lenglet, for helping me rethink North and Shaw's role and, in particular, chapter four; for her wonderful suggestion about the connection to the Cottonmouth Club, and for fact-checking so many important parts of the story (like the phone calls!) in addition to her meticulous edits. And extra thanks for the last-minute help fixing some vital problems!

Steve Leonard, for his excellent suggestion about verifying North and Shaw's identity, for giving me Parker Rhodes (hazel eyes and all!), and for being a North apologist—thank you, thank you, thank you!

Raj Mangat, for her keen attention to the timeline, for continuity and consistency errors (like the Highway Patrol!), and for pressing me to clarify the important stuff (Adam and Ambyr) and omit the irrelevant (like, maybe it was obvious he showered in the bathroom).

Cheryl Oakley, for asking important questions (like how Brey and Welch escaped), for catching information leaks (like Auggie spilling the beans!), and for catching so many missing words and typos!

Meredith Otto, for making me laugh with "amaze-balls," for the reassurance about North and Shaw's big conversation, and for her feedback about jabroni (even though I kept it).

Pepe, for so much tremendous help with the timeline (after I wrote this book on Twitch), and then even more help straightening everything out in the next draft, and for asking so many thoughtful questions (I'm sorry I couldn't answer all of them in this book).

Nichole Reeder, for spotting missing end marks (and other typos), for her help with the story's continuity, and for her concern about Shaw and his caffeine addiction (beware the unicorn latte).

Tray Stephenson, for catching my missing words, for spotting my plural-masquerading-as-a-singular, and for his kindness and concern about Shaw at the end.

Mark Wallace, for spotting all those absentee quotation marks, helping me clarify and smooth out my dialogue, and for being willing to be honest when the story got too "loud."

Wendy Wickett, for spotting so many dropped words / phrases / endmarks, for her wonderful suggestions for clarity, and most importantly, for her contractually obligated reminder about how to mark the passage of time.

Keren and Raye and Crystal, for catching errors that somehow survived into the ARC.

Last of all, thank you to everyone who joined me on Twitch as I wrote this book. It's a humbling and intimidating experience (read: gut-wrenchingly terrifying), and I'm so grateful for your kindness and support!

About the Author

For advanced access, exclusive content, limited-time promotions, and insider information, please sign up for my mailing list at **www.gregoryashe.com**.